"ANNIE, YOU'RE NOT DEAD . . . AND NEITHER AM I. . . ."

Turning around, she looked up, and her breath caught in her chest. He was too close, and with the hot stove at her back, there was nowhere to go. She stood there, almost paralyzed, as his finger traced the edge of the flannel ruffle at her neck. The sleepiness was gone from his blue eyes, replaced by open desire. As he bent his head to hers, she could feel the heat of his breath against her cheek.

"You're beautiful, Annie," he murmured huskily.

Her throat constricting, she closed her eyes at the warmth of his lips touching hers. His arms slid around her shoulders, drawing her stiff body against his. She felt the panic rising within her, possessing her even as he kissed her, his tongue teasing her lips, seeking the depths of her mouth. For an awful moment she was drowning, but as her hands came up to fight him, he left her mouth to whisper hungrily against her ear, "Let me take the pain away, Annie—let me make you whole. I can make you forget, Annie."

COMANCHE ROSE

Anita Mills

A TOPAZ BOOK

TOPAZ
Published by the Penguin Group
Penguin Books USA Inc., 375 Hudson Street,
New York, New York 10014, U.S.A.
Penguin Books Ltd, 27 Wrights Lane,
London W8 5TZ, England
Penguin Books Australia Ltd, Ringwood,
Victoria, Australia
Penguin Books Canada Ltd, 10 Alcorn Avenue,
Toronto, Ontario, Canada M4V 3B2
Penguin Books (N.Z.) Ltd, 182–190 Wairau Road,
Auckland 10, New Zealand

Penguin Books Ltd, Registered Offices:
Harmondsworth, Middlesex, England

First published by Topaz, an imprint of Dutton Signet,
a division of Penguin Books USA Inc.

First Printing, January, 1996
10 9 8 7 6 5 4 3 2 1

Cover art by Pino Daeni
Topaz Man photo © Charles William Bush

 REGISTERED TRADEMARK—MARCA REGISTRADA

Printed in the United States of America

Larry, you made this one possible.

San Saba County, Texas
September, 1870

Hurriedly gathering the laundry she'd hung out less than an hour ago, Annie glanced up at the dark, burgeoning clouds. The wind was already up, whipping the wet sheets against her legs, and the sky was turning decidedly ugly. The distant, flickering lightning she'd seen a few minutes earlier now shot down from the clouds, accompanied by deafening cracks of thunder. The baby behind her wailed loudly, while his four-year-old sister tugged at her skirt.

"He's scared, Mama!"

"Yes, I know."

Exasperated, Annie turned around. If she took him in now, she'd be washing everything again tomorrow, but if she didn't, he'd work himself into hysteria. She hesitated, thinking that if Ethan would come in, he could carry the baby while she saved the clothes. But as another clap of thunder shattered the sky, Jody crawled off his blanket, screaming.

"All right, we'll go in," Annie decided wearily.

"Mama, look!" Susannah exclaimed, pointing.

7

"Yes, it's going to come a toad-strangler, and I'll have lost a day's work," Annie muttered. But as she turned around, her heart nearly stopped. Racing across the farm field, whipping their ponies, were at least fifteen, maybe as many as twenty painted riders. *Comanches.*

Grabbing the baby, Annie reached for her daughter's hand. "Ethan!" she called out. "Indians!"

There was no time to look back, to wonder if he had heard her. She ran toward the house, dragging the child, while Jody's stranglehold tightened on her neck. Susannah struggled, shouting up at her, "Where's Papa? I want Papa!"

But Annie could hear the thunder of horse hooves closing the gap. Gasping, she fought for enough breath to keep running that last fifty feet. If she could just reach the door, if she could just get to Ethan's rifle, they still had a chance. If she could shoot a few of the Indians, maybe she could drive the rest away.

"Listen, Susannah," she gasped, "you've got to get inside and get Papa's gun for me—you've got to get Papa's gun!" Releasing the child's hand, Annie gave her a push. "Go on, run! Don't look back—just run," she panted. "Mama's coming, Mama's coming—go, Susannah—go!"

Terrified, the little girl looked over her shoulder and tripped on her own feet, falling just short of the front door. Desperate, Annie plunged past her, thrust Jody onto his play pallet, and grabbed the rifle herself. Racking the lever, she forced a bullet into the chamber, then ran back to the open doorway.

"Susannah, get in here!" she shouted.

But her daughter was cowering, too frightened to move. An Indian dropped low, groping for her, missing her arm by inches. He came back up, wheeling the small spotted pony, whipping it furiously with a knotted thong, and charged again, ready to pluck the child from the ground.

"Mama! Come get me, Mama!" Susannah begged hysterically.

Sighting the Comanche, Annie squeezed the Henry's trigger, missing him as he dropped over the animal's side again. But the bullet tore into the horse's side. It shrieked, reared, then went down, quivering. The rider rolled free, coming up in a crouch, sheltered by the dying pony.

While Annie hesitated, considering her chances of pulling her daughter to safety, he sprang into the open, firing his gun at her. The doorjamb splintered beside Annie's head just as she got off another shot, this time hitting the painted torso just above the dirty breechclout. At impact, the bullet knocked him several steps backward. Blood poured from the wound as he raised his gun again, then dropped his arm. He staggered a few feet, sank to his knees, and began rocking back and forth, keening a death wail.

Beside her, Jody squalled at the top of his lungs, demanding her attention. But she couldn't think of anything beyond the Indians in her front yard, not now. Bracing her body against the door facing, she took a deep breath, trying to calm herself. She couldn't make any mistakes.

"Susannah, get in here right now," she tried again. "If I have to come after you, you'll get a whipping."

"Mama, I can't—I *can't!*" the child sobbed. "I'm scared!"

Shifting the rifle to one hand, Annie stepped onto the small stoop, but a tug at her skirt stopped her. The baby had crawled off his pallet and was frantically trying to pull himself up between her legs, hoping to hide beneath her petticoat and skirt.

"Get down, Jody," she said firmly, stepping away from him.

"Up, Mama, up! Jo-Jo up!" the baby persisted, throwing himself against her leg. "Up!"

Her eyes on the Indians, Annie stooped enough to thrust him behind her, blocking his escape with her body. "Not *now*."

Another burst of wind banged the shutters and the back of the house, and for a moment her stomach knotted. When she'd boiled her clothes on the stove, she'd opened the windows to let out the steam, then forgotten to close them. If the Comanches got behind the house, there was nothing to keep them from coming inside.

Her pulse pounded in her ears, and her mind raced, jumbling her thoughts. She had to remember how many bullets she had left in the Henry. Fully loaded, it held sixteen rounds, she knew that much. If she were a crack shot, she could make every bullet count, but she wasn't. And yet with the ammunition box across the room in a cabinet, she couldn't afford to waste the fourteen in the gun's magazine. No matter how scared she was, she had to hold her fire until they were close enough she couldn't miss.

Suddenly, one of the Comanches broke away from the others to ride within fifteen feet. He waved his lance, shouting taunts at her. Holding her breath, she raised the rifle and fired, hitting him as he whirled his pony to rejoin the others. He slumped forward, then fell head first to the ground.

"Mama! Mama, he's got me!" Susannah screamed.

While she'd been distracted by the rider, she'd missed seeing the wounded Indian move, and now he'd pulled her daughter down by an ankle. As she watched in horror, his bloody, dirt-caked arms imprisoned her child.

"Mama! Mama!"

Annie raised the rifle to her shoulder, taking careful aim, holding him in the sight for several seconds. Her finger tensed on the trigger, then relaxed as she wavered. No, she couldn't do it—she might hit Susannah. She wouldn't fire unless he tried to kill her daughter, and if that happened, she was going to have to make the shot of her life.

She took a deep breath, holding it, striving to keep a cool head. As she lowered the gun, he sank back, rocking, resuming his death chant, impervious to the struggling child in his arms, while his blood soaked Susannah's dress. Annie hoped against hope that he would lose enough of it to pass out.

As they regrouped, she prayed fervently that her husband had seen them in time to hide, that he was safe somewhere near the field. And that he'd not try to come to her aid. Caught out in the open with nothing but a six-shot Colt, he wouldn't have a chance. No, it was up to her regardless of where he was.

A bullet shattered a front window, scattering shards of glass, bringing her back to stark reality. Pushing Jody behind her again, Annie pulled the breech lever down, shifting another cartridge into the chamber, then waited, her eyes on the Indians. An emboldened brave rode forward, posturing insolently, much as the other one had, but this time she held her fire. She wanted a clear shot at his chest.

When she hesitated, they apparently thought her out of bullets. They charged the house then, sweeping across her lawn, giving her no time to take aim. Overwhelmed by the suddenness of the attack, she could only fire and pump, fire and pump, as fast as she could work the lever.

Two Indians went down, but the others still came. Bullets and arrows hit the house, and a lance struck inches from her shoulder. Perspiration stung her eyes and made her hands so wet that the trigger was slippery within her aching fingers.

They were so close she could smell the stench of unwashed bodies, and she could feel the foam that flew off the horses. As a buck leaped from his pony's bare back, landing within three feet of her, she pulled the trigger again. There was an ominous click. The magazine was empty. Taking a step backward, trying to retreat behind the door, she swung the Henry like a club, aiming for his head.

"Mama, behind!" Susannah cried out.

An arm slid around Annie's neck, cutting off her scream, pulling her back, and she knew it was over. One of them had made it through a window. Struggling, she kicked and clawed until her head snapped back with the force of a blow. Then her world went black.

"I see a house over there!" Romero Rios shouted.

Hap Walker reined in, then leaned forward in his saddle, looking at the farmhouse ahead. The cold, steady rain dripped from his hat and soaked every inch of his clothing, but it was the only thing that still kept him awake. He ran his hand across his face, wiping the water over tired eyes. Every muscle in his body ached, but he wanted to go on. He wanted to get across the San Saba before the last trace of tracks disappeared in the mud. He shook his head.

"We've got no time."

"I ain't made of iron like you, Cap'n," Johnny Becker spoke up behind him. "I'm about done for."

"Me, too," A. J. Harris agreed. "Three days in the saddle's about all I can take. And my horse's all stove in."

"Maybe they got horses, Hap," Rios ventured.

"Yeah. If we was to rest up a bit—get some grub and some sleep—we might feel more like keeping at it," Ben Cummings allowed.

"If I could just spell Lucy, Captain, I'd be all right," Rios assured Walker.

That was the trouble with the state police, Hap reflected wearily. It was about as effective as the carpetbag government that created it, which wasn't saying a damned thing. Of the five men with him, only Romero Rios would have lasted a week in the old Texas Rangers Hap remembered. But since the war there hadn't been any rangers—or much law enforcement, either, to his way of thinking. Nothing like it'd been before. He half turned in his saddle.

"If we don't cross the river now, we'll never catch up to 'em," he answered shortly.

"Hell, Hap, they probably done killed the Halser girl already," Becker grumbled. "Ain't no sense to keep after 'em past three days."

"Until I see otherwise, I say she's alive."

After an exchange of mutinous glances, Jackson rode forward. "I ain't saying I ain't going a-tall, Cap'n, but I ain't going until I get a little shut-eye. Mebbe if we was

13

to wait a bit, help'd catch up. I don't cotton much to tangling with a whole passel of injuns on a tuckered horse. Like A. J. said, she's probably dead, anyway."

"I say we wait for help," Becker agreed. "Might be a posse's coming behind us. Way we been ridin', ain't nobody got any chance to help us out."

"And maybe if it was to snow in July, hell would freeze," Hap retorted. "What if it was your daughter they got?"

"I'd pray for her," Jackson declared. "But I wouldn't ask nobody to kill hisself going after her."

"Hap, there ain't but six of us, and more'n twenty of them—and they're a good day ahead of us, ain't they? Hell, afore we catch up to 'em, we'll be right smack dab in the middle of the Comancheria! There'll probably be a hunnerd more a-waitin' fer us! I don't know about you, but I got a real hankerin' to keep my hair, Cap'n," Harris argued.

Hap's gaze rested on Rios. "How bad's the horse?"

"If she had an hour, Lucy could go on, Cap'n."

"Well, at least that's something. Guess you're the only one that's not yellow-bellied," Hap muttered under his breath.

"Captain, that ain't right to say no such thing," Harris complained. "I been doing my damnedest to keep up—we all have. You can't fight Comanches with dead men."

Maybe Hap wasn't being fair, but he had promised the girl's dying mother he'd get Gretchen Halser or her body back. And every time he had to stop, his odds of keeping that promise went down. But looking at Rios' black mare, he could see she was nearly spent. "All right," he decided. "We'll stop in here, try to eat a bite, and see if we can buy some fresh horses."

"Sure could use some home cooking," Harris said. "I'm downright sick of wet biscuits and cold coffee."

"All I want to do is dry out and sleep for a week," Becker decided. "My butt's so tired I can't think."

"I knowed there was something wrong with your brain, Johnny," Jackson declared, "but danged if I knew it was in the wrong place. You hear that, Cap'n? He's sitting on it!"

"Yeah, I heard."

On approach, the rain had obscured the fact there was something wrong, but as they reached the muddy field, Hap could feel the hairs on his neck prickle. A big draft horse still hitched to a plow lay dead, its body bristling with arrows. And when he looked toward the house, he could see laundry sagging heavily on the line.

At first none of the men spoke, then finally Jackson said it: "Looks like they been through, don't it?"

"Yeah. Sure as hell looks like it, all right."

The house itself appeared untouched, and the laundry basket still had some clothes in it, giving an eerie unreality to the scene. Hap's eyes moved back to the field, scanning the rows until he saw a mound of clothing about a hundred feet from the animal. Easing his exhausted body from the saddle, he slowly walked down the muddly furrow, then dropped to his knees to examine the dead man. Turning him over, he found a gun underneath. It was still fully loaded. The poor devil hadn't even gotten off a shot. But there was something even more ominous about the body—aside from the missing scalp, it hadn't been mutilated.

"Damn," Rios muttered, coming up behind him.

"Yeah, they went after something else." Rising, Hap

wiped muddy hands on his buckskin pants. "Guess we'd better take a look at the house."

But Rios stood there for a moment, his lips moving silently. When finished, he leaned over and closed the dead man's eyes, making the sign of the cross over his face.

"He was probably a Baptist," Hap muttered.

"I know," Romero responded simply. "But I didn't figure it'd hurt to put in a word for him."

As they passed the laundry line and the soaked clothes basket, Hap noticed a small, soggy blanket lying beside it. And a china-faced doll with yellow hair was staring up from the wet grass. He stooped to pick up the little girl's toy. The cloth body dripped muddy water from beneath a blue checked dress covered with a little pinafore. A loose black lace dangled from a little high-topped doll shoe. He stood there, staring at it, his big hand smoothing the dirty hair back from that painted face. If he'd had anything in his stomach, it would have come up. Mastering himself, he managed to look at Rios.

"Guess they got a little kid."

The other man's toe lifted what looked like a hanky with a knot tied in it. "Your mother ever fix you one of these?"

"I don't know—what is it?"

"Your people call it a sugar titty," Romero responded soberly. "Must've been a baby here, too."

"Jesus." Wiping rain from his face, Hap looked around. "No sign of them or the mother," he said wearily. "Damn."

"Not unless she's in the house."

"The door's wide open."

The other three men were watching from the porch,

and it wasn't until Hap and Rios reached them that they reported, "Nobody inside, Cap'n."

"Yeah."

"Didn't see no horse in the pen, just a milch cow and some chickens. Funny, you'da thought they'da butchered it," Becker told him. "The cow, I mean."

"They were in a hurry."

"We ain't gonna catch 'em, Cap'n," Jackson declared. "Not the way that sky looks. Even if we was to have the horses, we couldn't do it."

The rain was pelting down hard, sending them ducking into the house. There, just inside the door, a number of spent cartridges were scattered over the floor. Somebody had put up a fight. Hap looked around the dim room, taking in all the little things that made it somebody's home. His gaze strayed to the piano. It was a fine piece of furniture, oddly out of place in the small room.

On top of it, a young couple stared from an oval frame. He thought he recognized the fellow in the field, but it was the woman's face that drew him. Despite the artificiality of holding that pose, she didn't look like so many folks when they had their pictures taken. She stood beside the man, her hand on his shoulder, smiling as though she meant it. There was a liveliness in those eyes that the camera hadn't missed. He picked it up, turning it over. On the back somebody had written a date in neat script.

"I found their Bible," Rios murmured. Opening it, he read, " 'Married—August 27, 1865, in Austin, Anne Elizabeth Allison to Ethan Wayne Bryce.' "

Hap was holding their wedding picture. Feeling as though he'd been spying, he carefully placed it back on

the piano, then stepped back. She was a pretty woman, a
real pretty woman—and the damned Comanches had her.

Looking at the opposite page, Rios scanned it. "Here—
it says they had two kids, Susannah Elizabeth and Joseph
Ethan. Looks like one would be four, the other not yet one.
Guess that's it. Nothing else written down, anyway."

"It's enough. With Gretchen Halser, that makes four
captives those sons of bitches have—and there's at least
six bodies they've left behind. I'm not going to wait. Those
that want to, come on. Those that don't—well, I guess
you'll bury Bryce." Jamming his soaked hat on his head,
he turned his back on them.

"Ain't nothing but mud out there," somebody muttered.

"Fred, let me take your horse. I've got to give Lucy a
rest."

"If you ain't back afore I leave, I'm taking her," Jackson
threatened.

Tying his wide-brimmed hat on, Rios tried to catch up
to his captain. "What do you want the rest of 'em to do?
Go for help?"

"They can go to hell for all I care!" Hap snapped.

"They'll probably head back to San Angelo," the Mexican decided, swinging up on Jackson's horse.

"Thanks." Hap caught the saddle horn and stepped into
the stirrup. Pulling his tired body up, he eased his sore
rear back into the saddle. "Reckon I owe you."

The San Saba was already high, lapping at a stand of
cottonwoods several feet out from its banks. Reining in,
Hap stared grimly at it, weighing his chances of crossing
it. Then he thought of the young German girl, and of the
pretty blond woman with two little kids, and he knew he
had to try.

"Better wait to see if I make it," he told Rios over his shoulder. Edging the big roan gelding closer to the swirling water, he leaned forward and patted its neck. "Easy, Red. Take it real easy."

The animal sidestepped skittishly, but he pulled it up short and tried again, guiding the horse with his knees. This time the roan plunged in and strained to swim against the heavy current. Cottonwood limbs torn from the bank butted Hap's leg and bobbed beside Old Red's outstretched neck. As strong as the animal was, they were being carried downriver. Hap coaxed and shouted, but the horse couldn't fight the current. Finally, at a bend in the river, he slid from the saddle into the swift water, then caught an exposed tree root and hung on. Free now, the big roan managed to catch a footing in the sand and lunge out of the water. With one last do-or-die effort, Hap pulled himself up the gnarled root far enough to brace his boots, then climb to safety. Exhausted, he collapsed on the wet ground and lay there, catching his breath. When he managed to sit up, he couldn't even see where he'd left Romero Rios.

Remounting, he walked Old Red along the water's edge for more than a mile, looking for tracks. The mud was smooth, swept clean by the water. Still determined, he rode away from the river at an angle, then came back, zigging and zagging repeatedly until he'd covered just about every place he figured the war party could have crossed. All trace of them had been washed out, making it impossible to know whether they'd gone due north or cut northwest. Either way they'd be headed for the Staked Plains, and once they got up there, there were a thousand places they could hide. And without Clay along, he'd never find them.

The defeat was a bitter one. He'd pushed himself hard, giving up food and sleep, racing an enemy with every resource he could summon, and he'd lost. The damned Comanches had a young girl, a pretty widow, and two little kids, and despite his promise to Mrs. Halser, he wasn't going to get any of them back. Disgusted, he turned back, encountering an equally dispirited Romero Rios.

"Took everything I had to get Fred's horse into the water," Rios explained. "By the time I got across, all I could do was look for where you came out. When I found your tracks went east, I went west, thinking at least we'd be looking at something different."

"Anything?"

"No. Only sign I found was yours. Everything else's been washed out."

"Yeah. It's like they reached the San Saba and vanished," Hap admitted wearily. Squaring his shoulders, he sighed. "Guess that's it, isn't it?" His expression sober, he added, "Sometimes, no matter what a man does, he comes up short, but knowing he tried doesn't make it any easier."

"No. What are you going to do now, Captain?"

Hap stared at the flooding river for a long moment, then decided. "If I can get back across, I'm going to see that the Bryce fellow gets a decent burial. Then I'll file a report before heading down to Laredo to meet Clay."

"If we don't get some sleep, we won't make it."

"Yeah. Reckon I'm going to have nightmares tonight, thinking about that wife in the picture. Her and the Halser girl."

Indian Territory
November 12, 1873

Cold, weak, and hungry, Annie Bryce lay shivering between vermin-infested buffalo robes, listening to the wind beating the hide walls of the tipi, wondering how much longer she could last with no food and no fire. Her stomach was so empty that it felt as though some wild creature gnawed at her insides.

It had been a full two days since Bull Calf had brought in one scrawny rabbit to feed himself, two wives, three children, and Annie. Sun in the Morning had gamely boiled it, adding small pieces of yep, dried grass, and God only knew what else to make a thin, tasteless soup. By the time somebody left a bowl outside for Annie, there hadn't been a single piece of meat left in it.

But last night had been the worst since she'd been with Bull Calf's band. She'd lain awake in her old, discarded tipi, listening to the hungry wailing of the children coming from the other one, hearing the pitiful attempts of Sun in the Morning and Little Hand to comfort them. Remembering her own little son, Annie had wrapped her arms around herself and wept also.

21

This morning, after coming back empty-handed, an angry Bull Calf had stood outside her tipi. He'd been lured off the Llano to starve, he ranted, drawn by the promise of winter rations—of "plenty good meat, smoke, and blankets." But when he'd tried to collect his band's share, the agent had refused to issue anything until the Indians gave up every white captive they held. And when the Comanche chief had declared he had none, he'd been accused of lying. If anyone was lying, Bull Calf insisted, it was the "Jesus man" at the agency. And now the band couldn't go back to Texas, either, because they'd had to eat most of the horses, and if they stole animals from Fort Sill, the soldiers would come after them.

He ended up telling her through the flap that he could no longer feed her. He wanted her to walk to the Indian agency by herself and tell somebody named Haworth that he'd never held her against her will, that he'd actually saved her life. Then, recalling that she couldn't talk, he'd given vent to his frustration, raising his arms and cursing the spirits who'd guided this crazy, useless woman into his life. Now his act of mercy was going to bring the wrath of the bluecoats down on him.

She'd been stunned by his outburst. Isolated from the others in the camp, she'd had no idea where she was, that she was so close to her own people. But the discovery was a bitter one, for she no longer had the strength to gather firewood, let alone try to walk miles in a storm. For three years she'd endured, doing whatever she had to just to stay alive, sustained only by the hope of being reunited with Susannah, of somehow taking her little girl home with her to the farm on the San Saba. Now she was going to die within miles of help, and she'd never know for sure what had happened to her daughter.

Nearly every night of those three years, Annie had relived the horror of Two Trees dragging her into the brush-filled ravine, of his naked, foul-smelling body brutally invading hers, while Susannah screamed for her. She still remembered pulling her bloody dress down and crawling up from that hell pit to the awful discovery that the war party had divided, and her daughter was gone—Two Trees had traded the child to a Quahadi for a stolen horse he'd admired. Since that time Annie'd clung to the notion that because the unknown warrior had paid for Susannah, he hadn't mistreated her, that her daughter was still alive somewhere in the vast Comancheria.

Hap Walker was afraid he wasn't going to make it. The temperature had dropped steadily since early morning, and the bitter, howling wind whipped his raw face. Shivering, he turned up the collar of his buffalo hide coat and leaned forward, hunching his shoulders over the saddle horn. By the looks of the heavy gray sky, a big norther was blowing down from Kansas, and when the full brunt of it hit, God deliver anybody fool enough to get caught out in the open.

But that wasn't the worst of it. He was sick. After three days in the saddle, the pain in his leg was white-hot, throbbing with his pulse, and he was so damned light-headed he was sick to his stomach. He felt worse now than when the Comanchero bullet had shattered his thigh last summer.

He was a stubborn fool, he admitted it. When he'd heard the government was offering an emergency price of five and a half cents per pound for beef on the hoof, he should have sent Diego Vergara to make the deal, but he'd had too much pride for that. Instead, he'd convinced Amanda he could do the job better than Vergara because he knew Black Jack Davidson, the commanding officer at Fort Sill, personally. In truth, he didn't have much use for the old martinet.

What he'd really wanted was to prove to himself as much as to her that he wasn't useless, that his life hadn't ended when the bum leg had forced him out of the Texas Rangers. After spending nearly half of his thirty-seven years fighting Indians and outlaws, he'd found retirement a bitter pill to swallow. He felt like an old warhorse put out to pasture before its time. After years of thinking he might like to farm or ranch, he'd discovered it was really rangering in his blood, after all. He knew now he wasn't cut out for anything else.

He forced his thoughts to Clay, knowing he was going to be as mad as fire when he got home and found Hap gone. But Amanda had a knack for handling him, something Hap had never expected. Yeah, the wild, blue-eyed young'un he'd found fourteen years ago in that Comanche camp was taming down, married to the Ybarra heiress and studying law now.

It was real funny how things turned out, he reflected. He'd never guessed when he stood between that kid and Barton, shouting, "Don't shoot! This one's white!" that the boy'd turn out to be like a younger brother to him. He remembered that day like yesterday.

"Outta my way, Hap!" the lieutenant ordered.

"He's white, I'm telling you!"

24

"He's a damned savage!" Barton raised his rifle, drawing a bead on the boy. "For the last time, outta my way!"

Before the older man could fire, Hap pushed the struggling kid behind him, trying to hold him there. "Then you better kill me with him. Otherwise, I'm reporting it," he declared. "And I'll say it was cold-blooded murder."

"They've had him too long, Hap," Barton argued.

"Maybe, maybe not. All I know's he's white," Hap maintained stubbornly. "You're gonna have to plug me first, Bill."

And all the while he'd been trying to shield the kid, the little devil had been kicking his legs, trying to bring him down. But in the end it was Barton who wavered, lowering the gun, growling, "If he scalps anybody, I'm hanging you for it."

The kid had given Hap one hell of a time, fighting him every inch of the way back to the ranger camp at San Saba. Hap's shoulder still bore the scar where the boy'd jumped him, then stabbed him with his own knife. He'd finally trussed the kid up like a wild animal and tied him over the side of a pack mule. The young'un raved in Comanche for two solid days before he finally lost his voice.

And it wasn't over when they got in, either. While he was trying to locate some relations to take the boy, the kid must've escaped seven or eight times, determined to get back to what was left of his Comanche family. His Indian name was Nahahkoah, or Stands Alone, but after the second time he ran away, the rangers jokingly referred to him as "Long Gone," and it stuck until they discovered he was really Clayton McAlester, the lone survivor of a Comanche raid nine years before.

It took some doing, but Hap found a maiden aunt in Chicago willing to take him. Grateful to see the kid go, the whole ranger company chipped in to make the train fare. The way Frank Kennedy put it, it was worth the money to be able to sleep with both his eyes closed again. They'd all gone down to the depot to watch Clay off, then got roaring drunk to celebrate afterward.

Miss Jane McAlester the aunt's name was, Hap remembered. Lord, but what he would've given to be there when Clay stepped off that railroad car. When Hap wrote her, there hadn't been any good way to explain that the kid tore into his food with his bare hands, slept naked on the bare floor under his bed, and spoke Comanche a damned sight better than English. But that spinster woman must've been made of pretty stern stuff, for she kept her wild nephew four years, somehow managing to get him about half-civilized.

After that he'd come back to Hap, and they'd enlisted in the Confederate Army and fought together in Hood's tough Texas Brigade. Then Clay'd followed Hap into the Texas State Police, and finally into the Texas Rangers when the state legislature reactivated them. He'd made a damned good ranger—he'd go after the toughest, meanest cusses ever born, and get 'em every time. About the only thing he wouldn't do was turn on the Comanches that raised him. Hap, on the other hand, went after them with a vengeance.

Now the irony of the situation wasn't lost on him. While Clay was reading law in Austin, it was Hap who was riding north to sell beef to feed Clay's Indians. And he did so with real misgivings. Ybarra beef might see the savages through the winter, keeping them alive so they could raid Texas after the spring thaw. But it was the government peace policy, not his, and the Indian Bureau had hired a bunch of damned Quakers to implement it.

The soft-headed Quakers thought they could love Comanches into submission, but they actually made things worse by turning a blind eye when so-called peaceful agency Indians took to the war trail. If they'd take away every horse and every gun before they issued any food or clothes, they could put a stop to a lot of it, but they didn't. Instead, afraid of offending their red-skinned pets, they'd declined the army guard sent from Fort Sill, a few miles away.

He sucked in his breath, trying to stay awake, and noticed suddenly there was something more than sleet in the air. Smoke. He was still some distance from the agency, he knew that much. Reining in, he leaned over his pommel, squinting his eyes, trying to make out the trail ahead of him. And what he saw made his blood run cold.

Fifteen, maybe twenty tipis right in his path. If they saw him, they'd probably come after him, and he was in no shape to make a run for it. They'd be sure to recognize him, then all hell'd break loose. Yeah, they'd have a real party with him, and they'd make it last awhile.

They even had a name for him, he knew that, too. Too Many Bullets, a tribute to the sixteen-shot Henry rifle he'd carried ever since the war. He'd probably killed fifty or sixty Comanches with it. Yeah, the squaws would be sharpening their knives, all right.

He didn't dare run. He'd just have to go in real peaceful-like and brazen it out. Clay always said it was a rule among Comanches that they had to welcome anybody, even a worst enemy, if he came in peace. Hap didn't much like the notion, but he was about to put that rule to a real test.

"Well, Red," he murmured, nudging the big roan horse with his left knee, "I reckon we're going in real quiet-like." Straightening his shoulders, he rested his hand on the saddle sheath holding the Henry, then eased the animal into a slow, deliberate walk. Now if he could only keep the damned Indians from knowing how sick he was, maybe he'd have a chance of getting to the agency.

Bull Calf was huddled morosely over his fire, trying to ignore the fretful whimpering of Little Coyote, his two-year-old son, and the reproachful looks cast his way by Little Hand, the child's mother. Across from him, Sun in the Morning, his younger wife, boiled dead grass and mesquite bark in water. Goaded, he rose and reached for his rifle. Despite the bitter cold he was going to have to find something to feed them, even if he had to steal a cow from the agency. If the soldiers came for him, it'd at least be for something he'd done.

While Bull Calf was still loading the gun, a boy burst into his tipi, exclaiming breathlessly, *"Tejano!"*

Rifle in hand, the Comanche chief stepped outside to watch the lone rider coming through the swirling snow. The white man wore a battered leather hat pulled low, a heavy hide coat, buckskin pants, and scarred brown boots. As the gap closed between them, the war chief's jaw tensed with recognition.

Tondehwahkah. He'd faced the *Tejano* and five other men from ambush once, and it had been enough to make Bull Calf remember him forever. When the brief battle ended, every ranger was still alive, but nine Comanches lay dead, and four more had been wounded so badly that Bull Calf had abandoned the war trail and retreated to the safety of the Llano.

Despite the defeat, Bull Calf had lost no face, for Tondehwahkah's deadly aim was so well-known across the Comancheria that Coyote Droppings, medicine man of the Quahadis, made medicine bags against the ranger's power. But they hadn't worked, and after a number of braves had died wearing them, nobody believed in them anymore. Tondehwahkah's medicine had proven greater than that of his enemies.

Behind Bull Calf, Fat Elk emerged from his lodge, waving his gun defiantly. Grabbing the man's arm, the chief forced it down, telling him tersely he couldn't kill the ranger on the reservation without bringing the soldiers. Disappointed, the other Indian muttered that Bull Calf was turning into an old woman unfit to lead warriors. But even as he said it, others shouted him down.

"He lets us starve like helpless children," Fat Elk retorted angrily. "For the good of the people, he should have killed the woman where he found her; instead, he has brought a bad spirit to live among us, working its evil. Can any doubt it? Before Woman Who Walks Far came, there were many buffalo, and a Penetaka did not go hungry—now they are few, and we are starving! Where are the deer? The antelope? Even the rabbits? They have fled because of this woman! The spirit that possesses her must leave or we will die!"

"You could have killed her yourself, but your medicine was not strong enough," Bull Calf reminded him. "You were afraid of her." Rubbing his chin thoughtfully, he mused aloud, "But now Many Bullets will take her back to her people, and Haworth will give us food."

"A brave man does not wait to be handed what he can take," the disgruntled Indian scoffed to the others. "Look at Bull Calf. Once he was powerful, but now he is weak. Once he led us down the war trail, but no more. Now he cannot even lead a buffalo hunt. No, he leads us to beg in our own land!"

As his words brought a murmur of assent from some of them, the rider entered the camp. Fat Elk's gaze traveled from the big roan to the man in the saddle, and his bluster left him. He was facing Tondehwahkah, and the white man had his hand on the gun with many bullets. He retreated as Bull Calf stepped forward.

Hap's eyes took in the line of suddenly silent, grim-faced Comanches, wondering what the hell he'd gotten himself into. Suddenly, a little boy in a tattered breech-clout and worn leggings, his ribs sticking out above a bloated belly, spat out, *"Tejano!"* A woman quickly thrust the child behind her, whispering, "Tondehwahkah," as though he'd come straight from hell. Yeah, they knew who he was, all right, and they weren't exactly glad to see him.

He was too weak to whip an ant, but he knew he couldn't show it. He had to act like he'd intended to be there. Seeing the big, ugly buck in front of him, he raised his left hand in greeting.

"Howdy. Name's Walker—Hap Walker."

The Indian thumped his chest proudly. "Me Bull Calf—heap big chief." Speaking in pidgen English and signing at the same time, he immediately launched into what sounded like a bitter complaint, punctuating it by hitting his palm with his fist. "People come, make peace. No food, no smoke, no—" He paused, groping for a word, then finished with, "No nothing!" His voice rose angrily, threatening, "For Bull Calf, no food, no peace!"

"Whoa, now, you've got the wrong fella," Hap protested, unable to follow the grievance. "Tell it to Haworth."

"Haworth!" the Indian snorted. "He say no food! You look," he demanded, pointing at another underfed child. "People come, make peace—no get food." The chief's hands moved, signing rapidly, then he insisted, "No got captive, only woman—she no captive." When Hap didn't respond, the chief's frustration erupted. "You tell him give food! Only got this many white woman!" he insisted forcefully, holding up one finger. "No more!"

As light-headed as he was, Hap managed to guess that the Quaker agent was demanding the release of captives before he doled out rations. "You better take her in," he advised.

"No take," Bull Calf declared adamantly.

"You don't want the blue shirts to come, do you?"

The chief shook his head. "No lock Bull Calf up like Satanta! You take—give Haworth. Tell 'um give food!"

Now it was beginning to make sense. Ever since Haworth's predecessor had allowed Colonel Grierson to arrest Satanta, both Kiowas and Comanches were suspicious of the soldiers at Fort Sill. Bull Calf was wanting to avoid any confrontation by sending his captive in with Hap. And he was in no condition to take her. He wasn't even sure he could make it that far himself. It was taking all he had to keep from passing out then and there.

"Yeah, well, I don't—"

But the chief had already turned away, barking out something to a skinny squaw, who ducked behind the tipi.

Returning his attention to Hap, he threw up his hands in disgust. "Woman no good to Bull Calf—bad spirit. You take. Bull Calf no want her," he insisted.

Hap had to get out of there. He was shaking from a fever as much as from the cold. He nudged Old Red with his knee, but before the horse could move, the Indian had grabbed his bridle, stopping him. "No go," he declared forcefully.

On the other side of Bull Calf's tipi, Little Hand hesitated, then lifted a tattered flap. "Saleaweah?" Then, "Saleaweah!"

"Go away," Annie croaked.

"Saleaweah!"

This time there was anger in Little Hand's voice. She didn't want to come any closer. Annie rolled over and looked through the interior darkness to the lifted tipi flap, where she could see the sleet coming down almost sideways. Cold air rushed past her, blowing at the hide walls. Annie watched the Indian woman hesitate, then edge gingerly inside, still holding the flap, ready to flee. Her black eyes flitted around the circular room as though she expected to be seized at any moment by whatever possessed Annie.

She picked up one of the rocks from the pile blocking a hole and threw it at Annie, striking her shoulder, shouting for her to get up, that Bull Calf wanted her outside. To make her point, she bent down for another stone, then dropped it when Annie sat up. Her broad, flat face broke into a broken-toothed grin as she changed her manner, speaking kindly now. Backing out through the flap, she beckoned as though coaxing a child to follow her.

Though Annie was fully dressed, clad in an odd combination of fringed leggings and an oft-mended buckskin shirt pulled over a faded calico dress, she shivered as she stood. Picking up her tattered army blanket, she turned the bloodstained holes away from her and wrapped herself in it. Pulling it close, she followed after Little Hand unsteadily. Her limbs felt almost too weak to hold her.

The wind peppered her face with tiny pellets of sleet as it blew between tipis. Beneath her frayed moccasins a thin layer of ice cracked like eggshells as she walked over it. Coming around the side of Bull Calf's lodge, she saw a knot of Comanches gathered around someone on horseback. Her breath caught and her heart pounded with the realization that it was a white man.

He was looking at her, and she heard him mutter, "She looks like death warmed over."

"She no sick, no hurt, only *loco*," Bull Calf declared defensively. "No hurt woman. Saleaweah," he said, beckoning to her. Turning back to the rider, he translated, "Woman Who Walks Far."

As she passed them, women pulled their children into the shelter of their bodies and looked away. Warriors touched medicine sacks and amulets to protect themselves from her evil spirit. But Bull Calf stood his ground, trying not to show fear. Of all of them, only he had been kind. She kept her head averted, afraid he'd look into her face and know she'd duped him.

Hap tried to study her through the fog in his mind. Her face was gaunt and dirt-streaked, her greasy hair a matted nest of God only knew what, and her tattered clothes were filthy. She didn't look much like a white woman until she raised her eyes to him. They were blue, and a furtive hope flickered in them. He didn't have to ask—he knew she'd been through hell. As he looked at her, he didn't trust himself to speak.

Behind her, Bull Calf explained, "She no talk—*loco*. You take woman, tell Haworth only one," he insisted. "He give food, give smoke white chief promise!"

"Look, I—" Knowing he had no strength to help her, he ran his tongue over cracked, wind-raw lips. "I'll try to send somebody back for you," he promised lamely. "I'm sorry." Her eyes widened, then she blinked back tears, shaming him. "I can't—I'm in no shape—" His voice dropped almost to a whisper as he looked away. "I'll get somebody. I won't forget—"

"No! You can't leave me!" Annie cried. "You're my only chance!" Lunging at him, she grabbed his leg and clawed his arm, pulling herself up as she put her moccasined foot on his boot. For a moment she hung there, both of them teetering awkwardly. Then she managed to get her leg across the roan's back. As he struggled to keep his balance, she settled her body behind the saddle and leaned forward. Pulling the blanket up to cover her head and shoulders, she slid her hands beneath his coat to grasp his gun belt.

Shocked that she'd spoken, Bull Calf reached out to her, but she leaned away. "Let's go!" she yelled behind Hap's ear. Her foot kicked Old Red's flank, and the horse broke free, jerking the bridle out of the Comanche's other hand. Hap caught the saddle horn and held on.

Still stunned, Bull Calf stared after them, then found his voice. "You tell white chief Bull Calf no take woman—you tell him! Tell 'um give food!" he shouted.

"You'll rot in hell first," Hap muttered under his breath. As he said it, the woman's knee bumped his left thigh,

34

making him sick to his stomach. It was all he could do to gasp, "Got a bad leg. Damned thing's sore as a boil. Got to watch out for it. Can't stand—"

Feeling him weave unsteadily, she reached around his waist and locked her thin fingers together across his stomach, holding him within her tight embrace. Despite the heavy hide coat, his body felt cold and his shirt was as soaked as if he'd been in the river.

"You sick, mister?" she asked over his shoulder.

He started to deny it, then swallowed the words with another wave of nausea. "Yeah, well, you don't look too good yourself," he managed finally. "Be damned lucky if we make it in."

"We've got to. How far to the agency?"

"I don't know," he gritted out.

All he could think was that he had to concentrate on getting there. He was so tired, so damned weak. He felt like some old man about to nod off, but he couldn't. He had to keep thinking. He had to keep his mind going somehow. With an effort he pursed his lips and tried to whistle "Dixie," but after the first bar he lost his place and had to abandon it.

As silence descended like a curtain between them, the sleet came down harder, icing everything it touched, even his mustache, laying a deceptively pretty glaze over rocks, bare limbs, and dead grass. If the heavy snow would just hold off a little longer . . . just half an hour longer . . .

They were going to make it. They had to. She'd come too far, endured too much, to give up now, Annie told herself fervently. She was holding freedom within her grasp, and God could not abandon her now. Closing her eyes, she prayed for the man in front of her, for her own safety, and for Susannah. Always for Susannah. She didn't know how long she prayed, only that she did.

His whole body shook as if he had the ague, and yet he didn't feel cold. He was sweating like it was July instead of November. Blinking to clear his mind, he tried to fix his thoughts on the woman behind him.

"Name's Walker, Hap Walker," he mumbled.

The wind carried his words away. "What?" she shouted.

He roused. "Hap Walker!"

The name seemed familiar, but it had been so long since she'd heard anyone speak her language. Hap Walker, he'd said. She hesitated, then blurted out, "I'm Mrs. Bryce, Annie Bryce!"

Bryce. He ought to know the name. Annie Bryce. He furrowed his brow, trying to break through the haze clouding his mind. Ethan Bryce. And in a flash of lucidity, he was standing on the porch of an empty house, looking across a yard, watching those bedsheets flap on that laundry line, feeling helpless. Yeah, he remembered when it happened, all right.

"Sorry, damned sorry," he mumbled. He slumped, nearly losing his balance, then he righted himself. "Damn."

Alarmed, she turned loose of him long enough to pull her blanket around his shoulders also. Tucking it in at the front of his neck, she could feel his pulse beneath her cold fingers. It was faint and uneven.

"Mister, you need a doctor right now."

"Just got to get there—just got to get there, that's all," he muttered thickly. Willing himself to hang on, he straightened his shoulders. "I'm all right," he insisted, but he knew he wasn't. He was sick enough to die.

The wind had lessened somewhat, but the snow was

picking up, coming down in large flakes, laying a white blanket over the veneer of ice. If they got lost in the storm, there wouldn't be any hope for either of them. She felt for the reins, and he didn't resist when she took them.

She had no idea where she was, but she could tell the horse was following a road of sorts, so she let the reins slacken in the hope that the animal would just keep going. Sooner or later they had to reach something, but right now all she could do was try to hold Hap Walker on his horse while she prayed for help. If he lost his seat, she knew she couldn't help him.

They rode what seemed like an eternity through nearly blinding snow. Her arms ached from holding him, yet she didn't dare ease them. Finally, her own fatigue made it nearly impossible to go on. Leaning sideways, she tried to look around him.

"Do you see anything?" she asked anxiously.

He didn't answer.

"Mr. Walker, can you hear me?" she shouted.

Nothing.

Frightened and unable to see much of anything, she reined in and tried to dismount. As she leaned to her right, his weight shifted, and both of them fell, landing in a tangle on the snow-covered ground. His heavier body pinned her there, forcing her to struggle from beneath him. As she rolled him over, he made no effort to help himself. She stood up shakily, then looked down. His eyes were closed, his face ashen.

"Mister, you've got to get up!" Bending over, she tried to lift his shoulder, but couldn't. He fell back like a sack of sand, unmoving.

Panicked, she turned, her eyes searching for some sign

of life somewhere. She hadn't come this far to die in a blizzard with a stranger. Tears of frustration stung her eyes, nearly blinding her, then she blinked. Wiping her hand across her face, she stared, scarcely believing what she saw. In the distance the faint outlines of several buildings rose through the swirling snow. They'd almost made it, but not quite.

She scooped a handful of snow and rubbed it over Hap Walker's face, trying to revive him. "Listen, I think I see the agency," she said loudly. "Come on, you've got to get up. We're almost there!"

His eyelids fluttered but did not open. "Go on," he mumbled. "Can't—"

"You've got to!"

It was no use. He wasn't going to move, and she couldn't make him. She straightened her aching shoulders and gathered her blanket closer. Grasping the horse's reins, she tried to pull the animal toward a rock so she could remount. It wouldn't budge, and she didn't have enough strength to fight it, either. Instead, it dropped its head to stand guard over Walker.

Now it didn't matter that she was too weak to walk more than a few steps. If she didn't, they'd both die. And she hadn't survived Two Trees for this. After casting one last, desperate look at Hap Walker, she squared her shoulders beneath the blanket and started for what she hoped was the Indian agency.

Her moccasins slipped and slid on the ice, forcing her to plod through the deeper snow, while the wind whipped the blanket back from her face. Fixing her mind on the agency, she kept her head down and walked. And walked. And walked.

As she stumbled into the agency yard, an Indian came out of the stable and found her. Too tired to fight or think even, she lunged past his outstretched arm, then fell into a snow drift. Summoning the last of her strength, she crawled on all fours to the door, where she collapsed against it. Reaching over her, the Indian rapped the wood with his knuckles. She almost fell inside when the door opened.

"My word, whatever—?"

She looked up, saw a white man standing there, and she managed to gasp, "I left Mr. Walker out there—Hap Walker—and—"

"Hap Walker!"

Catching her breath, she nodded. "I think—I think he may be dead by now. I couldn't help him—" She choked, unable to go on.

Somebody lifted her and carried her to a rocker by the fire. As the blanket slipped, she heard a woman's voice say, "Why, she's naught but skin and bones!" Too exhausted to respond, she turned her head against the hard back of the rocker and held on.

It was cold in the ambulance, and the heavy canvas covering beat like giant bird wings against its frame. Heavily bundled in wool blankets, Annie lay still, fighting to keep down the bowl of beef broth she'd drunk at the Indian agency. A medical corpsman, Corporal Nash, knelt between her and Hap Walker, trying to steady both stretchers as the vehicle rocked and lumbered awkwardly through the snow.

There was an unreality to everything. After months and years of dreaming and planning for this day, she felt an odd detachment, almost a strange, unexpected melancholy. The joy she'd first felt was tempered now by the realization that nothing would ever be the same again, that she'd lost Ethan and Jody forever, that she'd be going home without Susannah. She'd be facing her neighbors alone. And she held no illusions about that.

No, the hope of finding Susannah had sustained her throughout her captivity, and it had to sustain her now. If she gave up on that, she might as well die. She had to believe that either the state of Texas or the United States

Army would help her regain her daughter. Without Susannah she had nothing.

Lurking in the back of her mind had always been the fear that Susannah's captor might have murdered her like Two Trees had killed Gretchen Halser. Poor Gretchen. When the soldiers were closing in, Two Trees hoped they'd take some time to bury the white girl, giving him the chance to escape. Annie would have shared the same fate, but instead of cowering, waiting for that final blow, she'd attacked him, shrieking wildly, making him think she'd gone insane. As mean and violent as he was, he feared the spirit world, believing if he killed a possessed person, the evil spirit would take him instead.

So he'd abandoned Annie in a brush-filled ravine, and by the time she'd managed to crawl out of it, the troopers had already passed. Ironically, they never saw Gretchen Halser's body, nor did they hear Annie's cries for help. Left alone in the desert, she'd tried to walk out, taking the opposite direction to keep from being found by Two Trees. She'd believed if she went far enough, she'd encounter a fort—or at the very least, a white settler. And she'd been wrong.

She walked as far as her feet would hold her, losing all sense of time, but it must have been two or three days before a band of Penetaka Comanches found her. She'd never forget the bitter frustration she'd felt, looking up at the ugly, big-chested, bandy-legged Bull Calf. With her last ounce of strength she'd lunged at him, scratching his face, screaming invectives, hoping he'd be as afraid as Two Trees.

But despite his frightening aspect, Bull Calf was about as different from Two Trees as an Indian could be.

While he could boast of following the war trail deep into Texas, killing settlers and stealing stock, he never took captives, nor did he seem to delight in torture like so many others. To him the struggle with whites was simply a war, captives were more trouble than they were worth, and an enemy ought to be dispatched as quickly and efficiently as possible. By the standards of his people, he was downright humane.

So instead of abandoning Annie, he'd taken pity on her, telling her she could follow behind him and eat his family's leftovers. He'd even cut a scrawny pony from his herd and tied it to a tree for her. Hopelessly lost, she'd mounted the animal and trailed after the Penetaka band, never daring to speak for fear he'd discover she hadn't lost her mind.

Later, as she listened from a good distance behind him, she heard him explain to his indignant wives that he'd done it for his mother, who'd been scalped by Crows, something that condemned the poor woman to wander the spirit world forever. In showing compassion for Saleaweah, or Woman Who Walks Far, as he called her, he was easing his own guilt over his mother's death.

Not that he didn't share the Comanche fear of spirits. He never spoke to Annie without fingering the eagle feathers that gave him his power, and even then he maintained a certain wary distance. There had been times when she suspected he let her stay to prove his bravery to the others.

But that was behind her now, and it was time to stop thinking of those years. Resolutely, she turned her attention to the man across from her. By the time Mr. Haworth and two Indian policemen had carried him in,

Hap Walker was so sick he was hallucinating. Even now, after the medical aide had revived him several times with liquor of ammonia, he wasn't making any sense. From time to time he'd rouse enough to croak out orders to imaginary subordinates, then fall back, mumbling. His fever was high, Corporal Nash said, and that made him restless.

She was still trying to place him. When Mr. Haworth had sent one of the agency Indians up to the fort, he'd repeated several times, "Tell them it's Hap Walker—Hap Walker—and he's sick, bad sick. Tell them to send help right away. It's Hap Walker—can you remember to tell them that? Otherwise, they won't want to come out in the storm."

The wagon was slowing, then it halted. Nash relaxed his grip on her stretcher. "We're here," he announced. Turning his attention to Walker, he shook his shoulder, trying to rouse him. "Captain Walker—"

That was another thing—everybody called him "captain," although he wore no uniform.

"Captain Walker," Nash repeated loudly, "we're here."

"Uh?"

"You're at Sill, sir. If you can just hang on a little longer, we'll get you in."

"Pinned down . . . they got m'leg—"

"You're at Sill—Fort Sill, sir."

"Rios—where's Rios?" Walker's head twisted, but his eyes didn't focus. "Take my gun. I can't—"

"He's still out of it," the soldier decided, shaking his head. "I'd say Haworth was right. He's in a bad way, a real bad way."

"At least he's no worse than he was an hour ago."

43

He looked up, thinking she was saying he was neglecting her. "You doing all right, ma'am?" he asked politely.

"Yes."

There was a wariness in his eyes, as though he didn't know what to make of her. It'd been the same with Mr. Haworth, who'd been quick to voice the opinion that she belonged at the fort rather than on the reservation. Maybe he was afraid her presence might cause trouble with the Indians. It didn't matter where she went, she reflected wearily. All she wanted to do was regain her strength so she could press the government to search for Susannah. With enough food she'd be all right.

"Looks like you've got a welcoming committee, Captain Walker," Nash said, opening the canvas flap. "Even got Old Black Jack himself out here, and that's something, for sure. Yes, sir, you got a lot of folks caring about you, all right."

"Rios, tell Clay—"

"Now, don't you fret yourself, Captain Walker. You're going to get well. We got Doc Sprenger here, and if anybody can fix you up, it'll be him. He's a mite crochety sometimes, but he sure can patch a body up." Half turning to Annie, he told her, "They'll be ready to carry you in right away, ma'am."

She sat up, then leaned forward. She was so weak, so very weak, and she'd moved too quickly, making herself dizzy. "No, I'm all right," she said as Nash reached to steady her. "Tell them to see to him first. And I'd rather walk, if you don't mind."

"Ma'am, you're in no shape—"

In that moment she was afraid of the pity certain to come her way. And she knew she couldn't stand that any better than the censure likely to follow. "No," she declared resolutely, "I don't wish to be carried like an invalid."

Despite the bitter wind blowing heavy snow across the parade ground, close to twenty men, including the commanding officer, had waited for the ambulance. Staying in the warmth of her house, Cora Sprenger was standing at the window, watching intently, praying for the strength to welcome her guest.

"Dear God," she'd written in her journal while she waited, "it has been my misfortune to see one such wretched creature; I know not how I shall deal with another. The shame and degradation of a woman's captivity leaves such terrible scars on the mind and body that I am determined to save my last shot for myself rather than risk capture by those capable of such savagery."

The words had been incapable of expressing the horror she still felt whenever she thought of Millie Purvis's face. And she would never forget the scars that crisscrossed Millie's body. The squaws had done that, she'd said. To Cora it was beyond understanding how a female of one race could do such barbarous things to a female of another.

As she watched, Corporal Nash opened the canvas cover, and two soldiers climbed up into the ambulance. Cora held her breath, then exhaled when she realized the occupant of the stretcher they passed down was a man. For a moment she dared to hope Haworth hadn't sent the captive, that the Quakers were ministering to her, after all. But while one soldier jumped to the ground, the other turned back, and she knew she was about to receive the poor, pitiful creature. She looked away, fighting tears, unable to watch any longer.

After the dim interior of the ambulance, the snow was blinding. Grasping the hand offered her, Annie gathered her blankets closer, then put her foot on the icy step—and lost her balance. An officer lunged to catch her, swung her body up into his arms, and carried her past a line of sober-faced soldiers toward the surgeon's quarters.

"I'm all right, really," Annie insisted. "I can walk."

"It's slick out, ma'am. No sense risking a fall."

Embarrassed, she turned her face into the hard-finished wool of his blue coat and fixed her eyes on the gold cavalry buttons. One ordeal was over, another was just beginning. And she realized with resignation that there was nothing she could do now but hold her head high and ignore everyone who tried to pry the details of her captivity out of her. No matter what, she wasn't going to relive them again for anyone.

"Mrs. Sprenger!" he called out.

Cora's breath caught audibly. Behind her, Sarabeth Hughes hovered. "Well, she's here," Cora managed, moving toward the door.

It swung inward, admitting a blast of cold air as he stepped inside. Looking past Cora to his wife, Elliot Hughes said, "She's light as a feather, but Nash says other than being more than half-starved, she's in pretty good shape. Where do you want her?"

"Just down," Annie answered quickly. "I'm all right now. I can stand, really. I'm more tired than anything. But I—" She paused, aware they were staring at her curiously, then went on, "But I'm in desperate need of soap and water—and something clean, anything clean, to put on."

"You'd better rest first," Cora said firmly. "If you'll just help her to that chair, Lieutenant," she told Hughes.

But as he put her down, Annie stood her ground. "I'd rather wash up, if you don't mind it." Her hand crept to her matted hair, and she flushed self-consciously. "I'm going to need a comb—and some kerosene, please."

Sarabeth Hughes was the first to find her voice. "We thought—that is, we were *told* you were captured by Indians. It must have been terrible for you."

Annie didn't meet her eyes. "Yes," she said simply.

"But you don't look—that is, I mean . . . other than—"

"Hush, Sarabeth," Cora said, cutting her off. Looking again at Annie, she apologized, "I'm sorry, my dear, you must think us utterly rude, but we were led to expect— oh, dear, I'm making a botch of this, aren't I? You must forgive me. I'm just so glad to see that you aren't, well, *disfigured* like so many when they are got back," she managed somewhat lamely. Then, recovering, she tried again, blurting out, "Oh, my dear, we're so very glad you're back among us! It must have been terrible for you! And, gracious, where *are* my manners? I'm Mrs. Sprenger, and this is Mrs. Hughes," she said, smiling. "And of course, you've already met our gallant Lieutenant Hughes."

"Annie Bryce. I was Mrs. Ethan Bryce before—" Annie paused awkwardly. "Before my husband was murdered," she finished, exhaling. "We had a farm on the San Saba in Texas." There. She'd said about all she wanted to. She touched her hair again and forced a smile. "Please, I think I'd better take care of this first, or we shall all regret it."

Her meaning wasn't lost on Cora. "Yes, of course. I

think I have laid out everything you'll need, so if you'll just follow me, Mrs. Bryce, we'll get you all fixed up." Laying a hand on Annie's arm, she directed her toward an open door. "Now, we've plenty of room, so you just make yourself at home."

But Sarabeth was still regarding Annie suspiciously. "How long were you a captive?" she wanted to know.

"Since the fall of 1870."

"Three years," Cora murmured, shaking her head. "All I can say is you're far stronger than I would have been. It's a credit to you that you survived."

"I can't believe they let you live for three whole years."

"Sara—" There was no mistaking the warning in Lieutenant Hughes's voice. "I'm sure Mrs. Bryce has no wish to speak of her captivity—at least not yet, anyway."

"Well, I just meant—"

"Let us just say I survived," Annie cut in dryly. "And now I want to go home as soon as I can."

"Well, I certainly can't blame you for that," Cora declared briskly. "And I am sure that once you are sufficiently recovered, arrangements can be made. But right now we've got to see you get enough rest and food."

Annie hesitated awkwardly, then forced herself to impose further on Cora Sprenger's charity. "I, uh, I'll be needing to borrow some clothes until I can sew myself something to wear, but when I get home, I can send you the money for whatever you can spare. Right now all I have is what you see."

"I've already collected a few things and spread them on the bed for you to try on, my dear," Cora reassured her. "And as for money, well, there's no need, no need at all."

"No, really, we had money in the bank. I can pay for everything."

"Pish and nonsense! My dear, I cannot wear any of them anymore, anyway. Indeed, my greatest concern is that you will find the dresses sadly outdated. No, I won't brook any argument," she declared firmly. "Now, you go on in there, and you'll find everything at the ready. There's hot and cold water pitchers already filled by the washstand, and plenty of good lye soap for a start. And I put lard and kerosene, along with a comb and scissors, on the night table."

Annie tried to swallow the lump forming in her throat. "Thank you," she managed to whisper. "I'll be beholden to you forever, Mrs. Sprenger."

"Oh, go on with you! And while you are getting started, I'll be heating the rest of the water for the washtub. There, I think that's everything, isn't it? Oh, the towels. I put plenty of towels on the bed, too, but I expect you'll want the bath before you'll be wanting them, won't you?"

"Yes."

"And if you need me for anything, I'll be more than willing to help."

"No, I'll be all right, thank you."

"Well, in my time I've bathed the sick and tended the wounded, so there's not much I've not seen. I'm not the least bit squeamish about anything, I promise you." Afraid Annie was too weak to walk more than a few steps on her own, Cora took her elbow and guided her. "Goodness, they didn't feed you much, did they?" she said, looking down at Annie's arm.

"Not lately, anyway. They were all starving."

"Serves them right, to my notion. I wouldn't care if every last one of them perished from the earth," Cora declared stoutly. "But I'll have you fattened up again in no time, starting today. I've already made a good hearty broth, and my noodles are drying. I'll have them boiled within the hour." She stopped to peer into Annie's pale face. "They did give you something to eat at the agency, didn't they?"

"Yes."

"Good. We'll have some hot cornbread and milk with the noodles, so that ought to set all right in your stomach."

"It doesn't matter. I learned to go for days without food, then gorge myself when I got the chance."

"Well, you won't be going without food around here. Will—Major Sprenger, that is—lives by his stomach. But that's a man for you, I guess." Cora stopped at the door, then turned to Annie. "If you need anything more, don't hesitate to ask. There's a bell by the bed you can ring, and I'll be right here."

"Thank you."

As Cora Sprenger closed the door behind her, Annie could hear the other woman observe archly, "Well, she certainly seems to have survived three years with those savages rather well, hasn't she?"

"For God's sake, Sara, she lost her husband," Lieutenant Hughes retorted. "And she's thin as a rail. You act like you're disappointed she doesn't look like the Purvis woman."

"I wouldn't call being starved surviving well," Cora added.

"There's no telling how many of the savages she's been

with, is there?" Sara went on nastily. "No doubt that's how she managed to live—by letting them do whatever they wanted."

"That's enough. She can probably hear you," her husband said harshly. "Good God, Sara, you ought to be ashamed to think it, let alone say such a thing."

"Well, it's true, isn't it?"

"What would you have done under the same circumstances?" he countered.

"I would have chosen to die first, Elliott."

Despite having made the same resolution to herself, Cora murmured, "The desire to live is a strong one, my dear. I don't really think we can fault Mrs. Bryce for staying alive."

"The very notion of one of those filthy savages even touching me is more than I could bear," the younger woman insisted. "I should never feel clean again after that, and I'm sure I could never face Elliott or anyone else the rest of my life. No, I'd have killed myself."

"Well, she didn't. Come on, Sara, I'm going over to the infirmary to see what's going on with Captain Walker. You do have a sewing circle or something this afternoon, don't you?" he asked pointedly.

"It was the Indians that got him, wasn't it?" Sarabeth blurted out.

"I don't know, Sara. If it was, it didn't happen in the last day or two. Nash said he's running one helluva fever, and you don't get that overnight."

"Really, Elliott—"

"All right, then, he's got a high fever. Now, come on. I'm sure Mrs. Sprenger's got enough on her hands with

Mrs. Bryce without having to listen to you carry on about how you hate it out here."

"Why wouldn't I hate it here?" she demanded. "You didn't tell me there'd be nasty, dirty Indians all over the place, did you? You didn't tell me I'd be exiled to an outpost in the middle of nowhere! Well, I don't want to live here—I don't deny it! And if you won't take me, I'm going back to Ohio alone! There, does that surprise you?"

"You knew I was in the army when you married me, Sara," he responded evenly. "As a soldier I have to go where I am assigned." He turned to Cora apologetically. "I'm sorry, ma'am. I'll see she stays away from Mrs. Bryce. The woman doesn't need to hear things like that."

But Annie had heard it. Every word. And as much as she'd expected, even resigned herself to the very things the Hughes woman had said, they still stung. And this was only the beginning of what would surely be more to come. Fighting the urge to weep, Annie moved to the washstand, then stared in shock at the gaunt-faced stranger in the mirror.

Her hand crept to her hair, feeling the lice-infested, matted knots. She touched the taut, dirt-caked skin that clung to her cheekbones. Her fingers traced the hollows, then moved to the dry, cracked, bloodless lips. But it was the stranger's eyes that tore at her soul. They were too old to belong to her.

She reached for the pitcher of hot water and poured it into the washbasin. Then she picked up the soap and lathered it between her hands. It'd be hours before she got herself cleaned up, and then it would be only the part of her people could see. Sarabeth Hughes had been right about one thing—she'd never, ever be clean on the inside again, no matter how long she lived.

The door cracked open behind her, and Cora Sprenger carried a steaming kettle in. "I'd be glad to help," she offered again. Walking to the tin bathtub, she emptied the hot water into it. When she straightened up, she smiled reassuringly at Annie. "You're going to be all right. It just takes time," she said gently.

Annie's face crumpled then, and she gave up the fight. "But I don't have any time!" she cried. "I've got a little girl out there somewhere!"

"Oh, my dear—"

As Cora Sprenger's arms enveloped her shoulders, Annie turned her head against the older woman's bosom, and she sobbed uncontrollably. Rather than pushing her away, Cora stood there, holding her, smoothing the awful, tangled mass of hair against Annie's back.

Finally, Annie stood back, embarrassed by her outburst. Wiping wet cheeks, she managed to whisper, "I'm sorry. I don't usually cry, really." Turning back to the washstand, she touched her hair. "It looks hopeless, doesn't it?" she asked wearily.

"No. But we may have to cut it before we soak it with the kerosene. It'd be easier to get a comb through it then."

Annie closed her burning eyes for a moment, then shook her head. "No, if it takes me all day and night, I'm going to try to save as much as I can. Ethan loved my hair," she recalled painfully. "He said it reminded him of angels."

"Your Ethan loved *you*, my dear," Cora responded softly. Moving behind Annie, she looked at the mess for a moment, then decided, "If you can stand the pain of a comb going through it, I'll work with you to save it. And if that takes us all night, I don't mind in the least. I expect Will's going to be busy with Captain Walker for a while, anyway. When we are done, we can visit. If you want to, you can tell me all about your little girl."

"I can't—at least not now," Annie whispered. "Not yet."

M ajor Wilson Sprenger's first assessment was that Hap Walker was too sick for surgery. His second was that without it, the man might die from a rampant infection. He decided to operate.

"You've got yourself in one hell of a fix, Hap," the surgeon told the semiconscious man. "Take it easy, boys. Get him on the table without moving that leg if you can."

It was a futile order. Walker's body went rigid as his knee bent and his foot caught on the edge of the table, twisting his leg underneath him and pulling the muscle in his thigh. Before the two soldiers who'd carried him could straighten it out, he'd rolled onto his side and vomited. Sprenger noted with relief that he hadn't eaten much. While a third attendant cleaned up the mess, the surgeon kept talking, repeating Walker's name at every opportunity, trying to focus his patient on what he had to do.

"That the same leg where you took the Comanchero bullet, Hap?" Sprenger asked him. When Walker didn't answer, he spoke directly into his ear. "I'm going to take a look at it," he said loudly. "I'm going to see what's the matter with your leg."

Walker's eyes opened. "Clay—?"

"Boy's in Texas. You don't know where you are, do you, Hap?"

"Tell him, got to get word to him . . ."

"Tell him what? What do you want me to tell him? That you're sick? I expect we'll try to get word out as soon as the storm's over."

"Sanchez-Torres coming . . . New Mexico . . ."

"Sanchez-Torres is dead. Your boy McAlester took care of him last summer."

"He's dead? Clay—?"

"Way I heard it, McAlester blew him up, plumb to smithereens."

"Good." Hap closed his eyes.

Sprenger took out a straight-edged razor and stropped it. "I'm going to have to cut off your pants for a look-see, Hap."

"No," Walker croaked.

"Not your leg, your pants." The surgeon looked up at Nash. "Hold him real still, trooper. If he thrashes around, there's no telling what I'm liable to cut."

"Yes, sir."

"Walsh, get on the other side and hold that foot, but don't turn it. Yeah, that's it."

As cold as it was in the infirmary, Sprenger wiped his brow with his sleeve, then made a light stroke, slicing the weathered buckskin several inches below Hap's groin. Working carefully, he cut a flap that extended down to the knee. He laid the razor aside and lifted it back, exposing the leg beneath. About mid-thigh, he found a puckered scar. At a cursory glance, it appeared to be almost healed, but the flesh around it told a different story. It was hot and swollen with red streaks extending both upward and downward from it.

"Looks like it's going septic," he muttered. "Parker, get me the chloroform, will you? Soak the rag with a good capful," he ordered over his shoulder.

"Need the capital saw?" Nash asked.

Sprenger shook his head. "Not yet. I'd like to see what's down there first." Turning to the basin nearby, he washed his hands thoroughly with strong-smelling lye soap, then toweled them dry. "It's an old wound, so there's got to be a reason it's infected. And one way or another, I'm going to have to clean it out, or it's going to kill him."

"Looks like it should have been an amputation in the first place," Parker observed. "The bullet had to have hit the bone."

"Looks that way, doesn't it?" Returning his attention to Hap, the surgeon asked him, "Boydston over at Griffin fix this, or was it Abbott down at Stockton? I'd say one of 'em botched the business, and I'd sure as hell tell 'em about it if I were you."

Hap opened his eyes again, saw the surgeon's operating case, and for a moment he thought he was at Shiloh. "No," he gasped, grasping the surgeon's left hand. "Don't cut. Too many limbs out there already."

Sprenger pulled free. "If I don't have to, I won't," he promised. "Chloroform ready?"

"Yes, sir. Here it is, sir," the corporal responded promptly. "Right at your elbow."

Reaching back, the older man took the cloth, checked it, then leaned forward, pressing it over Hap Walker's nose. "Take a good whiff, and you'll be out cold before I get to the good part."

Instead, Hap began struggling, clutching Sprenger's arms, trying to rise from the table. But the two soldiers on either side held him down until he was still.

"Don't know why they always fight it, but they do," the doctor muttered. He lifted the cloth for a quick look, then nodded. "He's out. Parker, keep your finger on his pulse and stand ready with liquor of ammonia if it weakens."

"Yes, sir."

Sprenger surveyed the thigh again. "Another inch, and it would have hit the artery. Then he'd have bled to death," he murmured. "Nash—?"

"Yes, sir?"

"Put your thumb on the femoral artery in his groin and slow the blood through it."

"Yes, sir."

Turning to his case, the surgeon selected a scalpel. "After I make the incision, I'm going to dissect the muscle around the wound." As he spoke, he cut straight across the scar tissue, opening it, then stroked through the inflamed muscle beneath. He wiped his brow again and studied the exposed tissue. "Looks like the bullet went this way," he murmured, taking the dissection forceps to pull back the muscle. "Here, hold this, will you?" he told Walsh. "Keep it out of my way."

"Yes, sir."

He picked up the scalpel again. "Must be a piece of lead in here somewhere," he mumbled to himself as he cut deeply, taking the incision all the way to the bone. The knife punctured a pocket of pus, and the foul-smelling green exudate spurted. While both Nash and

Walsh gagged, Sprenger began whistling softly. After placing the scalpel on a tray, he dipped his finger into an iodine solution and probed the path of the bullet, feeling around the bone.

"Rough as a cob," he murmured. "Bone slivers everywhere—damned thing was in pieces. And there's lead in there, a lot of it." Hooking his finger, he pulled it up, bringing a bit of bone with it. "No wonder it didn't heal inside. There's constant irritation there. Must've hurt like the devil all the time. Give me the sequestrum," he ordered.

Parker produced the probe, then leaned over to watch as Sprenger used it to dig where his finger had been. One by one the surgeon pulled out several bone splinters, then the first lead fragment, and laid them on the tray. Within minutes, he'd added six more bits of bullet to the collection.

"Ever see anything like this, son?" he asked Parker.

"No, sir."

"Well, when I was with the 9th Massachusetts, I saw a lot of 'em. It was hell, son. I was cutting off limbs at four to the hour some days. Wasn't much else we could do in the field. No time so save 'em if I could've done it. Had a fifty-two percent fatality rate, which was about two percent better than the average, so I guess I did about as well as most of my colleagues."

"You going to have to take this one?" Nash wanted to know.

"If it doesn't heal. But I'm going to try to save it first. Parker, how's the pulse?"

"Even, sir."

"If he so much as blinks or looks like he's coming

around, give him another snort of the chloroform. Aha, yeah." This time Sprenger managed to pull out a large part of the bullet. "Doesn't look like anybody even tried to get it out, does it?" he muttered. "Makes you wonder what they teach in medical college anymore. Not much about lead poisoning, by the looks of it. Remind me to mention this to Boydston, will you? If he did this, he ought to be told about it, and if he didn't, he shouldn't have left the bullet in, anyway." He pulled the last piece out, then looked up triumphantly. "I'll bet if I put all of this together, I'd have about a .50—what do you think, soldier?"

"I couldn't say, sir. They just look like lead fragments to me."

"Yes, indeed. I'd say that Comanchero had himself a buffalo gun," Sprenger decided. "I'll have to show that to Hap when he wakes up." Wiping his face with his other sleeve, he returned to the wound. "Too late to do too much with the bone other than clean it up a bit, I guess." Looking up, he addressed Walsh. "You can put away the dissecting forceps, son, and make up about a cup of ten percent iodine solution. I'm going to flush this before I stitch it up. And I'm going to leave a little bit of the incision open—why is that, soldier?"

"You're asking me, sir?"

" 'Course I am. How's a man to learn anything if he doesn't think about it? Now, why would I want it to keep draining?"

"So the abscess won't form again, I expect."

"Damned right."

Whistling a peppy tune now, the surgeon quickly wiped the pus away with a cloth, then squirted the antiseptic into the area with a trocar several times. Finally, he patted the area as dry as he could and started stitching deftly. When he looked up, the three men were exchanging glances.

"Something the matter?" he demanded.

"No, sir." Caught out, Parker suppressed a smile.

"Then what's so damned funny, soldier?"

"Nothing, sir."

"Actually, sir," Nash answered, "we were just being grateful that this wasn't an autopsy."

"Oh? How's that?"

"Some of them get pretty rank, especially in the summer, sir. It's hard to follow a lecture when your stomach's in your throat."

"Think I talk too much, eh? Well, let me tell you, soldier, a man can't learn too much in this business. We've got too many people depending on us to keep 'em going."

As they fell silent, he finished with the leg. "Nash, give him a whiff of the ammonia, will you? Then fan him as he comes around. Walsh, I want a half grain of morphine in four drops of water drawn into the syringe."

The ammonia burned Hap's nose, making him cough. "That's enough," Sprenger ordered. Leaning over his patient, he said loudly, "Well, it's done, Hap, and if the infection goes down, you're going to be damned lucky, you know that?"

Walker's eyes fluttered but did not open. "My leg—?" he whispered hoarsely.

"You've still got it, but the next time you decide to carry pieces of lead in the bone, don't come to me. And for God's sake, stay off it awhile and give it time to heal, you hear?"

Hap's mouth was so dry he could scarcely form words. "What—?"

"A deep abscess. You nearly bought your ticket to the great beyond with a damned abscess." Straightening up, Sprenger took the syringe from Nash. "I'm going to make you real happy here, Hap," he murmured. "In a minute you won't give a damn about anything." As he spoke, he slide the needle under the skin and squeezed the morphine in. "They say a man can dream in color with this," he murmured, withdrawing the needle.

"You want me to clean up for you, Doc?" Parker asked.

"Yeah. You'd better boil those ten minutes instead of five." Looking at the others, he ordered, "Get him to bed, boys, and cut the rest of those pants off. It's time he bought himself another pair, anyway."

"Yes, sir. What do you want to put him in? A hospital shirt?" Nash asked.

"You'll have to. We'll draw off any pus that forms with the trocar tonight and again in the morning. Maybe if we keep that abscess empty, it'll try to heal. Otherwise, there's not a chance of saving the leg. Fever's a good thing—up to a point. If it goes over a hundred, give him three grains of quinine. You can repeat that in four to five hours." The surgeon paused, mentally reviewing his orders, then nodded. "Well, that's about all I can think of right now. I'm going to wash up, then I'll be seeing how Mrs. Sprenger's managing with the job I gave her. I ought to be back in an hour or so."

But after he'd washed and changed into one of the clean shirts Cora kept in his surgery for him, he had to take one last look at Hap Walker. The man was lying with his leg propped on a rolled blanket, and he was asleep.

It'd be touch and go, but if the blood wasn't actually infected, and if that abscess cleared up, Hap just might walk out of Fort Sill on both feet. He turned to leave, thinking he'd compliment the boys for elevating the leg—they'd done it without being reminded.

"It wasn't the great beyond, Doc," Walker whispered behind him. "I was going to hell."

"How do you know? You never got there," Sprenger countered without turning around. "Don't move it off that roll, whatever you do, and I'll be back after a while. I've got to take a look at the woman you brought in."

"Her name's Bryce—she's from Texas."

"If you can remember that, you were in better shape than I thought."

"No. I just heard her say it before I passed out."

Sprenger was almost out the door before Hap spoke again, and his voice was so low the surgeon wasn't sure he heard the words right.

"I tried to go after her, but I was too late—too damned late."

Still dressed in the blue cotton dress Cora Sprenger had provided her, Annie sat in the slat-back chair, rocking absently. She hadn't taken the laudanum—she didn't want to sleep yet. Everything was still too new to her, and all day long her mood had swung between the relief of freedom and the pain of loss.

She couldn't bring herself to go to bed. Her gaze strayed there, taking in the pretty handmade quilt turned neatly back, the starched ruffle beneath, the snowy sheets. The last time she'd slept in a real bed, she'd been under her own quilt, lying beside her husband.

That night she and Ethan had loved each other almost to exhaustion, then lain awake long after, dreaming of a trip to New Orleans. They'd planned to visit his younger brother's family, and Ethan had been looking forward to showing off her and Susannah and Jody. Now she could only wonder if anybody had notified Matthew that Ethan had died, if Matt had come to take care of their affairs.

As she looked around the room, seeing all the homey touches Cora had put in the Sprenger quarters, she felt her own loss now more than any time since those days after they took Susannah. She had no husband to hold her, no baby to tug at her skirts, no inquisitive little daughter to follow her about.

But she was free, she reminded herself, and she had to be grateful for that. Now she could look for Susannah. She could pester the authorities until they joined in her search. She could go home and regain her strength; then she could help in the search for her daughter.

The only sound in the house was the loud ticking of the big clock in the front parlor. Annie sat listening to it, hearing it strike the three-quarter hour, then the hour. It was ten o'clock. *Ten o'clock, and all's well Or if it isn't, you have to make it that way. You have survived for a reason.*

She couldn't stand the loneliness of that ticking. Rising, she went to the window and looked outside. The wind had died down, and the storm had passed, leaving behind a thick, pristine layer of snow on the ground. By moonlight a single sentinel made his rounds, crossing between buildings, then disappearing. It was a lonely night out there also.

She thought of Hap Walker lying in the infirmary, clinging to leg and life. Major Sprenger had talked a great deal about him at supper, reminding her where she'd heard the name before. Hap Walker, the Texas Ranger. She'd read his name in the Austin paper some years back, before the war even, when he'd made a daring rescue of two little girls taken by a Kiowa war party. As she recalled, he'd crawled into the camp, stampeded the Indians' horses, then grabbed both children in the confusion. Everybody had talked about it at the time.

According to the major, Walker had lived an incredible

life. A Texas Ranger at eighteen. Captain of a ranger battalion by twenty-four. A Texas volunteer in the Confederate Army who'd risen to the rank of captain there also. Twice wounded in the war, once at Atlanta, once at Sharpsburg, and yet he'd not come home until it was over. Recommissioned in the rangers just last year, he'd been forced out by the wound that still threatened his life. But people still called him Captain Walker.

"Hap Walker," Sprenger declared, "was the best Indian fighter in Texas, bar none—and a damned fine lawman, too," adding, "Folks could count on Hap. He'd die before he'd let 'em down. They don't come any better than Hap."

But when Cora had asked how he was recovering now, the surgeon's expression had sobered. "I'm worried—real worried," he admitted. "Maybe I should have just gone ahead and amputated. If that fever doesn't come down some by tomorrow, I'll have to do it, anyway, and hope to God I didn't make a mistake by waiting."

"But you said you'd found the source of infection earlier," his wife reminded him. "You said he had a good chance."

"That was before the fever shot up. It was one hundred three at six o'clock, and that's mighty high for a grown man. I told Nash to add sassafras to the quinine if it goes up any more, but I hate to make a man sweat when his body's short on water."

And so it had gone. The surgeon had just come from there a short while before he went to bed, but Annie'd been in her room and hadn't heard if Walker was any better. Now she wondered. She found it mattered a great deal to her. By what had to be divine intervention, Captain Walker had strayed into that small Comanche encampment, ending three years of despair for her. As sick as he had been, it was a miracle either of them had made it to the safety of the Indian agency. She wished she'd thanked him for getting her almost there. For what he'd done for those two little girls so long ago, saving them from being lost like Susannah.

As she turned away from the window, she saw the shawl Cora had given her earlier, saying she ought to wear it as long as the wind was in the north. But after three hard winters on the Staked Plains, even a drafty house seemed hot. Annie stared at it for a moment, then made up her mind. Whether he knew she had come to see him or not, she was going to thank him. She might not get the chance tomorrow.

Throwing the wool shawl over her shoulders, she pulled it close, then slipped out of her room. It was as though the house were empty except for the clock, and her heart kept rhythm with the ticking as she opened the outside door. Clutching her skirt to lift the hem out of the snow with one hand, holding the shawl closed with the other, she gingerly made her way down the steps and across the yard toward the hospital building.

At the door, she stopped to shake the snow from her skirt, then knocked loudly. Shivering now, she waited for someone to answer.

"Mrs. Bryce!" It was Corporal Nash, the man who'd ridden in the ambulance with her and Walker.

"May I come in, sir?"

He hesitated. "It's kinda late."

"Yes, I know, but I'd like to see Captain Walker."

"Doc know you're over here?" he asked suspiciously.

"No, he and Mrs. Sprenger have already gone to bed. He seemed terribly tired at supper."

He nodded. "Plumb tuckered out."

She stepped past him and removed the shawl. "How is he now—Captain Walker, I mean?"

"What did Doc tell you?" he countered.

"Not much," she lied. "What do you think?"

"I'm not a doctor, ma'am, I'm just a corpsman. But if I was the captain, I'd be afraid of following that leg to the grave. If it was me, I'd want it off before the danged thing killed me."

"Gangrene?"

"Looks more like blood poisoning—all streaked-like. Guess it's coming from that abscess. It was nasty, real nasty."

"He's not better, then?"

"Fever's up, and it don't look like it's going down any. Don't know whether it's that or the morphine I gave him a little while ago, but he's plumb out."

"Oh."

"But," he added, relenting, "I don't suppose it'd hurt none to look at him. Since Wright and Hansen were discharged to the barracks today, he's the only one in the infirmary right now."

"Thank you."

"I reckon I'd better cover him up some first, though."

Leaving her there, he disappeared through a door. She moved closer, getting a glimpse of the room. Kerosene lanterns flickered, sending the distorted shadows of empty beds up the wall.

When he came back, he was frowning. "Captain Walker's hotter than ever." He met her gaze soberly. "I kinda hate to wake the major up, but even if I get more sassafras down him, I don't know what he's going to sweat. He hasn't drunk enough to pass any water." As he said it, he colored in embarrassment. "Sorry, ma'am. I just meant he's not drinking."

"I understand."

He stood back to let her pass. "First bed." Following her in, he stood behind her. "Don't look good, huh?"

The ashy gray she'd seen earlier was gone, replaced by a flush that made Hap Walker look almost red under the orange glow of the lamp. She reached out to touch his forehead with cold fingertips, then looked up.

"I'd say if you don't get the fever down, he's going to convulse. He needs to drink something—anything."

"I reckon I know that, ma'am, but the captain won't swallow anything for me." He peered over her shoulder for a moment, then made up his mind. "I'm going to get Doc. If Walsh or Parker was here, I wouldn't wake him, but tonight's my night. He won't be happy about it," he added glumly.

"Wet some sheets in water first."

"Huh?"

"Cover him in wet sheets before you go."

He shook his head. "We got to keep his leg dry."

"Do you have any oil cloth? You could put that around the leg. You might have to cut it, but—"

"I want Doc to look at him first. I don't have any authority to do anything more than he ordered. And he can be downright contrary if things ain't the way he wants 'em."

"I'll watch Captain Walker," she volunteered.

"You know the captain?"

69

"Yes," she lied. "We're both from the same area of Texas."

He seemed somewhat relieved by the offer. "Well, if it looks like he's going into convulsions before I get back, the wood's on that table. All you got to do is stick it in his mouth so he don't swallow his tongue or bite clean through it."

"All right."

"I'll be back as soon as I get the major up. Mrs. Sprenger'll boil some coffee to get him awake, then he'll come over."

"All right."

"You'll be okay?"

"I don't see why not."

"Then I'm going to go get him," he said again.

As the sound of his boots receded and the outer door banged shut, Annie draped her shawl over the back of a wooden chair, then dragged the seat to the bed. Sitting down, she fixed her eyes on Hap Walker's face.

"Everybody says you are too good a man to die," she said softly. "And while I don't know you, I suspect they're right. I—well, I just came to thank you for riding into Bull Calf's camp this morning. If you hadn't come through, I'd probably have died there. I'd just about given up."

It was like talking to a statue. There was no sign he heard her, only the sound of labored breathing, the rise and fall of his chest beneath the blanket. He was so hot, so terribly hot. And his skin was parched from the fever.

Looking at the table, she saw a small water pitcher and a folded napkin beneath. "You've got to drink—you know that, don't you?" she asked softly.

She rose and poured water onto the napkin, soaking it.

Carrying the dripping cloth back to the bed, she turned Walker's head and pulled his lower lip out, making a pocket. Using a corner of the napkin, she dribbled water into his mouth, watching him intently. His tongue moved, then his throat constricted as the water went down. Sitting down again, she patiently worked to get nearly a half cup of it into him.

Red-faced and short of breath from running in the cold, Nash came back. "Doc's going to take a look," he announced from the door. Then, "What're you doing?"

"He's drunk a little," she murmured, pleased with herself. "It takes awhile, but he can swallow when he's not hurried. Did you tell Major Sprenger I was here?"

"No. Like I said, he's a mite touchy when he gets woke up. But Mrs. Sprenger'll give him a little coffee, and then he'll be all right."

"I still think we could use wet sheets to bring this fever down. My mother used to soak my brother in a tub of water, and it usually worked, but the captain's too big for that."

"I got no orders for it," he maintained stubbornly. "Besides, I told you, Doc's coming. Uh-oh."

The hospital door opened, then Will Sprenger stamped the snow from his feet. Coming into the infirmary, he took off his cloak.

"Didn't wait for the coffee," he muttered. "If I'd have known folks got sicker at night, I'd have never gone to medical college." Then he saw Annie. "What the hell are you doing here?" he demanded.

Fearing he was in trouble, Nash spoke up quickly. "She's a friend of Captain Walker." As the surgeon turned his scowl on him, he added lamely, "They grew up in Texas together."

"Oh? And where was that?" Sprenger asked, looking at Annie.

She knew he knew she didn't know Hap Walker. Nonetheless, she managed to say, "San Saba."

"Humph! Didn't know there *was* a San Saba back in the thirties."

"Actually, there's been a ranger camp there for several years—I don't know where he's from," she admitted baldly. "I may have given Mr. Nash a mistaken impression. I said Walker and I were both from Texas."

"Big place, Texas," Sprenger murmured. He took a deep breath, then exhaled heavily. "Well, I'd better take a look at him." Going around to the other side of the bed, he leaned over and listened to Walker's chest. "No pneumonia, anyway. Guess that's something." He rubbed his hands together briskly, then laid his palm on his patient's brow, holding it there for some time. His frown deepened. "He drink anything?" he asked Nash.

"She said she got something down him."

"About a half cup of water," she murmured. "I used a wet napkin."

Sprenger looked up from Walker to her, taking in the deep-set circles under her eyes, the tight, drawn skin that clung to the hollow cheeks, the fatigue revealed in every line of her face, and he relented. "Guess you didn't take the laudanum."

"No." She looked away. "I was afraid of the nightmares. I didn't want to sleep."

"Yeah." He could understand that. There was no guessing what her memory could recount if given a free rein.

"Yeah." Turning his attention back to Hap Walker, he frowned again. "Damn. Thought I'd got everything cleaned up in there." He leaned over and spoke loudly, saying, "Can you understand me? I'm going to have to cut."

Walker's eyelids moved, but did not open. "No . . . no . . . don't . . ."

"You don't want to die, do you?"

Hap managed to swallow. His mouth was too dry. He worked his tongue, trying to wet his lips. "Worse . . . things . . ." he whispered.

"Hap—" Sprenger hesitated, then sighed. "All right, I'll take another look first. But don't ask me to let you die. That fever's coming from somewhere."

"I gave him ten grains of quinine again after you left," Nash admitted. "And I was getting ready to go for more sassafras."

"He can't sweat," Sprenger muttered. "Guess maybe we could try a little boiled willow, sometimes that works. I sure hate taking him back to surgery."

"Do you want me to find Walsh and Parker?" Nash wanted to know.

"I'm getting too old to lift 'em anymore, so you'll have to." The surgeon reached for the blanket covering Walker. "You'd better go, Mrs. Bryce, this won't be pretty."

Her gaze dropped to Hap Walker for a long moment. "I'd like to stay, Major Sprenger," she decided. "And I've seen quite a lot of ugly things."

"I expect you have at that." Not knowing how long it would take Nash to find the other two, he nodded. "All right. In that cabinet over there, you'll find the herbals. One of 'em ought to say willow on it. Put a teaspoon of it in a cup, fill the rest with hot water, then strain it through cloth in about five minutes. Make it strong enough he doesn't have to drink a lot of it. You up to doing that?"

"Where is the water?" she asked.

"There's two pots on that stove—one's coffee, the other's water. Cups are on the metal stand next to it." As she moved away, he lifted the blanket. "Still say it looks better than it did earlier," he muttered. "Still here, Nash?"

"Getting my coat, sir."

"Anything draining?"

"He's still making pus."

"All right, go on." Retrieving the trocar from the table, he squeezed the bulb and inserted the tip into the wound. Drawing it back, he looked at the tube. "Still yellow."

"No chlor—no chlor—"

"Make you sick?"

Hap swallowed. "No."

"That's the wound?" Annie asked, looking over the major's shoulder.

"It's stitched up now. If I was to open it, it'd be pretty raw."

"The willow bark is steeping," she remembered to tell him.

"Good. Mrs. Bryce, there's a large black case in the surgery. Ought to be setting next to the tray on the stand by the operating table. Would you fetch it, please?"

When she returned with it, he spread the field kit open. "Got one thing left to try, Hap," he murmured, reaching for the scissors. "It'll hurt like hell, but it's not the saw." Going to work, he removed his earlier sutures. When he turned around, Annie was still there, watching. His first inclination was to order her away, but he had no one else to help him. "Get into my case and find the lint swabs, then look for containers marked Bromine, Potassium Permanganate, and Spirits of Turpentine. Put 'em all on that table."

Leaning forward again, he addressed Walker. "I'm giving it all I know, but if it's not better by morning, I'm going to have to take it off. Best I can do."

It looked like Hap nodded.

Rising, Sprenger went to a basin and washed his hands. He came back carrying the wash basin with him. Sitting down again, he soaped the area around the reopened wound, then dried it. "Hand me a swab, Mrs. Bryce," he said, reaching behind him. "And the bromine. Open it first, if you don't mind," he added. "But don't get any of it on you—it's caustic. Oh, and I'm going to need one of those little glass tubes—in the vial next to the one with the swabs."

As she watched, he soaped the lint tip, then plunged it into the incision, separating the tissue. Rinsing it out, he again dried the area. Inserting the pipette into the bromine, he withdrew a small amount.

"Brace yourself, Hap," he ordered, pushing the pipette into the incision. As it touched the bone, he lifted his finger, releasing it. Walker's leg jerked. "Got to burn out the infection—all I know to do now. You know, once I had to do this with a hot poker 'cause I ran out of bromine."

Without thinking, Annie grasped Hap Walker's hand. His fingers closed around hers, tightening painfully, while Major Sprenger repeated the application several times, probing the abscess and around the injured bone. By the time the surgeon sat back, her fingers were numb. He capped the bromide and handed it back to her.

"It's going to burn awhile. It eats away at the tissue like

75

acid on a nail. But to be sure I've got everything, go ahead and give me—" Sprenger considered a moment, then told Annie, "Give me the turpentine. Sorry to add insult to injury, Hap," he murmured apologetically, pouring a little of it into the incision, "but it's a good disinfectant. Don't guess I'll use the P.P., after all. If bromine and turpentine don't get it, nothing will, anyway." He looked up at Annie. "Might as well strain the willow tea while I restitch him."

"I got Mr. Parker, but couldn't find Walsh, sir," Nash announced, bursting through the door.

"Hell, I'm done now," Sprenger muttered, covering Hap. "Might as well send him back to bed."

"But—"

"Cauterized it with bromine." Sprenger rose to return his supplies to his field kit. "If it's still draining in the morning, we'll know it didn't work." He leaned over Walker. "Doing all right, Hap?" There was no answer. "Passed out," the surgeon decided. "Just as well, but it'll make getting anything down him a damned sight harder. Think you can do it without choking him to death, Mr. Nash?"

"I'll try, sir."

"Like feeding a baby—a little at a time. You know that, don't you?"

"I ain't even got a wife," Nash reminded him.

"I can give it to him, Major," Annie offered, carrying the cup back.

"You belong in bed yourself," Sprenger told her sourly. "So you might as well walk back with me. It's Mr. Nash on duty, anyway."

"Please, I couldn't sleep."

"If you won't take the laudanum, I can give you some chamomile."

"No. I'm all right, really."

Looking past her to Nash, he ordered, "If she changes her mind, see her home, will you? Mr. Parker, you'd better get a good night's sleep in case we have to saw tomorrow."

"Any change in orders for Captain Walker, sir?" Nash inquired.

"Give the willow bark tea every two hours until morning. Quarter grain of morphine at midnight, then again about five."

"Yes, sir."

Sprenger unrolled his sleeves and reached for his coat. "Unless you need me, I'll be back around six o'clock, soldier."

After the two men left, Annie sat beside Hap Walker's bed and began dipping the napkin in the willow bark tea, dribbling it into his mouth as before. When she looked up, Nash was watching her.

"You going to stay here all night?"

"I don't know."

He appeared uncomfortable for a moment, then blurted out, "There'll be talk. I mean, you're a woman, and I'm a man, and—"

"How old are you, Mr. Nash?"

"Twenty-three, ma'am."

"I was thirty last summer." Dipping the cloth into the cup again, she returned to her task. "Come on, just a little more," she coaxed Walker.

"You aren't exactly old enough to be my mother," Nash said behind her. "And after what happened—"

She sighed. "After what happened, I expect people to

talk, and there's not much I can do to stop them. What am I supposed to do—hide?"

"No, of course not. But—"

Laying the cup aside, she turned back to wipe Walker's mouth with a dry corner of the napkin. "I cannot help it that I wanted to live too much to die, sir," she said wearily. "But if it bothers you to sit here with me, you can go into the other room."

"I didn't mean me. I didn't mean *I* felt that way, Mrs. Bryce," he responded awkwardly. "I was thinking of you."

She felt a surge of anger. "Well, don't. I'm not a woman who thrives on pity."

"I'm sorry. It must have been very hard on you," he murmured.

She looked up at that. "I don't mean to talk about it—now or ever," she said evenly. "To anyone."

"I wasn't trying to pry, ma'am. I just meant . . ." He paused, then sighed. "Well, if you're going to sit up with him, I think I'll go into the surgery and straighten things around for tomorrow. I, uh, I guess if you need any help, you'll call for me," he added lamely.

"Yes."

For more than a quarter hour after he left, she worked to get the rest of the medicine down Hap Walker. When she was done, she rose slowly and went to the window. They sky was almost cloudless now, and the snow sparkled in the moonlight. Layers of ice weighed heavily on the branches of a small tree, bending them almost to the ground. The stillness was nearly overwhelming.

She turned back to Hap, then cast a furtive glance toward the surgery. She hesitated, then deliberately walked over and closed the infirmary door. Coming back to Walker's bed, she considered him for a moment before she reached for the wash basin.

There wasn't anything that said *she* couldn't bathe him, after all. Telling herself resolutely that he had nothing she'd not seen before, she poured water into the pan. Wringing out the cloth Major Sprenger had used, she began wiping the wavy brown hair back from his forehead.

While he wasn't what most people would call handsome, he had an appealing face—straight nose, strong jaw, well-defined chin. And despite a faint sprinkling of silver, the tousled hair gave him an almost boyish look. That and the smile lines at the corners of his eyes and mouth. She guessed he was probably between thirty-five and forty.

She lifted the blanket and unbuttoned the nightshirt, then washed his neck, throat, and chest. Her hands shook as she tugged the shirt up, exposing his lower body. She shuddered, fighting the revulsion, and forced herself to look down. Nestled in curled, brown thatch, his manhood was limp, benign. She took a deep breath. Telling herself that the only thing he had in common with Two Trees was his gender, she very carefully began washing his belly and his right leg. The injured one she didn't touch.

She didn't dry him, but let the air cool his wet skin, then gently pulled his gown down. Using a corner of the bedsheet, she fanned his face. Exhausted, she sat back to pray.

Please, dear God, she thought, *spare this decent man.* Even as the words went through her mind, she wondered what there was about a man she scarcely knew that had moved her to pray for him, when she could hardly find it within her to pray for herself. It was, she supposed, all those things Major Sprenger had said about him.

The only light in the room was the yellow flame flickering valiantly within the sooty lamp chimney, the only sound Hap Walker's harsh, ragged breathing. She squeezed her dry, itching eyes tightly shut, trying to wet them, then leaned forward again to touch him. She didn't know why she'd expected anything different, but he was still hot.

The heightened nerves that had driven her through the day were giving up the fight for her mind and body. It was as though every fiber ached, every thought came with an effort. She knew she ought to summon Mr. Nash to watch Walker, then walk back to the Sprengers. But again the thought of sleeping in that featherbed was almost too much to bear.

The image of a smiling, scrubbed Ethan standing in Reverend Helton's Austin parlor, holding her cold hand in his warm one, telling the preacher they wanted to wed, came to mind. She could remember every detail of that day, from the figured waistcoat and navy blue serge suit Ethan had bought for the occasion to the pleated lawn waist, the cornflower blue twilled silk basque and matching skirt she'd made herself from the Butterick pattern she'd ordered in the mail. Ethan had gallantly told her the outfit matched her eyes.

After the few words were spoken, pledging them to a lifetime together, Mrs. Helton had dabbed away tears and pronounced them the handsomest couple in her memory. They'd had coffee and cake there, then taken a drive through the countryside in a smart gig Ethan had rented at the livery across the street from their hotel. They'd dined early on roast beef, boiled new potatoes, and candied carrots, all scandalously washed down with a bottle of burgundy.

But it was what had come after that had both shocked and delighted her. When she'd first discovered what was expected of her, she'd recoiled, but he'd coaxed and teased and tantalized her until she forgot her disgust. He'd made it seem so right, so pure, so very wonderful. And in that week in Austin, he'd given her Susannah.

That was then. With Two Trees the same act had been defiling, dirty, and disgusting. And when she'd missed her courses, his two wives had pummeled her so unmercifully that she'd hemorrhaged enough to miscarry, and she'd actually been grateful for it. The very thought of his baby within her had made her thoroughly sick. No, she never wanted to think of that again. But there was no justice in a world that let Two Trees live and made Ethan Bryce die.

"Why, Ethan—why? Why did it have to happen to you—to us?" she whispered brokenly.

A sob welled in her chest, rising, fighting to get out. Unable to suppress it, she leaned forward, resting her arms on Hap Walker's bed, and let go. She cried so hard she shook the mattress beneath him, but she couldn't stop. Not until she got all of it out of her.

"Wa—" Hap Walker's hand came up, then dropped. His mouth worked, trying to form the word. "Wa—water," he rasped.

Embarrassed, she sat back and wiped her wet cheeks. But his eyes were closed. He wasn't really conscious, just unbearably thirsty. Her hands shaking, she managed to pour a little water into the cup, then dipped the napkin into it again. As she pulled down his lip to squeeze the liquid into his mouth, his hand touched hers.

"Wa—water."

He began to struggle, attempting to rise, falling back.

His fingers closed on her wrist, pulling her hand to his mouth. Standing up, she bent over him, slid her other arm beneath his shoulders, and tried to lift him. He wasn't a big man, but she was weak. Finally, she put a knee against the bed for leverage, then threw her shoulder beneath his, bracing him up. Freeing her hand, she reached behind her for the cup.

"Sip, don't drink," she cautioned him, bringing it to his lips. "Just a little at a time."

He tilted the cup and guzzled greedily, his Adam's apple bobbing as he swallowed every drop. His eyes still closed, he leaned back against her.

"Thanks," he whispered.

She eased him to the mattress, then stepped back to put the cup on the table. Turning to him again, she touched his forehead hopefully. The fever didn't seem any better.

"Are you hurting? Do you want me to fetch Mr. Nash?"

"No." He'd said it so softly, she wasn't sure she'd heard it, but then he whispered it again. "No."

As tired as she was, she decided to wash his face and neck again. Her shoulders and back ached as she wrung out the cloth in the basin. As soon as she finished, she was going to have to force herself to make the walk back to the Sprengers' house. She couldn't fight it anymore. She was beyond dreaming now.

She dragged the wet cloth over his forehead, his cheeks, his chin, then back to his ears and down to the hollow of his throat. That was it—she couldn't do anything more.

But rather than leave, she sank back into the chair and just sat there. She leaned forward to touch him again, then her head dropped to the edge of the mattress. In a few minutes, when the weakness passed, she'd go.

The major and the corporal found her at six in the morning, her head resting against Hap Walker's body, his fingers touching her blond hair.

"Mrs. Bryce," Sprenger murmured, shaking her gently.

"Unnnhhhh."

Reaching over her, he touched Walker's forehead.

"Well, I'll be damned," he said softly.

"What is it?" Nash asked.

"He's sweating. His gown's soaked. As soon as Walsh gets here, you'd better change him."

The significance wasn't lost on the corpsman. His face broke into a smile. "You did it, sir. You did it."

As Annie Bryce sat back reluctantly, yawning widely, Sprenger's gaze took in the fatigue mirrored in her face, then the empty cup and the cloth in the washbasin. "I'd say I didn't do it alone, soldier."

It was becoming increasingly obvious that Lieutenant Colonel Davidson, Fort Sill's commanding officer, was avoiding Annie. After two days of unsuccessful attempts to gain an appointment with him, she finally went to his office, determined to stay until he saw her. Whether he wanted to take it or not, she intended to file an official report on her captive daughter, requesting the army's assistance in the child's recovery.

She'd waited an hour, sitting in a straight-back chair with her hands folded in her lap, praying and hoping the colonel would do more than listen politely and send her on her way. From time to time she looked up and caught the aide watching her furtively. Their eyes would meet, then he'd hastily look away to busy himself at his desk. It was as though he didn't want to speak to her.

"Are you quite sure he knows I am here?" she asked finally.

"Yes, ma'am."

She didn't know much about Black Jack Davidson, as he was called, other than he'd served on the frontier even before the Civil War, and he was reputed to be a harsh, unpleasant man. But she figured that as long as he'd been in the business of fighting Indians, he'd surely be inclined to help her. At least he knew what she'd been through, so she wouldn't have to tell him much about her captivity. And he ought to sympathize with Susannah's plight.

It seemed as though another eternity passed, but the door to the inner office remained closed. She was beginning to wonder if he was in there at all.

"Excuse me, but how much longer do you think it'll be?" she tried again.

"I couldn't say," was the brusque answer.

"It's a rather long meeting, isn't it?"

"The colonel's a busy man."

"Yes, of course."

She'd just have to wait, no matter how long it took, and she knew it. But she was beginning to fume. If he was aware she was there, it seemed unconscionable that he couldn't at least let her know when he'd be done, instead of letting her sit there forever. She refolded the handkerchief for the hundredth time before looking up again. The young man behind the desk was eying her speculatively.

"Is there some reason why you keep staring at me?" she asked irritably.

"No, ma'am."

Maybe she was imagining it, or maybe she was just overly cross this morning. Reaching up, she tucked an errant strand of hair under the edge of her bonnet. She felt like a fidgety child on a hard pew, wondering how long before church would be over. Glancing at the clock, she noted it was past eleven. She'd been there two hours, and before long he'd be going to eat. Her stomach was already growling.

"Would you inquire of the colonel if it would be more convenient for me to come again this afternoon?"

"He'll be going over to the agency then."

"Oh." Her fingers twisted the damp handkerchief. "All right, then would you be so kind as to ask him how much longer he'll be?"

It was obvious to Billy Thompson that Davidson didn't want to see her, but she'd been waiting so long he could almost feel sorry for her. But as prim and demure as she looked sitting there in that dress buttoned up to her chin, he knew she'd probably spread her legs beneath every buck Comanche in old Bull Calf's band. The thought had been turning his stomach ever since she walked in the door.

"I take it that you don't intend to find out for me," she decided.

"Uh, no, not exactly. But the colonel, well, he's a stickler for discipline, ma'am. He don't want me breaking in on him unless he calls for me."

"I see."

"Ain't nobody around here that likes him," he went on, unbending somewhat. "If he was to smile, it'd break his face. Now, Old Ben Grierson—the one that was here afore Black Jack—well, he had a smile for everybody. Too many, some people thought," he added judiciously. "Guess there was some as thought he was an Indian lover, but it wasn't that. Same way with the Negroes in the Tenth— long as they behaved themselves, he treated 'em right. When they didn't, then he could be hard on 'em."

"I don't care whether he smiles or not," Annie said

tiredly. "I just wish he'd give me fifteen minutes of his time." She glanced up at the clock, then exhaled heavily. "I'm beginning to wonder what on earth he's doing in there."

"Got Doc Sprenger—Major Sprenger, that is—with him. Guess they're arguing over the yearly health and hygiene report."

"Oh."

"It's always like that, ain't it? The docs want to clean up everything, and the commanders don't care as long as they can put the cavalry in the field when it's needed. I guess Doc Sprenger wants the higher-ups to rule against enlisted men keeping pigs on the post. Says the filth gets into the water, and we had a bad bout with dysentery awhile back."

"And Colonel Davidson doesn't agree? Surely—"

"Naw, he don't want anybody telling him how to run his post. He ain't going to let anything bad go into Washington."

"And you, what do you think?"

Billy shrugged. "They don't pay soldiers to think, ma'am." He saw her look at the clock yet again. "All right. Guess it wouldn't hurt none if I was to say they needed Doc over at the hospital. Reckon he'd be glad to hear it, whether it was the truth or not."

"Thank you."

When she smiled, he was struck by what it did to her eyes. If she had a little meat on those bones, she'd be downright pretty. But he didn't know a man alive that'd be able to forget she'd had a Comanche buck inside her. He knew he sure as hell couldn't. He pushed away from the desk and stood up.

"Guess more dysentery's as good as anything," he said. The thought struck him as funny. Given the timing, Black Jack wouldn't like hearing that.

"I really appreciate your help," she murmured.

The thought crossed his mind that it might be interesting to find out just how much appreciation he could get out of her, then he dismissed the notion. It'd be like bedding a whore who'd been with Grierson's Negroes, and there were just some things that were beneath him.

As she watched, he tapped lightly on the closed door, then opened it just enough to ease inside. It clicked shut behind him. She sighed and closed her eyes briefly, hoping she was going to get in now.

In the inner office, the colonel eyed his aide irritably. "What is it?"

"Beggin' the colonel's pardon, sir," Thompson began deferentially, "but they're needing the major over at the infirmary."

"Can't it wait?" Davidson demanded.

"What is it?" Sprenger asked, rising.

"Big mess—looks like another run of dysentery, sir." It was all Thompson could do to keep a straight face. "Guess it's spreading again."

"Must be bad meat from the last shipment," the colonel muttered.

"If it was bad meat, they'd have got it after dinner. More'n likely it's the damned pigs you're letting 'em keep all over the place," Sprenger retorted. "And you can't say I didn't warn you."

"If you put that down, it's insubordination, Will. I'm not having a bunch of staff officers come out and tell me how to run the place."

"What are you going to do if you come down with it?" the surgeon countered. "Pretend you don't have it?"

Davidson eyed him balefully for a moment. "No," he answered evenly, "I'm going to order all private livestock moved off post and away from the water. Does that satisfy you?"

"Thank you."

"And you are going to report we passed the health inspection," he added flatly. Seeing that Thompson was still in the room, he demanded, "Well, soldier, what else?"

"It's Mrs. Bryce, sir. She's still waiting."

"Damn. Tell her I'm occupied right now."

"She's expressed her intention to remain, sir. She's been here most of the morning already."

"She's actually quite a remarkable woman," Sprenger observed. "She's got a lot of grit. You have to admire her for it."

"Do you know what she wants?" Davidson asked his aide impatiently.

"No, sir."

He turned on the doctor. "She's staying at your house, isn't she, Major? Well, she must have said something, I'd think. What is it?"

While Sprenger had a pretty good idea what she intended to ask for, he wasn't giving it away. The way he looked at it, once Davidson saw her, the old martinet might be moved to gallantry. Even if he wasn't, she at least deserved a chance at him. He shrugged. "I'm not home much, and when I am, Mrs. Bryce tends to keep to herself. Cora might know something, but if she does, she hasn't mentioned it. If you want my opinion, I think you ought to see her."

"Tell her to come back," the colonel decided.

"Beggin' your pardon, sir, but she's been by every day already," Thompson dared to tell him. "She ain't giving up easy."

Sprenger nodded. "She'll keep coming back until you give her an audience. It says something for her that she survived three years with the Comanches, Colonel. You might as well find out why she's out there and get it over with."

Black Jack Davidson digested his surgeon's advice as if it gave him a stomachache. Finally he sighed heavily. "It's unfortunate, this captive thing. I never know what to say to a woman after that, you know. Hell, it's hard enough to look at 'em, knowing what's happened."

"You have to remember that she didn't ask to be captured."

"I keep thinking of the Purvis woman—and the unfortunate Miss Baker." The colonel looked up. "Her brother had to put Lucy Baker in an asylum, I was told."

"It doesn't surprise me. But Mrs. Bryce is made of sterner stuff. I don't know how she managed it, but she kept her mind. Aside from malnutrition, she's in pretty good shape. In fact, the way she's eating now, I'd say she's already put a few pounds back on. Along about Easter, she'll be a fine-looking female again."

"Really? I didn't get a good look at her the other day, but I've heard she's skin and bones."

"She's thin," Sprenger conceded. "But nothing like those poor men I treated after they came out of Andersonville. They were skin and bones, as you put it. They couldn't even walk out, but she's in a fair way to regaining her strength."

Unconvinced, Davidson asked wearily, "What do you say to her? Beyond offering condolences, I mean? Major, I'm a soldier, not a diplomat."

"You just listen. There's not much you can say."

"I don't know what good I can do for her, anyway. If it's justice, I can't give it," the colonel admitted bitterly. "With the Indian policy we've got here, my hands are tied. As long as Bull Calf and the others agree to come onto the reservation, I'm supposed to protect them." He sighed again. "I suppose I could arrest Bull Calf," he mused, "but putting him away is another thing. You saw what happened with Satanta, didn't you?"

Sprenger nodded. "They paroled the bastard."

"It's those damned Quakers. I'd like to bring the lot of them out here and leave them up on the Staked Plains. Those that came back alive would be singing a different tune, I can tell you."

"They'd probably just blame the Texans for making the Indians hostile."

"And I'll tell you something else," Davidson went on, betraying more than a little pique, "if General Sherman would give me the free hand he's going to give Mackenzie come summer, I'd take care of the Indian problem. They'd either come onto the reservation and stay put, or they'd die."

"I expect that's what Mac will do, don't you?" the surgeon observed mildly. "And he's as methodical as a damned machine, when you get right down to it. He'll have the supplies to outlast 'em on their own land. No, you're dead wrong. Sherman's picked the right man." Seeing that Davidson's color was heightening, he tossed the smallest of olive branches. "If anything, the general needs you right here. Without you, who's going to watch the Quakers?"

"Damned near anybody," the colonel grumbled.

"No, it takes a strong man to keep idle troops disciplined and in fighting trim. There's more discipline here than there's ever been."

"Humph."

"What do you want me to tell her, sir?" Thompson asked, reinserting himself into the conversation.

"The dysentery can wait, Major." Having made up his mind, Davidson turned back to Sprenger. "All you're going to do is give 'em copper and opium, anyway."

"That depends. Sometimes sulphuric acid and laudanum are more effective," the surgeon murmured.

"Write it down, and Thompson can take the orders over for you. I'm sure there's somebody there that can dose 'em."

"Probably," Sprenger conceded.

"Good. Then you won't mind hearing what Mrs. Bryce has to say," the colonel declared. "All right, tell Thompson here what's needed, and he'll go after he sends her in."

"No need to write it down. Tell Parker and Nash to mix up pills the same as always—one-eighth grain copper sulfate and one-eighth grain opium. That'll do for a start, anyway. Tell 'em if that doesn't work, I'll be on over in a little while."

"Yes, sir."

While they waited, the colonel drummed on his desk with his fingers. "Cora getting along all right with her?"

"Of course. And she's doing a damned good job of keeping the gossips at bay."

"I didn't know that was a problem."

"As a rule, women aren't very kind to women. Most of 'em want to smile to her face, ply her with questions, then go away shocked, so they can spread nasty stories that have the ring of truth. But Cora won't give 'em the chance."

"I don't remember it being like that with the Purvis woman," Davidson murmured.

"That's because they couldn't stand to look at her. Mrs. Bryce, on the other hand, is rather pretty—thin but pretty. But you can see that for yourself."

Annie watched the door open and the aide come out. Passing her, he went to his desk, where he wrote something down quickly. Straightening up, he looked her way. "If you'll just step inside, Colonel Davidson is available now, ma'am," he told her. "You can leave your cloak out here."

Wiping damp palms on the skirt of her gown, Annie rose. "Thank you, sir. I'd begun to think I was wasting my time."

"He's a busy man," Thompson reminded her, moving to hold the door. Leaning familiarly toward her, he lowered his voice. "If I was you, I'd be real friendly, if you know what I mean."

She drew back stiffly. "No, sir, I'm afraid I don't."

His hand touched her arm lightly, then slid to her elbow before he dropped it. "It's going to take a lot of honey to sweeten the old wheezer up."

"Really?" She regarded him coldly for a moment, then smiled faintly. "Unfortunately, I tend to prefer vinegar, I'm afraid. It works wonderfully to cleanse corruption—of any sort. Honey, on the other hand, seems to feed it."

As she swished past him, he stared blankly. He closed

the door after her, trying to figure out what she meant. All he knew for sure was that he'd been set down. "Awful highfalutin for a Comanche's whore, ain't you?" he muttered under his breath. "Well, I'll just bet when you get down to Texas, those cowboys'll take care of you real good."

Both men stood as she entered the office. The colonel came around his desk to greet her with a perfunctory handshake. Before he could say anything, she quickly introduced herself.

"I'm Mrs. Bryce—Mrs. Anne Bryce."

"Mrs. Bryce," he acknowledged. "What a pleasant surprise indeed. You are acquainted with Major Sprenger, I believe?"

"Yes, of course." Still ill at ease from the aide's remark, she forced a smile. "I look across the dinner table at him every evening. Major," she murmured, inclining her head slightly.

"Hello, my dear." To Sprenger she looked even more pale than usual. He smiled back warmly, trying to encourage her. Half turning to the other officer, he asked, "Does she look like skin and bones to you, Colonel?"

Usually stiff-necked and aloof, Davidson found himself staring at her. She was somewhat tall, but the dress was far too large for her, betraying the fact that she was at least twenty, perhaps twenty-five pounds underweight, and the hand she'd offered him was small, almost skeletal. Still, she was possessed of hair the color of ripe wheat, eyes as blue as cornflowers, and features that would have done a sculptor proud. But it was her manner that struck him the most: She met his gaze coolly, without wavering. After everything that had happened to her, she wasn't like the others he'd seen. She wasn't hanging her head in shame, and she wasn't cowed.

"No," he said finally. "You were quite right." Gesturing to a seat beside the surgeon, he said, "Would you care to sit down, ma'am?"

"Thank you."

As she sank into the chair, both men returned to theirs. Davidson found his gaze straying to her face again, trying to decide what it was about her that drew him most. It was the eyes, he decided. Within those blue depths was a sadness, a wariness he'd missed but moments before. He almost wished he could help her.

"So," he said, leaning back, "what can I do for you, Mrs. Bryce?"

She'd not expected him to dispense with the usual civilities so quickly. Taken aback somewhat, she felt awkward, uncertain how best to proceed. Then she thought of her daughter.

"I don't blame you for wondering why I've insisted on this interview," she began carefully, looking down at her clasped hands. "Although this is somewhat difficult for me, sir, I expect I should explain what happened before I ask for your help." She lifted her eyes to meet his. "You know, of course, I have been a Comanche captive for some time—"

"My dear, there is no need, no need to relive the horror—none at all," Davidson assured her, trying to cut off something he didn't want to hear. "I've been on the frontier long enough to have a pretty fair notion."

"I don't intend to relive anything I don't have to, believe me."

"Good. Good." He nodded, wondering where she meant to lead him.

"I'm not here to speak of me, sir—I'll never speak of that," she said quietly. "I was in no worse situation than any female captive. Perhaps I was even better off, for I learned to survive." She looked down again as her fingers worked the handkerchief, betraying the agitation she was determined not to show. "My husband was thirty when it happened—the same age I am now. A thunderstorm was blowing across the San Saba River near our house, and I was outside tending to the laundry with our two children. Susannah was four then, and Jody had been born just after the Christmas before. He would have celebrated his birthday on December twenty-eighth that year."

Will Sprenger laid a hand on her arm. "Don't put yourself through this, my dear," he said gently. "We know it was a Comanche raid."

She caught her lower lip between her teeth to master the rising emotion that threatened to overwhelm her. She shook her head. "No, I'm not telling this for me," she said, low. "I'm telling it for Ethan. For Susannah. For Jody." She forced herself to look across the desk again. "If I'd been in the house—if I could have gotten to the gun sooner—they might have survived. But Ethan was in the field—I don't guess it matters now what he was doing, does it?"

She was too controlled, her voice too even, her muscles under his hand too taut. Afraid her composure would shatter and she'd start weeping, Will reached into his pocket and drew out his handkerchief. When he tried to give it to her, she shook her head.

"I'm all right," she insisted. Lifting her hand, she held up the wadded cotton. "As you can see, I have brought my own." Going on, she recounted what happened without embellishing any of it. "Anyway, it had started to storm, so I was hurrying to take down my clean sheets when my little girl saw the Comanches coming. I ran to the house for my husband's gun—well, that doesn't make any difference now, either. The children and I were captured, anyway."

"A tragedy, Mrs. Bryce—a tragedy," Davidson murmured.

"They never stopped for anything. We rode night and day because they were afraid they were being tracked," she continued. "We didn't have anything to eat except a little buffalo jerky. They wouldn't even let me clean Jody when he soiled himself. And I lost my milk." She closed her eyes, and her already low voice dropped to a whisper. "They killed my son, Colonel Davidson, and he was an innocent baby. All he knew was that he was wet and hungry."

"Believe me, Mrs. Bryce, you have my deepest sympathy," he responded soberly. "I'm terribly sorry."

"And the little girl?" Sprenger forced himself to ask.

"It was a large war party—there were some Kiowas, and Comanches from several other bands. When—when the Indians separated to discourage pursuit, one of the other Comanches took Susannah with him." She took a deep breath and let it out slowly. "Sometimes when I close my eyes, I can still hear her screaming for me. But I couldn't help her—I couldn't even help myself."

"Red-skinned bastards," Will Sprenger muttered under his breath.

"Later, when I learned enough of the language to speak it, I asked who'd taken her. I was told it was a Comanche named Lost Dog, and he was either a Quahadi or a

Noconi, but that's all anybody would say." She looked up, meeting Black Jack Davidson's sympathetic gaze. "I want her back, Colonel. I want your help finding her."

"Of course you do," Sprenger murmured soothingly.

"She's all I had to live for—everything. I stayed alive because she was out there somewhere, and I couldn't just abandon her. Colonel Davidson, I have lived amid filth and vermin. I have eaten everything you could imagine, and then some—even bugs and grass and uncleaned buffalo guts. And I have endured things I would wish on no other woman on this earth. For three years—*three years,* sir—I have survived with no other purpose than to find my daughter. Now that I am free, I am asking—no, I am *demanding*—that a search be conducted for Susannah Bryce before it is too late."

Davidson cleared his throat uncomfortably, then tried to explain why he couldn't help her. "It isn't really a matter for the army, Mrs. Bryce—or at least it isn't yet. Under the current Indian policy, my orders are to protect those Kiowas and Comanches who have come onto the reservation. I can act only on application for help by the current Indian agent, Mr. Haworth, and he is opposed to asking for so much as a single guard. Likewise, troops stationed in Texas cannot cross the Red River, even in pursuit of hostiles. While I don't agree at all with the policy, my hands, and those of every officer out here, are effectively tied. Whether I approve or not, I am ordered to see the government delivers adequate food and protection to reservation Indians while they rest between raids," he admitted regretfully. "Believe me, it is not a task I relish, but I am a soldier, my dear, and I will do my duty."

Annie couldn't believe what she was hearing. "But if a

child is held captive, surely then the camps can be searched, can't they?" she demanded incredulously.

"No. Not unless Mr. Haworth should ask it."

Seeking to soften the blow, Will Sprenger laid a comforting hand on her arm again. "I doubt you would find many Quahadis on the reservation, my dear. Quanah Parker has chosen to keep his people away, and they are openly hostile."

"But I might have misunderstood. It might not even be a Quahadi." Clenching the handkerchief tightly, she tried not to break down. "One of the other bands could be holding her. She could have been sold, or traded, or—"

"You have my sympathy, Mrs. Bryce—my complete sympathy," Black Jack Davidson assured her again.

"I don't want sympathy, I want my daughter, sir—and I don't care how it happens, but I intend to get her back," she declared, her voice rising. "I want my daughter back where she belongs."

"Of course you do," he murmured soothingly. "Perhaps if you applied to Haworth, he might attempt to pressure the so-called peaceables into giving her up—if she's on the reservation."

"He's withholding rations now," Sprenger pointed out. "I don't think it's helping. They just deny they've got anybody."

"If she's not on the reservation, it would be a Texas matter," Davidson added. "And again, the army there is in a defensive posture right now. As I said, I expect that to change, but so far it hasn't. Next summer there could well be a campaign undertaken against the hostiles, but until then—"

"Then it will be too late! If the camps are overrun, she'll

be killed with the Comanches! *Surely* you must see—*surely* you must understand—I've got to get her out before then! I cannot just wait for it to happen. Please, there's got to be something. I desperately need help before it is too late, sir," she pleaded. "Susannah's only seven years old, and I don't want her to die with them. Surely you can understand that, Colonel Davidson."

"Forgive me for saying so, Mrs. Bryce, but she may well be dead by now," he responded with unusual gentleness.

"No."

"Three years is a long time in an Indian camp."

"She's got to be alive! She's got to!"

He appeared to consider for a moment, then pressed his fingertips together and leaned across his desk. "If you are determined to assume that, Mrs. Bryce, then you must accept the probability that the child has become as savage as they are. After three years it's more than possible you wouldn't even recognize her."

"She's my flesh and blood, Colonel. I'm her mother," she said more calmly. "I *know* I would know her, no matter how long they've had her. And I know I can make her remember me."

"I understand—and I wish I could offer you some hope, believe me."

Her anger flared. "I *have* hope, sir—it's help I need! And I intend to get it. If I have to write the governor of Texas, or my congressman, or the Secretary of War even—I'm going to get it! If need be, I shall go to Washington to apply directly. But whatever it takes, I shall not give up, ever," she said evenly. Rising, she added stiffly, "I suppose I should thank you for letting me waste your time, Colonel

Davidson, but I cannot bring myself to do it. Good day, sir."

As she opened the door, he sat very still, saying nothing. It wasn't until he heard Thompson tell her not to forget her cloak that he could bring himself to speak. "You were right, Will," he said finally. "Anne Bryce has a lot of grit." He sighed heavily, then looked at Sprenger. "It'd be like looking for a needle in a haystack, wouldn't it?"

"Yeah." Will leaned forward to pick up his hat. "Guess I'd better make sure she's all right. When what you told her sinks in, she's going to take it real hard."

"The Texans probably won't help her, either," Davidson acknowledged. "There aren't enough rangers to risk sending them on a three-year-old trail."

"No."

"It'd help if she even knew whether it was the Quahadis or the Nokonis," the colonel mused. Suddenly, he heaved his frame up from the chair, asking, "Can Walker have visitors yet?"

"He's on the mend. He can't get around, but he's on the mend. Why? He's not in any condition to help her, I can tell you that for sure."

"No, but maybe he can tell me whether he found Bull Calf on or off the reservation."

"Like I said, you're too tough to die," Will Sprenger observed wryly. "Damned if it doesn't look like you've beaten this."

"Either that or I'm too ornery," Walker agreed. Sitting on the edge of his hospital bed, he looked up, and his expression sobered. "Thanks, Doc. A week ago, I wouldn't have bet two bits on my chances."

"Yeah, well, I wouldn't have, either," Will admitted. "I thought we'd be cutting off that leg come morning, and I figured it'd be touch and go even then. Guess it was the bromine that finally did it—that and Mrs. Bryce," he added slyly. "Woman was weaker'n an ant, and more than half sick herself, but she sat up all night with you, trying to bring that fever down one drop of water at a time. Bathed you, too." Turning around, he searched for his magnifying glasses. "Don't suppose you remember any of it, though."

"I knew I was sucking on a rag. The water tasted like laundry soap, but I was too dry to care. And I halfway came to during the bath, but I was too out of it to know who was doing the washing."

"Guess she must've thought she owed it to you." Hooking his glasses over his ears, Will returned his attention to the matter at hand. "I want to get a good look at those stitches, Hap," he murmured. "I know some of my colleagues like to leave 'em in a while, but I'm of the opinion that if they stay too long, the skin tightens around them, and you do more damage than necessary getting 'em out." Lifting the blanket and sheet covering Walker's leg, he bent closer to examine his handiwork. "Hmmm. Yeah, I'd say it looks damned good right now. When's the last time you ran a fever?"

"I don't know—Wednesday or Thursday, I guess."

"I could look it up and find out for sure, but I think it's been long enough, anyway. How's the leg feel?"

"Better than any day since the bullet hit it."

"Stand down. I want you to tell me what it feels like with your weight on it."

"It feels all right."

Will looked up at that. "You've been on it, haven't you?"

"Not until yesterday."

"Dammit, Hap! Who's the doc around here, me or you? When I give an order, it's an order!"

"It's too damned hard to use the pan with another man looking at you," Hap muttered mulishly, not meeting Sprenger's eyes. "Besides, I wanted to know if I could walk, or if I was going to be a cripple forever."

"I'm supposed to be the judge of that," Will grumbled. "All right, what did you find out? It hold you up like you want?"

"It's sore, but yeah, it holds me up."

"You used crutches, didn't you?"

"Tried to—a couple of times, anyway. Kinda hard to get 'em in the privy with me, you know."

His mouth drawn into a thin line, Will picked up his scissors and small forceps. "If you move, I'm liable to stab you—you *can* sit still, can't you?"

"Barely."

Working deftly, the surgeon cut and picked out each stitch, pausing to drop the tiny pieces of silk thread onto the tray. Noting Walker gripping the edge of the mattress, he asked, "This hurt?"

"No."

"Never figured you for a liar," Will murmured, finishing up. "Now," he said, straightening, "I'm only going to say this once, and you can do what you damn well please, but you'd better stay on those crutches a week at least. If something busts open in there, I'll be *damned* if I'll fix it again. See that you remember that, Captain." Turning around to wash his hands in the basin, he acknowledged, "I expect it's not easy for a hard-living man like you to sit around and do nothing."

Hap took a deep breath, then let it out slowly. "It's harder'n you'd ever think, Doc—harder'n you'd ever think."

"Don't like selling cattle much, do you?"

"No. Only thing good about it is I can kinda keep my eye on Clay."

"He did all right for himself, I'd say, but I never figured you'd wind up working for him. I never took you for a cattleman."

Sprenger had touched a spot rawer than the one in his

leg, and Hap didn't want to expose it further. "How is she, anyway?" he asked, abruptly changing the subject.

"How's who?"

"Mrs. Bryce."

Will considered for a moment, then allowed, "She's damned disappointed, but I expect Davidson told you about that. If it'd been me, I'd have told her I'd file a report—or look like I was doing something, anyway. The woman's lived on hope, and damned if he didn't dash it right down. Man's too concerned with his damned regulations to act more'n half human. He thinks telling her he's sorry is enough."

"I wouldn't be too sure of that, Doc."

"But other than that, she's coming along better'n I'd expected," Sprenger murmured, returning to Annie's condition. "Don't guess you were in any shape to notice much about her, but she's a real pretty woman—be a fine looker once she puts a little meat on those bones. I thought for a moment she was even going to soften up Black Jack, but I don't guess that's possible."

"That's what everybody said—that she was real pretty, I mean. I guess her husband was good-looking, too, but it was hard to tell it by the time Rios and I found him. Yeah," he said, exhaling. "They left Bryce lying in a field, facedown in the mud. By the looks of it, he was still alive when they tore his scalp off."

"God."

"Worst of it, it was too late to go after the wife. Maybe if Clay hadn't been down in Laredo, things might've turned out different. He thought like 'em—knew where they'd hide—but we didn't. Hell, it rained about three or four days along in there, washing their tracks out. The

San Saba was high, too, and by the time we got across it, there was no sign left to follow."

"You can only do so much, Hap. If you were in my business, you'd know that."

"It doesn't make it any easier. Besides, she had two little kids with her, and knowing that made it even worse."

"Damned savages killed the baby."

"Davidson told me. I guess the little girl's still out there."

"If she's alive."

"Yeah. 'Course if the kids survive, they adopt 'em and treat 'em just like flesh and blood. If she's alive, she's a Comanche."

"That's what old Black Jack told her."

"Yeah, I know. I think he felt pretty bad for saying it," Hap ventured. "Hell, I know he did."

"The way he and Haworth get along, he's not even going to ask for help at the agency. Not that he'd get it, anyway," Sprenger admitted. "Now Cora's all upset that Mrs. Bryce wants to go home to Texas. She was looking forward to having the company for a month or so. It's hard for a woman out here on a post, what with the other women either being Negresses or gossipy officers' wives, most of whom are twenty or more years younger than Cora. She's taken a real liking to Annie. For one thing, we lost a girl back in '53, which would have made her about Annie's age. For another, Cora thinks she needs mothering right now."

"She probably does. It's going to be damned hard on her in Texas."

"I've already seen some of that around here. But to tell

you the truth, I don't think she cares. All she wants is that little girl."

"Yeah, women kinda pine for the young'uns," Hap agreed. "They never get over losing 'em. So she's going home right away?"

"Well, there's a supply train of wagons coming up from Fort Griffin now that the road's passable. I was thinking of telling her about it. They'd probably take her back that far, anyway, and then I know somebody'll be going down from Griffin toward Concho before long." Seeing that Hap frowned, Will demanded, "What's the matter?"

"I don't know, Doc. Some bullwhackers are real hard cases. And given where she's been, they're apt to have notions. Maybe you ought to send her with the mail."

"It'd be out of her way." Sprenger considered for a moment, then nodded. "But I see what you're saying."

Hap reached for the crutches propped against the wall, then slid off the bed.

"Where do you think you're going?"

"To the privy. Then I'm going to see if my borrowed britches fit. If they do, I'm going for a walk."

"Like hell."

"Yeah. I figured I'd go over to the store and get myself a razor and a bottle of whiskey. At least that way I'll be a good-looking drunk."

"Or a crippled one."

"I'm all right."

Will's mouth turned down at one corner. "You and the Bryce woman must've been cut from the same cloth. You'd both be saying you were all right if you were dying."

Hap shrugged. " 'Way I look at it, it's a whole lot better than complaining, Doc."

"Only if it's the truth." Removing his surgeon's apron, Will folded it up, then laid it aside. "If it looks like you're going to fall, call for Walsh. He's out there passing out paregoric for the runs again."

"Remind me not to eat in the enlisted men's mess," Hap murmured.

"It's not the food, it's the water. People've been keeping pigs, and the waste drains into the creek. Hell, you got enlisted men drinking and bathing in it, but since Davidson gets his water from the well, he refuses to see the problem. But I finally got his attention on the health and hygiene report, so I guess he's giving everybody a week to find someplace else to keep the animals until they're butchered."

"Yeah, he wouldn't want anything bad going in on anything official."

"Tell you what, you get around on those crutches without falling, and I'll tell Cora to set another place at dinner." Sprenger reached for his hat and carefully placed it over his thinning gray hair. "I'll tell one of the boys to come on early and help you over. We eat about six-thirty, and Cora's pretty much set about that." Turning back to Hap, he added significantly, "Be a whole lot better for you than swigging on a bottle by yourself. Besides, it'll give you another look at Annie Bryce. You owe her, you know."

"Yeah." Actually, Hap had been thinking about that, but there was something about facing a woman who'd seen him buck naked that made him uncomfortable. It was as though she'd seen the worst of him already. And what made it even harder was the guilt he felt for what had happened to her. But if she was going to leave, it was time he got around to thanking her. "Yeah."

"Good." Moving to remove his coat from the peg by the infirmary door, Will glanced out the window. His hand stopped in midair. "Well, I'll be damned."

"What?"

"Haworth's going to be mad as hell. They're bringing in one of his pets—in irons."

Cursing the damned crutches under his breath, Hap hobbled up behind the surgeon for a look. Sure enough, surrounded by at least a dozen troopers, a manacled Comanche sat astride a bony pony, his impassive face giving him a majestic look despite the ragged blanket that covered his shoulders.

"Looks like you were wrong, Doc," he murmured.

"About what?"

"Black Jack's arrested Bull Calf."

Annie was sitting alone in her room, composing a letter to the Bank of Austin, asking for an appointment to go over her affairs as soon as she got home, when Cora knocked on the door. As she looked up, the older woman came in.

"I know it won't begin to make up for what happened, but at least they've caught him," she said. "I thought you'd want to know they've arrested the savage responsible."

For a moment Annie was at a loss. "They've arrested whom?"

"Colonel Davidson said to tell you that you don't have to face him. If you give a sworn statement, he believes it will be enough—at least to hold him, anyway," Cora explained. "Indeed, he wanted to tell you himself, but I thought perhaps the shock might overset you, so I said I'd prepare you."

"Prepare me for what? Who's been arrested?" Annie asked again.

"Even if you wish to avoid testifying, which you very well might, the colonel still believes the arrest may force them to yield your daughter. It's been done before."

Annie's hands gripped the arms of the rocking chair. For an awful moment she thought of Two Trees, and it was as though she was hollow, totally empty inside. But it couldn't be—she'd never even mentioned him to anyone. And he'd be the last Comanche to come anywhere near the reservation.

"I don't think—"

"Oh, dear, I knew it was going to be a shock." Moving behind Annie, Cora placed a comforting hand on her shoulder. "My dear, they've found the Indian called Bull Calf. Colonel Davidson just had word of the Tonkawa scouts that they were coming in with him."

"*Bull Calf?* But—" For a moment Annie was at a loss, then she protested, "But he wasn't—oh, Lord, no!"

Cora nodded. "He said it was the least he could do for you after all you have suffered."

"Well, I wish I'd been asked, for I could have *told* Colonel Davidson—they're bringing him in now?"

"Yes, he didn't want to say anything until it was done."

"But it's not right, not right at all!" Quickly setting her writing supplies aside, Annie rose to go to the window, and what she saw made her heart sink. There in the middle of the parade ground, two troopers were wrestling Bull Calf from his horse, and despite the fact that his hands were shackled, he was putting up a fight. Finally, one of them cracked the barrel of a pistol against the side of his head to subdue him. "No, he doesn't deserve this," she said under her breath. "I can't let it happen—I can't." She started for the door.

Confused by her guest's manner, the older woman hesitated, then asked, "What are you doing? Surely you're not going out there?"

"I've got to stop them!" Annie flung over her shoulder.

"Don't—you'll take your death without a wrap!" Then the words sank in. "*Stop* them? Have you lost your mind? No, you don't want to make a spectacle of yourself!" she called out. "Annie, come back!"

"But they're wrong!"

"They brought him in because of you!" Hugging her arms against the cold, Cora hurried after her. "Annie, wait!"

It was as though her words disappeared in the chill wind. Before Cora could catch up, the younger woman reached the cordon of soldiers around the Indian. As she watched with dismay, Annie Bryce pushed her way through the men, crying, "Let him go! You don't know what you are doing!"

Bull Calf's black eyes glittered as he lunged toward her, his manacled hands raised as though he would strike. Two troopers caught him from behind, pulling his elbows back. He stared hard for a moment, then demanded angrily, "Is this how you would repay me, Woman Who Walks Far? Look at you. You deceived me, and now you have told them lies! Fat Owl was right—you brought misfortune among us! You blinded me with pity when I should have killed you!" he finished contemptuously.

The Comanche words stung. Facing him, she fought tears as she reached a hand out, speaking his language haltingly. "It is true that I could speak—that I was not possessed of spirits—but I was afraid. I did not know that I would find kindness in Bull Calf. I had no reason to expect it. I saw the scalps on Bull Calf's lance, that they were white, and I wanted to live. But you let me stay. Out of pity you fed me."

"Not one hair of your head did I harm. Nothing did I ask, and this is how I am thanked for it."

She swallowed and nodded. "And I will tell them that. I will tell them Bull Calf is my brother," she promised. "I will tell them I suffered no ill at your hands." Her hand closed over the cold iron on his wrist. "I swear it."

Expecting gratitude, Davidson was making his way toward her when he saw her touch the Indian. He recoiled as a shiver of apprehension ran down his spine. He'd risked Sherman's certain displeasure by violating his orders, but he'd been prepared to lie and say his men had taken the Comanche chief after he'd fled the reservation. And now that it was done, she was saying they'd made a mistake. He felt betrayed. And angry. As his temper rose, she saw him.

"Colonel Davidson," she said, "I appreciate what you have done, but this is the wrong man. You've got the wrong man."

"It's Bull Calf, isn't it?" he demanded harshly.

"Yes, but—" Taken aback by the anger in his voice, she hesitated, knowing it would be difficult to find the words to convince this stern man he'd made a mistake. "It wasn't Bull Calf who killed my husband, Colonel. It wasn't Penetaka Comanches who raided our farm. The war party was mostly Quahadi and Nokoni—and a couple of Kiowas, I think. But no Penetakas. This man is innocent."

Davidson's jaw worked visibly before he could bring

himself to speak. "I'm afraid I don't understand, Mrs. Bryce," he responded with tightly controlled fury. "This is the man who held you captive—you were found in his camp. Are you saying you were there willingly? That you were not misused there?"

Those gathered to watch fell completely silent, and she could feel the hostility around her. In the eyes of every man there she was condemning herself by defending Bull Calf. Her chin came up and she dared to meet Black Jack Davidson's eyes, seeing the outrage there.

"Yes," she responded simply.

It wasn't what he wanted to hear. "Look at him—he's a savage!" Davidson said furiously. "He's got the blood of God only knows how many whites on his hands! How in God's name could you—?" He choked on the thought.

"He's innocent of mine," she countered quietly. "I was abandoned, left to die by a man called Two Trees. I wandered for days, lost and alone without food or water, until the Penetakas found me. And there were those who wanted to kill me, but I pretended to be crazed. Then, afraid of my evil spirit, they wanted to leave me to die as Two Trees had, but Bull Calf didn't abandon me. He let me follow him and his family."

"He starved you half to death," the colonel retorted.

She shook her head. "None of us had any food at the last. When the hunting was bad, I was a burden to him, but he let me stay. Once we reached the reservation, he encouraged me to walk to the agency. If I'd had the strength, I would have come on my own, but by then I was too weak from hunger to make it."

She wasn't telling him anything he wanted to hear. She was making him look like a damned fool. He stared hard into those blue eyes of hers, but she held her ground. Finally, it was he who looked away.

Afraid of drawing Davidson's ire, one of the troopers turned to Lieutenant Hughes to ask, "Where do you want to put the prisoner, sir?"

The colonel squared his shoulders ramrod straight and fixed the man with a glare. "Strike the manacles, soldier," he snapped. "Then get the red son of a bitch out of my sight."

With that, he turned and stalked across the ground toward his office. It wasn't until the door slammed that anyone spoke. Elliott Hughes exchanged glances with Captain Harrison, who exhaled audibly, then ordered, "Release the prisoner and escort him off the post. I don't know what the colonel's going to tell Haworth, but I sure as hell don't want to be around when it happens."

Relieved, Annie turned back to Bull Calf. "They're letting you go," she told him. In front of everyone, she held out her hand again. For a long moment the Comanche just stood there. Finally he took it, clasping her fingers in the white man's gesture of friendship.

Then it was over. A soldier stepped between them to unlock the irons. As soon as his hands were free, Bull Calf swung up on the pony, and without waiting for any escort, he dug his moccasin into a bony flank and laid the braided quirt across the animal's shoulder. At the edge of the parade ground, he wheeled around for one last defiant gesture, then rode off.

Taking their cue from Davidson, soldiers and onlookers drifted away, most without looking at her. Cora Sprenger took a step toward her, then stopped.

"Well, my dear, you've certainly made your road a lot

rougher," she said finally. "Colonel Davidson will never forgive you."

"It doesn't matter. I'm going home, anyway." Shivering now, Annie rubbed her arms. "For three years Bull Calf was the only good thing that happened to me," she added, sighing. "I just repaid the favor. But if you want me to remove myself from your house, I'll understand."

"No, of course not." Cora forced a smile. "I know you did what you thought you had to, and I just wish you didn't have to regret it. Well," she said, "I'm going inside. It's too cold to stand out here, my dear. I think I'll make a good, strong toddy. Right now we both probably need it."

"All right."

As the older woman started back to her house, Annie paused to watch Bull Calf. His bravado gone, he was riding slowly southward on the plodding pony. As much as she despised his people, she felt sorry for him. Clasping her arms across her breasts, she turned to follow Cora Sprenger.

"Wait up!"

Startled, she stopped for a moment, then saw Hap Walker awkwardly hobbling across the yard on crutches. By the looks of it, he was going to require a lot of practice before he mastered them. He was nearly breathless by the time he reached her. She waited warily, expecting him to condemn her. When he didn't say anything, she observed, "Well, you are getting around at least, Captain."

"Like a racehorse," he muttered dryly. "But it'll get better. It's got to."

The winter sun seemed to reflect in the pale hair that framed her face. And her eyes were as blue as a summer sky. Doc Sprenger had been right—she was a pretty woman.

"I guess I know what you're thinking," she told him.

"I'd be surprised if you did," he countered, a smile slowly spreading across his face, crinkling the corners of his eyes. He looked up at the sun for a moment, then back to her. "You look real different from when I saw you in that Indian camp. I couldn't even tell what color your hair was then."

"You couldn't tell much of anything then, could you?"

"Not much," he agreed. "I don't remember much before the next morning." He glanced at the sky again. "Yeah, I was kind of waiting for you to come back after that. Makes more sense to visit a man when he's awake, doesn't it?"

"Major Sprenger said you were recovering," she murmured.

"I guess you've been busy," he allowed, "but I was kind of hoping I'd get a chance to say thanks. You've got healing hands, you know that?"

"No."

"Well, you do. And I just wanted you to know I appreciated everything you did for me that night. Doc says you were more'n half-sick yourself."

"I had to do something. I couldn't sleep." It was too cold outside, but she didn't want to leave him standing there. "Mrs. Sprenger's making hot toddies right now. Uh, I don't suppose you'd care to join us?" she asked him. "I'm sure she wouldn't mind."

"Never drink the stuff. 'Way I look at it, it's a waste of whiskey."

"Oh."

"I don't like anything with mine, not even water," he admitted ruefully. "I guess it's all in what you get used to."

"I don't know. If you put every drop of spirits I ever drank in a cup, it wouldn't be full. If it doesn't have water and honey or sugar to go with it, I can't get it down."

"Fool thing to do, you know."

Somehow she knew he wasn't speaking of hot toddies. "Yes, well, I think everybody shares that opinion. I know you think I ought to have let them put him in jail, but I couldn't."

"There you go again."

"What?"

"Thinking for me."

"Well, it's pretty obvious. Look, I'm freezing. Why don't you come in, whether you want the toddy or not?"

"I would, but I'm coming for supper, so I reckon I'd better get myself a razor somewhere first."

"Oh. Then I guess I'll see you there, Captain."

He waited until she was about fifteen feet away. "I guess you read the wrong mind," he said then.

She half turned back. "I beg your pardon?"

"I was thinking after what the Comanches did to you, it took a lot of goodness—and a lot of guts—to stand up for old Bull Calf. Most folks in your place wouldn't have lifted a finger to help him, whether he was guilty or not. I'm not even sure I would have, and I don't have nearly as much at risk as you do."

"I couldn't have lived with myself," she said simply.

"No, I reckon not. My ma would've said you had character. She admired that in a person—and so do I."

She found herself actually smiling. "Well, thank you, sir. It's quite kind of you to say that."

Bracing his crutch under his arm, he reached to lift the front of his battered hat. "See you at supper, ma'am."

This time he watched her all the way into the house. Character. Yeah, that's what she had, all right. And it was going to cost her. Now the unpleasant speculation would pass for the God's truth everywhere anybody heard about her and Bull Calf.

As the door closed behind her, he adjusted the crutches beneath already sore arms and hopped on one foot toward the post store. Yeah, he was in bad need of that shave, and a bath, too, not to mention that he could sure use a pint of good whiskey right now. But the whiskey'd have to wait until after supper. Cora Sprenger didn't seem like the sort to tolerate a drunk at her table.

When he finally made it to the store, all the talk was about Annie Bryce, and it was as bad as he'd expected. As he opened the door, he heard the post sutler declare, "Now we know why she wasn't messed up like the Purvis woman. She was keeping old Bull Calf warm at night and liking it."

Those around him nodded. "Yeah," somebody said, "it must've plumb broke her heart when he traded her for food."

"Here now, no way to talk about a white woman," one brave soul protested.

"Ain't much of a white woman now."

"Gone three years, way I heard it," another offered. "Kinda makes you wonder how many papooses they got on her, don't it?"

"Yeah. Mebbe that kid she's wanting back is half-red."

"No."

The sutler turned around at the sound of his voice.

118

"Damned if it ain't Hap Walker!" he called out. "If you ain't a sight for sore eyes—damn, but I head you were nearly done for, Hap!"

"Can't believe everything you hear now, can you?" Hap swung his frame between the crutches and groped for the counter, pulling himself along it until he faced the small knot of men standing with the trader. "I'd take it real kindly if you'd lay off lying about Mrs. Bryce," he said evenly. "It makes me want to horsewhip the lot of you."

A low murmur spread through the room, and then a curious silence descended as they stared at him. Finally, one fellow found his voice. "Now, dammit, Hap, you saw her out there with the Comanche!"

"Talking to him like she was one of 'em!" someone shouted from behind him.

"I reckon in three years a body'd learn the language," Hap retorted. "Be downright stupid not to."

"All that stuff she told old Black Jack, 'bout how—"

"He let her live," Hap cut in curtly.

"And we all know why, don't we?"

"No, you don't know a damned thing about it." Reaching into his pocket, he drew out a silver dollar and tossed it to the sutler. "Still renting out the back room?"

"Yeah."

"Good. I'll take it, along with a razor and some soap. And there's another one just like it for anybody that's got a clean pair of pants my size. No holes in 'em." He looked at the trader again. "Yeah—and I'll be needing a bath."

"All I got's a tin tub and a bucket."

"Throw in hot water, and you got yourself a deal."

"Cost you twenty-five cents."

"I got it. Oh, and when I get back from supper, I'll take

a bottle of the best whiskey you've got on that shelf," Hap added. The corners of his mouth turned down, forming a wry smile. "Don't suppose you carry any eau de cologne, do you?"

"Ain't much call for it out here," the man allowed. "Got some fair-smelling liniment, but that's about it. 'Less I was to count the lilac water I keep for the ladies," he amended, remembering it suddenly. "Say, you ain't taken to stinking yourself up, have you?"

"A man gets tired of smelling like his horse sometimes. Yeah, I'd take some lilac water in my bath, I guess. My ma was always liking lilacs," Hap decided. "Anybody want to say anything about it?"

"Damned if it don't sound like you're going courtin', Cap'n."

"No."

"I might have some pants as would fit you," a man in the back of the room offered.

"Clean?"

"Never been worn," he assured Hap. "My ma sent 'em for Christmas."

"Jack, your ma's been dead five years!" somebody yelled out.

"Well, the pants is still good. Like I said, I ain't never worn 'em! I was a mite heavier than she remembered me when I got 'em," he explained, looking at Hap. "You can try 'em, and if a dollar's too much—"

"Thanks."

"Bring the razor and soap back to you, Hap," the sutler offered. "Might take awhile to heat the water."

"Better bring the bottle, too, in case you're closed up when I get back from supper."

"I wouldn't eat in the enlisted men's mess. Half a dozen of 'em are down with the runs," the man with the pants advised him.

"I'm not."

"Naw, he's Hap Walker. They'll let him eat with the officers," somebody said.

"Well, it ain't much better. I heard last night all they had was boiled potatoes and cabbage with a little salt pork. Supply wagons are late this month. Better get Captain Harrison or Lieutenant Hughes to take you home with 'em. They got wives, you know."

"You all right, Hap?" the sutler asked suddenly. "You look a mite peaked. Maybe you better go on back."

"Yeah, I'm all right."

As he struggled with the hated crutches, he heard somebody murmur, "Never thought I'd see Hap Walker crippled up like that." Gritting his teeth, he kept going.

Later, as he sat in the tub, soaking in tepid water, his eyes strayed to the bottle on the table. For two cents he'd forget the Sprengers and drink his supper. But then he thought of Annie Bryce, the way she'd stood there, smiling for that brief moment in the yard. The image faded as quickly as it had come, and he was standing on that porch, looking at those wet bedsheets flapping on that laundry line.

It was only five-thirty, and he knew it. But it was a matter of either coming on over or staying in the room he'd rented, staring at a full bottle of whiskey, wanting to drink all of it. Still, as he knocked on the Sprenger door, he was so ill at ease he wished he was almost anywhere else.

After years of living in buckskin pants and open-necked shirts, he was standing there looking like a cross between a preacher and an undertaker in new black serge trousers and a borrowed frock coat, reeking of the lilac water. He probably smelled like a whore from the Hog Station. And to make matters even worse, the woman who'd washed his shirt had starched it as stiff as paperboard. When he moved, he swore he could hear it.

He took off his hat and smoothed his hair back with his hand. That was the only thing he'd gotten from his mother he'd ever regretted. The unruly waves looked a whole lot better on a woman than on a man. And the hell of it was nobody on either side of his family had ever gone bald, so he was probably stuck with every last dip and flip for as long as he breathed.

Wiping flour from her hands onto her apron, the major's wife finally answered. The smell of fried chicken wafted out to greet him.

"Captain! Oh, dear, Will's not home yet."

"I reckon I'm a mite early," he murmured apologetically, maneuvering the crutches inside.

"Actually, you are. But that's quite all right," she added hastily. "Here, let me take your hat."

As it was the only thing that felt like it belonged to him, he yielded it almost reluctantly. Again he tried to smooth his hair. "Mrs. Bryce about?" he asked casually.

"She's about done peeling potatoes."

"Oh."

"Well, do come on in and make yourself at home in the parlor," she offered, seemingly distracted. "Let's see, the chicken's in the skillet, the biscuits are cut, the beans are boiling, and the potatoes are ready to go on when Will gets here," she murmured, more to herself than to him. "Yes, I think that's everything." She looked up at him. "Would you care for a glass of something before dinner? Will's got some sherry—or some blackberry wine he made himself last summer. And there's coffee, of course."

"I'm a whiskey man myself."

"Well, there is that," she conceded. "I think Will has some scotch."

"That's all right, coffee'll do just fine," he decided hastily.

"I'll send Annie out with it." She paused, then looked up again. "I suppose there's quite a lot of talk, isn't there?"

"Yeah."

"One could have wished she hadn't done it," she said tiredly. "But there's no help for that now. I'd hoped she could be persuaded to stay through Christmas, but she wants to go home. I suppose it's for the best," she added, sighing. "Though how she's to get there, I'm sure I don't know. No matter how much the sun shines now, it *is* the dead of winter, so there's no telling how long it's going to last. But that's not your concern, so I don't know why I'm bothering you with it."

"No, but I reckon the road'll be downright dry in a couple of days."

"She's a woman alone, Captain. It's not like it is for a man. She cannot just get on a horse and ride there."

"I was telling Doc she ought to go with the mail down to Stockton, then take the stage back over to San Antone."

"I hadn't thought of that. Yes, I suppose it would serve, but it's quite a distance out of her way," she mused. "Well, in any event, she'll do what she wants, I suppose." Seeing that he still stood, she flushed guiltily. "There's no need to play the gentleman for me, Captain," she assured him. "It must be terribly uncomfortable on those crutches."

"Yeah." He didn't need her permission twice. Keeping the sore leg straight out in front, he eased his body down onto the settee. "Thanks."

"I must say you are looking much better than I expected, sir. A little over a week ago, we were all praying for you."

"I'm a pretty tough old bird, I guess. As soon as I can throw these things away, I'll be going back to the Ybarra myself."

"Will tells me you sell cattle now."

"Yeah." She was making an effort to be gracious, but he could see she was busy. Besides, even though he'd brought it up, he didn't want to talk about the Ybarra or the cattle business. "Look, if you need to do something, I don't have to be entertained, ma'am," he told her. "I've spent half a lifetime by myself, so I don't mind it. In fact, it feels good just to sit a spell by the stove."

"Well, Annie ought to have them in the water by now—the potatoes, I mean. I'm sure she'll want to come out and say hello, anyway." With that, she turned toward the kitchen.

"Tell her she doesn't have to."

Yet as he waited, there was a certain anticipation—and a certain dread. It was funny how a man could do a hundred things right and yet remember a single failure. For three years he'd told himself he and Rios had done everything they could, and he'd believed it. But now he'd seen Anne Bryce, and instead of a faceless name, she was flesh and blood. And rain and mud and swollen rivers didn't seem enough of an excuse for what had happened to her baby and that little girl of hers.

"Hello, Captain," she said quietly from the doorway.

He struggled to stand. Even though he'd seen her three times now, he hadn't really taken stock of her beyond the blond hair and the blue eyes. Her height surprised him—she came within three or four inches of being as tall as he was, and her thinness made her seem even taller. Now that he had the time to study her, he felt even more awkward than ever.

She'd fixed her hair, parting it in the middle, twisting it into a coil at the back of her neck. It was both severe and appealing, and the thought crossed his mind that not many women could wear it like that. Only the good-looking ones. Yeah, it was her fine features that let her get away with it. That and the eyes—only a blind man wouldn't notice her expressive eyes. He didn't know how she'd managed to make Bull Calf think her crazy with those eyes.

"Is something the matter?"

"No," he said finally. "I was just thinking you cleaned up really pretty." God, but he sounded ignorant, almost stupid. "Sorry, hope you know I didn't mean it to come out like that," he murmured sheepishly. "Kinda hard to know what to say to a woman when a man gets to be my age without a wife. Guess I haven't been around too many ladies."

"I thought you did all right outside."

"Yeah. I'm not real used to sitting down in a parlor, trying to say the right thing. I usually just speak what's on my mind and get it over with. Then I get to regret it."

The corners of her mouth lifted in a faint smile. "I don't think you have much to apologize for. Everybody admires you, Captain." Moving into the room, she set down the tray on the low table. "Cora wasn't sure whether you took cream or sugar in your coffee."

He eased back onto the settee, then looked up. "Just sugar, lots of it. The boy I helped raise can't make a decent pot of the stuff, so I got used to sweetening it to kill the taste. But he turned into a good man except for that, and coffee's not everything."

"Clay McAlester?"

He brightened visibly. "Heard of him?"

"From both sides."

"I reckon the Comanches didn't forget him any more than he forgot them."

"No." She hesitated for a moment before taking the

126

other end of the settee. Leaning forward, she poured the dark, steaming liquid into a delicate china cup, then set it and the sugar bowl in front of him. "You'd better fix this to suit you," she decided.

"Thanks. You're not having any?"

"No. Cora and I have tea steeping."

He dipped three spoons full of sugar into the small cup, then stirred it. When he tasted the coffee, it was like syrup, just the way he wanted it. She watched, seemingly fascinated.

"You could use that on pancakes," she said finally.

"Sometimes I do," he admitted. He took another sip. "You doing all right?"

"Yes, but I'm ready to go home."

"You can't blame Davidson, you know. It's the damned peace policy. But come summer, that's going to change."

"That's what I'm afraid of. I feel like I'm in a race to do something before it happens. I feel like the hourglass is running out."

"There's not much you can do to stop it," he said quietly. "But maybe when they're pushed onto the reservation, the kid will turn up. That's about the only way anybody could find her."

"I can't wait for that. I can't take the chance that she won't survive, sir. I have to find her first." She stared unseeingly at the stove for a long moment, then shook her head. "I can't wait. When I get home, I'm going to Austin."

"You can't trust politicians, Mrs. Bryce. You'd be better off going to the papers. Believe me, I know. I took a lot of abuse from the politicians—after the papers got wind of things and printed 'em up."

"I want to see the governor first. I want to tell him about Susannah, and I want to hear what he says."

"It won't be much."

She turned on him then. "You don't know that—you can't know that! She's a Texas citizen, Captain Walker. She's a little girl!"

"Look, I'm sorry."

"Sorry? *Sorry?* Everybody's sorry, Captain, but nobody wants to do anything about it! Well, I'm going to haunt them. I'm going to beg and plead and rant and rave until somebody helps me—and if nobody will, then I guess I'll just have to help myself. But even if the whole world is deaf, I'm getting my daughter out of there—and I'll do it if I have to go alone, Captain Walker," she told him fiercely.

"Be hard to find her after all this time."

"You sound like Colonel Davidson."

There was no mistaking the bitterness in her voice, and he wished there was something positive he could tell her, but there wasn't. "You know, Mrs. Bryce, the chances of getting that little girl back—well, it's probably not going to come about. I reckon it's harder for a woman, but it'd be a whole lot better for you if you could just go on. You've still got your land and your house, and that's something. You may never see her again. You may never know what happened to her. And it may have happened right in the beginning. Pining for her won't change that. It'll just make you sick."

"No, she's alive. She has to be. He traded a horse for her, so he wanted to keep her."

"Maybe. But even if she was their own kid, there's a lot of things that happen to 'em. That's why you don't see many Comanches who've got more than one or two offspring—but you know that," he reasoned with her. "Even if they took care of her, there's no guaranteeing she survived. Hell, you know how they live."

"I'm telling you she's alive!"

"You've got to look ahead, not behind you. Someday there might be another man come along to help you work the place—you know that too, don't you? You're a fine-looking woman, and—" He stopped, suddenly aware of her stricken face, of her hands twisting the blue cotton skirt in her lap.

She closed her eyes and swallowed. "No," she whispered, "I don't want that ever again. I just want my daughter."

"You got let yourself grieve first, then forget—and I'm not saying that's easy. But instead of going to Austin on a wild goose chase, take care of yourself. Take the time to get well. And pretty soon time will take care of the rest of what ails you. Some fellow will come along that knows none of this was your fault, and then—"

Her fingers closed on the fabric, clenching it tightly. When she spoke, her voice was flat and toneless. "I would rather die first. Nobody's going to touch me like that again, ever. I think if a man kissed me, I would vomit. No, I *know* I would."

"All right, look, I didn't mean to upset you. I just think you're going to keep hurting yourself."

She swallowed again. "Well, you did—and you have."

"Look, you don't have to talk to me about any of this if you don't want to. I was just trying to tell you you've got the rest of your life left ahead of you." When she said nothing, he went on, admitting, "I feel pretty guilty about what happened—I want you to know that. I feel like it was me that let you down."

"You?" Her eyes widened. "Why would you think that?"

He took a deep breath, then let it out. "I was there, Mrs. Bryce. About a day after it happened, I was there."

"Yes, but by then—"

"I was with the state police then. Six of us had been tracking that war party for days—had followed it all the way from South Texas when we stumbled on your place," he remembered. "Yeah, we were about a day behind 'em, I'd say."

"You were too late, Captain."

"Yeah, I know, but that doesn't make me feel any better. I keep thinking I ought to have found you and the kids— and that German girl they took before you."

"Gretchen Halser."

"Yeah. The Comanches got her ma—left her for dead, but she was still alive when we found her. Wiped out everybody but the girl. It told the woman I'd find her, but I didn't."

"She didn't survive."

"I'd sure like to get my hands on the buck that killed her. But I don't guess that'll ever happen," he conceded, sighing.

"His name was Two Trees."

"Still alive?"

"I don't know. I hope not." She looked at her hands for a moment, then said fiercely, "I prayed to God he would die. Every day I prayed he would die."

"Yeah. Like I said, I was at your place. Me and Romero Rios buried your husband under a cottonwood tree in the backyard, near where you had your flowers. I passed by there last summer, and I think you'd be pleased with where we laid him. It's a pretty spot, looking toward the river."

"Yes," she managed, her throat constricting. "Yes, it is. When it was hot, we used to eat out there on a blanket. Susannah liked to bring me the wild roses."

"They're still growing—must've been a hundred blooms on 'em when I was there." Compelled to make a clean breast of everything he felt about it, he went on: "But when we found your place, everything was mud, and the river was coming up fast. I got across it, but there wasn't a trace of tracks anywhere on the other side. Finally, I just went back, and we buried your husband."

"Thank you."

He looked down at the rag rug on the floor, then exhaled heavily. "I guess I'm wanting you to know every one of us hated giving up on you and the kids. I rode the boys pretty hard for three days trying to catch up to that war party, and then the rain came."

"I don't blame you, Captain Walker," she said quietly. "You'd never have caught up, anyway. They never stopped. They didn't eat or sleep for the first two days. They wouldn't even let me change Jody's wet clothes." She closed her eyes again, this time to hide hot tears. "They killed my baby," she whispered.

"Yeah, I know."

"It wasn't his fault." Her mouth contorted as she fought the flood that threatened to overwhelm her, but the dam broke, sending shudders through her. "They killed my baby, Captain Walker—they killed my baby!" she choked out. "They wouldn't let me feed him!"

He slid down the sofa and reached out to touch her shoulder. "Don't—" he said gently. "Look, I'm sorry for bringing it up."

"I-I cannot help it! There isn't a day that goes by that—that I don't think about it—that I don't wish I'd been able to stop them, but I couldn't!" She raised anguished, tear-reddened eyes to his face. "Don't you understand? I should have done something, anything to save him! But there *wasn't* anything I could do—nothing!" she cried. "I saw it happen and—and I couldn't stop it!"

"Shhhh, don't—"

His arm circled her shoulder, turning her against his body, pulling her close. She stiffened momentarily, then clutched his arms, digging her nails into his flesh, holding on as though she were drowning. Burying her face in his shirt, she sobbed uncontrollably.

"Captain, whatever—?"

Cora stopped in the doorway. Hap looked over Annie's shoulder, meeting her eyes, and shook his head. She withdrew without another word, leaving them alone again. If Walker could make the woman deal with her grief, it was a good thing, Cora reasoned.

He tried another tack. "Go on, cry. Get it all out," he said softly. "It's all right, you've got a right to cry." One of his hands stroked her hair, smoothing it against her head, while the other rubbed the hollow between her bony shoulder blades. "If I could, I'd kill every last one of 'em for you."

He didn't know how long she wept, only that his arms ached from holding her. Finally, the shudders subsided into shivers; then she lay still and exhausted against his shoulder. He cradled her like that in a silence broken only by the steady ticking of the big clock.

If he hadn't had to move the leg, he could have held her forever. But as he shifted his weight, she sat up guiltily. Wiping her wet cheeks with the back of her hand, she said self-consciously, "I've, uh, soaked your shirt. I'm sorry."

He looked down, seeing the wet place where her face had been. "I reckon it'll dry. It'd be a good thing if you softened it up some, anyway."

Her forced smile twisted. "I'm sorry," she said again. "I always thought if I let myself weep, I'd never stop. I guess I was right, wasn't I? I'm truly sorry."

"For what? You had that coming to you, probably for a long time. Besides, I didn't mind. It was like I was still good for something." Reluctantly, he removed his arm from her shoulder and sat back also. Looking again at the stove, he said quietly, "I've never been through anything like what happened to you, so I can't even imagine it. It had to be hell."

"It still is. Without Susannah, it still is." Sniffing, she fumbled in her pocket for a handkerchief, then blew her nose loudly. "I'm sorry," she apologized again.

"You know, you and Gretchen were the only white females I didn't make 'em pay for. I guess that's always going to bother me."

The intimacy had passed, replaced again by the awkwardness between strangers. She sat on the edge of the sofa, twisting the blue cotton between her fingers again, unable to think of anything more to say. Finally, she rose and walked to the window.

"How long do you think the weather's going to hold?" she asked suddenly.

"Hard to tell."

"The snow's melted, and the ground is nearly dry now."

"Just about."

"I want to go home."

"I know."

"I want to plant flowers on Ethan's grave."

"Yeah, I reckon you ought to."

"It's a wonder the coyotes didn't dig him up. They dug everything else up—even the plow horse he buried the winter before."

"They tried, but they couldn't get at him. Rios found a big metal trunk in your house, and we locked the body in it."

"That belonged to Ethan's mother. When they divided her things up, he wanted it." She sighed. "I guess in a way it was fitting. The trunk was all he had left of her, and they're both gone now. I'm beholden to you for taking care of that."

"No."

"But you didn't have to do it."

"I always thought it was part of the job. I guess I hope if I died like that, there'd be somebody to do the same for me."

She couldn't stand thinking it anymore, not right now, anyway. She stared into the twilight, watching a soldier light the lantern marking the hospital. "I hate winter. It turns dark so early," she said low. "The sun's gone already."

"Kinda like life sometimes."

"Yes."

"Eventually it passes, and spring shows up. Then it's all pretty and green again, and we forget the cold and the darkness. It's bound to happen."

"I hope so, Captain—I hope so. You don't know how much I want the sun to shine."

Hap stared at the three fingers left in the bottle, wondering why he was still sober enough to think. He took another long pull, savoring the trail of liquid heat running all the way to his stomach. No, it wasn't the whiskey's fault—it was his. His mind was too occupied to let the spirits work.

He looked toward the curtainless window, seeing the starlit sky, and he wondered if Anne Bryce was sleeping. It was long past midnight, so he guessed she probably was. God, he felt worse about her kids than anything else he could think of, and he had ever since Davidson told him about it. And seeing her hadn't eased that, not at all.

God, he could still feel her thin body against his, and he could still hear her cry for that dead baby. No, it didn't matter how many times he told himself he'd done everything he could have; it didn't even matter that she'd said the same thing. Back then he hadn't been used to failing, and that one loss had stuck in his craw more than anything else. Gretchen Halser was dead. Little Joseph Bryce was dead. Susannah Bryce might as well be. And Anne Bryce was left to live with her losses.

He had to get her out of his mind. Sitting up, he leaned into the window, looking up at the night sky. That big, full moon hung like a giant ball beneath one lonely cloud, making it seem almost as bright as day out there. Just by looking at it, one would think the night air was warm, but he knew it wasn't. When he'd left the Sprengers after supper, the wind was cold.

Old Washaya, a colorful Tonk scout, had predicted a warm spell, and the post sutler insisted the Indian had an uncanny knack of knowing the weather, so much so that even Black Jack Davidson wouldn't send out a patrol if Washaya said it was coming a storm. Hap hoped the Tonk was right. Winter'd just begun, but he was already sick of it.

He looked beyond the fort itself, squinting at the faint light coming from the lantern on the Hog Ranch. This time next week the girls would be having company out there. Only then it'd be real swine, and not the human kind they were used to. And Davidson wouldn't care when they complained of the stench.

It was hard to figure what made a woman do that for a living, and even poverty didn't seem enough of an excuse to let a parade of unwashed strangers use her, knowing she was no more than a convenience to any of them. Even if she was passable-looking when she started, she wouldn't stay that way long. Most of the old whores he'd seen were drunks at best, disease-ridden drunks at worst. But maybe they got even in the end, because according to Doc Sprenger, every year syphilis killed more men in the army than "arrows, bullets, malaria, and all the other fevers put together."

Then there was Anne Bryce. A decent Christian woman forced to endure the unspeakable to stay alive. It didn't seem right that some folks couldn't or wouldn't make the distinction between her and those whores out there. She'd probably end up going someplace where nobody knew her to escape from the stigma.

Filled with a longing for the trail, for a night spent over a campfire rather than in the back room of a damned store, he swigged more whiskey down. After all those years of raising hell with Indians and desperados, he still had enough wildness left to yearn for a little meanness in his life.

Jim Miller, his first captain, used to say, "Ain't much difference between a ranger and an outlaw, 'cepting it's the outlaw as gets himself hanged. Rangerin' is nine-tenths guts and one-tenth law, but it's the guts that will keep you alive." Unfortunately, right after he'd said it, Jim got himself ambushed by Kiowas over by the Big Spring, and his guts weren't enough to save him. To stay alive in the business, a man had to outthink his quarry. And be willing to kill him without remorse. There'd never been any time to second-guess anything he'd ever done. Right or wrong, once it was over, it was over.

But now the Halser and Bryce raids were bothering him again, leaving a hole in his gut that wouldn't go away. Anne Bryce wasn't getting that kid back, but it'd take her years to finally give up. Until then she'd be pounding her head against a lot of closed doors, and nobody'd answer. Nobody.

He'd tried to tell her it wouldn't do any good to ask for

help in Texas. Hell, the whole frontier battalion was twenty-five men, and they couldn't even keep up with the rustling and the raids the way it was, let alone spare any men to ride up into the Comancheria with nothing but a dim hope of finding one little girl. But she didn't want to hear it, and he couldn't blame her. If it had happened to him, he'd have combed every inch of desert and canyon all the way up into the Indian territory, keeping at it until he either had a live kid or dead body to bring back. Or until he was dead himself.

He knew only one man who could go up there and come back with his hair. And no matter how bad Hap felt about Anne Bryce, he wouldn't ask Clay to do it. Not with a new wife, with a baby on the way. And he couldn't go himself, not even if he'd wanted to. No, she was just going to have to do what he told her—go on without the kid.

He started to take another pull off the long-necked bottle and found it empty, something that did nothing to improve his morose mood. He stared at it for a minute, then threw it against the cast-iron stove. The glass shattered, sending shards across the rough-hewn floor. Disgusted, he lurched to his feet, started to reach for his crutches, then knocked them out of the way. No, by God, he wasn't going to hobble around on the damned things anymore. He was going to walk on the feet the Almighty gave him.

He had to get out of there before the walls overwhelmed him. Holding onto the bedstead, he made his way to the door and let himself out. The store was deserted now, and like everybody else, Harper was probably somewhere huddled by a fire. Hap's gaze traveled over the shadowy barrels, the counter, the sacked hams hanging from the ceiling, to the bottles lined up like soldiers along

shelves against the wall. He could just help himself to another one, but it wasn't going to help. What he needed
was Texas.

He went back through his rented room and out the
back way. Cold, raw air slapped him in the face, taking his
breath away. And the alcohol hit him then. He reeled,
then steadied himself. For a moment he stood there, looking up at that big moon, then started across the open
ground. He walked unsteadily, working to keep his balance, trying not to favor the gimpy leg. Before he realized
it, he was standing in front of the Sprenger house. And he
knew why he'd come there.

Pulling himself up by a post, he pounded on the door,
shouting, "Annie, Annie Bryce!" at the top of his lungs.
When there was no answer, he went around the side of
the house and stood outside her window. "You want to go
to Texas, Annie?" he yelled. "I'm going that way! By God,
you want to go—I'll take you!"

At first she thought she was dreaming. Then as his
shouts penetrated her consciousness, she recognized his
voice. She groped for a match, struck it against the bottom of the night table, and lit the kerosene lamp. About
that time the clock in the parlor struck three o'clock.
Throwing back the covers, she padded barefoot to the
window and opened it a couple of inches. She confronted
a disheveled Hap Walker.

"What in the world—? Captain, what are you doing out
there?" she demanded in a loud whisper.

"I'm damned drunk." As he spoke, he weaved slightly,
and it looked as though he would fall. But he caught the
edge of the house and held on. "I'm taking you to Texas,

Miz Bryce," he declared, slurring his words. "All you got to do is say you want to go with me."

"Can't this wait till morning?"

"I'm going. Soon as I can, I'm going."

"Well, you'd better sleep off the liquor first," she told him severely. "Go on, before you wake up the Sprengers."

"You coming with me to Texas?"

"We'll discuss it tomorrow."

"I'm taking you. As soon as I can get a wagon, I'm taking you there," he insisted.

"You won't even remember this in the morning," she muttered. "You'll have the worst headache of your life."

"You think the damned leg won't hold me? Go ahead, say it," he challenged her almost belligerently. "Say it."

"You're standing on it. Please, the major needs his sleep, and so does Mrs. Sprenger."

She was too late. A door opened and closed on the front porch. Then a lantern cast his shadow up the wall as Cora, still tying her flannel wrapper, peered around the corner.

"Captain Walker! What on earth—? What's the meaning of this, sir?"

"Going home," he mumbled. "Going to Texas."

"He says he's drunk, and I believe him," Annie told her through the window.

Cora moved the lantern, illuminating his face, then the rest of him. He was coatless and his clothes were badly wrinkled, as though he'd just got out of bed. He blinked bleary eyes, trying to focus on the light. He looked about ready to pass out.

"Obviously," she agreed. "And he has no business walking around on that leg." Half turning, she called out,

141

"Will, come out here. It's Captain Walker, and he needs help!" Afraid Hap would stumble, she caught his arm and held on. "Will!"

"I'm all right," Hap said thickly. "Just taking Miz Bryce home, that's all. Going to Texas."

"What's the matter, Cora?" Will Sprenger mumbled sleepily. "What're you doing out there?"

"Holding Mr. Walker, and you're going to have to give me a hand. Otherwise, he's going to fall down and break something."

"What?"

"He's drunk, Will!" she snapped in exasperation.

He passed a hand over his eyes, then took a better look. "Hap, where the devil are your crutches?" he demanded.

"Threw 'em away," Walker muttered. Turning back for another look toward Annie's window, he stumbled and almost took Cora Sprenger with him.

"Will! He's falling!"

But the major was quick on his feet. "I've got him. Come on, Hap, you'd better get inside before you take pneumonia," he murmured, throwing a shoulder under his patient's arm. "Take it real easy on that leg."

"You coming, Annie?" Walker called out.

"Mrs. Bryce isn't going anywhere in the middle of the night, Hap. Come on."

Half walking, half dragging the drunk man, Will managed to get him up the steps and through the door. Her lips drawn into a thin line of disapproval, Cora followed them inside.

"Do you want me to make coffee?" she asked.

"I want to get him down first."

Annie threw a dress over her nightgown and came out

to the parlor. The big clock said seven minutes past three. "I'm sorry, truly sorry," she told the Sprengers. "I cannot think what got into him."

"Rotgut," the surgeon muttered. "How much of the stuff did you drink?" he asked Hap.

"Not enough."

"Half a bottle?"

"No."

"More?"

"Yeah. It's all gone."

"You had the whole pint by yourself?"

"More'n that," Hap muttered.

Sprenger turned to his wife. "Must've been a fifth. You'd better get some milk—and bread and butter."

Hap blinked, trying to focus his eyes on her. He lifted his hand, then let it fall. "I'm all right—just going home."

"It's a good thing you put away all that fried chicken," the doctor told him. "Otherwise, you'd be poisoned. You trying to kill yourself?"

"No." Slumping on the settee, Hap ran his hands through his hair, trying to think. He was beginning to feel sick. "I got to get home, Doc," he mumbled.

The surgeon laid a hand on Hap's arm and said soothingly, "Why don't you lie down right here, and we'll throw a blanket over you? We'll talk about this in the morning."

"Feel like hell." Shaking off Sprenger's hand, he looked up at Annie. "Got to get a wagon—can't—can't ride m'horse." He combed his hair again with his fingers. "Can't think right now."

He looked more like an unruly boy than a man in his thirties. Yet in spite of his bleary eyes, he was obviously sincere about taking her with him. As Annie studied him, one corner of his mouth turned downward, making a silly, crooked smile.

"Well? You coming?" he asked her. "You going to answer?"

Cora returned with a tray and set it down on a table. "What is she supposed to say to a drunk who shows up at three o'clock in the morning?" she countered tartly. "She probably thinks you've lost your mind."

His eyes still on Annie, he promised solemnly, "Take you to San Saba. Want to do it."

"Annie, he's drunk," Cora said. "He doesn't know what he's saying."

There was no question he'd had too much—or that he might not even remember the offer come morning. Still, she found herself nodding. "All right, as soon as you can drive a wagon."

The smile broadened to an outright grin. "Good."

"Annie, have you taken leave of your senses?" Cora demanded. "What if something happens? If an axle breaks or, well, neither of you is in any condition to deal with any kind of trouble. You are better advised to take the mail. Will, tell her—"

"Oh, for God's sake, Cora! Let her humor him," he snapped.

"No, I meant it," Annie said quietly. "When he's able, I'd like to go."

"Will, this is nonsense."

But her husband seemed to be mulling over the notion without discarding it outright. "Think you can handle a team of oxen, Hap?"

"Yeah."

"Will, he doesn't even know what you're asking him!"

The major rubbed his beard thoughtfully. "Well, I'd wait until mid-week at least, but I suppose if you'll take it easy—and if the weather doesn't turn bad again—you can make it. You'll have to stop and move that leg every now and then."

"Will! He can barely walk. What if something happens?"

"If I have to, I can drive a team of oxen," Annie spoke up. "I've done it once before, when Ethan bought me a piano in Austin. We took turns on the way home."

Cora rounded on her. "And you've not regained your full strength, so I don't see how you even think you could control the beasts."

"Leave her be, Cora. She knows her mind, and so does he."

"Not right now he doesn't. Indeed, I'd be surprised if he knew his name," she countered archly. "Besides, there'll be talk. One female alone with one man—well, it just won't look right! At least with the mail, it could be said she bought passage."

"There'll be talk, anyway. But right now you'd better get some of that milk down, Hap. And then we'll cover you up and let you sleep it off. Come morning, we can talk."

It was too late for any milk. The whiskey was already roiling in Hap's stomach, and if he didn't get out of there, he was going to be sick on Cora Springer's floor. Clenching his teeth shut, he managed to mutter, "Thanks." Desperate now, he lurched from the settee and bolted for the door as fast as the leg would let him.

"Will, you'd better go after him. He doesn't even have a coat!"

"Leave him be, Cora. A man don't like to be bothered when his whiskey's coming up."

"But—"

"I'm going back to bed, and so are you. And if Mrs. Bryce has any sense, she'll follow the example." With that, he headed for their bedroom. "He'll be all right," he flung over his shoulder. "He's a damned fool, but he'll be all right."

Outside, Hap caught the bar of the hitching post and hung his body over it. His head down, he retched, heaving as wave after wave of nausea hit him, emptying his stomach. Exhausted, he stayed there, sweat pouring from his face, until he was sure there was nothing left to come up. Finally, he caught his breath. Leaning down, he scooped a handful of dead grass and ran it over his face. When he straightened up, he felt like he might live a little longer. Come morning, he'd probably wish he hadn't.

Shivering, he hunched his shoulders and limped unsteadily back to his room. Anne Bryce was probably thinking he'd lost his mind, but it didn't matter what she thought of him as long as she let him take her to San Saba. He owed her that much.

After he sobered, it took him nearly two days to get rid of the hangover of his life. It was another sign he was getting past his prime, he supposed. There'd been a time in the not very distant past when he could have drunk a bottle down, then been up at dawn to follow a trail. Not anymore.

He'd have felt a whole lot better if he hadn't made a damned fool of himself in front of Anne Bryce and the Sprengers, but despite his aching head he remembered most of what he'd said, enough to know he'd committed himself to taking Mrs. Bryce back to Texas. Not just committed, either—he'd insisted. All the way to San Saba. And San Saba was one hell of a long way from the Ybarra.

But the weather remained mild, too warm for the latter half of November, and it hadn't snowed or rained since the norther twelve days before. And since he'd made up his mind to go, he figured it'd be better to make the trip sooner rather than later. The roads, even when dry, were hazardous—badly rutted and filled with stumps. When

147

wet, they were damned near impassable. He knew seasoned bullwhackers who'd lost whole loads when they hit a bad place.

On Wednesday he rode Old Red a mile or so down toward the reservation, making a final check of the road. It was a sort of trial for him, a test of whether he could sit the horse if he had to. Satisfied he could, he came back and told Annie they'd be leaving the next morning at dawn. That afternoon he proceeded to fit out a wagon for the hundred and twenty-three miles to Richardson, which was just the beginning. After that they still had to get to Griffin, then to Concho, following the military supply routes. For a man who could barely walk, he'd cut out a big job for himself.

She'd questioned whether he was up to a journey of such distance, pricking his pride. Despite his own misgivings, he declared he was going to Texas with or without her. Satisfied, she packed up, promising to be ready when he came for her.

It hadn't taken her long to throw two donated dresses, one of Cora's old chemises, a petticoat, three pair of drawers, and the ugly red flannel nightgown into the borrowed carpet bag. With a hairbrush, toothbrush, a square of homemade soap, and a washcloth, they represented everything she presently owned.

Setting the carpet bag by the door, she retired early, then tossed and turned much of the night because she was too excited to sleep. For the first time since her capture by Two Trees, she felt truly free. She was finally going home. She'd see those things she'd clung to in her dreams—her piano, the brand-new cooking range, the heavy oak furniture, the lace curtains she'd crocheted, the quilts she'd made while she carried Susannah.

The horses, two cows, and her chickens she'd left behind wouldn't still be waiting for her, she realized, but the barn and coop probably remained. She'd have to go into Austin, take stock of her money, then probably get a loan for enough supplies to get through the rest of the winter, but she didn't foresee any problems there. The money she and Ethan had borrowed to buy the place had been paid back early.

Come spring, she'd have to make up her mind whether to sell or not. A lot depended on whether she could persuade the authorities to search for her daughter. If they did, she wanted to keep the place. Susannah had been born there, after all, and surely she'd remember it. She'd need that anchor, that tie to her past, after spending nearly half her young life with the Comanches.

When the clock struck four, Annie gave up trying to sleep. Shortly after, she was dressed and creeping into the Sprenger kitchen to fix herself coffee and a hard-boiled egg. Not that she was hungry. She had to force herself to sit at the table and eat, and then the egg lay like a rock in her stomach.

Her thoughts turned to the Sprengers. They'd both been kind, Cora even more so than the major, and she was going to miss them. But it was time to move on, to look forward instead of back. Without Ethan she had to focus on making a life for herself so she could make one for Susannah. But that didn't make parting from Cora any easier. It was going to be like leaving her own mother again. She was still at the table, staring into nearly cold coffee, when the older woman found her.

"I *thought* I heard noises," Cora said.

Caught out, Annie smiled ruefully, admitting, "I was trying not to wake you or the major. Both of you need your sleep."

"As if I wouldn't want to say good-bye," Cora chided. "And Will's up and already shaving." She glanced at the peeled shell on Annie's plate. "I'd planned on making you a better breakfast than one egg. That's not much to travel on, especially when one travels with a man. They aren't like us—they never want to stop, you know. And I expect it'll be even worse with Captain Walker, because the rangers are not known for any notions of comfort at all."

"It can't be worse than following a war party," Annie murmured.

"At least let me fry some bread and salt pork. If you can't eat them now, you can at least make a sandwich for later."

"I guess I'm just excited. It's been a long time since I've been there. In some ways it seems like I just left, you know. I can close my eyes and remember everything in my house."

The older woman regarded her wistfully for a moment, then sighed. "I suppose you are all packed up, aren't you?"

"Except for my toothbrush and hairbrush. I still have to use those."

"I find myself wishing you'd stay—at least through Christmas, anyway. But . . ." She sighed again. "But I quite understand how it is."

"As much as I want to go, it's hard to leave," Annie admitted. "You've been very kind. I don't expect the same generosity when I get home."

"No." Cora sat down across from her. "It wasn't entirely

150

kindness, my dear," she allowed somewhat sadly. "To a degree it's been selfishness, for I've enjoyed your company. So many of the other military wives on the post are terribly young, and I don't have much patience with most of them. They arrive with such silly notions of what life is like, and then they are so disillusioned all they want to do is complain about everything from the weather to the isolation. Sometimes I just want to shake the nonsense out of them."

"The Hughes woman comes to mind."

"Exactly. When I was a young army bride, I considered it a noble calling, Annie. The need was—and still is—very great for good surgeons, and I knew Will could fill that need," she said softly. "It was my duty to make it possible."

"I imagine there were times it was hard for you."

"Not really—or at least no more for me than for Will. And we had four children—three that lived to grow into what I hope are good men. Even though one was born out on the Kansas prairie with soldiers holding blankets to shield me, and another in a tent during a blizzard, I wouldn't change my life for anyone's, Annie. It's been a grand adventure."

"I always thought that was the way a marriage was supposed to be—a grand adventure, I mean," Annie said quietly. "Ethan and I had such plans for the children and for growing old together."

"Oh, my dear—"

"No, I'm all right now. I've accepted that it won't happen, that he's gone. I know I'm not going to wake up from the nightmare one morning and find him beside me—at least not in this life, anyway." Annie stirred her cold coffee absently. "I loved him more than anything, Cora, and it's hard to go on without him and Jody. But at least I had them for a while."

Cora nodded. "I've always wondered what it would be like without Will. During the war, when he ran field hospitals in the thick of terrible, terrible battles, I was so afraid." Her mouth twisted. "I've always loved Will, you see—from the first time I danced with him at my coming out in Boston. Of course, my father was less than pleased. Although Will was in medical college, he'd already declared an intent to go into the army, and Papa wanted me to marry well."

"Mine wanted me to choose a lawyer in Austin rather than what he called a 'dirt farmer,'" Annie recalled. "But the lawyer he liked didn't suit me at all."

"It's always that way, isn't it? In my case, Will enlisted as soon as he completed his degree and was posted to Fort Hays, Kansas, something that gave my father enormous relief," the older woman went on. "Papa said it was a wild place, fit only for Indians, and he thought the distance would make me forget my 'foolish infatuation,' but it didn't. Finally, when Will came back to Massachusetts on leave, we faced Papa together, seeking his blessing. Of course, he didn't give it, but at least we tried. We wed at the Congregationalist minister's parsonage, then left for Kansas the next day."

"Ethan and I were married like that," Annie said softly. "Only it was a Baptist preacher's parlor in Austin."

"I guess that's what I like so much about you. You're a lot like I am, only you've faced more than I ever will. In spite of everything you still hold your head up."

"Thank you."

"I just hope you can keep it there." Cora reached out and clasped Annie's hand. "I admire you, my dear. I don't know how you managed to survive."

"I didn't want to die," Annie answered simply.

"But you chose not to give up."

"It wasn't much of a choice, really. The war party had taken a young German girl earlier, and she was so afraid—so very afraid. I couldn't let her know how frightened I was, not even after"—pausing, Annie looked away—"after they killed Jody," she finished, her voice dropping to a whisper. "I knew if she was hysterical, they'd kill her, too."

"You're very brave—you know that, don't you?"

"No. I did what I had to, nothing more."

"Is she still alive?"

"No. He killed her later, anyway." Afraid to remember any more, Annie stood up. "I guess I'd better finish getting ready. Captain Walker said he wanted to get an early start."

Knowing that the younger woman's confidences were at an end, Cora let her go, then rose to cook her husband's breakfast. What Annie needed, whether she knew it or not, was another husband, she reflected as she laid pieces of pork in the iron skillet. But it was going to be hard to find one big enough to overlook what the Comanches had done to her, and that was a shame. With a new man and a new name, Annie could get on with her life, and people would eventually forget. Without them, they never would. For a moment she thought of Hap Walker, then shook her head. He was too bitter—and he didn't seem like a man who'd want to settle down.

Outside, at five-thirty, it was cold and dark, with the

moon still visible in the sky. But Hap already had the four-oxen team under yoke, the canvas around the wagon bed secured, and Old Red and a mule he'd bought tied to iron rings at the back. Ready, he stowed the Henry rifle and his old army pistol under the seat, swung up, and drove up to the Sprengers' door. He was early, and he knew it. He'd probably be lucky if Annie Bryce was even awake.

He eased down from the seat, thinking he'd get a cup of Cora Sprenger's coffee while he waited. As he raised his hand to knock on the door, he heard something heavy hit the back of the wagon. He spun around, drawing the Colt.

"Oh, it's you. Sorry."

"Well, there's nothing wrong with your hands, anyway," Doc remarked sardonically. "You're pretty fast, Hap."

"Yeah." He eased the gun back into the holster.

"Kinda skittish, though."

"I'm thirty-seven—and alive."

"That's right. Most of 'em don't last that long, do they?" Sprenger murmured.

"No. Not many, anyway."

"Then I guess you could consider yourself real lucky, if you wanted to look at it that way."

"I don't. If I'd known that the bullet was going to do this, I'd have had Rios stake the damned Comanchero that gave it to me out on an anthill. Instead, I just shot him."

"You're a bitter man, Hap."

"You could say that. It's not easy to be washed up, Doc."

"I wouldn't say that. It's the leg, isn't it?"

"What did you put in the wagon?"

"Cora offered Mrs. Bryce some blankets, but she wouldn't take 'em—said she'd taken too much already—so I put the box back there, anyway. I reckon if it turns cold, she'll be glad enough to have 'em."

"Yeah."

"It's going to get better, you know," Sprenger told him. "The infection's gone, and if you'll stay off the damned thing, give it time to heal, that limp's going to improve. In time it won't even hurt except when the weather changes."

"That's a lot of comfort, Doc."

"It ought to be."

"It'd be a whole lot more if you could say I'd be back in the saddle again."

"That's a young man's job, Hap. You don't want to be following outlaws into New Mexico the rest of your life. You've done more than anybody I know, but it's time to hang up those guns and settle down."

"Is Mrs. Bryce ready?" Hap countered impatiently.

"She's had the bag by the door since last night." Sprenger sighed. "You aren't much for free advice, are you?"

"I figure it's about worth what it costs." He was being touchy, and he knew it. He knew also that he owed the surgeon more than he could repay. "Look, don't mind me, Doc. I'm just not much for talking until I get a little coffee in me."

"Eat anything?"

"I bought a couple of biscuits—they're in my pocket. I figure I'll eat 'em after a while."

"Haven't traveled much with a female, have you?"

"No."

"Then you're in for a real education. Come on in. Cora'll fix you a couple of eggs at least." Stepping past Hap, the major opened the door. "I'll tell her to set another place."

"Coffee's enough."

He wound up standing in the kitchen door, drinking from a little china cup, while Cora Sprenger quickly fried thick slices of salt pork, then put them between buttered bread. As he set down the cup, she wrapped four sandwiches in two napkins and handed them to him.

"At least you'll have something in your stomach," she told him. "Since you don't think you have enough time to sit at the table, you can eat on the way. The extra two are for Annie. She didn't want anything either, but I told her I was going to make them, anyway."

"Thanks."

"It's a long way to Richardson, Captain Walker." Putting his cup in the dishpan, she asked over her shoulder, "How long do you expect it'll take you to get there?"

"If nothing goes wrong, and if the supply wagons haven't made the road too bad, I reckon I can make four miles an hour," he allowed. "With about ten hours of daylight, that'd be forty miles. Probably about three days," he guessed. "Four, if Mrs. Bryce has to stop a lot."

"She won't." Wiping her hands, Cora turned back to him. "She's not one to complain."

"That's good."

"I'm ready," Annie announced from the door. "I just have to take out my bag." Seeing that he had the wrapped sandwiches in his hand, she dared to ask, "I'm not late,

156

am I? I thought you said dawn, and it isn't light out yet, is it?"

"I'm a mite early. I figured we better get on down the road. Probably be close to Sunday before we get there, anyway." He followed her into the small hall, and as she bent to pick up the carpetbag, he stopped her. "That all you're bringing?"

"Well, it's all I have," she murmured.

"Here, you take the food, and I'll throw that in the wagon for you. No sense in lifting anything you don't have to."

On the porch, Annie's eyes misted as she turned to the Sprengers. "You've both been so kind to me," she managed. "Nothing I could ever do would be enough to repay you."

"Fiddle," Cora declared, embracing her. Her lips brushed Annie's cheek, then she stepped back. "Now, you come back whenever you can, you hear? The spare room'll be waiting for you."

"I will. Thanks."

"And write when you get home. Will and I want to know that you're all right."

"I will."

"Yes, well, I hope everything works out for the best, my dear. Good-bye and God bless."

"Thanks. I won't forget either of you, ever," Annie promised.

The major gripped her hand. "Take care of yourself, my dear."

"And God keep you." Annie tried to smile, but her mouth twisted. Afraid she was going to cry, she stepped blindly off the stoop. "Good-bye."

Hap caught her arm, then cupped her elbow to give her a boost up. "Hold the reins until I get around to the other side," he told her. Now it was his turn, and he wasn't any good at things like this. He turned his back toward the major and nodded. "Thanks, Doc. I'm not much of a hand to write."

"Well, neither am I. But you take good care of Mrs. Bryce, and we'll be even up, Hap. If you're still able to walk when you get to Richardson, you tell 'em it was me that fixed you up. If that leg gives out, then keep quiet about it."

Hap grinned. "You want me to brag on you, huh?"

"Well, I don't want to be blamed, anyway." Will held out his hand. "Take time to get down and walk every now and then, will you?"

"Yeah."

Hap clasped the older man's hand, then let go. Moving in front of the oxen, he made one last check of them, then swung up into the wagon. Taking the reins from Annie, he settled in beside her.

"You might want to sit in the back, where it's warmer. If you didn't get your sleep out, my bedroll's back there," he offered. "You don't have to feel like you got to keep me company."

"I'm fine. Besides, I like to see where I'm going."

"Not much to see until the sun comes out," he observed laconically. He glanced upward briefly, then flicked the whip out over the backs of the oxen. "Reckon it'll be out before long. Within an hour, anyway." Exhaling, he squared his shoulders. "Well, we're underway. You'll be sleeping in Texas tonight."

"Yes."

She pulled the heavy cloak closer and wrapped her arms in the folds as the wheels began rolling slowly. The wagon creaked on its axles, then seemed to catch up. Behind her, the canvas cover filled with the wind. She was on her way home.

Watching them cross the parade ground, Will Sprenger laid a hand on his wife's shoulder. "It's going to be all right. Hap'll see she gets there."

"I know."

"She felt like she had to go, Cora."

"But it's going to be so hard for her," his wife managed huskily. "We both know she's not going to get that little girl back." Pulling away, she went inside, leaving him standing there.

Annie held on to her seat and studied the rugged mountains to the west, thankful they wouldn't be crossing them. The reservation land was flat, with a slight slope downward, but that didn't help the way the wagon rode. The dried ruts left by the earlier supply train made for rough going. Finally, to avoid the deeper gouges where some of the vehicles had apparently sunk all the way to their axles, Hap pulled completely off the road and followed alongside it. Not that that was much of an improvement. When the soldiers had cleared the roadway, they'd left a number of dead stumps on either side of it. Every time the wheels struck part of one, the whole wagon bounced, sometimes clear off the path.

"Riding all right?" Hap asked her after a particularly nasty jolt.

"Yes," Annie lied. "I'm holding on."

"You'd better. My hip bones feel like they're hitting my ribs, and there's a whole lot more meat on mine than yours."

"You've never ridden an Indian saddle, have you?" she countered.

"No. That bad, huh?"

"Well, they're not padded—and they're made out of wood and bone."

"Yeah, I've seen some. Guess they've been toughening up their behinds since before they can walk."

"Yes."

"Cold?"

"No." She shifted her body uncomfortably on the hard wooden seat. "How long do you think it will take?"

"To reach Fort Richardson?"

"Yes."

"Well, it's not like on horseback. Alone on Old Red, I could make it in about twenty-four or twenty-five hours, if I didn't stop to sleep."

"That's a hard way to travel. I know. Comanches do that a lot."

"Yeah. I was usually going somewhere I had to get in a hurry. If I wasn't chasing somebody, I was carrying a warrant somewhere. Usually it was to make an arrest legal before a damned lawyer howled about it. I had a couple of boys that were a lot better following the intent than the letter of the law."

"Like Clay McAlester? I think I read a few things about that."

"He was just one of 'em. I had a Mexican I could count on most of the time, too—he's the fella that helped bury your husband. But both of 'em were real bad about wiring for warrants after they'd already dragged somebody in or killed him trying."

"But you must have enjoyed it," she pointed out. "You stayed with it a long time."

"Sixteen years—since I was eighteen. 'Course there were three years spent in the war, but I wasn't counting them."

"You don't seem that old, really."

"I'm thirty-seven."

"That still doesn't seem old. I'm thirty."

"At least you don't look it. If you'd wear that hair down on your shoulders, you'd look like a kid compared to me."

"Well, I'm not, though it's kind of you to say it. But you seem to miss it—being with the rangers, I mean."

"Yeah. Funny how a man doesn't know what he wants until he loses it. Then it's too late," he observed soberly. "There was a time when I used to dream of owning my own place, of running a few cattle and watching things grow."

"And now that you've got the time to do those things, you don't want to," she murmured. "It's hard to know what to wish for until you get it."

"Yeah. Now I dream of lying under the stars out in the desert, listening to the night sounds, wondering how close I am to whoever I'm tracking. Trying to figure out if those coyotes are animals or if it's the damned Comanches. Guess I'm a hard man to satisfy. Not easy to understand, huh?"

"I don't know. I think I've always wanted roots, something to cling to. But I was never very adventurous, not at all. All my dreams were centered on Ethan, the kids, the farm. I just took it for granted that that's the way it was meant to be."

"It is. People like me are just different, I guess. I never

managed to settle down. I always thought I wanted to, but I never got around to it. Now I'm too old and set in my ways to be much good at it."

"You've got to have dreams, Captain. It's the dreams that keep us alive."

"I don't know about that. Sometimes I think they just give a body expectations that can't be satisfied," he mused. "Sometimes they never happen."

"There's a chance—until you're dead, there's always a chance," she pointed out reasonably. "You have to believe. I believe I'm going to see Susannah again, Captain—I believe it."

He held the equally strong conviction that she wouldn't, but he wasn't going to say it again. Not while it was all she had to cling to. By the time reality really set in, with any luck she'd be able to go on, to accept it. Even as he thought that, the irony of it wasn't lost on him. He wasn't doing much of a job accepting the change that had come to his own life.

"Yeah, well, I always believed by now I'd have a wife, a couple of kids, a house with all those gewgaws women stick in to make it a home—you know, quilts and doilies and flowers, things like that. Now I know it's not going to happen."

"Why not?"

"If I was cut out to be a husband, I reckon I'd have found somebody by now."

"Did you ever look?" Realizing how nosy that sounded, she apologized quickly. "I'm sorry. That wasn't any of my business."

"Yeah, I looked around from time to time. But I was always fixing my sights on women that wouldn't look back,

I guess." Again he felt that twinge that came whenever he thought of Amanda. "Maybe I aimed too high. I always hankered after somebody real pretty, but they never hankered for a weathered saddle tramp like me." Afraid he'd shown too much of himself to her, he leaned forward, hunching over the reins. "At least you had what you wanted for a while," he said, pushing the burden back on her.

"Yes. But not nearly long enough. It was only five years, Captain. I only had him five years."

"A body can put a lot of living in five years."

"We did. And I loved almost every minute of my life then. Ethan. The kids. The house. The farm. I can even remember walking down the furrows, just looking at the corn coming up, thinking that was the way God meant people to live, that that was why He gave us the land."

"Yeah, but you were meant to live like that." He stared westward toward the mountains for a time, then mused aloud, "There's something about pitting your mind against a Comanche and coming up the winner that I can't get from a cow or a row of corn. Same thing about outlaws— they test you, they make you think, they make you use everything you've got before you get 'em. When you kill one of 'em, you know you've rid the world of something evil, and you know what you did was good. And you know you got 'im because you were better, faster, and smarter. It feeds a need in you. Don't guess that makes much sense to a woman, does it?"

"I don't know—maybe. You're the first lawman I've ever visited with, so I've never thought about what the life was like. My people were all shopkeepers and farmers."

"Rangers are a different breed, ma'am. Most all of 'em

I've known need to walk on the edge of the crevice, looking down, wondering how close they can get without falling off."

"The danger makes it exciting," she said matter-of-factly.

"Damned right."

"Well, if that's what you really want, maybe when your leg is finally healed, you can go back to the rangers."

"No. I kinda burned my bridges when I left." Rather than get into that, he straightened up and half turned to her. "I reckon we ought to be there sometime Sunday. I'd like to say you'd be in time for church, but I can't promise it."

"That's rather longer than I expected," she admitted, somewhat disappointed.

"It's more'n a hundred twenty miles between Sill and Fort Richardson. Then you've got to get to Griffin—and from there to your place on the San Saba."

"Isn't Fort Griffin out of our way?"

"Well, it's not a straight line down, that's for sure, but there's supply roads to follow," he explained.

"Oh."

"Yeah, so there's probably another three days to Griffin, then maybe two or three more to the San Saba, making for about eight or nine days in a wagon, providing the weather holds and the animals stay healthy. If not, it'll take longer."

"I see."

"And you'll need a couple of days to rest your backside both places, so you'd better figure for that, too. What does that make it, about two weeks?"

"Yes," she responded without enthusiasm.

He cast a sidewise glance her way. "If the place is still

standing after three years, it'll be there waiting for you two weeks from now, I reckon."

"I'm sorry, I didn't mean it that way," she said quickly. "I just want to get there. I just want to see it."

"I know. But there's going to be times when I've got to rest m'leg."

She was being selfish, and she knew it. Ashamed, she tried to look at the journey from his side. "It's hurting, isn't it? Doc Sprenger said you need to stop often."

"It's going to hurt some whether I'm sitting, lying down, or walking on it. I just don't want to make it worse, that's all."

"I'm sorry."

"Wish you'd quit saying that. If it's not your fault, don't apologize. Just because I was griping a couple of minutes back, it doesn't mean I want pity, Mrs. Bryce."

"I wouldn't call it pity, Captain Walker."

"What was it?"

"Sympathy. There's a difference."

"Damned if I know what it is," he retorted.

"All right, it's not exactly sympathy, either, then. Maybe I should have said it's concern. Surely I can be concerned for your health, can't I?" she reasoned.

"Well, if I were you, there's other things I'd worry about more. Like rivers, for instance. We've got the Red between here and Richardson, and there's the Brazos north of Griffin, and after that come the Colorado and the San Saba. This time of year a river can be a mite contrary. Sometimes you've got to float the wagon and swim the oxen over. And sometimes they balk at going."

"I don't swim very well—not at all, Captain Walker," she admitted. "I've always been afraid of deep water. Even when the Comanches made me go across, I was terribly afraid of the water."

"That's why I brought the mule. It'll swim for you—a damned sight better than one of those little Comanche ponies, to my way of thinking. A mule's stronger."

"I'll never forget trying to cross the Pecos."

"The Pecos is a damned mean river."

"Yes, it certainly is—mean, that is," she agreed.

"It just sort of lies there under those steep banks, waiting like a snake to get you. If you got over that one, you'll get over the rest of 'em a whole lot easier."

"I hope."

"Yeah, we ought to make it to your place by the middle of December, no later than the twentieth, anyway. I'll get you settled in, chop some wood, maybe take you into town for some supplies. You know, see you fixed up for the winter before I go on. Maybe you could play me a couple of Christmas carols on that piano before I head out."

She hadn't really given any thought to Christmas. She'd be spending it in an empty house, surrounded by things certain to bring back memories of Ethan and her children. Like the piano he'd struggled to bring back from Austin for her. And as much as she wanted to be home, she was suddenly afraid she couldn't stand that part of it.

"My ma used to play the piano," he went on. "Even though we were Baptists, she like those old Martin Luther hymns. Ever play 'A Mighty Fortress Is Our God'?"

"Yes."

"She used to sing some old Scottish ballads, too," he recalled. "Don't suppose you know 'Barbara Allen'?"

"Yes."

"I'd sure like to hear 'em again. It's been a long time."

It didn't seem like much to ask, not after he'd gone to the trouble of getting her home. "I'll try to play them for you," she promised. "I may not be very good at it, though—and I don't know if the piano's kept in tune all this time."

"I got a tin ear, anyway," he allowed. "I'd just like to hear the words with the music."

"You won't have much time to get to the Ybarra, will you? Do you think you'll make it for the holiday?"

"No. It doesn't matter all that much—wouldn't be the first time I was out on the road then. Matter of fact, I've probably spent more Christmases out than in, if I was to count 'em up. Since most of the boys had kinfolks, I tried to cover for 'em." He shrugged. "Things like that don't mean much to me, anyway—leastwise not since my ma died."

"But don't you want to be at the Ybarra?" she asked curiously. "At least Clay McAlester will be there."

The image of Amanda came to mind, and for a brief moment he felt the regret. Before she'd married Clay, he'd had some hope there, enough to make a damned fool of himself. No, as much as he loved both of 'em, he didn't care much about seeing them together at Christmas.

"It doesn't matter," he maintained stubbornly.

"You don't have any family at all?"

"No. Just Clay—but he's got a wife now, and there's a baby on the way. Oh, they'd want me there, no question about it, but it's not the same. Don't get me wrong—she's a fine girl, and I wish I'd been as lucky as he is, but now there's a big house, fancy stuff all around—everything's a whole lot different." He stared off, seeing nothing. "I'm real happy for him," he said finally. "A lot of folks never thought he'd amount to much, and he showed 'em."

"Like the newspapers," she murmured.

"Yeah, like the damned *Austin Republican*," he agreed. "If I had a dollar of every lie they printed about him, I'd own half of Texas."

"They thought he was pretty rough, didn't they?"

"Yeah. And they weren't too happy with me, either. They never understood what the rangers faced—and the state police, too, for that matter."

"Well, at least they didn't call you an Indian-loving savage."

"I'd be about the last person anybody'd say that to," he countered. "Leastwise, if he wanted to live, anyway, But Clay had his reasons for liking 'em. Hell, the Comanches raised him. Me, I'd as soon crawl on my belly through a ravine full of rattlesnakes as be within smelling distance of a Comanche, or a Kiowa. Only place I want to see one of 'em is down the barrel of a rifle."

"But you came to Bull Calf's camp, Captain," she reminded him. "I thought God had answered my prayers when I saw you."

Before he could explain anything, one of the front wheels hit something, and the force sent the wagon into a deep rut that threw her against him. He grabbed her and braced her with his body as the wagon bed teetered, then came slamming down with a bone-jarring crack over the axle. Her first thought was that they'd wrecked, but the wheels kept turning, and the oxen plodded ahead as though nothing had happened.

"You all right?"

She righted herself within the circle of his arm. "What was that?" she asked shakily.

"I don't know—a rock or a stump probably." Easing his arm from her shoulders, he transferred the reins between his hands. "Guess I wasn't watching what I was doing," he muttered.

"Well, I didn't see it coming, either."

A prolonged silence descended as he turned his full attention to the road, leaving her to her own thoughts. The tightness of his grip, the lean hardness of body had startled her. Because of his obviously painful limp, because he'd been so sick earlier, she hadn't thought of him as a strong man. But he was, and if he hadn't caught her, she'd have been thrown from her seat. Sitting back, she rubbed her arm where his fingers had dug in. She was going to have a bruise. She knew, because Two Trees had given her a lot of them.

Forcing her mind away from that, she kept her eyes on the mountains, telling herself they were pretty, wondering what they were called. Just as she was about to ask, he suddenly spoke.

"You know, it'd be a whole lot easier if you'd just call me Hap. Everybody else does, and we're going to be spending a lot of time in this wagon. No sense wasting words, is there?"

"It seems rather personal—rather forward for just an acquaintance, doesn't it?"

"Any more so than if I was to call you Annie?"

"I guess not."

"Besides, I reckon we'll be friends by the time we get there. Otherwise, it'll be a damned long trip."

"I hadn't thought of it like that, Hap," she said, trying it out. "It's rather unusual, isn't it?"

"Yeah. It's not really my name, but I've had it for so long that I don't answer to much else. Comes from being the youngest, I guess. All five of us were boys, and Ma went through the whole roll every time she wanted one of us. When I was little, I wasn't sure if I was Marcus or Julius or Antony or Claudius or Horace."

"Those sound like Roman names."

"Yeah. She was a schoolteacher—came out here from Tennessee. She liked those Romans a whole lot. Anyway, I didn't complain much as a kid, so she was always saying to folks, 'Look at him, he's such a happy little fellow.' It got to where my brothers started calling me Happy, and it stuck. Finally, it just got shorted to Hap."

"So which one were you?" she asked curiously.

"My real name?"

"Yes."

"Like I said, I only answered to Hap," he responded, grinning. "I wasn't nearly as crazy about the Romans as she was."

"Do you keep in touch with the others?"

"Kinda hard." He sobered suddenly. "I'm the only one left."

"They're all dead?" she asked incredulously. "All of them?"

"Yeah. Jeff Davis wrote my ma, thanking her for giving four sons to the cause. I was the only one that came home. I kept the letter after she died. Every once in a while I get it out and read it, but it doesn't help much. I still miss all of them—and her, too. And my pa," he added hastily, "but he was gone a lot when I was growing up."

"I'm sorry."

"Yeah. Maybe that's why I never worried much about dying." Embarrassed now, he turned the subject again. "You sure you're riding all right?"

"I'm fine. This is a whole lot better than a Comanche saddle, Captain."

"Hap," he reminded her. "Just Hap, Annie."

"Hadn't you better stop to stretch your leg?"

"No." Then, realizing maybe she had to answer a call of nature but was too embarrassed to mention it, he told her, "Look, any time you need to get down, just speak right up. I, uh, haven't traveled much with a woman, so I might not notice if you were getting uncomfortable—or anything like that. I don't know much about a woman's needs."

"I expect they're about the same as yours."

"But you'll tell me?"

"Yes."

"Good."

He let it go at that. She was a lot easier to talk to than he'd ever expected, and if he didn't watch himself, he'd be bending her ear all the way to the San Saba. And after everything that had happened to her, he didn't really figure she'd want to know all that much about any man.

The afternoon of the second day out of Fort Sill, about ten or fifteen miles after they'd crossed the Red River without incident, the sky clouded over, and the temperature dropped. Still well above freezing, it was nevertheless a cause for concern. If the sky poured, and it looked like it would, the road could become impassable. Hap squinted up at the retreating sun, then at the flattening horizon. Riding behind a plodding team of oxen was too damned slow to suit him. If it was just him and Old Red, the weather wouldn't matter half as much.

He glanced over at Annie Bryce, who rested her head against the canvas support. Her eyes were closed, indicating she was asleep. He thought about waking her up and urging her to get inside, but he didn't. She didn't seem to like it much back there, and he couldn't blame her. It was too dark, too close, and the air smelled of the musty straw in the mattress. With the added redolence of oxen dung wafting backward into the wagon, where it couldn't escape, the atmosphere inside reminded him of a cow barn after a rain.

He had to admire her. As thin as she was, she obviously tired easily, but she never complained. It was he who always stopped for everything—to eat, to walk, to rest, to relieve himself, to sleep. Then she'd busy herself fixing food or whatever he needed before she walked behind the wagon to take care of her own business. Last night she'd helped him unyoke the animals, feed and water them, then tie them out to graze. And when the wolves got too close, spooking the oxen, she'd crawled out of her bed in the back and covered him with the Henry while he brought the team nearer to the wagon. She was pulling her share like a man, something a body wouldn't expect from looking at her.

Only she wasn't a man. She was a damned pretty woman, and it wasn't easy to ignore that, no matter how much he was trying. If he'd met her under different conditions, if he hadn't known her circumstances—and if she hadn't made it real plain that she never wanted to think about a man again—he might have entertained a notion of flirting a little with her. At least that way he could tell himself he was forgetting Amanda.

But right now the last thing Annie Bryce needed was a half-crippled man hanging after her. And the last thing he needed was a woman afraid of being touched again. As open as she was about so many things, she was pretty closed about that. He could still feel her slender body within the circle of his arm, and he remembered how quickly she'd sat up when the danger passed. And the way she'd tensed when his hand brushed hers on the seat. She didn't have to say anything. He knew as long as there was no gender between them, she'd be all right. But if he ever crossed that line and became a man to her, she'd either fight or run.

He could smell the rain in the air now. Yeah, it was about ready to hit, all right. He nudged her with his elbow.

"Better get in back before you get wet," he told her.

"Huh?" She sat up, rubbing her eyes. "I'm sorry, I must've dozed off."

"Yeah. Reckon you needed it what with the wolves and coyotes keeping you awake last night."

"It wasn't that. I was awake anyway."

"Straw's pretty hard when it gets packed down. Guess I should have tried to get a feather mattress, but I didn't think of it."

"The mattress was fine, Hap. It was me—I couldn't sleep."

"Because you were going home?"

"Yes."

The first big drops of rain spattered the canvas. "Go on. Otherwise, you'll get wet," he urged her again. "You can't afford to take sick on the road."

"I won't. I never get sick. I've been tired, hungry, and scared sometimes, but never sick. I never even caught the measles when Susannah had them."

"Yeah, but you didn't weigh eighty pounds then."

"I'm over ninety now. I weighed myself on the grain scales at Fort Sill." Her mouth twisted wryly. "I'm not the one who was at death's door two weeks ago, you know. I just hadn't had much to eat for a while. You were the one with the fever," she reminded him.

"Yeah, well, it looks like it could come a gully washer,

175

so I'd just as soon you got out of it. It'd be real nice if you'd just humor me."

Giving credence to his prediction, a lightning bolt shot through the sky, followed by a sharp crack of thunder. She stiffened, suddenly transfixed, while her stomach knotted, nearly making her sick. To control the wave of fear that coursed through her, she gripped the flat board seat with both hands so tightly that her knuckles went white.

"Go on. I—" He caught her stricken expression and stopped. "You all right?"

"Yes."

Her answer was so low he could scarce hear it. He nodded. "You're afraid of storms, aren't you?"

"Yes."

"I guess I understand that. Claude was like that—three years older 'n me, but whenever there was lightning and thunder, he'd crawl into bed with me and say he was there to keep me from being scared. Hell, as the youngest of five boys, I wasn't afraid of anything. But he was this big, strapping kid, and he didn't want any of us to think he was a coward. I'd try to sleep, but with every new roll of thunder, he'd get this stranglehold on me, making it damned near impossible."

As another bolt shot to earth, she winced, then closed her eyes. "I wasn't always like this," she whispered, swallowing.

He reached over with his free hand and disengaged her fingers from the seat. "Go back there and put the pillow over your head until the storm passes," he told her. "No sense sitting here watching it," he added gently.

"It's silly, isn't it?" she managed. "I'm thirty years old, not a child."

"No. Far as I know, Claude never got over it. I used to be crawling up a hill under fire, thinking about how he hated the thunder, wondering how he stood the cannons."

"I think if I could just get home—"

"Go on. When it's over, you'll be all right."

"All right." As she stood up and turned toward the opening in the canvas, she muttered under her breath, "I despise being weak."

"Here now, none of that, you hear? You're not weak, Annie. Hell, you're the strongest woman I ever met."

"No, I'm not."

A heavy roll of thunder shook the road beneath them, sending her diving into the depths of the dusty wagon. Scrambling onto the hard straw mattress, she pulled her blankets over her head, then turned on her side and rolled into a ball. Shaking all over, she tried to reason with herself. She wasn't lying in the mud, pinned down by Two Trees' body. And every fiber of her being wasn't crying out against what he did to her. She was in a wagon heading home, and Hap Walker was with her.

The worst of the storm had passed, followed by a light, steady rain, the kind that soaked in. Now there was a little respite, one that wasn't going to last. Before long, it'd be dark, but he didn't want to stop and make camp. He didn't want to wake up in the morning and find the road had turned to mire while he'd slept. Yet once night set in, it'd be too risky to travel. And he wasn't alone. He had Annie Bryce to consider. The way his own stomach was growling, she was probably starving.

Reluctantly, he pulled up, then called over his shoulder, "You awake back there?"

"Yes."

"Hungry?"

"Are you?"

"That's no answer. I asked about you, not me! Hell, I know I am!"

"I could eat." Crawling forward, she stuck her head through the opening. "It's too wet to make a fire."

"Yeah. There's beef jerky and salt bread in the sack, along with some dried apples I bought at the post store. That all right with you?"

"Yes," she answered without much enthusiasm.

"Guess you've eaten a lot of jerky, haven't you?"

"Quite a bit." That was perhaps the greatest understatement of her life, but she didn't want to hurt his feelings. "I don't really mind it."

"There's a couple of tins of something called Borden's Meat Biscuits. I picked them up while I was at it. Mind you, I've got no notion what the stuff tastes like, but it's got to be better than what we had in the war, because they're selling it."

"I can't say I've ever had any, but I'd be willing to try some. It'd be a change, anyway."

"You need to stop, don't you?"

"Don't you?" she countered.

"Damn. You can't ask for anything, can you?"

"Yes. I just don't want to cost you any time unless I have to. I figure I can last as long as you can, and then we'll only have to stop once," she explained practically. "You wouldn't like it if I was wanting to get down every mile or so, would you?"

"No. But it seems like I'm making all the choices."

"All right, then. I'm very hungry, I need to take a walk

if you see any woods, and I'm cold. There, have I complained enough to suit you?"

"Barely."

"Well, if I said anything else, I'd be lying."

"That cottonwood stand look all right to you?" he asked abruptly.

"It's kind of sparse."

"You could go behind the wagon."

"Not this time."

"All right. Hold the reins."

He waited until she climbed onto the seat beside him before transferring the traces to her hands. Jumping down, he headed toward the group of naked trees, then stood behind one, his back to her. Uncomfortable with this reminder that he was a man, she turned her head and studied the white line of light beneath the low-hanging clouds. The sun was almost gone, so they'd have to make camp. Her gaze took in the flat area, the slope of a hill coming down, and she felt uneasy.

"Your turn," he said, climbing up beside her again. "Better hold up your skirt, because it's muddy as hell over there."

"At least it's too cold for snakes."

"Yeah. While you're gone, I'll get out my knife and open one of those tins. I was told you didn't have to heat the stuff, so that ought to make it easy enough. We ought to be done with supper before the rain starts in again."

"Are we going to camp here for the night?"

He looked around, then shook his head. "Too open—there's no cover. If a Comanche were to come over the hill, it'd be too late by the time I saw him. I reckon we'll eat and then try to find a better place."

Her relief was obvious. "That's what I thought."

"Why didn't you say something?"

"I just did."

"No, you just asked." As she gingerly reached the ground, he looked down at her. "I'm not a man that needs to be cottoned to, Annie. You need to say something, say it. I put on my pants one leg at a time, just like everybody else. You've got nothing to be afraid of with me. I'm no damned Comanche."

"All right."

"Something's the matter, isn't it?"

"No. But I don't put pants on."

For a moment he didn't follow her. Then he thought he understood. "Freedom doesn't come easy, does it? It's too soon for you to know what you want."

"I want to go home, Hap."

"And I'm getting you there. That wasn't what I was saying, and you know it. Damned if I know what to make of you, Annie."

She gazed up at him, then dropped her eyes. "I don't know, either."

"Was it the storm?"

"Yes. It makes me remember."

"Look, if it'd helped anything, I'd have put my arms around you and held you until it stopped—like Claude used to do with me."

"That's the last thing I want," she said, turning away.

He waited until she reached the cottonwoods. She looked back, seeing if he'd watched, then started to lift the skirt. Out of the corner of his eye, he could see the ruffled leg of her drawers. Resolutely, he turned his attention to rummaging behind him for the sack containing the tins. When he found one and straightened up, he caught a glimpse of bare thigh and the curve of a bottom. She'd gotten the drawers off and was trying to squat while keeping her clothes out of the mud. It had to be hell being a woman.

By the time she got back, he had the tin open and two spoons out. "Guess if you get the canteen, we're fixed for supper," he told her as she grasped the iron ring and pulled herself up. Looking into the can, he observed, "They don't seem like much, but I guess we'll find out."

"At least it's not jerky," she murmured, settling in beside him. Reaching down, she retrieved the water container. Seeing that he still eyed Borden's Meat Biscuits with some misgivings, she asked, "Do you want me to go first?"

"I want you to take a stand on something," he muttered. "Don't leave it all to me."

"All right, give me the tin." While he watched, she dug her spoon into the can and came up with a doughy blob. Carrying it to her mouth, she took a large bite, then held it without chewing. "Here," she said, "your turn." Slowly, she began to work it around between her teeth, then gulped from the canteen, washing it down with the water. "Well, go on," she urged him once she'd swallowed.

"Yeah." Telling himself he was hungry enough to eat raw horsemeat, he scooped a goodly amount from the can into his mouth. As soon as it touched his tongue, he knew he'd made a real mistake. Rather than chew the stuff, he tried to swallow it whole, but it didn't want to go down. And the little amount that hit his stomach provoked an immediate rebellion. Leaning over the side of the wagon, he spat out as much as he could. "Damn," he said, reaching for the water.

"You didn't like it?" she asked innocently.

"You just did that to me, didn't you?" he choked out. "Your turn," he said, mimicking the way she'd said it. "What the hell did I ever do to deserve that?"

"You bought them."

"You didn't think much of 'em, either, did you?" he demanded, recovering.

"Well, I expect they could support life," she allowed.

"Want the rest?"

"No. Not right now, anyway." She eyed the can. "Maybe you were told wrong. Maybe we were supposed to cook them."

"It'd be a waste of the fire," he declared, glaring at it. "If I was on the trail, and that was all I had left in the pack, I'd catch bugs before I'd eat those things."

"You obviously haven't lived on bugs," she murmured. "No matter how we fixed them, I couldn't forget what they were. And I've eaten nearly everything these last three years."

"Then meat biscuits ought to suit you. Here," he said, handing her the tin.

"I'll get the jerky," she decided. "At least I know what it's made of."

"Yeah. Too bad oxen only eat grass and grain. If I wasn't afraid of poisoning 'em, I'd try it on 'em, anyway. Damn, but I spent a dollar apiece on those cans."

"That's robbery."

"Yeah. Well, I guess I'll just leave the rest out for the wolves. Maybe it'll kill off a few, and we won't have to listen to 'em."

"Wolves eat anything, and none of it ever bothers them.

182

They'll probably like it so well they'll follow us all the way to Fort Richardson," she predicted.

Whatever had been bothering her seemed to have passed. He felt relieved about that, anyway. Leaning over, he scraped the rest of the contents from the tin onto the ground. When he straightened up, she was cutting pieces of jerky with his knife. He could feel his breath catch in his chest. In the dusk, silhouetted by the last bit of light, her face was truly beautiful.

He lay beneath the wagon, listening to a steady drip of rain. Despite the oilcloth under him, he could feel the water oozing through the dead grass. Above him, in the relative comfort of the wagon bed, he supposed Annie Bryce slept. He couldn't. He was too cold, too wet, and in too much pain to let go of conscious thought.

Despite the darkness, he should have violated the accepted rule of wagon travel and gone on, even if he'd had to walk with the oxen. They had too many miles to cover to spend any time bogged down to the wagon axles in mud. And if it didn't stop raining, that would happen. He felt it in his bones. No, if the leg was any barometer, the weather was going to be wet for a while.

In the distance, a rumble of thunder signaled yet another storm about to come through. He rolled onto his side and peered from beneath the wooden frame. Yeah, right now the lightning was flickering like a lantern flame, licking the clouds along the horizon, lighting them for an instant, then fading. As he watched, he traced a flash through a black, roiling mass. The ugly thought of a tornado shot through his mind. It wasn't the right time of year, but then the weather hadn't been exactly normal for

November, either. Now he studied the cloud intently, wishing for more lightning. No, there wasn't any tail—not yet, anyway. But by the time it got to them, it was going to pour like a river. Gully washer wouldn't be the word for it.

He rolled to sit up and rubbed the offending leg. The wind was picking up, blowing a fresh blast of rain against the canvas top. The mule raised its head, its nostrils flared, and snorted nervously. It smelled the storm, too. For a moment Hap considered moving the oxen from the clump of mesquite trees, then decided against it. If lightning struck there, he'd know God didn't intend to let him get Annie Bryce home.

Old Red's manner reassured him somewhat. The big roan had his head down, eating in the rain. It took a lot to rile that horse. It always had. He'd once known a fellow who insisted men bought horses that reflected themselves. He guessed there might be a grain of truth in that—everybody said he was easygoing, slow to anger. What nobody realized was there was a reason for it. Once he let go of his temper, there was no getting it back.

Finally, unable to stand the ache, he pulled himself from beneath the wagon and stood up, gathering the so-called waterproof poncho about his shoulders. Needing to walk, he moved to the small mesquite grove to check the tethers. Yeah, that was better. The leg had been in some sort of bind, that was all. Now that he'd gotten the kink out of it, he could walk all right. The discovery was a great relief to him. Maybe it really was healing right this time.

The wind was coming cross-wise now, whipping the stiff poncho like a sail, beating him with it. The sky lit up, and the ground shook under his feet from the force of lightning streaking down from the huge thunderhead. The wagon rocked. Hurrying now, almost running, he headed for it. It was as though the sheeting rain pushed him.

He grabbed the handhold, stepped on the iron bar, and swung himself up through the canvas flap, pulling it closed after him. "Annie?" he asked softly. "It's me, Hap. Are you all right?"

It was pitch black inside, making sight impossible. But he could hear her. Groping his way between boxes, he found the straw mattress first. Then as he crawled to the end of it, he touched her. Recoiling, she screamed. Cursing under his breath, he dug for dry matches under the poncho, found one, and struck it with his thumbnail. It blazed, sending a flash of light in front of him. Never in all his days had he ever gotten a reaction from anyone like he was seeing now. Her knees drawn against her chest, Annie cowered wide-eyed, her hands held up to shield her.

"My God." Holding the match, he crept closer to her. "It's Hap. You're all right, Annie—you're all right," he said quickly. As the flame went out, he pulled off the rain wrap, eased his body down next to hers, and threw a comforting arm over her. "It's just a Texas storm, that's all." She went rigid, almost as though she were convulsing. He caught her clenched hand, forcing it down beside her.

"That's better, a whole lot better. Now you just lay there." Pulling the blanket from between them, he turned her away from him, then drew her backside against his stomach. It was like wrestling a board. "Now, I'm just going to do like Claude, I swear. I'm just going to hold you."

She was panting from panic, and he could feel her

heart pound beneath his arm, but he lay still, holding her, saying nothing while the canvas above beat the iron frame and the wagon bed creaked and groaned. Outside, the storm hit with full force, raging and railing like an angry god. As the noise grew worse, he bent his head to her ear, saying, "It'll be over in a little bit, and I'll turn you loose. Everything's going to be okay. I won't let anything hurt you, Annie—not even me."

His breath was warm, his voice soft and reassuring, but the arm across her chest was strong, tight against her breast. A low sob formed deep within her. Drawing her clenched hand to her mouth, she bit on her knuckles, trying to stifle it.

"Everything's going to be okay," he said again. "Don't do this to yourself, Annie."

"I-I can't help it!" she sobbed, letting go. "I can't help it! Nothing's ever going to be all right again!"

"Shhhhhh."

"You don't know—you don't know!"

"Take it easy—just take it easy." Still holding her tightly, he tried to smooth her hair with his other hand. "You're not with them anymore. You're with me, Hap Walker—the happy fellow, remember?" Afraid he was making it worse by holding her arms down, he relaxed his embrace. "Better?"

Instead of pulling away, she turned into him, burying her head in his chest. His arms closed around her again. There wasn't anything more he could say. All he could do was let her weep against him as she'd done at the Sprengers. He felt completely helpless in the face of her pain.

Closing her eyes, she clung to him, seeking the comforting warmth of his body. Spent, she went limp. He was almost afraid to breathe lest he set her off again. Despite how little she weighed, his arm beneath her was going numb. To ease it he stroked her hair where the pins had fallen out, tumbling part of it over her shoulders. It felt like satin beneath his callused fingers.

Gradually he became conscious of her breasts pressed against his chest, of the woman's curve to her thin shoulders, but as long as she lay quietly like that, he couldn't push her away. He was a man, not an animal, he reminded himself. And she was like a lost child. She needed to be healed, not seduced. She had enough trouble in her life. But there was no denying she was a woman, and it had been a long time since he'd held any woman like this. He'd never gotten this close to Amanda.

Forcing his thoughts away from the woman in his arms, he tried to focus on what he was going to tell Clay. Since this last thing with his leg, he'd pretty much made up his mind he didn't want to sell cattle for anybody. Life was too unpredictable, too short to spend it doing something he had no real feeling for.

No, he wasn't being honest. He hated it. Whether it was because he had to look at Amanda every day he stayed at the Ybarra, or whether it was because he found the business boring, he hated it. Clay was going to be disappointed in him, but dammit, the job wasn't much more than a pension in disguise. Besides, Diego Vergara was a whole lot better at selling cattle than he was. It wouldn't be like he was leaving Clay in the lurch.

Rangering was out, he knew that. Even if he could regain his commission, it wouldn't be fair to those asked to serve under him. A man needed to be able to keep up with his men, and his days of living weeks on end in the saddle were pretty much over. But it had come to him last night as he'd stared up at the stars. The way Texas was being settled, there was a real need for a different breed of lawman. And it wasn't impossible to see himself as a sheriff somewhere. Somewhere where he wouldn't have to climb boulders and ford rivers and ride for days.

He still had fast hands and a sharp eye—and he still had the nerve to kill a man if he had to. Yeah, last night he'd made up his mind: He was going to spend the winter working with the leg. Then, come spring, he was going to look for a town that needed him. To survive, a man like him had to be needed, or he might as well shrivel up and die.

The wind was tapering down, the rumble fading, but Annie Bryce didn't move. He was beginning to think she'd either passed out or exhausted herself into sleep. Very gingerly he eased his arm from beneath her, then edged away to sit up. Leaning over, he pulled the blanket up over her shoulder. It wasn't until he was creeping from the wagon that she spoke.

"I'm sorry," she said, low.

"For what? For something you can't help?"

"For being a burden."

"Don't ever say that, Annie. Don't ever say that again," he said almost harshly. "It's their fault, not yours. It's what they did to you."

Unable to deal with his own turmoil, he quickly swung down. The rain had been so heavy the water stood several inches deep. By morning, when it sank in, the ground would be soaked to mush, he reflected wearily.

He walked to the mesquite grove again and found the

animals had survived. Circling it, he came back to face the wagon. There was a hole in the sky where the storm had been, and the shadow of the moon was visible above a feathery haze. A couple of brave stars peeked cautiously from behind a few remaining, far more benign clouds. God willing, it'd clear up completely.

The oilcloth was still beneath his bedroll, but water stood on top of it. He stared at the soaked blankets for a moment, then sighed. It was too damned cold to spend the night in wet bedclothes. He'd have to sleep inside.

This time he mounted the step slowly, crawling into the musty depths of the wagon bed. He pulled off his muddy boots and his damp flannel shirt, then felt in the dark for the box Doc Sprenger had loaded. Finding it, he took out two wool blankets and a heavy quilt, which he carried to the straw mattress. On his knees, he rolled one of the blankets in the darkness, then found Annie. She flinched as his hand brushed her bare leg, but didn't actually move away. She was clinging to the edge of the mattress.

"It's all right," he assured her, laying the rolled blanket the length of her back.

"No," she choked out.

"Here." Unbuckling his gun belt, he reached over her and placed it in front of her. "That's a brand new spanking Colt revolver with five .44-caliber shells in it. If you find me on your side of the bundle, use it." When she didn't respond, he shook out the quilt and other blanket, covered himself, and lay down, his back to hers. "Now, let's get some shut-eye. Come morning, we're going to have one helluva time getting this wagon out of here."

Her hand on the holster, she lay awake long after he fell asleep, listening to his strong, even breathing. Beyond the fact he was a man, she had no reason to fear him. And given all he'd already done for her, she wanted desperately to trust him. But he was so different, so unlike Ethan. He'd been a Texas Ranger. And a man didn't get to be a ranger captain with kindness. Beneath Hap Walker's kindly, almost folksy, easygoing manner, there had to be a pretty rough man.

The muddy road had made for hard traveling, and several times they'd had to unload the wagon, push it through the mire, then reload it. Once, when even that failed, they'd stood calf-deep in mud and dug it out. When they finally rolled into Fort Richardson two days late, they were filthy and exhausted. While Annie waited in the wagon, Hap met with the commanding officer to arrange for her stay there. Coming back, he told her he'd found a place with people the colonel characterized as "a nice young couple, a lieutenant and his wife, both of whom come from Arkansas."

But as soon as Annie met them, it was immediately apparent that Lulene Davis was no Cora Sprenger. Despite Frank Davis's assurances otherwise, his wife was obviously less than enthusiastic about welcoming a fallen woman into her home. Upon introduction she smiled thinly, looked her guest up and down with raised eyebrows, murmured something about "your unfortunate experience," and quickly turned her back, leaving the lieutenant to show her undesirable guest to her room.

Having nowhere else to go and not wanting to burden Hap, Annie spent most of the next two days there while he continued living in the wagon, affording her only an occasional glimpse of him from the window. She felt somewhat abandoned, but as Mrs. Davis failed to invite him to call or dine with them, there wasn't much she could do about it.

As nearly as she could tell, he was spending most of his waking time either at the post store or off the fort at what Mrs. Davis characterized as "an extremely unsavory cantina." When the lieutenant attempted to defend the place, his wife wouldn't hear of it. "Everyone knows what those painted hussies are, and everyone knows exactly why the men go there," she retorted. "I'm quite certain it isn't for drink, which can be bought from the sutler."

Lulene rarely spoke to Annie, preferring to direct her conversation to her husband, saying such things as "Pray ask Mrs. Bryce to pass the potatoes, will you?" or "I'm sure Mrs. Bryce would prefer to retire when dinner is over." Trying to make up for his wife's ill manners, he took it upon himself to be a gracious host, which only increased the woman's dislike. It was so uncomfortable there that Annie desperately wanted to leave.

No one came to call, not even the colonel's wife, and while that wasn't entirely unexpected, it was hard to deny the anger Annie felt. As unjust as it was, she knew she was considered no better than those cantina girls Lulene Davis condemned. That it had been against her will didn't seem to matter. She'd been with an Indian, and that made her unfit for white society. She'd heard it in Sarabeth Hughes' voice, and she was seeing it in the Davis woman's manner.

192

Wednesday evening, supper was early, and Lulene came to the table dressed in a pretty braid-trimmed basque jacket, striped silk weskit, frilled lawn waist, and demi-bustled skirt. Taking off matching navy gloves, she laid them carefully beside her plate.

"You look fine tonight, Lu," Davis murmured appreciatively."

She flashed a smile at him. "Thank you."

"I take it you don't mean to sit at home like that, my dear?"

"Of course not. Really, Frank, if you paid any attention to matters of your soul, you'd know that it isn't our Mr. Johnson tonight."

"Oh? I must've missed the notice."

"You ought to come, you know."

"Lu—"

"Well, you ought to," she declared positively. "You haven't set foot in church since last Easter."

"And Johnson talked for two solid hours," he reminded her.

"Probably because he knew it was his only opportunity to instill any godliness in half the men there. I know at least ten of them had never been before."

"And after that sermon they haven't been back since."

"No. Really, you'd like tonight's preacher—he's from the Baptist Speaker's Bureau in Little Rock. He's from home, Frank."

"Christmas and Easter, Lu, that's all I promised you."

"Yes, I know, but—"

"No buts," he said, interrupting her. "You look after your soul, and I'll look after mine."

"Well, you cannot stay home. I mean—" She cast a significant look toward Annie. "Well, you know what I mean."

"No, I don't. I fail to see what Mrs. Bryce has to do with my going to church, my dear."

"Frank!"

"Well, I don't. If you want to drag somebody with you, why don't you take her?"

The woman reddened, and the expression on her face looked as though she'd just sucked on a persimmon. "Really, Frank, I don't think that would be at all wise," she said tightly. "But as I don't have all evening to sit here and argue with you, I shall just go by myself—as usual, of course."

"I still don't see—"

"Well, I do. Why don't you pass the meat plate to Mrs. Bryce? Maybe after supper you can go over to Major Hammond's. I understand there's a card game there, and I'm sure it will be more suited to your tastes, anyway."

"He's already got a full table."

"Oh. Well, I was just thinking of you, of course," she murmured through thinly drawn lips. "I'm sure Mrs. Bryce will wish to go to her room, and I hate to leave you alone here."

Her meaning wasn't lost on Annie. The woman obviously expected her to throw herself at Davis the instant she was alone with him—or vice versa. "Actually," she spoke up, "I would like to go to church, Mrs. Davis."

"Tell her it's out of the question, Frank."

"I don't see why."

"Well," Lulene floundered, trying to think of a reason, then declared, "well, the seats are by subscription."

"To a church meeting?" he asked incredulously.

"I told you, he's a guest speaker," she responded peevishly. "Now, will you please let it go by?"

"Then let her have my seat. If I've paid for it, I ought to be able to give it away."

"It doesn't work that way, Frank. Besides, I'm sure since Mrs. Bryce knows no one here, she'd be uncomfortable. She probably isn't even a Baptist. Now, are you going to pass the meat, or shall I reach across the table for it?"

"Actually, I *am* a Baptist, Mrs. Davis," Annie admitted.

Lulene's expression was pained. Appealing to her husband, she said, "Surely you can see why it wouldn't be appropriate, Frank." Picking up the platter, she thrust it toward Annie. "Here, do take some roast so that we may get on with eating. I really don't have much time tonight."

"Before you go, you ought to take out your Bible and read out of John—I think it's in chapter eight," Frank said, addressing his wife.

"What?"

"Excuse me," he murmured to Annie, rising. When he came back, he had the book opened in his hand. Leaning over Lulene, he placed it in front of her. "Read verse seven, my dear."

She looked down, then flushed angrily. "It's not the same thing," she snapped.

"No, it's not. At least you realize that," he muttered, taking his seat again as she quickly closed the Bible. "But you cannot just pick what you want to believe and leave out the rest, can you?"

Furious with him, Lulene stood up. "I don't need a lecture from—from an unbeliever, Frank! I'm not the one who doesn't go to church!" With that, she stalked from the table.

There was an awkward silence for a moment before he looked at Annie. "I'm sorry, Mrs. Bryce, truly sorry. If I'd known it was going to be like this, I'd have asked the colonel to ask someone else. I guess Lu doesn't realize it could happen to her out here."

"Yes. Well, I'm quite sorry also, but I cannot say it was totally unexpected. I grew up in Texas, you know. I know how people feel."

"But when I made the offer to Captain Walker, I didn't think she'd act anything like this, ma'am."

"It's all right, Lieutenant." Reaching across the table, she retrieved his Bible. As she opened it, the front door to the house slammed, telling her Lulene had left. She thumbed the pages until she found the book of John, then the chapter he'd mentioned. Following her finger down the page, she found the passage where Jesus was asked about punishing the woman taken in adultery.

So when they continued asking him, he lifted himself up and said unto them, He that is without sin among you, let him cast the first stone at her.

Blinking back tears, she looked up at him. "Thank you, sir."

"And I meant it when I said it wasn't the same thing," he said quietly. "Adultery is hardly the word for what happened."

She made up her mind then. "I'm not very hungry, Lieutenant. If you'll excuse me—"

"No need to go to your room on my account, Mrs. Bryce. I was sort of thinking about going out to the cantina myself," he admitted sheepishly. "I figure I've got a good, stiff drink coming to me."

"I wasn't planning on going to my room, sir." Her eyes met his again. "I'm going to church. I'm just as much a Baptist as anyone else. What time does the Wednesday service start?"

"Seven."

"I should have plenty of time to get ready."

He watched her leave, then sat for a time, staring at his Bible, wondering if he'd done right by encouraging her to go. Finally, he pushed his untouched plate back and went to fetch his coat. If he found Walker at the cantina, he was going to tell him it wasn't fair to her to make her stay with Lulene. He was just damned sorry any of it had happened.

A soldier stood outside the chapel, ringing what looked like a dinner bell, as a line of worshipers filed by him. While there were more women than men, there was a goodly sprinkling of blue coats in the small crowd.

" 'Evening, major. Ma'am. 'Evening, sir. Ma'am," the fellow called out as people passed.

Annie forced a smile. "Good evening," she said politely. "Are the pews assigned?"

"No, ma'am, the first as gets in gets the seats," he assured her. Then, peering more closely at her, he seemed surprised. "Say, you're the Bryce woman, ain't you?"

"I'm Mrs. Bryce," she acknowledged.

Once inside, she took a printed program from a prim-looking female by the door, then made her way to the back pew. Taking a place beside three other women, she bowed her head and closed her eyes to pray for

Susannah's return. When she looked up, the three ladies had moved away from her, all of them sitting quite close to each other, leaving a space of several feet between them and her. It was hard to miss the message.

Pretending indifference, she looked around the chapel, taking in the lanterns lit at the end of every pew. Unlike the women, they were warm and inviting. Leaning forward, she retrieved a hymnal and opened it, turning the pages, seeing the familiar songs of faith and praise. She'd played most of them on her piano.

What one was it that Hap Walker liked? "A Mighty Fortress Is Our God." Yes, it was in there. And all the Christmas carols. He wanted her to play them for him, too.

As she looked up again, people in the rows in front of her quickly turned around. The woman closest to her opened a filigree watch case with gloved hands, and Annie caught the time. Six minutes to seven. She had another six minutes to sit there in silence while the curious stared at her.

Outside, Hap Walker crossed the open area between cantina and fort, limping and cursing under his breath. He'd been peaceably playing cards and drinking decent whiskey when Frank Davis had told him about Lulene's behavior to Annie. Blast the woman—no, blast both of them. He was leaving a winning hand to go to church.

" 'Evening, sir," the soldier told him, adding, "You'll have to check your gun at the door."

"Like hell," Hap muttered.

By the time the startled bell ringer recovered, Hap was already inside. Recalling where he was, he paused to smooth his hair, then looked around. She was there, all right, sitting by herself in the back row, while those three hens crowded against each other down at the end. That was one thing he'd never understood about women—there didn't seem to be much sisterhood between them. Resigned, he went to her side of the pew.

"Move over," he said tersely.

"What are you doing here, Hap?" she whispered.

"I came to sing."

"Oh." She slid over to make room for him. "I thought you said you couldn't."

"Couldn't what?"

"Sing."

"I can't," he muttered.

She could smell the liquor on his breath, but he didn't seem drunk. It didn't matter, she decided. She was extremely grateful to see him.

"Thank you," she murmured.

"Yeah."

There was a stirring among the small congregation, and then a woman moved to take a seat at the piano. A man in a black frock coat stepped forward to the lectern to announce, "Number one forty-two, folks, all verses."

As Annie opened the hymnal, Hap leaned over for a look. "Never heard of it," he declared, disappointed.

"Neither have I."

"You lead, and I'll try to follow."

"It's not a dance," she whispered. The woman closest to her turned and glared. "All right."

The song was too high, and his voice cracked trying to reach the notes. He gave up the effort to listen to Annie, who could hit them all cleanly. She had a pretty voice—a real pretty voice. When he closed his eyes, it was like listening to his mother sing again. And then it was over, and she was closing the book.

"You didn't have to quit, you know," she said, low.

"You were doing all right without me."

"God doesn't care."

"A man doesn't like to make a fool of himself."

He'd about forgotten how long-winded a preacher could be, he discovered to his regret. Once the fellow in the black coat got started, he waxed eloquent for well over an hour, haranguing his captive audience about the cost of sin, enumerating just about every transgression anybody'd ever think of. About halfway through, Hap took a peek at his watch, then resigned himself to endure, vowing silently that it'd be a long time before he made this mistake again.

His thoughts left the sermon, turning to the woman beside him. The lantern light seemed to reflect off her pale hair almost like a halo, and the irony wasn't lost on him. Nobody but him was seeing it. They were too determined to look down their noses at her. But she sat straight, her shoulders back, her head up, listening to the preacher, almost daring anybody to tell her she didn't have the right to be there.

He'd been angry with her earlier, but as he watched her out of the corner of his eye, he was damned proud of her now. She had real grit. After everything that had happened to her, she could still face folks down. She wasn't going to play dead for anybody.

She was poking him, pointing at the hymnal. He glanced down, seeing the title. "Break Thou the Bread of Life." "Surely you know this one," she whispered.

"Yeah, but I can't sing it, either. It's too slow."

After Communion, the prayer lasted another ten minutes, and then came the inevitable invitation to be "saved in Jesus." And a recessional he could actually manage with some authority. As he gave full range to the refrain of "Holy, holy, holy, Lord God Almighty, early in the morning our song shall rise to Thee," he was almost reluctant to close the book.

He felt pretty good now that it was over. The chapel was emptying, the people lingering outside in small groups. Seeing that the three women were eyeing him speculatively, he flashed them a smile, then took Annie's elbow.

"You didn't have to do that, you know," she murmured.

"Smile?"

"No, come on my account."

"What makes you think I did?"

"You saw Frank Davis, didn't you?"

He started to deny it but didn't. "Yeah. Why didn't you tell me about her? No sense putting yourself through that."

"I haven't seen you since I got here," she reminded him. "Besides, I doubt if anybody else is exactly wanting my company, either."

He had no answer for that. It was cold enough outside that he could see his breath. Guiding her past the curious, he nodded to them but kept going. "Guess we'll be leaving in the morning," he said finally.

"You don't have to leave for me, Hap. You need to make it easy on yourself."

"It doesn't make much difference. If I hang around here, I'll just play poker and get drunk. There's not much else to do around a fort in winter."

"You're sure?"

"Yeah. I reckon we ought to get an early start. Think you can be ready to load up by six?"

"My carpetbag?" she asked, smiling. "I'm sure of it."

"Good. I'll tell Davis I'll be by about then. There's some rough country between here and Griffin, and I still aim to have you settled in your house by Christmas."

They were almost to the Davis house when he stopped. "You better get on inside and get some sleep, Annie. Six o'clock'll be coming early." But despite his words he made no move to leave. Instead he stood there, looking at her.

"You're a fine-looking woman, Annie Bryce," he said softly. "A real fine-looking woman."

It was as though the world stood still for a moment. Afraid he meant to touch her, she froze, her expression stricken. "Don't," she whispered. "Please don't."

"Don't what, Annie?" His hand reached to brush a stray strand of hair back from her forehead. "You've got nothing to be afraid of with me, Annie."

He could see her swallow, and the terror in her eyes was real. He dropped his hand and backed away. "Hell, I'm just drunk, don't mind me," he told her. "Good night."

"I'm sorry."

"Be sorry for things you can help."

"I'm dead inside, Hap."

"See you in the morning, Annie."

But as he left her, he knew he would have kissed her if she'd let him. And it would have been wrong. She wasn't ready for anything like that, and neither was he. Any man wanting to bring her back to life was laying himself out a hard row to hoe.

She watched him walk toward the low building beyond

the post grounds, wondering if it was the girls that drew him there. Not that it was any of her business, anyway, she reminded herself. Yet as he disappeared into the darkness, she felt an acute, aching loneliness.

Gray, weathered boards showed through where the whitewash had faded on the exterior of the house. And the yard was strangely empty. The clothesline was bare, the big tree in the front of the house gnarled and naked. Her gaze moved to the barn and the pen surrounding it. They were deserted, too. There wasn't a living, breathing creature on the place. She'd known it would be like this, but she still was unprepared for what she saw.

"I reckon you'll want to go inside," Hap said behind her.

"Yes."

"Key's under the jar. I had Rios lock it up when we left. I didn't figure anybody ought to be going in."

"There was a time when I never thought I'd ever see this place again," she murmured.

"I'll get the key for you."

"It seems so empty."

"Last time I looked, your things were still there." Moving around her, he stepped onto the stoop and felt beneath a heavy crockery jar. "Yeah, it's here, all right." Straightening up, he unlocked the door.

It creaked on its hinges as it swung inward, admitting a slice of winter light that spread across the dusty floor. Her heart pounding, Annie followed him in, and her spirits sank. In her memory everything had stayed just as it was before. She was unprepared for what she saw.

Cobwebs hung from every horizontal surface and clung to the walls. As she walked across the room, her skirts stirred gritty dirt, nearly choking her. She stopped at the piano and reached her hand to trace the carved beadwork along the top, leaving a trail of fingerprints in the thick layer of dust.

As he watched her move through her house, stopping to touch each piece of furniture, each bit of bric-a-brac she'd collected, each scarf and doily she'd made, he felt like an intruder. "It's all here, isn't it?" he asked finally.

"Yes—yes, it is."

"You want to go through the rest of it?"

"Yes."

She didn't look nearly as happy as he'd hoped to see her. "It's a nice place, Annie. You had it fixed up real pretty, you know."

"Yes."

"It's going to need a little cleaning up to make it look like that again," he added in an understatement. "But you can do it. In a week it'll be home again."

"I hope."

"Tell you what—you make a list of what you need, and I'll go into town and get it. Then we'll spend a couple of days getting everything back in order before I leave for good."

"All right."

"I'll get the fire going, bring in some of the food from

the wagon, and help you get started. You'll be all right while I'm gone, won't you?"

"Yes."

He came up behind her and laid his hands on her shoulders. "Something's the matter, isn't it?"

"No, I'm all right."

But she was moving around almost as though she were in a trance. Instinct told him to leave her alone, to let her work out whatever was ailing her. He dropped his hands.

"Well, first things first," he said. "I'd better see about some wood before you take your death of cold in here. Until then you'd better keep your coat on."

If she heard him, she didn't respond. Instead, she walked into another room, leaving him standing there. Maybe he'd been wrong to bring her home in winter. Maybe if the sun had been shining, things would have seemed better. Maybe she was just now facing the reality of being alone. Maybe the task of cleaning up the place was too much after the long trip from Fort Sill.

He took a deep breath, and nearly choked from the dust in the air. Yeah, he'd better get some wood in. With a fire in the stove and some food on the table, things might seem different to her.

"When I get back in, I'll try to help you get some of this swept out," he promised.

She heard the door close after him. Standing in the doorway of her bedroom, she took in the heavy wood bedstead. Her quilt was still there, only now the background was tan instead of white. She walked closer, studying the fine stitches she'd made, the intricate blue and white stars in the pattern. Then she pulled it off the bed and threw herself onto the feather mattress. Sobbing, she pounded

COMANCHE ROSE

the pillows with clenched fists. It wasn't fair that this was all she had left.

The wood in the pile behind the house was bleached with age, the bark on it long since eaten by something. It was too old, too porous to burn right, but if he could put it with something else, maybe it wouldn't go so fast. He went to the barn to look for Ethan Bryce's ax, found it and an iron log splitter, then carried them back outside. It had been a long time since he'd actually chopped wood, since he'd lived at home with his ma, but it wasn't something a man forgot.

It took awhile to find what he wanted—a stunted cottonwood tree already more than half-dead, apparently struck by lightning some time before. The first swing of the ax told him something he didn't want to know. As the muscles pulled across his back, he knew he was going to hurt when he was done. But all the time he was growing up, his ma had always said good, honest hard work never killed anyone. Now he was going to find how just how right she'd been.

It took him nearly two hours to fell the small tree, split the trunk, trim kindling, and make logs that would fit into a stove. Yet as much as his arms ached, he had to admit it made him feel good, as though he was still worth something. He made several trips to the woodpile, stacking everything neatly for her. With what she had, maybe it'd last a little while, at least long enough for him to make a supply run and get back.

As he came around the corner of the house with his arms full, he stopped dead. Hanging from the clothesline, bedsheets and a quilt flapped in the cold wind. It was ev-

207

ery bit as eerie a scene as when he'd been here three years before.

"What the devil—? Annie, what the *hell* are you doing? Are you out of your mind? Dammit, you can't wait for help can you?"

She was on the front stoop, bending over a rolled rag rug, struggling to pull it out through the open door. As he came up the step, she turned around, and his anger faded on the instant. Her eyes were red-rimmed, her face splotched. She'd obviously been crying.

"Annie—"

"No, I'm all right now, really," she said stoutly. "It was just the shock of seeing everything, that was all. Now, the sooner I get my life in order, the better it'll be. I just had to see it, to face it."

"What do you think you're doing?"

"Well, I couldn't sleep with that much dust and grit on my bed, so I thought I'd at least air the bedclothes out. And the rug. I can't sweep until I can clear the floor."

"Get back inside before you let all the heat out of the house."

"There isn't any heat."

"Well, there's going to be," he muttered. "That rug weighs more than you do, Annie."

"I know."

"Is that how it's going to be when I'm gone? You're going to be trying to do everything by yourself?"

Exasperated, she pushed stray strands of hair back, then looked directly into his eyes. "I don't see anyone else, do you? I'm alone now. I'm going to have to learn how to do everything, anyway."

"I told you I'd stay a few days to get you settled."

She looked at the wood in his arms. "I don't have a right to ask you to do things for me, Hap. I already owe you for more than I can ever repay."

"Did I every ask for anything?"

"No."

"Look, it didn't cost me but fifty dollars for the wagon, and I'd be eating, anyway. I'll just stop over at Concho before I head for the Ybarra, and some bullwhacker'll give my money back."

"I wasn't thinking of money."

"Maybe it was something I wanted to do. Maybe it was something I needed to do."

"Why?"

"Hell, it doesn't matter why, does it?" he countered almost angrily. "I got you home, didn't I? I can still do that, anyway."

"This isn't like you, Hap."

"How would you know? All you've seen is a damned cripple," he muttered, brushing past her. "I've got to build a fire. And then I've go to go somewhere and get you enough supplies to last awhile."

"A cripple?" she echoed incredulously. "Is that what you think you are?"

"Sorry I brought it up. I don't want to talk about it." Dropping the wood on the floor, he opened the stove door. He dug into his overloaded coat pockets for twigs and dead grass, then crouched to arrange them in the firebox. "Hand me one of the smaller pieces, will you?" he said over his shoulder. "I don't usually make my fires inside."

"Is this what you want?" she asked, finding a foot-long section of limb.

"Yeah. About three or four of 'em."

She was right behind him now, so close that when she bent over him, he could feel her breath on the back of his neck. It sent a shiver down his spine. Ducking away, he nearly stuck his head into the stove.

"Your leg's hurting you, isn't it?"

"No."

"You're feeling sorry for yourself."

"Yeah."

Fumbling beneath his coat for the matches in the flannel shirt pocket, he found one. He struck it against the stove, waited until the flare became a flame, then held it to the tinder. As the grass caught, he blew lightly on it and tossed the rest of the wooden match in. About the time he thought the whole thing had burned out, a small yellow finger of fire licked its way up a twig. Half closing the door, he set the damper handle.

Rising from the dust, he brushed his buckskin pants with his hands. "All right, I guess I can help you with the rug. Just don't try to bring it in by yourself."

She opened her mouth, then shut it. "I won't," she said finally.

"Good, you're too skinny to be pulling on things like that. Afterward, you'd better sit down and make out your list."

"You're not going today surely."

"Yeah, I figure it'll take a couple of days, anyway. But I'll unload the wagon first."

"But you haven't even eaten!"

"I've still got jerky." A faint smile curved his mouth. "But I'll be sure to leave the Borden's Meat Biscuits here. I figure I'll be back before Christmas, so you won't have to eat 'em."

"Thank you."

"You got any neighbors close by?" he asked suddenly.

"The Willetts live about five miles to the east—why?"

"Just wondered. Know 'em very well?"

"Well, I used to. Now—" She hesitated. "Well, now I don't know—that is—"

"Yeah."

"Mr. Willett used to come over and help Ethan get in the corn; then Ethan would go back with him and they'd do his field, too. They were quite nice, really," she recalled somewhat wistfully. "Sometimes she'd come over with her husband, and we'd visit while the men were outside."

"Maybe I'll stop in and tell 'em you're home."

"They may not want to see me. They may be like Lulene Davis, you know."

"Maybe, maybe not. At least you'll know."

To combat the awful loneliness, Annie threw herself into putting her house in order. By the time she finally went to bed the first night, she'd exhausted herself by dusting, sweeping, and mopping the parlor and her bedroom. Too tired to dream, she slept soundly until morning. Then, after a breakfast of boiled coffee and dry soda crackers, she started all over again.

Hap Walker had left most of his things there while he made the trip into Veck's Store. Making up a laundry tub with hot water, she pared a bar of lye soap into it, then unrolled his clothes when she unpacked hers. Despite the cold wind blowing down from the north, she had them all washed and pinned on the line well before noon. Then, while her bed linens soaked in one washtub and her dishes in another, she turned her attention to emptying and sorting everything in her chest of drawers.

Going through Ethan's clothing was the worst thing she'd faced so far, but it had to be done. Until she got past that, she couldn't go on. She had to get the finality fixed in her mind. Resigned, she unfolded each shirt, looked it over, then refolded it on the bed, wondering if perhaps Hap Walker might be able to wear them. Or if he'd even want to.

Hap was a strange man, a puzzle to her. Words like kind, tough, bitter, and determined came to mind whenever she thought of him. Just when she'd decided he was perhaps the kindest man she'd known, kinder even than Ethan, she'd see another side of him. Like his remark about being a cripple, the harshness of his judgment of himself. The undeserved disappointment, as though nothing else he'd ever done counted for anything now. All he could see was the limp, and he was too blind to realize it was getting better.

That was like a man, though. A man was raised to think he could do everything, to see himself as a failure if he couldn't. She'd seen that in her father, a successful shop-keeper who'd silently chafed under the boredom of standing behind that counter. In his dreams of glory he'd always seen himself as a lawyer posturing dramatically before a jury. Her mother had never shared that vision, and he'd never tried to live it.

But Hap Walker was different. In his own time he was almost a legend, an Indian fighter, a lawman whose name was as recognized in parts of Texas as Jim Bowie's or Davy Crockett's, not because he won independence for Texas, but because he'd fought to make it safe. Without men like him the place would be empty of ranches and farms, way stations and towns. The way she saw it, he had nothing to be ashamed of, nothing at all.

She set the pile of shirts aside. When he got back, he could try them on and take any that he wanted. The same with the rest of Ethan's clothes. Then she'd know all the work she'd put in them wasn't wasted—and she wouldn't have to look at them anymore. He'd take them with him to the Ybarra.

Her thoughts froze momentarily, and she felt an awful panic. It was odd—she thought she heard a wagon, but he hadn't had time to make the supply trip and get back. Keeping close to the wall and away from the windows, she moved quickly to get the shotgun he'd left for her. Her whole body shaking, she broke it open and checked the load. She had shells in both barrels.

"Miz Bryce! You in there, Miz Bryce?" a man called out.

Her heart pounding so hard she could hear it, she edged to the window and lifted a yellowed curtain. Jim Willett was standing on her porch, and his wife, Mary, was sitting on the buckboard in her front yard. She'd been so lost in thought she hadn't heard them until they were there. Relief washed over her, followed by a new anxiety. What if they'd come just to gawk? What if they looked at her as Lulene Davis had?

"You'd better knock, Jim," Mary reminded him.

Telling herself there wasn't much she could do about what anybody thought of her, Annie smoothed her hair back from her face and went to the door, ready for the worst. Wrenching it open, she managed to force a smile and look Willett in the eye.

"Well, if you ain't a sight for sore eyes! Mary, come here—she's all right!" Grinning at Annie, he pulled off his hat. "Glad to see you home, ma'am."

Behind him, his wife hurried toward the stoop, carrying a basket. "Why, when Captain Walker stopped in to tell us, we couldn't believe our ears! Jim and me figured you were done gone forever, Annie!"

"Hard enough to believe it was Walker," he allowed, taking the basket. Holding it out, he added, "Packed you a mite to eat, ma'am, 'cause he said about all you had was some kind of canned biscuits, and that didn't sound good a-tall."

"Thank you," Annie said, taking it. Afraid she was going to cry, she stepped back. "Come in."

"Better get the rest of the stuff, Jim," Mary reminded him. She stood there for a moment, looking at Annie, then burst into tears herself. "Lordy, but I prayed for this. I been praying ever since it happened, but I never thought—" Unable to go on, the woman threw her arms around Annie. "Welcome home, honey—welcome home," she choked out.

Annie's arms slid around her, embracing her, holding her, hanging on. "Thank you," she whispered. "From the bottom of my heart, thank you, Mary."

Still patting her as though she were a child, the Willett woman assured her, "It's not what I'd like to bring, mind you, but Jim wanted to get right over this morning—said I could fix what you wanted when I got here." Releasing her, she stood back to wipe wet cheeks. "We brung you some chickens. You'll want most of 'em fer laying, but I'm going to wring one of 'em's neck and fry it up for supper. I don't figger them heathens fed you any fried chicken."

"No. Oh, Mary, you don't know how glad I am to see you!"

"Reckon so. If I'd a knowed you was coming home, I'd a been over cleaning the place up, getting it ready fer you. Lawks-a-mercy, but you coulda knocked me over with a feather when Walker said you was home! Now, you just put that food wherever you want it—it's just pork sandwiches, mind you—and I'll get busy. We got a lot of work to do here, Annie, but we'll get it." Her gaze traveled from Annie's face downward, and her smile faded. "Starved you, they did," she decided. "Well, it won't take long to fix that, neither."

"I think I've gained back about half of what I lost."

"Well, you got a ways to go." Mary wiped her streaming eyes again. "I'm so sorry about the kids, Annie. I reckon God's got a special place for that little boy."

"Yes."

Rather than dwell on that, the woman looked past her. "Good, I see you've been busying yourself already. Only thing to do right now—keep busy until you get to where you don't think. Leastwise, that's all that helped me when I lost my boys."

"You lost them?"

Mary nodded. "Diphtheria, both of 'em. Austin caught it first, then Billy—first winter you was gone, Annie. It was real hard, real hard. I ain't over it yet, but—" She patted her stomach shyly. "But after trying hard fer nigh to three years, it looks like God's giving me another chance."

"I'm happy for that. You were a good mother."

"No better'n you." Recovering, Mary Willett moved farther into the room. "I seen those clothes on the line. You been washin' already this morning?"

"Yes."

"Looks like you got this part about in order," Mary murmured approvingly. "I brung a little linseed oil. Soon as I get a rag wet, I'll go over the wood fer you, get it polished up real nice. Then we'll wash the curtains and things, get 'em starched and ironed up. By tonight it'll be like you never left it." Her gaze returned to Annie. "Me 'n' Jim

216

stopped by the church afore we came over to tell the reverend the good news. He'll be spreading the word you're home, so folks'll know to get over and help out."

"Thank you. I'll look forward to seeing everybody."

Mary frowned, then owned, "Well, I wouldn't count on everybody, mind you. There's always some as ain't got any Christian charity, no matter how often they make it to church. But I reckon they ain't worth knowing, anyways."

"I know."

"Now, Annie, you can't think about 'em—they ain't worth wastin' your mind on. There's always some as is so nasty-nice they can't put themselves in anybody else's place. The way I figger it, they got a surprise comin' when they get to them pearly gates upstairs—St. Peter's going to be givin' 'em a one-way ticket down, don't you know?"

"It doesn't matter to me," Annie lied. "I can't worry about what I can't change."

"Exactly. It wasn't easy, mind you, but that's what I finally had to decide after we buried the boys. If I hadn't, I'da gone plumb crazy."

"All right, Mary, where'd you want to put all this stuff?" Jim asked from the door. Looking past her, he told Annie, "She brung darned near ever'thing but the washtub."

"And you woulda thrown that in," his wife reminded him. Turning to Annie, she explained, "It ain't all that much—just things I didn't figger you'd have right now."

"A lot of corn and beans she put up last summer," Jim declared proudly. "Eggs from the layers, bread, round o' cheese, crock o' butter, a little flour to hold you over," he added, ticking them off on his fingers.

"We figgered anything left here was weevily, you know," Mary said quickly.

"I don't know what to say," Annie responded slowly. "I never expected this."

"You want me to turn the hens loose?" he asked.

"I haven't even looked at the henhouse yet."

"I'll see to it. Looks like it's still standing, anyways."

"Ain't you fergettin' something, Jim?" Mary prompted him.

"Huh?"

"You know, in t'other basket."

"Oh."

"Really, this is too much. Hap's gone in to get what I need." Seeing the other woman's smile falter, Annie hastily embraced her. "I'll never be able to repay you for this, never."

"It ain't all that much."

"It's the kindness, Mary. I don't even know what to say."

"You done said thanks, and that's more'n enough."

"Ah-hem." Behind them, Mary's husband cleared his throat. "Reckon this was what you was wantin', ain't it?"

"Well, bring it on over, and let her take a look. Mind you, they ain't much, but I thought they was real purty for what they are." Taking the basket from him, Mary lifted what looked like a small blanket. "Bless me if they ain't sleepin'."

Curious, Annie looked over her shoulder as she reached inside. All she could see was an old pillowcase wrapped around something.

"They're just cats," Jim explained.

"Cats?" she repeated faintly.

"You don't like 'em?"

"Oh, yes."

"There you are . . . come on now," Mary said, lifting a

little black ball of fur. Slate-blue eyes opened and tiny claws came out as the kitten tried to climb her shoulder. Nestling it against her chin, she reached into the basket again, this time to retrieve another almost like it. But as she held the second one up, Annie could see the little white toes. Both had more hair than any cats she'd ever seen. "Now," Mary demanded triumphantly, "ain't they the prettiest little things? Where they came from I don't know."

"That old gray barn cat," Jim said.

"I know that—I was meaning you wouldn't expect 'em to look like this. Look at that fur." Disengaging the one on her shoulder, she held it out to Annie. "Now, you don't have to take 'em—or you can have just one if you want—but I figgered you'd like a little company."

"They're beautiful."

"Both boys, if you was to believe Jim. Like I said, you can have one or both. I was just hatin' to split 'em up. Real unusual, ain't they?"

"Mary, they're just cats," Jim protested.

"Surely you don't want to part with them."

"Oh, he's been complainin' ever since they was born seven weeks ago—says we got too many. Why, if I hadn't stopped him, he'd a drowned 'em."

"You're sure?"

"You want 'em?" Mary asked hopefully.

The one Annie held had its eyes fixed on her face. The long black fur made a circle around its little head, giving it an owlish aspect. It was, without doubt, the prettiest kitten she'd ever seen.

"Of course I want them," she assured the other woman warmly. "They are really beautiful."

"They're just cats," Jim insisted. But as he said it, he was grinning. "Even if they are a mite purty."

"Thank you."

"Well, that's settled, then. While me 'n' Annie's putting things away and doin' what's needed, you'd better go back home and fetch Henry for her."

"Henry?"

"Well, you gotta have milk, and we can spare 'im."

"Oh, now that's too much! I can't take your cow. Really."

"Ain't a cow." Heading for the door again, Willett said succinctly, "Goat."

"You better take 'er. He don't like 'er neither," Mary confided. "You got to keep 'er tied, or she's a-eatin' ever'thing."

"Oh."

"But the milk's good—a little rich, that's all. That's where the cheese I brung came from."

"Oh. I've never milked a goat, but I'm sure I can learn."

"Nothing to it. Just don't let 'er nip you." Taking charge now, Mary headed for the kitchen. "I'd better get started, 'cause he's going to want to head home right after he gets back. 'Course, I aim to make him stay till supper," she confided. "I reckon the fried chicken'll make him hold still that long, anyways."

"I'd like that."

"Be the second time in two days we've et chicken—fixed one fer Captain Walker last night."

"I expect it pleased him."

"Oh, it did. Said he'd been livin' on jerky all the way down from Fort Sill."

"Or at least a lot of it," Annie murmured.

"You oughta seen Jim, honey. I thought he'd plumb pass

out when the man allowed as how he was Hap Walker. You'da thought the pope was callin'—no, it was more'n that, Jim wouldn't give a snap fer no pope. But now Walker, well, that's somethin' else."

"Yes, he is."

"Now, there's a man as they don't make no more. And there he was a-sittin' at my kitchen table. Who'd've ever thought it? 'Course, Jim was disappointed that he wasn't carryin' the gun he killed Big Coyote with."

"No, this is a new model, he said."

"He don't talk much about being a ranger, does he? Why, a body'd think he'd want t'brag about it, but he don't." When Annie said nothing, she turned back to her. "Ain't a hard man to like, is he?"

"No—no, he's not."

"Said he might be stayin' fer Christmas. Be a good thing if he was t' take a shine to you, Annie. Man like that could stop a lot o' talk."

"Or start some."

"You're still a pretty woman, honey. And from the way he was soundin', Jim was thinkin' maybe he was gettin' sweet on you."

"No—at least I hope not. I couldn't bear that." Ignoring the other woman's sharp look, Annie stooped to set the kitten down, then watched as it scampered across the floor after its brother. "They are lively, aren't they?" she murmured, turning the subject away from Walker.

It was dark when Hap came over the hill and saw the lighted windows of the farmhouse. The smell of burning wood wafted upward, sweetening the cold air, welcoming him. As tired as he was, he felt a certain satisfaction at being there, at knowing he'd been able to bring Annie Bryce home. He'd been three years late, but he'd gotten her home where she belonged.

Yeah, he was feeling pretty good about that at least. For the first time since he'd taken that Comanchero bullet, he felt that he'd done something useful. That and making the supply run. She was going to be surprised when she saw he'd gotten back early—and even more surprised when she saw what he'd gotten from trading the oxen.

As he drove down the narrow, overgrown path to the barn, a chicken flew up, startling him—then he remembered. The Willetts had said they had some to spare, and they must have brought it over. Annie ought to feel pretty good about that. At least she'd have somebody to speak to after he left.

He unhitched the team and led them into the darkened barn. Old Red smelled him and raised his head, then went back to eating. It took a lot to bother that horse. The mule, on the other hand, moved skittishly, backing up against the wall. He turned the two draft animals loose in stalls, then stumbled into the pile of hay. He guessed Willett must've done that, too. Unable to see the pitchfork, he scooped up two arms full and threw them over the gates. That'd have to hold 'em till morning, when he'd do a better job of it.

Suddenly, he felt a tug on his coat, and the hairs on his neck stood on end. His hand eased downward to his holster, then he spun around, gun drawn.

"What the hell—?"

Something had a hold on the coat, and it wasn't turning loose. He struck it with his hand, hitting a knot on its bony skull, but it held on. It was some kind of animal.

Feeling like an idiot, he sheathed the gun and felt in his pocket for a match. Striking it, he looked downward into a pair of round black eyes. It was a goat, and it was trying to eat through the buffalo hide.

"You damned near got yourself killed, you know that?" he muttered, backing out of its reach.

Retracing his steps back by the flatbed wagon, he made his way to the house. "Annie!" he shouted. "It's Hap, I'm back!"

It didn't take her long to get the door open, and she was obviously glad to see him. He took off his hat as he stepped inside, utterly unprepared for the change in the place.

"Whew, you've been busy," he said in an understatement.

"The Willetts came over, and Mary spent most of yesterday helping me—no, she spent most of the day *getting* everything done," she explained. "Here, let me find a place for your coat."

"Yeah," he murmured, shrugging out of it for her. "That varmint you got out there tried to eat it."

"You must mean Henry."

"The damned goat."

"Henry. It's a milk goat."

"Henry?" His eyebrow lifted.

"It probably should have been Henrietta, but I think it was mis-sexed when it was born. Anyway, it's obviously a female now." Hanging his coat on the peg by the door, she added, "I didn't think you'd be back before tomorrow, if then."

"Yeah, well, I got rid of the oxen, so I made better time. Got rid of the wagon, too. Fellow over at Vest's wanted 'em." When she said nothing, he prompted her. "Well, don't you want to know how I got back?" A corner of his mouth fought to smile. "Go ahead, ask me."

"You rode a horse."

"With supplies? You still haven't learned to read minds, have you?"

"All right, if you sold the wagon and oxen, how did you get here?"

"I didn't say I sold 'em, Annie." He lost the battle and grinned. "Traded 'em for a team of draft horses—and a buckboard you can manage."

"Draft horses!"

"Yeah. I was talking to the Willett fellow, and he allowed as how he'd be willing to help you farm the place, but all he had was a couple of plug plow horses. I figured between you, you could use these. Pretty fine pair, and you can pull the buckboard with 'em."

Her eyes widened, then she looked away. "You didn't need to do that, Hap."

"I know I didn't. But maybe I wanted to. Maybe I kinda felt like I owed you."

"Owed me? For what?"

"Hell, Annie, I didn't need 'em—and it saved me a trip back down to San Angelo."

"But you don't owe me anything, Hap—I owe you! I've been nothing but a burden to you! *I owe you!*"

"If I'd done my job to start with, you wouldn't be in this fix."

"No. I can't take all this from you, I can't."

Hiding his disappointment, he shrugged. "I'm not making another trip back to trade 'em again, Annie."

"But—"

Moving past her, he dropped into a rocking chair close

to the stove. "I'll bring in your things after while, but right now I'd like to sit a spell. Maybe eat a bit, if you got anything you don't have to fix," he added, looking up at her.

There was something boyish in his face, in that tousled hair of his, that made it difficult to be angry with him. "I'll pay you back, I swear it," she muttered. "All right," she conceded, coming to terms with what he'd done, "and you can have whatever you want. There's cold chicken, bread, and beans—or I can fry you an egg."

"I don't care." He leaned back lazily in the chair. "I'm not a hard man to please, Annie. Just don't put yourself out."

"Then pick something." In spite of herself, she found herself smiling. "I'm not a mind reader, remember?"

"What kind of chicken?"

"Fried. We had it last night, but it's been kept cold outside."

"Drumsticks?"

She shook her head. "White meat."

"Suits me. With beans. I don't mind 'em cold. I reckon I've eaten a full ton of 'em like that."

"They're green beans, Hap."

"Oh. Well, I'm not above trying it, anyway."

"I'll heat them. It's the least I can do for you," she decided.

He was tired, damned tired, but he was glad he'd pushed himself to get back. He closed his eyes for a moment, then opened them to look around the room. Savoring the smell of freshly polished wood, of the freshly washed curtains, of the hot iron stove, he felt a pang of regret. This was the way it was supposed to be. This was the way a man was supposed to want to live.

As tired as she was, she couldn't sleep. Her house was in order, her pantry full, and none of that meant much. In the stillness of night, lying in the bed she'd once shared with Ethan, she felt a stifling, overwhelming loneliness. She didn't want to live like this. She wanted her life back as it had been. She wanted the impossible. At the very least she wanted Susannah.

Finally, unable to stand it any longer, she rolled out of bed and reached for her old flannel wrapper. Tying it around her, she felt with her foot along the ice-cold floor for her knit slippers, then bent to retrieve them. Shivering, she made her way in the dark to the parlor. There was a faint glow showing beneath the door. Opening it a crack, she peered inside. She could see the lighted kerosene lamp on the table, and feel the warmth of the stove.

Surely Walker wasn't still up, not at this time of night. It had to be well past midnight, she guessed. Moving cautiously, she crept into the room, then saw him in the rocking chair. By the looks of it, he'd fallen asleep there. She started to retreat.

"Oh!" She jumped, startled, as a kitten ran across her foot.

"One of 'em get you?" Hap asked, sitting up.

"I thought it was a mouse."

"Fast little devils, I'll give 'em that," he murmured.

"I didn't know you were still up."

"Yeah. I was just sitting here by the fire, thinking about going to bed. I figured you were asleep a long time ago."

"I couldn't sleep," she admitted. "I was going to warm myself some milk. I don't suppose you want any, do you?"

"Goat's milk? I don't think so." He held up a long-necked bottle. "This works better, anyway."

"Liquor?"

"Whiskey."

"You drink quite a lot, don't you?"

He appeared to consider it for a moment, then shrugged. "I don't know. I guess you could say so."

"I would."

"Man's got to have some vices, or life's not worth living. What about you, Annie—you got any vices?"

"You're drunk, aren't you?"

"No." He heaved himself up from the chair and walked toward her, holding the bottle out. "Don't waste your time on goat's milk, Annie. You want to forget? Try this. You can drown a lot in a bottle."

"I don't want to." Certain he'd had too much to drink, she offered, "If I made coffee, would you drink it?"

"No. I told you, I'm still stone-cold sober." Holding the bottle within inches of her face, he showed her. "See, most of it's still in there. What made you think I was drunk, anyway?"

"I guess I just sort of expected it."

"He drink?"

"Who?"

The hand that held the bottle gestured toward the piano. "Him—your husband."

"No—not very often, anyway. I never saw him drunk."

" 'Course not. He had you, didn't he?"

"I don't think that had much to do with it."

"Sure it did. Happy men don't drink. Ask me, I can tell you. I used to be a happy man, you know."

"Until you got shot?"

"I don't know—maybe. No, it was before then," he decided. "Here, you want to sleep? Make yourself a toddy."

"I wouldn't know how. Come, on, I'll get a pan and boil some coffee."

"Cookstove's cold. You want me to make a fire for you?"

"I can boil it in here."

"I kinda like the kitchen. There's something nice about sitting at a table in the middle of the night," he said. "I'll make a fire."

"All right. And I'll make coffee."

"Didn't I ever tell you I don't like the stuff?"

"Actually, I think you did," she remembered. "You put three spoons of sugar in it at the Sprengers' house."

"Yeah. Anybody that ever traveled with Clay learned to hate it. He makes it like mud." His eyes traveled over her, taking in the pale hair that fell over her shoulders, the faded flannel wrapper, the high-necked nightgown showing at the top. "You got no business out here with me. You know that, don't you?"

"I don't know where I'd go. It's my house," she reminded him. "All right, since you don't care for coffee, how about tea?"

"Tea," he repeated blankly.

"Well, it's not goat's milk—and it's not coffee."

"Yeah, why not?"

He followed her into the kitchen and set the bottle on the table. While she lit a lantern, he turned his attention to the cookstove. "Still some coals, so it's not dead—just limber."

"Limber?"

"Passed out, but revivable."

She watched him go to work on the fire, thinking he didn't really seem intoxicated, even though his behavior was rather odd. He was in some sort of mood, she decided, and more than likely it had to do with his leg. Men just didn't deal well with their ailments. Unlike most women she knew, they felt having anything wrong with their bodies somehow diminished them. And it had to be even harder for somebody who'd lived the way he had.

It was cold in the kitchen, but he didn't seem to notice. She sat there, rubbing her arms, waiting for the heat. Finally, she got up from the table and moved around, setting out the metal tea container, the pot, the cups, and the sugar bowl. Then she dipped water from the bucket into the kettle.

"Is it going?" she asked hopefully.

"Yeah."

He opened the flue, then fanned the cookstove door. She could see the flames. Using a knife, she pried the lid off the tea, then looked inside. After more than three years, it was so dry it was brittle. Hoping hot water would revive it, she put three spoonfuls into the china pot.

"Would you like bread and jam with this?"

"I don't care." He took the kettle and set it on the top

229

of the stove, then sat down at the table. "I didn't know you could keep jam that long," he said, eying the jar.

"Mary—Mrs. Willett—brought it over. We threw out everything on the shelves while you were gone."

"Even the meat biscuits?"

"She took them home to try. When I told her you'd paid a dollar for the tin, she didn't want to see it go to waste."

"I don't know, Annie," he murmured, shaking his head. "That may be the last you ever see of 'em. You may be plowing that field by yourself."

"I warned her, Hap, I swear I did. She seemed to think she could doctor it up enough that they could eat it."

The light from the lantern was casting a moving halo over her hair, giving her an almost otherworldly beauty. As he looked at her, he forgot Amanda Ross, Clay McAlester, and just about everything else. She was still too young, too pretty, to let herself just wither up. No matter how bad it had been, no matter what had happened to her, she couldn't be dead inside. There still had to be life in her. And right now he wished more than anything he could be the man to find it for her.

"Is something the matter, Hap?"

"Huh? No."

"You had an odd look on your face."

"Did I?"

"Yes."

"I guess I was thinking what a nice place you've got here. That's the way it's supposed to be, you know. A man, a woman—a house, a couple of kids," he mused.

"Yes. But sometimes it doesn't work out that way—at least not like it ought to."

"I guess I'll always wonder what I missed out on. At least you had it for a little while, you know."

"Not nearly long enough." To change the subject, she said abruptly, "Day after tomorrow, it's Christmas."

"I know. Christmas doesn't mean all that much to me, Annie."

"No."

"It was different when Claude and my other brothers were around. We had a lot of good times. Then after the war Ma died, and there didn't seem to be much sense in it." He fell silent for a moment, then added soberly. " 'Course, when I found Clay, he was still a kid, but he was about as heathen as a body could get. Hard to celebrate the birth of Jesus with a kid that believes in wolves that talk to him.'

"Even now?"

"Oh, not now. I reckon they'll have a real celebration down at the Ybarra. Nothing like a wife and a kid coming along to make a believer out of you." His mouth twisted wryly. "Hell, he even turned Catholic for her."

"She must be quite a woman."

"Yeah. She is."

Deciding the water must surely be hot, Annie rose and took the kettle from the cookstove. Carrying it to the table, she poured the steaming water into the teapot, then closed the lid. As she put the kettle back, she heard him say, "You're quite a woman yourself, Annie." She froze, then told herself he didn't mean anything by it. All he was doing was comparing her to Clay McAlester's wife, and she'd brought that on herself.

Picking up the teapot, she poured a small amount into

one of the cups to check the color. "It's pretty weak," she decided.

"That's all right. I aim to doctor it up."

"You'll just have sugared water," she warned him.

"Maybe not. Just fill it halfway."

"That's all?"

"Yeah. That's enough," he said, stopping her. Leaning across the table, he retrieved the sugar bowl and dipped out two spoons. "Ought to be enough," he decided.

"I'd think so, anyway—for no more than that."

"Yeah." He picked up the bottle, then added enough whiskey to bring the mixture to within a half inch of the brim. "I'll let you know if I like it." Taking a sip, he held it in his mouth, savoring it. "Not half-bad. Want to try it?"

"No."

"Suit yourself."

"I will."

"You're a hard woman to understand—you know that, don't you?"

She felt a measure of relief. "I expect I am. Most of us are."

"Here . . ." He poured part of her tea back into the pot, then before she could stop him, he'd splashed whiskey into the cup. "Live before you die, Annie. Go on, it won't hurt you." As she tried to push it away, he covered her hand, holding it. "It'll make you sleep, Annie. It'll make you forget." Releasing her, he leaned back. "What do you have to lose? If you don't like it, throw it out."

It seemed almost reasonable. Finally, she nodded. Carrying it to her lips, she took a tiny sip, then made a face "Ugh!"

"Here." Leaning forward again, he handed her the sugar. "Put some of this in it."

Sweetened, it wasn't bad. And it was warm, almost comforting once it hit her stomach. By the time she'd finished the cup, the atmosphere in the kitchen was pleasant, mellow, with the smell of steam, the heat from the stove.

He was feeling it, too. He'd done it only to help her, he told himself, and yet as he watched the tension ebb from her body, as he saw the wariness leave her eyes, he was intensely aware of his own desire. And yet he knew he had no right to touch her, to push her into something she didn't want. She'd hate him for it.

"Think you could sleep now?" he asked in a voice not his own.

"I don't know—maybe."

"Want a little more?"

Not wanting to return to the loneliness of her bedroom, she hesitated. "Just a little," she finally decided.

He poured it for her, added the whiskey, then leaned back to watch her, his expression lazy. "We're a real pair, Annie—a real pair."

"How's that?" she asked, her gaze meeting his over the cup.

"We're both crippled. Only you can see it on me."

"But you're getting better. You're getting well."

"Am I? If I am, I sure as hell can't tell it."

The way the light hit his face, he didn't look anything like his thirty-seven years. With that tousled hair and almost sleepy blue eyes, he seemed more like a little boy in need of comforting. Her heart went out to him.

"You've got a lot of living left in you, Hap," she said

softly. "You're not done yet. You haven't made half your mark on this world."

His mouth was dry as he watched her, and he wanted to see her move, to take in the grace of her slender body. "You're running out of tea. Would you like some more hot water?"

"I can get it." She rose unsteadily, and the effect of the whiskey hit her as she turned toward the stove. She caught the edge of the table as the room tilted, then waited. "Whoo," she managed. "It's the liquor, isn't it?"

"Probably. Making you giddy?"

"Yes." Seeing the humor of being tipsy in her own kitchen, she giggled. "I feel downright silly, Hap— downright silly."

"Anybody ever tell you how pretty you are when you laugh?" Even as he said it, it sounded stupid to his ears, but he couldn't help himself. She *was* about as lovely a woman as he'd ever seen. And he was feeling the effect of her even more than that of the whiskey. "You ought to laugh more." With every inch of his body acutely aware of what he wanted, he stood up behind her. "Annie," he said thickly, "you're not dead, and neither am I."

She turned around at that, and as she looked up, her breath caught in her chest. He was too close, and with the hot stove at her back, there was nowhere to go. She stood there, almost paralyzed, as his finger traced the edge of the flannel ruffle at her neck. The sleepiness was gone from his blue eyes, replaced by open desire. As he bent his head to hers, she could feel the heat of his breath against her cheek.

"You're beautiful, Annie," he murmured huskily.

Her throat constricting, she closed her eyes at the

234

warmth of his lips touching hers. His arms slid around her shoulders, drawing her brittle body against his. She felt a wave of panic rising within her, possessing her even as he kissed her, his tongue teasing her lips, seeking the depths of her mouth. For an awful moment she was drowning, but as her hands came up to fight him, he left her mouth to whisper hungrily against her ear, "Let me take the pain away, Annie. Let me make you whole. I can make you forget, Annie."

A wrenching sob broke free, sending a convulsive shudder through her, as she returned his embrace for a moment. Then she pulled away, leaving him bewildered. "No!" she cried, ducking beneath his arm. "Don't touch me—don't touch me!"

Before he could stop her, she'd run from the kitchen. He stood there, trying to master his still raging desire, then went after her. By the time he reached her bedroom door, he could hear her weeping hysterically. Disappointment warred with shame, and shame won as he listened to her. Subdued now, he felt an intense need to comfort her.

"Annie . . . he said gently, approaching her bed.

She way lying facedown, her head buried in her pillow, her shoulders shaking so hard the whole bed shook. Feeling lost, helpless, he sat on the edge of the feather mattress and leaned over her.

"Annie . . . Annie . . ." His hand smoothed her tangled hair over the flannel wrapper. "I'm sorry."

The apology had no effect on her. It was as though she hadn't even heard it, as though she didn't realize he was touching her. She was somewhere he couldn't reach, and yet he had to try. He sat there, stroking her shoulder without passion. as though she were a child. His desire gone, he was completely sober.

"I guess I had too much to drink, Annie. Believe me, I never intended to scare you. I wanted to love you, Annie, not to hurt you."

It seemed like forever, but the crying finally stopped, and she lay quietly beneath his hand. Now there was a dead, empty silence within the room, broken only when he sighed.

"Look, I don't blame you for not wanting me," he said finally. "If I'd had any sense, I'd have known it was too soon. Hell, I did know, but I was looking at you, wanting to think you could look twice at me." Unable to put his own loneliness into words, he straightened up, then stood. "Well, I just want you to know it won't happen again— that's all."

She waited until he was nearly out of the room before she turned over. "No," she said, her voice breaking, "it isn't you—it's me." As he turned back to face her, she swallowed, then nodded. "You're not a cripple," she whispered. "I am."

"Yeah, I know."

"I don't want to be like this, Hap."

"You got a long time to be alone."

"I don't want that, either. I'd give anything to start over."

"Yeah." He squared his shoulders, then exhaled heavily. "Good night, Annie. If I'm not here when you get up, I reckon I'll be on my way to the Ybarra."

"You don't have to go. You can still stay for Christmas."

"No. You aren't the first woman I've made a damned fool of myself over, but at least I've got a rule about it— it's never the same woman twice."

The door closed behind him, shutting her in darkness. As she lay down again, she felt utterly lost. And when he left, she was going to be utterly alone. All she'd have left would be her dream of finding Susannah, and she wasn't sure that was enough to sustain her. But it had to be.

It was a long time before she slept, and just as she was about to leave the conscious world, she felt tiny steps coming across the covers. And in the silence of night a small, furry body settled against her shoulder, purring loudly. Her hand crept to stroke the long, silky fur, gaining the reward of a sandpaper tongue on her neck. Telling herself it was enough, she gathered the animal close. And yet when her mind wandered again in the netherworld before sleep, it was Hap Walker's voice that haunted her.

Let me take the pain away, Annie. Let me make you whole.

If only it was that easy. If only she could have let him. But that part of her life was over. For now. Forever.

Spring came early at the Ybarra-Ross Ranch, with temperatures reaching well over eighty by mid-March. That was one of the things about Texas—if a man didn't like the weather in one part, he could travel a hundred miles and find something different. And Hap was about as restless as he'd ever been in his life. He was more than ready to travel. Somewhere. Anywhere.

Right now it was looking like it'd either be Blanco or maybe Karnes County. Both places had offered him a sheriff's job, Blanco at forty dollars a month, with a place to live behind the jail, Karnes at sixty-five, but he'd have to find his own lodging. Blanco County lay in the hill country—with hot weather, rough ground, and big stock ranches. Karnes had Helena, a tough town situated near the Chihuahua Trail and the San Antonio–Indianola Road, filled with cowboys, drifters, gamblers, and gunfighters. For a lot of them life in Helena was short and cheap. He knew that firsthand—he'd been there.

As soon as Amanda had the baby, he'd feel that he could leave Clay and get on with his own life. Clay wouldn't much like it, but Hap was thinking about taking a long, hard look at Helen's offer. His last letter from the town council there had indicated they might be willing to go another ten dollars a month "to engage someone of your reputation." It wasn't much pay for a man's life, but he didn't need the money. What he needed was the action.

It'd be different being a county sheriff, with just a county seat and a little land to police. Facing rowdies in streets and saloons required different skills than tracking Indians and outlaws through canyons and deserts. But he hadn't seen anybody he couldn't face down yet, and when he did, he figured then it'd be time to retire. Not now, not while he still had his nerve.

It'd be a little out of his way, but he was going to stop at San Saba just to see how Annie Bryce fared, nothing more than that. It was funny—she'd been on his mind a lot lately, more than he'd expected. He guessed he wanted to know if she was making it on the farm, if Willett was getting her corn planted as he'd promised. No, he was lying to himself again. He wanted to see if she was as pretty as he remembered, if she still had the same effect on him. Or if it'd be like Amanda.

He was over Amanda now, had been ever since he got back to the Ybarra. He'd come in between Christmas and New Year's, expecting to feel like the odd man out, but he hadn't. He'd looked at her, admired her for what she was—Clay's wife—and felt nothing other than relief. That was the way it ought to be, and it was. Maybe he'd look at Annie, and he wouldn't feel anything there, either.

"You've turned awful sober on me, Hap."

"Huh?"

"You're not yourself."

He looked up, seeing Clay. "Man can't raise hell all the time," he responded noncommittally.

"Something's eating on you."

"No."

"You haven't had a bottle in weeks."

"That ought to tell you something—if something was eating on me, I'd be damned drunk. Besides, look who's talking. You don't drink much yourself."

"Amanda and I don't want you to leave," Clay said quietly. "That's what's on your mind, isn't it?"

"I'm not much of a cattleman," Hap muttered.

"You don't have to be. I'm not asking you to be."

"That's about all there is around here. Not much need for anything else."

"With me over at Austin so much, I need you to kind of look after Amanda and the baby when it gets here. You're the closest thing to kin we've got, Hap."

"She does all right on her own, Clay. She doesn't need me—and you don't either. You just want me underfoot where you can keep an eye on me." Hap heaved himself up from the chair and walked to the window. Looking out over the wide brick-paved courtyard to the hazy purple mountains in the distance, all he saw was Ybarra land. "You don't need to take care of me, Clay."

"You're like a father to me, Hap."

"I'm nine years older, that's all."

"You can't go back to the rangers—it's a young man's job. Hell, *I'm* too old for it. You paid your dues. You spent your time in the saddle."

"I'm not going back to the rangers," Hap muttered. "If that's what you're afraid of, I'm done with 'em."

"There's something going on, I can see it. Every day you've been riding out into the desert, practicing your aim—practicing your draw."

"Yeah."

"And all this mail. You never were much to write when I was a kid. All the time I was in Chicago, I think I heard from you twice."

"I figured Miss McAlester was talking good care of you."

"I missed you back then. I didn't like Chicago." Clay came up behind him. "Two more letters came for you today—one's from Rios."

"That where you got the notion I was going back to the rangers?"

"No. I've seen this coming ever since Christmas."

Still staring outside, watching the sleepy activity of several Mexican ranch hands, Hap exhaled heavily. "You know, I never tried to rein you in, Clay. Even when you were a wild youngster, and I was taking a lot of griping about it, I never tried to rein you in. I always kinda figured you had to find out who you were and what you wanted to do."

"Yeah."

"And when you wanted to follow me, I never tried to stop you, even though I wanted to. Every time you left out, I knew it might be the last time I'd see you, but I didn't figure I had the right to tell you you couldn't do it."

"No."

" 'Way I look at it, you think the boot's on the other foot now. You think maybe I'm not what I used to be, that I'll go out and get myself killed, don't you?"

241

"I worry about that leg, Hap. It damned near got you twice, you know."

"The leg's fine. All I got's a limp left. And that don't bother me like it used to. I reckon I've come to accept it, just like I was born with it." Hap swung around to face him. "If you care about somebody, you don't hogtie 'im, you know. If he gets careless and gets himself killed, you got a right to mourn 'im, but that's about it. Now, have we got that straight between us?"

That he was right didn't make it any easier. "Yeah, I guess so."

Hap's eyes narrowed as he studied the younger man's face. "You understand, don't you? You aren't just wanting me around because you're here, are you?"

"No."

"You never want to go back out yourself?"

Clay found himself looking away. "Yeah, sometimes I do. I guess there's always going to be that wildness, that meanness in me. Sometimes I just ride out to those mountains and sit up there, looking up toward the Comancheria."

"Then it wasn't fair to marry her."

"That why you never married?" Clay countered.

"No. I was always looking at the wrong woman."

"I've got no real regrets, Hap. If it was a choice between anything out there and Amanda, she'd win. When I get real restless, I just look at her, and I know I don't want anything else."

"Well, I don't have that. I'm going back out, Clay. I've got me a job lined up, and I'm inclined to take it. I may not walk straight, but I can sure as hell still shoot straight." As Clay looked up, he nodded. "Yeah, they're wanting a sheriff down at Helena. It's not the rangers, but at least it's in the right line of work."

"I see."

"I don't need your blessing to take it."

"I thought you wanted to farm once. You even saved your money for it."

"Four thousand dollars. And I've still got it."

"If you need more—"

"Clay"—Hap's mouth twisted wryly—"how the hell do you think I'm going to walk behind a damned plow?"

"The same way you're going to walk down the street with that Peacemaker strapped to your leg. But there's no talking to you, is there? Here—here's your damned mail," Clay said, handing him the two pieces. "I should have known you weren't going to stay. Rios said you'd be worse than me when it came to settling down."

Hap waited until he was nearly out of the room. "I'm sorry," he said simply.

Clay swung around, and his smile warmed his blue eyes. "*Vaya con Dios,* Hap. I'm giving you what you gave me—but when it's done, and you can't complain about it, I'll be dragging your dead carcass back for burial at the Ybarra. I want you to know that."

"I guess that's fair enough."

"Amanda's planning on you being here for the baby, you know."

"I don't know about that," Hap responded evasively. "He'll get here without my help, anyway."

"It's the closest you'll ever come to being a grandpa."

"Maybe. But I'll tell you one thing: If you name that kid after me, I'll disown the both of you."

"I don't think that's on the list, Hap. If it's a boy, it'll be John—probably John Ross, for her father."

"Good. That's got a real nice ring to it. I always thought Horace sounded like a damned sissy."

As Clay's footsteps receded on the hard stone floor, Hap turned back to the window. It was a mighty big place the Ybarra–Ross. Clay'd done well enough for himself that Hap could leave him on his own now.

Almost as an afterthought, he remembered the letters in his hand. Looking down, he saw Rios' handwriting, but it was the other envelope that intrigued him. Crudely printed in a hodgepodge of small and capital letters, addressed to HEP WOKKER at the EBARA–ROSE, it stood out. Thinking it probably came from an illiterate cohort from his days at the state police, he ripped it open and read it.

Deer Mr. Wokker,

Jim sed I shud writ becuz we ar worrit abowt Annie Brice. The stade wudent hep her so shes gowin bak to th Injuns to luk fer her liddle gril. She pud a ad in th papr fer hep, but twar no anser thet we no uf. She wonts tu go annyhow. We wuz hopin yu cud hep owt and mebe git Cly Malster to do hit fer her. She tol Jim she wuz leevin cum th ind of th munth. Hop you ken hep.

It was signed simply "Mary Willett." If she couldn't spell anything else, the woman at least got her own name right. Scarcely believing what he'd just sounded out, Hap read the remarkable message again. If the Willett woman could be believed, Annie Bryce had made up her mind to go back to the Comanches rather than abandon her daughter to them. It wasn't rational, but he could see her doing it.

"Damn!" He balled the letter up and started to throw it across the room, then smoothed it out for yet another look. "She's lost her mind! She's lost her damned mind! How the hell does she think she's getting there?" he shouted to the empty room.

The Willetts wanted him to ask Clay. They were wanting Clay to ride up into the Comancheria on a wild goose chase for a kid that was probably already dead. Well, he wasn't going to ask him. Not now, not when he had his own baby coming. No, Clay had too much to lose. His days of riding off into the desert to track anybody were over.

Hap had to talk her out of it. He'd offer to take her to Austin himself so she could appeal to the legislature. He'd offer to approach the rangers for her. Anything to keep her from getting herself killed. Jesus, what could she be thinking of? But even as the thought went through his mind, he already had the answer. She knew time was running out, that she couldn't wait for a bunch of bureaucrats to decide to help her.

She'd been desperate enough to try to hire somebody, Mary said, but she hadn't got any takers. Hell, a man'd be a fool to sign on for something like that, no matter how much she offered. Getting caught by Comanches was a hard way to die, the hardest way he could think of. There wasn't enough money on earth to make a man risk that willingly. And yet she was going back to face them herself, after all they'd done to her.

This time when he stared out the window, he didn't see the courtyard, the vast expanse of sun-baked land. He didn't even see the distant mountains. He saw a pale slip of a woman, her pretty face framed with a halo of wheat-gold hair. And he was lying beside her in that wagon, holding her while she sobbed with remembered terror. He was in her kitchen, wanting her, reliving the feel of her lips yielding ever so briefly to his.

"You're a damned fool, Annie," he said softly. "A damned fool."

And from some corner of his mind, a voice spoke to him. *Not nearly as much as you, Hap Walker, because you won't let her go alone. No matter what it takes, you won't let her go alone.*

The end of the month. That didn't give him very long to get over there, to try to talk her out of it. And if he couldn't, he didn't even want to think about it.

"Bad news, Hap?"

He spun around to face Clay. "No," he lied. "But I just found out I've got a little unfinished business over on the San Saba. Reckon I'll be leaving out early in the morning." Expecting an argument, he added defensively, "Nothing much. I'll leave word where you can reach me over there. I'll be wanting to know about the baby."

"Yeah." Clay hesitated, then ran his fingers through his short blond hair. "I, uh, I just came back to say I'm sorry, Hap. I guess I know how you felt every time you sent me out."

"Most of the time I felt pretty good about it. You never let me down—never."

"You taught me a lot."

"I hope so."

The younger man shifted uneasily from one booted foot

to the other. "I guess I just thought if I was settled down, it was time you were, too."

"I know."

"Hell, if you don't get your head blown off over there, Helena might be a good place for a man like you. Maybe when you're not trying to cover half of Texas, you'll have time to find yourself a woman. They have a way of settling down men like us, Hap. Maybe you'll have a Horace, Jr."

"You're never going to let me live that down, are you? I should've never told her."

"Yeah, I always thought Hap stood for a family name," Clay said, grinning. "You know, something like Hapgood maybe. When you weren't around, Rios and I used to guess a lot about it."

"Well, now you know," Hap retorted. "Just don't expect me to answer to it. And don't go putting it on my tombstone, either. I won't rest easy under Horace—be like being buried in somebody else's grave. Hell, what am I talking about? More'n likely I'll be burying *you*." He hesitated, sobering. "Tell you what—I haven't had a good drink in nigh to three months. Tonight me and you'll split some good whiskey for all the good times. Wouldn't seem right anyway if I was leaving a place without taking a hangover with me."

"Sure. What did Rios want?"

"Huh? Oh, I don't know. I didn't get around to reading it. Guess I'll take a look at it now." Sliding his thumbnail under the flap, Hap pried it up, then pulled out two sheets of paper. Giving them a cursory glance, he murmured, "Well, I'll be damned."

"What?"

"Here, you read it. You ought to get a real good laugh out of this."

Taking the letter, Clay read aloud.

Hap,

I thought I'd better warn you before I sent him your way, but there's a man been asking about you. I guess he's been talking to some of your friends, by the sound of it. Anyway, he's wanting to publish a book of your memoirs (hope I spelled that right). Maybe I should have said your life story, *amigo*.

He says it ought to appeal to folks back East, what with you being a war hero, Indian fighter, gunfighter, army scout, and Texas Ranger. Funny I didn't realize you'd done all that until I got to thinking about it, and I guess that's right. I think you ought to do it, just to set the record straight, because the way he's talking, if you don't, he's going to write about you anyway.

His name is Woods—Elmo P. Woods, but don't call him Elmo. He goes by E.P. Anyway, unless I hear different, I'm going to tell him how to find you. I expect he'll be out sometime in April.

I just got back from El Paso, and would have stopped in at the Ybarra, but I had a prisoner with me, and I was afraid Clay might kill him. You can tell him I caught Sanchez-Torres' brother coming across the border from New Mexico.

The service isn't the same without the two of you. I'm almost missing Clay's coffee. I know I miss swapping stories with you. The kid I've got with me now doesn't have any.

"As ever, your friend, R.R." Clay handed it back, grinning. "He's right, you ought to do it. Guess this means you'll be putting off leaving a little while, anyway."

Hap shook his head. "If he wants a story bad enough, he can catch up to me. Besides, I don't know that I want to be in any dime novel. Might give folks the wrong idea about why I did the things I've done."

"Or the right one."

"I'm not much of a hero, Clay. I always just tried to do what I could to make things right. Sometimes it worked out, sometimes it didn't." Hap looked down at Rios' letter. "I don't reckon folks'd want to read that, do you?"

"I would. I'd save a copy for my son, if I have one. I'd want him to read it someday. Then maybe he could understand me a little easier. I've always tried to be like you, Hap."

The affection in the younger man's voice was almost more than Hap could bear. Rather than acknowledge it, he pocketed the letter, muttering, "Hell, I'm not done living yet. How the dickens am I supposed to know how everything's going to turn out? Somewhere out there there's probably a bullet getting ready to write the final chapter."

"You don't have to go."

"Yeah, I do. But I'll be seeing you at supper, and then there's that drink afterward I'll be holding you to. Later, when I'm old and gray and cantankerous, I'll be back here boring your kids with my stories. Drive 'em plumb crazy, having to listen to me."

"I'd like that, Hap. See you at supper."

As Hap started toward his room at the other end of the sprawling house, he felt immensely relieved. He and Clay had come to an understanding, and that made leaving a whole lot easier. If he never made it back, they'd have that last bottle to remember. For a moment he paused, thinking of Clay's kid, knowing he might never see him. Maybe he'd start that book, even if he never got a chance to finish it. It'd at least be something to leave to Clay's boy.

The San Saba River twisted and meandered through the pretty, peaceful valley. It was benign now, nothing like that September day when he'd found it flooded. As he splashed across Peg Leg's Crossing, he couldn't help thinking about that, remembering the awful exhaustion, the terrible hopelessness of knowing he'd failed. He felt a whole lot different this time.

There was a real anticipation, an exhilaration at the thought of seeing Annie again. For a hundred miles he'd thought of nothing else, and now he was nearly there. As Old Red cleared the bank, Hap reined in and slid to the ground. He'd been in the saddle four days, and he didn't want to ride in on her looking like a damned saddle tramp and smelling like a polecat.

After he tied the horse in a stand of chaparral, he stripped down buck naked and, carrying a chunk of lye soap, he eased his body into the river. The water was cold as he ducked under it, then came up. Thoroughly wet, he soaped himself from head to foot, then tossed the bar onto the bank. A few more quicks dunks, and he crawled out, shaking himself like a dog.

Letting the hot air dry his skin, he filled his pan with water, positioned his mirror on his saddle, and lathered his face. *It's a waste of time. She's going to think you're a rough-looking cuss, anyway.* Yeah, but there was no sense going in looking any worse than he had to. He paused to study his face in the mirror, wondering if the mustache made him look older. Deciding it did, he got rid of it. The way he looked at it, he needed every bit of help he could get. For good measure, he splashed on some of the lilac water he'd bought at Fort Richardson. Given the heat, he probably needed it.

The hair he couldn't do much about. When wet, it lay in ringlets against his head. Sighing, he took his comb from the saddlebag and tried to stretch the curls out, to slick them down into the hated waves. He'd meant to get some Harrison's Hair Balm to fasten it down with, but none of the places he'd stopped had any. So it was just going to have to do what it wanted to, he guessed. It had a mind of its own, anyway.

Giving up, he pulled on clean clothes, stowed his gear, and swung back into the saddle. Annie Bryce might not be impressed, but he'd got himself all gussied up for her. Now all he had to do was persuade her she wanted to give the folks in Austin another try before she took off for the Comancheria.

Knowing it would be awhile before she came back, if ever, Annie hoed the weeds from the flower bed on Ethan's grave. She wanted to at least leave it looking nice. Kneeling to brush away the last of them, she poked the pointed end of a trowel into the ground she'd softened the night before with water. Then she carefully separated the uprooted wildflowers she'd gathered, plugging each plant into a hole. It was something she had to do, in case she didn't make it home. At least they'd reseed themselves, and there'd be something pretty there to mark the place.

Satisfied with her handiwork, she stood up and dusted her dirty hands on the apron covering her blue gingham dress. Well, that was that. Now, as soon as Jim Willett came to get the cats, the goat, and the chickens, she'd be ready to make the trip into town for provisions.

Standing back, she faced the wooden cross the rangers had placed under the tree. In black paint Hap Walker had printed, ETHAN BRYCE, HUSBAND AND FATHER, D. SEPT, 1870.

"I'm going back for Susannah, Ethan," she said softly. "I'm going back for our little girl. I know she's alive, Ethan, I can feel it."

"Annie! Annie Bryce!"

Startled, she whirled around, her heart in her throat. And for a moment she didn't know whether to laugh or cry. Riding that big roan horse, Hap Walker was coming across the field. Gathering her skirts, she ran to meet him, then stopped self-consciously just short of the pen fence. Her first inclination was to hide her hands. Instead, she pushed her damp hair back from her face and waited. He swung down and walked toward her.

His memory hadn't done her justice. She wasn't skinny now, and a few months of good food had put more color in her face, making her lovelier than ever. He stopped a few feet in front of her, drinking in everything about her, like a thirsty man at a well. The way that bright, hot sun played off her hair, the slightly flushed, damp skin, those bright blue eyes, the swell of rounded breasts beneath that prim, schoolmarmish dress, the slender waist. Just looking at her made his mouth as dry as cotton.

"You're looking damned good, Annie," he finally managed to say.

She smiled. "You're looking pretty good yourself, Hap." He seemed bigger than she remembered. His collarless white shirt was open at the neck, showing sun-darkened skin. Her gaze traveled upward. "You got rid of your mustache," she said foolishly.

'Yeah, what do you think?"

"It makes you look different."

"Better or worse?"

"Just different." She stepped back. "I didn't think you'd be back, you know."

"I was kinda passing through," he lied.

"Oh?"

"Yeah. I've got a job offer over in Karnes County. I'm thinking about being a sheriff there."

Her eyes widened. "That's Helena, isn't it?"

"Yeah. They get a little trouble every now and then," he added in an understatement.

"A lot of killing, anyway—or at least that's what I've read." Recovering somewhat, she started to hold out her hand, then thought better of it. "Well, I'm glad you stopped by. Come on in, and I'll put on some coffee." She caught herself and looked up at him. "I forgot—you hate coffee, don't you?"

"Yeah, but water's fine."

"You can stay for supper, can't you? I mean, you don't have to go right away, do you?"

"I got a couple of extra days."

"Good." Given the way they'd parted just before Christmas, she felt awkward. "Well, you're welcome to stay here, but I was planning on leaving in the morning. I guess I could stay another day maybe, so we could catch up. I'd like to hear about how things have been going for you."

"Yeah, I was coming by to talk to you about that—leaving, I mean. Tell you what—you get in where it's cooler, and I'll put Red in the barn. Then I'll be right on in."

"I need to wash my hands, anyway. I was trying to get some flowers planted before I left."

"Go ahead."

He watched until she'd disappeared into the house before he led his horse toward the corral. Well, he was here, and he'd seen her, and she still had the same effect on him. Now he just had to figure out how to deal with it. It was one thing to meddle in a body's affairs when he was asked, quite another when he wasn't. But he was going to make it his business, anyway. He wouldn't be able to live with himself if he didn't.

On his way to the house, he stopped at the pump and got his hands wet enough to slick his hair back. And just outside the door, he unbuckled his gun belt and took it off. Inside, he hung it on the coat peg, then went into the kitchen. Annie'd washed up and was standing at the table, slicing a loaf of bread. She looked up, smiling.

"I thought you probably hadn't eaten, and I made this this morning. With a little jam and butter, I was hoping it'd hold you till supper."

"Thanks."

She reached for the crock of butter, murmuring, "If

you'll kill a chicken, I'll stew it and make dumplings for you. I've got a real good recipe for them."

"Always liked dumplings," he admitted. "I'm not a hard man to please, Annie."

She turned around at the way he said that, then noticed, "You're not wearing your gun. I hope you didn't leave it in the barn, because Henry will have already eaten the holster by now. If it weren't metal, she'd eat the Colt, too. She'll probably try, anyway."

"I brought it into the house." He tried to smile but couldn't quite make it. "Actually, I was thinking it wouldn't look right to come courting with it."

She froze, her eyes widening, and the color drained from her face. "What did you say?" she asked, her voice barely above a whisper.

He hadn't meant to be so blunt about it, but now that he'd blundered, there wasn't much he could do but lay out his case. He took a deep breath, then plunged ahead.

"You need a man, Annie. I know what you've got in mind—you're wanting to go up into the Comancheria to look for your little girl. Well, you can't do it alone—be a fool thing to try it. A woman out there in a buckboard's a sitting duck for 'em. Before you start yammerin' Comanche at 'em, they'll have you killed, and then where will your kid be?"

"At least I'd be doing something. At least I'd be trying to get her. I can't leave her to be murdered by the army. But it's not your affair, Hap."

"Hear me out. I'm not much for speechifying, but I've thought a lot about this, Annie. I'd a whole lot rather be trying to get somebody in Austin to do something, but—"

"They won't. I've already been there," she said bitterly.

"I wrote the governor, the president of the state legislature—everybody I could think of. You ought to read what I got back from them. They don't care, Hap—they don't care! I finally went to see them in person, and it didn't matter! They *still* didn't care! It's like they all think I ought to just forget she ever lived—but I can't!"

"Yeah, I know."

"Do you? Or are you like every other man who's come around here since I've been back? They all seem to think I need a man, too, that I'm some kind of harlot that can't live without—without—"

"I don't think you're a harlot, Annie. I never thought that. But you didn't let me finish—I've got something to say."

"I'm sorry. I just don't want to argue with you or anybody, that's all," she said wearily. "I'm tired of waiting. I've got to do something."

"Those fellows wouldn't be coming around if you were a married woman, you know. What I'm trying to tell you is I'll go for you, if that's what you want. If that's the only way, I'll go, Annie."

"You'll go?" she echoed, stunned.

"Yeah. If that's what it takes, you can count me in."

"But *why?* I don't even have any claim on you, Hap."

It was now or never, and he knew it. "I reckon if I was your husband, you'd have all the claim you needed." Not daring to meet her eyes, he studied the checked tablecloth. "I've got a lot of rough edges to me, Annie, and I'm not trying to deny it. But you aren't going to find any gentlemen that'll go up there for you. I will."

"Oh, Hap—"

"I'm what you need, Annie. I can be as mean and ornery as they are. And I've never been a coward. Anything I've ever said I'd do, I've done. If I can't, I'll die trying. I'm thirty-seven, and you're thirty. 'Way I look at it, we've both got a chance to start over, and we ought to take it." Daring to look up now, he added, "And I haven't had but one bottle of whiskey since the last time I was here, so you won't be getting a drunkard."

Closing her eyes, she swallowed. "I can't, Hap, I can't."

"Because you can't stomach the thought of me?" he dared to ask, his heart pounding.

"No, not that. I can't stomach the thought of any man. If Ethan were here, I'd not be able to bear it." Tears began to roll down her cheeks, and her body shook. "I can't," she whispered. "I'd just cheat you."

"Here, now." Moving behind her, he laid a hand on her shoulder. "Cheatin's when a man doesn't know what he's getting, Annie. Me, I've got a fair notion." Turning her around, he slid his arms around her shoulders. "I've been a gambling man all my life, Annie. I'm willing to take the chance I can make things different for you."

"But what if I can't change? What if I never get over this? What if every time you look at me like—like you did last Christmas, what if it makes me sick to my stomach?"

Holding her close, he stroked her hair with his hand. "I don't know what they did to you, but I'm stubborn enough to believe I can make you get over it."

"But what if you cannot?"

"I've never forced a woman in my life. If you never change, I won't have any less than I've got right now."

"Why, Hap? Why would you want to do this?" she whispered into his shoulder.

"I want a home, Annie. When this is over, I want a

place to come home to. Me, you, and the kid." And as he held her, saying the words he knew Annie wanted to hear, he almost believed he could find the little girl. "You don't have to answer right now. I reckon you're needing time to think it over."

He was rock solid, making her feel safe within his embrace. Savoring the strength of his arms around her, she rested her head on his shoulder. "I was going to get provisions in the morning. I've already made arrangements for Mr. Willett to come for the animals. I couldn't just leave them here."

"You can stay here with 'em. As soon as you tell me, I'll go."

"I have to go. How else will you know her? I have to go, Hap."

"Then we'll do it together."

"I don't know, Hap—I don't know."

"Like I said, I've got time. They aren't expecting me in Helena for a few more days. And if you decide to take me, I don't have to go down there at all."

As she sat beside him on the buckboard seat, the tension between them was palpable, as though they were two tightly wound coils, either of which could break at any moment. They'd made most of the trip in silence, each afraid to say anything that might disappoint the other.

Her mind was in turmoil and had been ever since he'd sprung his totally unexpected proposal on her. Unable to sleep all night, she'd tossed and turned until both of the cats had abandoned her bed in disgust. If she didn't stop worrying over it, she was going to make herself physically sick.

The morning sun was white-hot, beating down on her back, baking her shoulders. She looked up from beneath the broad, curved brim of her sunbonnet, noting the cloudless sky. There wasn't any relief in sight. And to make matters worse, if it was already hot in this part of the state, the west Texas desert was going to be unbearable.

She cast a furtive glance at Hap. He was wearing a

black frock coat, which had to feel miserable, but his expression was set, stoic. It was hard to believe this was the
same man who'd stood in her kitchen asking her to marry
him. Now he seemed so purposeful, so sure of himself.

Her gaze dropped to the traces in his hands. He had
strong, capable hands. On this morning it seemed as
though everything about him was decidedly masculine.
The scuffed boots, the black pants that clung to his legs,
the butt of his Peacemaker above the tooled-leather holster, the frock coat straining across his hunched shoulders. Even the straight, even profile of his face.

The only thing relieving the unrelenting masculinity of
the man was that hair and those sleepy blue eyes. When
he'd come out of the house, his hair was wet, slicked back
as though he'd tried to glue it down, but now that the hot
wind had played with it, it had dried to a soft brown, ruffled and wavy. And whether he knew it or not, it looked
a lot better that way. If she hadn't been so wary of everything, she'd have told him that it made him look ten years
younger than the way he'd had it.

"Something the matter?" he asked.

She jumped guiltily. "No."

"I was beginning to think I'd sprouted devil horns the
way you were looking at me."

"No. I was admiring your hair."

"Now I know you're fibbing, Annie."

"No, you've got pretty hair."

"Pretty," he repeated. "Just what a man wants to hear."

"I mean it. It's very becoming."

"Yeah, well, I always sort of hated it. My brothers used
to call me—" He caught himself. "Well, I'm not saying it.

Anyway, I finally had to lick 'em before they quit. It always made me feel like a damned girl—the hair, I mean."

"My father would have been happy to have hair like yours."

"Not if he had it."

"He was bald."

"I used to wish I was."

"I guess we all wish for something we aren't," she observed. "I always wanted to be shorter."

"I don't know why."

"I had a cousin everybody made over. She was an itty-bitty little thing, and my mother kept saying she was so pretty that I got the notion I must be ugly."

"You're the prettiest woman I know."

"I wasn't trying to get a compliment, Hap."

"Denying what you are doesn't change it." Straightening his shoulders abruptly, he frowned. "Did you bring your list?"

"Yes."

"I don't know as it's such a good idea—traveling by wagon, I mean," he said slowly. "I've done a lot of tracking out in that country, and there's places where a wagon'd make a man a damned good target. Like all the rivers we'll be crossing. I know it's hard traveling for a woman, but I think we'd be better off taking a horse and a mule apiece like we did in the rangers."

"Oh?"

"Yeah. You're traveling light enough to make a run for it, and you can switch back and forth between 'em so you've got a fairly fresh mount when you need one."

"What do you do for clothes?"

"What did the Comanches do?" he countered.

"They didn't change very often—and they had fleas and lice, Hap."

"Take two or three dresses and leave the damned petticoats at home. Wash when you get a chance."

"There's not much water up there," she reminded him.

"It doesn't take much, if you know what you're doing."

"What about food and drinking water? I don't want to drink out of a buffalo paunch."

"Well, you have to take extra canteens into a desert, but you can live off the land when it comes to food."

"I did that—for three years."

"I've done it most of my life."

She considered a moment, then looked at him. "You're serious, aren't you?"

"Well, I was just thinking if we found your daughter, they might not be reasonable about handing her over. We could be riding hell for leather to save our necks."

"But can you ride that far on horseback? What about your leg?"

"I can stand it. We'll get a good supply of jerky, some coffee for you, pick up just enough flour and salt for hardtack, buy as many canteens as we can tie onto four animals, and get us a couple of good mules. Hell of a lot easier, Annie."

"I guess I was just thinking of me driving the wagon. But I guess you've had more experience than I've had. Most of the time when—when I was with them, I was lost."

"Won't even have to keep to the roads this way," he assured her. "We'll have a better chance of finding the kid by going up into those canyons."

"How well do you know the Comancheria, Hap?"

"Better than the army."

"You're going for sure, then?"

"It's up to you."

She took a deep breath, then looked away. "I could pay you—there was some money in the savings. I'd tried to hire somebody before this, you know, but nobody answered."

"There's not enough money on earth to make a sane man go up there, Annie."

"But you'd go."

"For you. All you've got to do is say the word."

"But I don't know if I could ever be a wife to you!" she cried. "What if you come to feel cheated? What if you come to hate me?"

"I'm not much of a man to hate anybody. Only the damned Comanches and the Comancheros, and I reckon if they'd have given me any reason to, I'd have tried to understand 'em. It was just damned hard to bury what was left of a family after they got done with 'em, so I gave up allowing any reason for it." Settling his shoulders, he flicked the whip out over the team, hurrying them along. "So if you're asking whether I can stand it if you can't love me, I guess I'm saying I mean to try. It'd be something just to have a place somewhere, to say I've got a pretty wife. You're a woman who'd make a man proud to say it, Annie."

"I wish I believed that was all it took to make a man happy," she said wistfully.

"I guess you can't know until you try."

He turned the team down a narrow, dusty wagon path at an angle to the road. Surprised, she asked. "You're not going to Veck's?"

"Not if I can help it. It's too far."

"There's not much in this place, I can tell you."

"No store?"

"Not much of one, anyway. Nothing like Veck's. You've never been here before, have you?"

"Passing through in the middle of the night. 'Way I remembered it, there was an old trading post, a blacksmith's shingle over a lean-to and a half dozen houses."

"That's Buell's Crossing, all right."

"Trading post ought to have what we need."

She'd never liked Lake Buell, not even when Ethan had been alive, and since she'd been back, she'd had to drive him off her porch once at gunpoint when he'd shown up drunk and amorous. But she couldn't bring herself to say that to Hap.

"It probably does," she said finally.

"You don't want to go there?"

"Well, he's always got rough-looking men hanging around the place, but I don't guess it really matters. It *is* a long way to Veck's," she conceded.

"You don't have to go in. No sense putting up with anything you don't have to." Slowing the team down to a walk, he offered, "Tell you what—I'll park under a tree, and you can wait outside in the shade."

"All right." Opening the drawstrings of her bag, she dug around inside her purse. "I brought forty dollars—you can get everything for that, can't you?"

"Put it back. I've still got a letter of credit I never used from when I was working at the Ybarra. I reckon it won't be any good after a while."

"I don't want you paying for this. I don't want to be beholden to you, Hap. Here," she said, pressing the banknotes into his hand.

It didn't make much sense to him. She was asking him to risk his life going up into some of the roughest country on God's green earth, but she didn't want him spending his money. He opened his mouth to point out her lack of logic, then shut it, saying nothing. Instead, he tucked the folded money into his pocket. They'd probably need it later, anyway.

Passing the low adobe building that said BUELL'S CROSS-ING in crude letters, he found a good-sized oak tree and pulled the wagon to a halt. Swinging down, he tied the traces to a low-hanging branch, then looked up at her.

"I don't plan on being long. I've got a good notion of what we need."

"All right."

She watched him walk back to the store, wondering if she was doing the right thing, if she was being at all fair to him. He still favored that leg, and after having ridden all the way from the Ybarra, he'd seemed to be in pain last night. While he hadn't said anything, he'd retired early, and yet when she'd gotten up for a glass of goat's milk to settle her stomach, she could see the glow of the kerosene lamp beneath his door.

He was quite a man, she'd give him that. After all the things she'd heard and read about him, he didn't seem half as wild as he'd been painted. He was too easy to like to be all that dangerous. But he apparently was. How had he put it?

I can be as mean and ornery as they are. And I've never been a coward. Anything I've ever said I'd do, I've done.

His words seemed to echo in her mind, reassuring her,

telling her it was fate that he'd come back to help her. He was tough, and he knew the land. He was her best chance of ever finding Susannah. She thought of Ethan, wondering what he would have said. It probably wasn't the sort of thing that had ever crossed a mind intent on a future that never came.

Ethan. Given the distance of three and a half year's separation from her memories, it was harder and harder to bring his image to mind. After three months of forcing herself to lie in the bed she'd once shared with him, she no longer dwelled on that, either. Which was just as well, she told herself stoutly. Every time she dreamed of what it had been like, the yearning had turned to terror, and it was Two Trees' hideously painted face hovering over her. Then she'd wake up screaming, drowning in sweat.

She looked around, wishing she'd not been such a coward, that she'd marched right into Lake Buell's store with her head held high. But she hadn't, and now she'd just have to occupy her thoughts in this sleepy, dusty little crossroad.

Hap Walker had left something that looked like a tablet under his seat. Curious, she retrieved it. Telling herself he hadn't really made any attempt to hide it, she looked inside. His decidedly masculine scrawl drew her, and she found herself reading what looked to be an essay he'd written.

I came into this world where the Sulphur and Red rivers meet (Paris, Texas now) on the Fourth of July, 1836, the youngest of five sons born to Henry Wagnon Walker, at various times a surveyor, a patriot in the war for Texas independence, a preacher, and a dirt farmer, and his wife,

Hannah Goodwin Walker, a schoolteacher from East Tennessee. She did her best to pass on her love of books to me, hoping maybe I'd read law or become a doctor. My father wanted me to be a Baptist preacher, but I knew early on I wasn't suited to it.

I was the hell-raiser of the bunch, so much so that my father was relieved when I ran off to join the Texas Rangers in 1853. I guess he figured it was that or I'd be swinging at the end of a rope as an outlaw. My mother cried when I left home, and I'm not sure she ever forgave me for picking what she considered a rough calling.

But I liked the freedom of being a lawman like that. Back in those days the Indians, particularly the Comanches, the Kiowas, the Lipan Apaches, the Kickapoos, the Mescalero Apaches, and the Tonkawas raided throughout Texas, stealing and killing, then fading either up to the Llano, over to New Mexico, or down to Old Mexico. While the Tonkawas have been known to eat their enemies, I would still have to say that the meanest Indian of my experience was, and still is, the Comanche.

His narration left off there, with a notation of the current date. If he'd been writing a letter to someone, it was going to be a long one. It was a curious document, but perhaps the most surprising thing about it was that every word was spelled correctly, and the prose, while lengthy, was correct. For all his seeming folksiness, Hap Walker was more literate than most Texans. She supposed he owed that to his mother.

Feeling somewhat guilty for reading it, she carefully put the tablet back, then resigned herself to at least a half hour of sitting under the spreading oak tree. She just hoped that Lake Buell didn't mean to give him any trouble.

"He'p you?" Buell was saying.

"Yeah." Hap took out Annie's list and a pencil, then marked off about three-quarters of it. Handing it across the counter, he asked, "Got any of this?"

The man studied it for a moment, then allowed, "Some. Canteens. Flour, by the fifty pounds only. Buffalo jerky in paraffin. Salt. Coffee. Now, tin plates I ain't got. Out o' cornmeal right now. No whiskey?"

"No."

Buell scratched his head. "Mebbe I could do you some good on the cornmeal. Jack!" he called out. "That Mexican got any cornmeal?"

Several men, obviously cowpunchers, looked up from a card game. "Naw," one answered, swatting a fly with his hand, squashing it on the table. "Lake, you got to do something about the damned flies. Damned things is bigger 'n buzzards."

The front door banged on its hinges, and a leather-skinned man sauntered in. "Hey, Lake! Never guess what I just saw outside. Looks like yer sweetie's done come to town!"

"Huh?"

"The Widder Bryce."

Hap didn't like his tone. "The lady's with me," he said evenly.

"Lady!" Buell snorted. "Hell, that ain't no lady, mister! Annie Bryce ain't nothing but a Comanche's whore!" he declared to the snickers of the fellows at the table. "Why, all you got to do is go out there with a bottle of cheap whiskey, and—"

His head snapped back with the force of the blow. Staggering, he backed into a shelf of tinned goods, knocking it over. For a moment he just stared, then his face turned dark red. "No gimp-legged son of a bitch's gonna hit Lake Buell," he growled, lunging across the counter. He came at Hap like a charging bull, swinging a beefy fist. It missed.

Hap's second punch caught him in the gut, followed by a third to his jaw, and the battle was joined. Bellowing now, the big, hulking shopkeeper got down to business by swinging a chair, breaking the rungs over Hap's shoulder. Hap's good leg kicked him, catching Buell behind the knee with the toe of his boot, sending him crashing to the ground, but the big man wouldn't stay down.

The fight was dirty, brutal, and short, ending when Buell grabbed a long-necked bottle, broke it on the edge of the table, and swung the jagged edge at Hap's throat. Ducking under the arc of the bottle, Hap butted him, knocking the wind out of him. As Buell sagged, he caught him hard in the gut with the boot, knocking him to the floor. A couple of swift kicks to the head, and it was all over. Buell tried to get up, then fell back, blood gushing from an obviously broken nose. Hap stood over him, fists clenched. But the bigger man leaned over and spit a broken tooth into the dirt.

"Jesus, mister, I ain't seen nuthin' like it," Jack muttered, looking away. "Ain't nobody beats Lake. Nobody."

But Hap's eyes were still on the proprietor. "I'd be real careful what I said from now on, Buell. The lady's a Walker now." Reaching into his pocket, he took out his letter of credit from the Ybarra and dropped it into Lake's lap. "I'll take that order now, and I want it carried out to the wagon, you hear? And if you so much as looked cross-eyed at her, I'll kill you," he added evenly.

As he walked out, the place was dead silent, but the hairs on Hap's neck prickled in warning. He dropped his hand and spun around, leveling the Colt as Buell edged for a shotgun. Lake dropped it like it was red-hot, then stammered, "I didn't mean nuthin', mister. I was just picking it up off the floor."

"Jesus, did you see that?" somebody gasped.

Hap returned the gun to his holster and kicked open the door. As it banged on its hinges behind him, he heard Jack say, "My God, Lake, he coulda kilt you! Look at this paper, Lake, look at it!"

"I'm gonna kill me a gimp-legged man," Buell muttered. "I'm gonna cut 'im in half with a load of buckshot."

"Lake, I'm telling you that's Hap Walker—you know, *Captain* Hap Walker! The Texas Ranger! Jesus, Lake, you don't wanna fight him!"

"Better apologize to 'im, Lake," somebody said. "Looks like he's up and married her. Guess you're out, huh?"

"A hell of a fighter—kicks real good with that gimp leg of his, Lake. Real quick with that gun, too," Jack pointed out.

"Shut up!"

Hap had heard enough. He started for the wagon, feeling an exhilaration he hadn't felt in almost a year. He was Hap Walker, and his name still meant something.

"My word, whatever . . . ?" Annie gasped when she saw him. "Your hands—"

He looked down, seeing the blood on them. It looked

like he'd slaughtered an animal with his bare hands. He must've done that when he broke Lake Buell's nose. Swinging up onto the seat beside her, he frowned.

"If you married me, Annie, it'd at least stop the talk."

"You got into a fight in there, didn't you?"

"Yeah."

"Because of me." It was a statement, not a question.

He started to deny it, then nodded. "Wasn't much of a fight. I reckon he'll be bringing the stuff out directly."

"It was Lake Buell, wasn't it?"

"It didn't amount to much, Annie. I just rearranged his mouth a little, that's all." As he looked up into the sheltering oak leaves, his mouth turned down at the corners. "I could've killed him. Maybe I should've."

"No. It was just words."

"You shouldn't have to put up with that." Turning to face her, he regarded her soberly. "I told him you were a Walker now."

"I see."

"You know I've never been much of a liar."

He was the kindest man she knew, and he'd just fought for her honor. As she looked at him, she realized just how lucky she was in that moment. "Then I guess you aren't now," she said quietly. "I'd be honored to be a Walker, Hap."

"Don't suppose you know where there's a preacher—or a justice of the peace, do you?" he asked, grinning now.

"Yes, but I don't want him at my wedding." A wry smile lifted one corner of her mouth. "Lake Buell's justice of the peace here."

"Damn."

"But there's one over at Baker's Gap."

"Baptist preacher?"

"No. A justice of the peace." Now that she'd agreed to marry him, she felt downright relieved. "I never had anything to do with Lake Buell, Hap."

"I never thought you did."

The big man came out with a loaded wheelbarrow. He'd taken time to wash himself up some, but there was no mistaking the damage to his face. His nose was flattened and leaning to one side, while his mouth still oozed blood from a cut on his lip. Without a word he went around to the back of the wagon and unloaded Hap's order, then came up front and held out a fistful of bills.

"You got sixty-five dollars coming back," he said. As Hap took the money, Buell looked up at Annie. "Afternoon, Mrs. Walker," he said somberly. "Captain."

"Afternoon, Lake," she murmured.

Muttering something unintelligible under his breath, Buell turned and walked back to his store.

Ralph Baker's house, a fourteen-foot-square adobe structure with a weathered lean-to in front, doubled as his place of business. Sitting in the middle of a flat, dusty, wide spot in the road, it was the only building in Baker's Gap so named because he'd once had hopes the land he owned would become a town with his name on it. A weathered sign with the optimistic designation of LAND OFFICE hung at an angle from a rusting chain. Beneath it, on cardboard, Ralph had added, "Justice of the Peace and Notary Public Available Inside."

Hap looked around uneasily, wishing he could do it right for her, wishing they were in a church somewhere instead of in this little dirty, squalid, depressing place. He

273

was about to turn around and leave when she put her hand on his arm.

"It's all right," she murmured. "I don't mind."

That was all it took. At her touch every fiber of his being became acutely aware of her. And he didn't want to wait, to give her a chance to change her mind. He wanted to be bound to her. That he was giving himself a long road with no more than a chance to win her didn't matter. When he went out into the sun again, he wanted her to have his name. The rest would come later.

And so, in a dingy, cluttered room, standing between an old desk and a trestle table, with Baker's Mexican wife for witness, Hap Walker held Annie Bryce's hand, pledging himself to her forever.

"Yuh got 'er a ring?" Baker asked, interrupting the short ceremony.

He didn't. Looking down at his own hands, he saw a heavy sterling band with the lone star of Texas carved in an onyx stone. It was about the only thing he had left of his father's belongings, it and an old watch that didn't run.

"Yeah," he decided, slipping it off. "It'll be a little big," he murmured apologetically to Annie. "Maybe you can wear it on another finger until I can get you something better."

"All right, yuh put hit on 'er hand, then yuh just say whut I tell yuh," Baker told him.

Hap had to hold it on her ring finger while he repeated the words. Then, afraid it'd come off when he was done, he moved it to her forefinger. It was still loose. When he got outside, he'd have to tie something around it.

Annie closed her eyes against the squalor while he repeated his promise to love her forever. This was so different from that other time when she'd been young, when she'd loved Ethan Bryce more than anything. But even as she thought it, a voice within her mind told her she was doing the right thing. She was starting over.

"Now, Miz Walker," Baker said, intruding on her thoughts, "mebbe yuh'd want tuh say thuh wuds, ennyway, e'en yuh don't have no ring tuh give 'im."

As Hap shook his head, she made up her mind. "Yes," she said, her voice low. "I think I ought to." Reaching into her bag, she took out her house key, moved it to one side of the ring, then maneuvered it onto his finger. Whispering, "I'll get you one, too," she looked back to Ralph Baker. "I'm ready."

Her throat ached as she whispered the words; then it was done. Baker looked over a lopsided pair of glasses to announce, "Reckon yuh-all's man and wife now, Mr. Walker. Yuh may embrace thuh bride."

Hap hesitated, but Mrs. Baker gave him a nudge, then giggled. Feeling utterly awkward, he took a step toward Annie and slid his arms around her. Leaning into her, he brushed her lips with his. Her hands caught his elbows and held on for a moment before he stepped back. He tried to smile but couldn't.

"Yuh got tuh sign th' papers afore yuh go," the justice of the peace reminded them. "And that'll be three dollahs."

As Hap counted out the bills, adding one for good measure, Annie signed her place on the certificate, then filled out a line in Baker's record book. While Hap signed his side, Mrs. Baker offered to make them coffee, and Annie politely declined.

Baker winked. "Reckon yuh's wantin' tuh get on with thuh res o' thuh business, huh?"

Anita Mills

"Come on, Annie, let's get out of here," Hap said tersely.

The sun was bright, the sky almost white when they emerged from the Baker house. Taking her arm, he walked quickly to the wagon and handed her up. Swinging up beside her, he picked up the traces and slapped them across the team. It was a good five minutes before he could bring himself to speak.

"I'm sorry," he said finally. "You deserved a lot better than that. We should have gone over to the fort and asked the chaplain to do it right. You'd have had an altar and a preacher, and it'd have felt like you were getting married anyway."

She looked down at the marriage certificate in her hand. Carefully unfolding it, she smoothed it across her lap. "Everything seems to be in order, Hap. I'm pretty sure it's legal. It's got his seal, anyway."

"Yeah, but it was a helluva way to do it—no ring, no pretty dress, no preacher. I wish I could do it over."

Her signature seemed to leap out at her. Anne Elizabeth Allison Bryce Walker. The woman had cautioned her to make sure she put down all of it "just to make it legal, in case anything was to come up." Annie Walker. Annie Walker. It'd take a little while to get used to the sound of it.

Then she noticed that he'd written. Horace R. Walker. "So you were the Horace," she said softly.

"Yeah. Helluva name to stick on a kid, huh?"

"Actually, it was a pretty venerable name. I think there were some Roman heroes with it well before the poet."

"Yeah, well, I'm not Roman, Annie."

276

"What does the R stand for?" she asked curiously. "Robert?" she guessed.

"Worse. Randall. Not much of a choice, huh? Where she came up with it, I don't know. No Randalls in the family that I ever knew of. Hell, maybe it came out of a book, or something."

"I don't mind it."

"Yeah, well, when I was a kid, I wanted to be a Bob or a Tom or a Bill. Even Claude was better than Horace." He stared out over the dry, dusty road ahead. "You don't have to worry any. I won't be wanting to name any kid of mine Horace—or Randall."

A child. She froze momentarily. Of course he'd want a child. It was to be expected—every man wanted to leave something of himself behind when he left the world.

He glanced her way and caught the stricken look on her face. Guessing the reason, he sought to reassure her. "Look, I'm not expecting it to happen right away, Annie. I figure we got some things to work out between us first. I've got time to wait until you're ready."

But even while he was saying it, he was taking in the beauty of her hair, her face, her woman's body, and he knew he didn't want to wait. She was his wife, and he wanted her. More than anything.

The sun was slipping below the softly rounded hills above her farm when he turned the wagon down the narrow lane to the house. "Mr. Willett has been here," she said suddenly. "Henry's gone." Sighing, she sat back. "I guess he's taken the cats, too. Spider's a pest, but I'll miss Twain terribly."

"Yeah, well, I never was much for cats myself," he admitted, "but I expect they were a lot of company for you."

"Yes. Twain especially. At night when I'd be reading, he'd climb onto my lap and snuggle next to the book. I named him after the writer, you know. I was reading *Innocents Abroad* the night after Mary brought him, and I guess because I was laughing, he had to investigate."

"And Spider? Odd name for a cat, I'd think."

"Not if you ever saw him with a ball of yarn. He tends to drape it around things. He's a terrible mischief maker."

"Well, I wouldn't worry about 'em. I expect they'll be waiting for you when you come back."

"I hope so. I'll hate it if they forget me."

"I had a dog like that—left him at home when I ran off

to join the rangers the first time. Came home a year later, and the damned thing growled at me," he recalled. "Took him a week to remember me."

"That's what I mean. And they're not very old."

But as he set her down, then took the team to the barn, she had another concern. Jim Willett had left a scrawled note for her on her front door.

"Cudnt find nowt but th wite-towed un," she read.

That was Twain. He'd taken Twain but not Spider. Hurrying inside, she began calling, "Here, kitty, kitty, kitty! Spider! Kitty, kitty, kitty!" Nothing. Not so much as an answering squeak. Knowing Jim, he'd probably let the kitten outside, and something had gotten it. He had the notion that if something didn't survive, God hadn't meant it to, anyway. That explained the order of things to him. And to him God never meant for man to have a cat in the house.

"Hap, Spider's missing!" she said as he came in the door. "Mr. Willett didn't take him."

"He'll turn up."

"Would you check the barn?"

"I was just down there."

"Oh, yes, I hadn't thought of that."

"He'll turn up," he told her again. "Probably after supper."

It occurred to her then that they hadn't eaten anything but bread and jam sandwiches since breakfast, and it was nearly six-thirty now. "You're hungry, aren't you?"

"I could probably eat something," he allowed.

"I don't know what to do about Spider. I don't let him out except to take care of his business, and then he comes right back in."

"After supper, if you don't find him, I'll take the lantern

out and look," he promised. "But right now I'd kinda like to wash up."

"Yes, of course," she murmured, still distracted. Recovering, she decided, "Maybe he's out hunting."

"Probably."

"When he smells supper, he'll come in," she decided.

"What is it?"

"Well, since we were leaving in the morning, I hadn't planned on making a big mess of anything. I thought maybe I'd heat the beans I put down the well last night, maybe fry some greens and make some cornbread to go with it. You like wilted greens, don't you?"

"With bacon?" he asked hopefully.

"Yes."

"And vinegar?"

"Yes."

"Yeah, my ma used to fix 'em like that."

"So did Ethan's mother." As soon as the words were out of her mouth, she wished them back. She didn't suppose he'd want to hear much about Ethan anymore. "My mother wasn't much of a cook," she added lamely.

"It's all right, Annie, I don't mind," he said. "It's not like we were a couple of kids. We both lived a long time before we crossed paths." He forced a twisted smile. "Your face gives you away, you know."

"Does it?"

"Yeah. You're wondering if I'm expecting you to put your memories away somewhere, aren't you?"

"Yes."

"I'd think there was something wrong if you hadn't loved him, Annie. I'm just wanting to be part of the rest of your life, that's all."

She could feel a lump rise in her throat, and her eyes felt hot with unshed tears. "Thank you," she managed.

To cover the awkwardness he felt, he decided, "Well, I'd better get washed up." He held up his hands. Lake Buell's blood had been rinsed off at Ralph Baker's pump, but his knuckles were raw and swollen. "Don't suppose you got anything for this, do you?"

"Yes. It's horse balm, but E—but we used it for everything. It heals cuts and sores." She took a step closer to inspect his knuckles. "That hurts, doesn't it?"

"Not bad. I've done a lot more damage to 'em before," he assured her.

"Lake looked pretty beat up."

"I wanted to kill him."

"Yes, well, I'm glad you didn't." Moving away, she rummaged in a cupboard and found the jar of balm. "I keep it in here for cuts and burns," she explained, coming back with it. "I burned my hand a couple of months ago putting wood in the stove, and after I stuck it in some snow, I put a little of this on it. It was healed in less than a week."

"Good. We better take some of it with us."

"Yes." She looked up at him. "Sit down, and I'll work on those."

"You don't need to."

"But I want to."

He sank into a chair and leaned forward to rest his elbows on the checked tablecloth, his hands up in the air. She filled a pan of water from the bucket and brought it to the table. Sitting down across from him, she reached out to feel of his knuckles. He winced.

"This could be broken, you know," she said.

"No. I can move my fingers." To demonstrate, he flexed his sore hands. "Fellow had a damned hard jaw, though."

"He's quite a respected fighter in these parts," she murmured, dipping a washcloth into the water. "This may sting," she told him, rubbing lye soap on it. "I thought I'd get everything good and clean, put a little iodine on it, then rub the balm in."

"Big men move slower and fall harder. I reckon we won't . . ."

But as she took his hand in hers, he lost his train of thought entirely. She had her head bent so he was looking at the shining crown of hair beneath the kerosene lantern. He had to close his eyes lest she look up and see the naked desire there. All he could think of was how close she was. All he could feel was the warmth of her fingers against his.

"Fight again?" she finished for him. "I wouldn't bet on it. He's got a mean temper and a real high opinion of himself. But you shouldn't have let him pick a fight with you, you know. I've always heard he was a dirty fighter."

"I guess I got lucky. I picked the fight with him," he managed, trying not to look at her.

"The skin's split here. I probably ought to bind it."

"No."

"No?" She looked up at that.

"Just let the air heal it," he muttered. "And the balm."

"You're sure?"

He wanted to go across that table, to gather her up and hold her, but he'd promised her time. Instead, he pulled his hands away and stood up. "You've done enough," he said harshly. "I'll finish up." Then, knowing how gruff he sounded, he added, "I don't want to put you out doing something I can do for myself. You just go ahead with supper." Reaching out, he grabbed the jar of balm and headed for the door. "I'd better look in on the team," he said lamely.

"You just put them up."

"Yeah, but I didn't look to see if there was any water."

"Would you bring the beans in from the well when you come back?"

"Sure." Out of the corner of his eye he could see her taking down the lantern. "Where are you going?"

"To pick the greens. There's some just out the back door."

"Oh."

He went around to the front of the house and sat on the stoop to rub the soothing ointment over his knuckles. Then he walked slowly to the barn, where he knew he'd already done everything. Inside, he leaned against the door to old Red's stall, talking to the big roan, trying to take his mind off Annie.

"Guess we'll be leaving in the morning," he told the horse. "It's not going to be just you and me anymore, you know." Red snorted, then moved closer to the door, hanging his head over it. Hap scratched the area between his eyes. "Yeah, I know, you're thinking I'm an old fool, aren't you? You figure if I was to get this far, I could have made it the rest of the way without a wife, don't you? Here I've been telling myself I was too restless to stay at the Ybarra with Clay, and now I'm wanting to settle down on this little farm. Don't make much sense, huh?"

In answer the big animal bumped his hand with its nose, trying to get him to keep scratching. Hap ran his hand down the bone, caressing the short, stiff hairs.

"I haven't been honest with her, you know," he went on. "I'd about as soon take my chances in a nest of rattle-snakes than go up there looking for that kid, knowing she's going to be disappointed. It'd be easier to strike gold in California than to find a little girl that's been with 'em this long. But I've got to try, anyway, 'cause that's why she's married me. Hell, maybe I *am* a fool."

He lingered in the barn until he felt sure enough of himself to go back to the house. He didn't want her to catch him panting after her like a dog waiting for a bitch in heat. He wanted more than that, anyway. He wanted her respect, he told himself. But in his heart, what he really wanted most was for her to love him. If he could have rolled back time and started over, he'd have wanted to be Ethan Bryce before the damned Comanches came.

It was dark, and the air was unusually heavy when he came outside. He took a deep breath, smelling the wood-smoke coming from the chimney, the scent of damp dust that came before a rain. Unless it blew on over, a storm would be moving in before morning. Even as he looked up, he could see the faint flashes of heat lightning along the horizon. The rain probably wouldn't amount to much, he decided. Just enough to settle the dust.

He stopped at the well and pulled the sealed crock up from the cool water, then carried it inside. The smell of frying bacon and baking cornbread greeted him at the door, welcoming him. This was the way a man was meant to live, and tonight he wanted to savor it.

But once inside, once he saw her standing at the cook-stove, her hair clinging damply to her temples and her neck, it started all over for him. There was something about knowing she was his wife that made it hard to re-

member he wasn't supposed to touch her. Not yet, anyway. She needed time.

"It's about ready," she said over her shoulder. "I thought
you'd gotten lost outside."

"I was just checking on things, figuring what I needed
to do to get ready before we leave," he told her. "Anything
I can do?"

"No. I've already set out the plates. I don't guess you
saw Spider out there, did you?"

"No. No sign of him."

"I'm afraid he's lost," she said, sighing. "I don't want to
go off and leave him out there."

"I'll look around again after I eat," he promised.

If he'd been asked what dinner tasted like later, he'd
have had no answer. Trying not to look at her, he wolfed
it down, then grabbed the lantern.

"If I'm not in right away, you don't need to wait up for
me. You've had a long day."

"And you haven't?"

"I'm used to it. Anything you do to call him up?"

"Just kitty, kitty, kitty—at the top of my lungs."

"Okay." He hesitated at the door. "Look, don't worry
about tonight. I was figuring on sleeping in the other bedroom, anyway."

"Yes."

"I've got no ideas," he lied.

"I know. You're a good man, Hap, better than I have any
right to expect."

"Don't say that," he said sharply. "It's not your fault."

"You deserve better."

"There's nothing wrong with you, Annie—nothing that
time won't take care of, anyway."

Bolting for the door with the lantern, he let himself outside. He held it in front of him as he walked the perimeter of the yard, calling, "Kitty! Kitty! Kitty!" until he felt like a damned fool. Every now and then he stopped to listen, hearing nothing besides the lonely howl of a distant coyote. The heat lightning still flickered too far away to even hear any thunder. "Kitty! Kitty!" Damn, where could the stupid little thing be? "Kitty! Come here, cat!"

The irony of what he was doing wasn't lost on him. Here he was, a bridegroom for the first time in his life, and he was spending his time walking around in a pitch-dark night on rattlesnake-infested land, looking for a damned black cat. He was just glad there wasn't anybody around to see him. Leaves rustled in the cottonwood tree by Ethan Bryce's grave. Holding the lantern higher, Hap looked up. A big owl blinked back at him.

At least maybe she'd be in bed by the time he went inside. Maybe he wouldn't have to look at her, thinking how much he'd like to be undressing her, how much he'd like to be exploring that pale, pretty skin of hers. The desire that washed over him left him spitting cotton. He found his way to the pump by the well and worked the creaking handle vigorously, then stuck his whole head under it, trying to drown the heat that was overwhelming him.

Her light was still on. Damn it. Why couldn't she just go on to bed? As he watched, she came to the window, opening it to let in the soft breeze. Her white cotton gown billowed around her. Instead of moving away, she lifted her arms and fanned the gown to cool her body. Then she picked up a hairbrush and stood there, brushing her hair with the light of a kerosene lamp behind her.

"Kitty!" he shouted angrily. "Spider, where the devil are you? Kitty!"

Annie heard him and leaned into the window. "If somebody called me like that, Hap, I'd run," she chided him.

"Yeah, well, he wasn't coming the other way either," he muttered.

"You can't see anything out there, can you?"

"Not much."

"I guess if nothing's got him, he'll turn up in the morning. I'll come out and look for him then," she decided. "You need your sleep, too."

"Are you ever going to bed?"

"Yes."

"Then do it."

She was taken aback by the tone of his voice. "All right. I was just brushing all the tangles out."

"I'd say you've about got 'em. Look, I don't want to come in until you've got your door closed, all right? I'm a man, Annie, not a saint."

Her eyes widened, then she backed out of the window. "I'll close it now."

It wasn't really what he wanted to hear, but he'd made his deal with her and he intended to keep his word. Going back around to the door, he let himself in. Her light was out now, leaving the house in total darkness except for the lantern. Lighting his way to the other bedroom, he put it on the little table, then sat down on the edge of the bed to take off his boots.

She probably thinks you're the biggest fool on earth, Hap Walker, his voice told him. *You'll burn a long time before she looks at you like you want her to.*

Still clothed in the black pants and the now wet collar-

287

less white shirt, he lay down, staring up at the fantastic pattern the flickering lantern flame made on the ceiling. He was a patient man when it came to tracking Indians and outlaws, he reminded himself. He had to keep that same patience if he wanted to win her.

Finally, still wide awake, he got up and found his tablet. Carrying it back to bed with him, he pulled the lantern closer, wet his pencil, and began to write. At the rate he'd started, he'd have his whole life told in twenty pages, he decided. But maybe once he had the main things down, he'd go back and fill it in with stories a boy'd like. Things such as what it had been like on the farm where he grew up. Things like what it was really like to spend half a lifetime in a saddle.

It sounded like a rifle crack in the room with him. Hap sat bolt upright in bed as lightning lit the sky outside. The wind screamed, forcing the window curtain straight out into the room. His first thought was a Texas twister was coming through. He made a jump for the window, closing it just as a wall of water hit.

The wind roared like a steam engine, and the house shook. Above, the roof groaned. Groping his way in the dark, he made his way to Annie's room.

"I think it's a twister!" he shouted, reaching for her. "Get under the damned bed!" As his hand closed over her arm, she fought back, screaming. "For God's sake, Annie, it's me, Hap!"

He managed to drag her from the bed, and he rolled underneath it, taking her with him, pinning her down with his leg. She went limp then and lay, passive and quivering, under his weight. Something crashed outside the window, and for a moment he thought the house was going. Throwing his body over hers, he shielded her head with his hands.

It was over within minutes, but it had felt like an eternity. The wind receded, leaving an eerie, silent calm. "Just wait," he whispered. "There may be more."

"No," she moaned, turning her head. "No, please."

"It's all right, Annie." His hands smoothed her hair. Her face was wet. "Shhhh." Easing off her, he drew her into his arms and brushed his lips over her eyes. He could taste the salt of tears. "I'll take care of you, I swear it," he murmured against her cheek. "You're my wife, Annie— you're a Walker now. You don't have to think about the other, ever."

He kept speaking softly, his lips moving over her face, tracing gentle, passionless kisses from her nose to her jaw to her ears. Gradually, she relaxed against him, and his arms closed around her, holding her close to his body.

"I think it's over," he said finally.

"Yes," she agreed in a childlike voice.

He eased away reluctantly and rolled from beneath the big bed. "Well, since you're all right, I guess I'll have a look outside, then go back to my room. Morning's going to come damned early." Standing up, he leaned down to lend her a hand. "Come on."

It was so dark in the room that he could barely see the white nightgown. She stood there for a moment, not moving, then he heard her say, "Don't go—please."

"God, Annie," he groaned. "Sweetheart, you don't know what you're asking."

"I just want you to hold me. I just want to be held."

He sucked in his breath, held it for several seconds,

then let it out. "All right. But don't you want to know if the place is still standing?"

"I don't care, Hap. I don't want you to leave me."

He couldn't say anything. Instead, he felt for the bed and eased his body onto it, rolling to the other side to make room for her. Using his fist, he pounded a place for his head in the feather pillow. When he looked back, all he could see was the shadowy form of the nightgown as she climbed in beside him. Resigned to a long night, he turned on his side and reached for her. She burrowed against him. He could feel the swell of her breasts pressing into his chest.

"Is this all right?" he asked hoarsely. "Are you sure you can sleep like this?"

"No. I don't want to sleep, Hap. I don't want to dream."

"Then I guess I don't, either," he managed.

His arms were so strong, so secure, his body so warm, that she wanted to stay there forever. The storm was over, the wind blowing across the room cool now. She lay there listening to his heartbeat, thinking he had to be the kindest man on earth. And she knew she'd cheated him.

"I wish I were different," she whispered. "I really wish it was just you and me, and I could begin my life again."

"You can, Annie." His hand smoothed her hair over her shoulder. "Let me make it happen for you." Even as he said the words, the ache in his breast was nearly unbearable. "Let me be a husband to you, Annie."

She swallowed. "I don't think I can, Hap. I'm afraid I can't—I—"

"You're the bravest woman I ever met," he murmured into her hair. "Let me show you, Annie. Let me show you it can be good again."

His hand slid from her hair down her back, stroking the soft cotton where it clung to her rounded hip. He was so aware of her that his blood pounded in his ears, nearly drowning out thought. She was as still as stone within his arms.

"I want you, Annie, but as God is my witness, all you've got to say is stop."

"I can't," she responded brokenly. "I can't say it."

His hand kept moving over her back and hip, caressing her body as his mind fought to master his. Ever so slowly she began to relax, giving him hope. He eased his body lower in the bed, until he could feel her breath on his face. As he pressed his lips against her wet cheeks, he felt he would burst. His arms tightened around her shoulders, and his mouth sought hers, tentatively at first, then eagerly, and by some miracle she was clinging to him, kissing him back.

He'd meant to be tender, cautious even, but he forgot everything beyond the heat in his blood, the feel of her warm body. And he wanted to know all of it. His eager hands gathered the cloth at her hips, working it up, baring her legs, her thighs, until he could touch skin that felt almost as hot as his.

It had been a long time since she'd been held like this, since she'd felt a man's strong hands on her body. Pretending he was Ethan, she responded with an eagerness nearly as great as his. His hot mouth was pressing impassioned kisses from her ear to the sensitive hollow of her neck, while his hands moved over her hips, molding her body to his. Her fingers kneaded his shirt, moving the length of his hard, muscular back to the waist of his pants.

If she'd screamed, "Stop!" at that moment, he wouldn't have heard her. He slipped his hand between her thighs, found the wet softness there, and forgot everything but the pounding in his loins, the incredible heat of his desire. With his other hand he fumbled with the buttons in front of his pants, freeing himself, worked them downward, and all but tore them off. Then he parted her legs with his knee and rolled over her.

She panicked, and her whole body stiffened as he pinned her beneath his weight. Her cry of "No!" was muffled by his mouth as he took possession of her body. Images of Two Trees flashed through her mind, sending a wave of nausea through her.

But he wasn't Two Trees. And as much as he wanted all of her, he felt the change in her body. Willing himself to stop, he lay still within her as he sought to calm her.

"It's just me, Annie, and I love you," he said softly. "God, how I want you, Annie. More than anything."

At the sound of his voice, she was in her featherbed again, and he was her husband. Her arms came up to twine around his neck, pulling his head down to hers. "Love me, Hap," she whispered. "Make me whole again."

He began to move, slowly at first, savoring the quickening of her passion, until he knew he could wait no longer. Grasping her hips, he rode, straining against her bucking body, losing himself in what he did to her. Panting like an animal, he could hear himself cry out. He could feel the pulsing release carry him to ecstasy, and then he was floating back to earth, cradled within her body.

She lay so still beneath him that he was afraid he'd hurt her. Resting his weight on his elbows, he tried to see her face in the darkness. And the tenderness he felt was overwhelming.

"Are you all right, Annie?" he asked anxiously, terrified of the answer.

"Yes." Her hand came up to stroke his jaw, to rest against his cheek. "I'm all right."

"It was too quick, wasn't it?"

"No," she lied. "It was just right."

Rolling off her, he pulled her close and rubbed his chin against her tangled hair. His heart still pounded, and his breath still came in quick, short gasps, but he felt unbelievably good. "No, it was too quick, but I couldn't help it," he said again. "It's been a long time since I've had a woman, Annie. A real long time. But I want you to know I never had anything like this. Never." His hand twined in her hair, pressing her head against his chest. "I'm real glad I found you, Annie."

She felt safe within his embrace, as though as long as he held her there'd be no nightmares. And her throat ached with the overwhelming gratitude she felt.

"I'm glad, too," she managed to whisper.

With the cool breeze blowing across their bodies, he lay there, holding her, savoring the feel of the woman he'd married, feeling incredibly lucky. But like the wedding itself, he knew he'd not done it right, that he'd not really satisfied her. And he didn't want her to have any regrets come morning. His hand moved lower, sliding over her hip, stroking it almost absently.

"You know what I'd like to do, Mrs. Walker?" he asked softly. "I'd like to take off the rest of my clothes, get you out of that nightgown, and love you again. I reckon this time I could do a whole lot better by you."

In the darkness he couldn't see her smile, but there was no mistaking the way she ran her fingers through his thick, wavy hair, or the way she parted her lips beneath his. And he didn't care about tomorrow or any day after. They were the only two people in the world tonight.

He came awake slowly, at first only dimly aware of the tickle in his ear, then of the hair in his face. He opened his eyes into a mass of black fur. As he reached to move it, he frightened the creature, and it sank its claws firmly into his head. Afraid it would go for his eyes, Hap groped for his wife's shoulder.

"The cat's come home," he mumbled sleepily.

"Spider?" She rolled over, saw his predicament, and giggled. "You've got a cat hat, Hap. You look like Davy Crockett."

"Ouch! You little devil!" Catching the half-grown kitten with one hand, he tried to disengage its claws with the other. Lifting it free, he looked up into a pair of round orange eyes. "Damnedest cat I ever saw," he muttered. It stared at him for a moment, then began to wriggle, struggling to get loose. "Not half-friendly, are you?"

Opening its mouth, it gave him a full view of fangs, snarling at him. "Damned if you don't think you're a panther," he decided, grinning up at it. "Spider, eh?"

Leaning to retrieve a small ball of yarn from the knitting basket beside the bed, Annie held it up for the kitten to see, and tossed it across the room. Spider gave a half twist, then escaped from Hap's hands to scamper after it. Annie lay back watching him.

"It won't take long before he's got it undone and hanging from half the things in this room," she murmured. "Then you'll understand."

But Hap wasn't looking at the cat anymore. Seeing her bare shoulder above the covers sent a fresh wave of desire washing over him, nearly robbing him of breath. And he wanted to explore every inch of her body, to feel her beneath him, yielding her softness, coming alive with passion, slaking his need of her.

"See? There he goes," she said, turning to Hap. Her smile froze, and her eyes gave him a glimpse of sudden fear. Unconsciously, she pulled the sheet up. "Oh."

She had to be thinking he was an animal after the way he'd had her twice last night. Willing the heat from his body, he sat up, his naked back to her, shielding his rigid manhood from her sight.

"If you were to close your eyes, I'd get up," he said finally.

"Hap—"

"No, it's all right. I reckon we've got a long day ahead of us, anyway. So while I'm out in the privy, maybe you can get dressed and make the coffee. I think there's enough tinder in the box to get the stove going again."

"I'm sorry, Hap. I couldn't help it," she said simply.

"I know." He twisted his neck to look back at her, and forced a smile. "Guess I can't have a storm all the time, can I?"

She looked away at that. "I wanted it as much as you,"

she said, her voice low. "I wanted you to hold me, to make me forget everything. And you did."

"Yeah. Close your eyes, Annie." Leaning down, he groped on the floor for his pants, maneuvered his feet into the legs, then stood to pull them up. Buttoning the fly, he kept his back to her until he shrugged into his wrinkled shirt and it hung down to hide him from her. Trying to keep his tone light, he told you, "Come on, you'd better get around if you want to go today."

Outside, he took his time, lecturing himself that if he didn't go easy, if he didn't give her enough time and distance to heal, he was going to ruin everything. He had no right to want more than she'd given him. He wanted her to love him, not have a disgust of him.

At the pump, he ducked his head under the stream of water and came up shaking his wet head, slicking his hair back with both hands. Then he leaned down to rinse the night taste from his mouth. Yeah, he was all right now. He could face her.

The kitchen was empty, the firebox barely warm from last night's late supper. She was probably washing up. He threw a handful of dead grass and twigs into the cookstove, waited until they caught, then added several small sticks of wood. While the fire got going, he rummaged in the cupboard, found her sack of coffee, and put a couple of spoons in a pan. Adding a couple of ladles of water from the bucket to it, he set the pan on the top of the stove.

"I put your coffee on, Annie!" he called out.

There was no answer. He walked back to the bedroom, expecting to find her setting at the little dresser, brushing out her hair—or something like that, anyway. She was sitting up in bed, the sheet pulled taut over her breasts and tucked under her arms. His mouth went dry all over again.

"God, Annie," was all he could think of to say.

"It wasn't right to turn you away," she said, not meeting his eyes. "You've got every right to expect—"

"I don't know what to expect," he cut in. "I don't even know what to give." Trying not to look at her, he exhaled heavily. "Look, I never was much of a ladies' man. Maybe I was never around enough of 'em—I don't know. I was out on the trail a lot, and when I got to town, I wasn't much for keeping company with whores—never understood how a woman could do that for money, I guess. Oh, I don't want you to think I was some sort of saint. My nature got the best of me sometimes, Annie."

"You don't have to say this, Hap," she said quietly.

"Yeah, I do. I just want you to know I'm willing to learn, to do what it takes to make you happy. If it's just holding you sometimes without the other, I'll try to do it. If it's loving you once a night, once a week, or even less than that, I'll try getting along that way, too." He swung around to face her, forcing another twisted smile. " 'Way I look at it, a man like me's just damned lucky to have a woman like you."

Hot tears stung her eyes, and the ache in her throat was nearly unbearable. "No," she whispered, "I'm the luckiest woman alive. I don't want to turn away from you. I want to be whole."

"I don't want to hurt you, Annie. I don't want to make it worse."

"Hold me, Hap—hold me now," she said softly.

"You don't have to do this."

298

"I want to."

His fingers tangled in the button holes of his shirt until he finally just pulled it over his head. Turning away, he hastily undid his pants, then allowed himself to face her in all his glory, giving her the chance to change her mind. "I've got a lot of scars on me, Annie," he said. "I'm not real pretty."

"You don't have to be." She tried to smile and couldn't. "A man's not supposed to be pretty."

As he walked toward her, his pulse raced, pounding the blood through his veins. He wasn't going to be groping in the dark now. He was going to see and explore all of her, and as he loved her, he could look into her face and know if he was pleasing her.

Sitting on the edge of the bed, he reached to lift the sheet. She closed her eyes and let go of it. Easing his body down next to her, he leaned over to push the pale, tangled hair back from her face. Her closed lids were bluish, her lashes almost gold against her pale skin. His gaze dropped lower, taking in the rounded swell of ivory breasts, the smooth, almost taut skin below them, the flat plain of her belly, and he could scarcely believe she was his.

He brushed his thumb over a soft, pink nipple, watching it tauten. Her body seemed to quiver beneath his hand. Gingerly sliding lower in the bed, he turned his face to her breast and teased the hardening button, running his tongue over it. She gasped, then her hands grasped his hair, holding his head there. Fighting the urge to hurry, he was determined to explore her thoroughly, to know every inch of her. His teeth lightly nibbled the nip-

Anita Mills

ple, then his mouth closed over it, and he sucked eagerly, while his hand felt her belly quicken.

The murmured words, the almost awkward couplings of the night, had left her utterly unprepared for the effect he was having on her now. It was as though her whole being was centered where he sucked—and between her legs. Her fingers opened and closed in his thick, wavy hair as she felt the wet warmth lower. It had been a long, long time since she'd felt anything like this. As he brought forth her desire, she urged him on.

"Kiss me, Hap," she said. "Kiss me now."

He pressed his mouth against her breast, her collarbone, into the hollow of her throat, along her earlobe. His warm breath sent a shiver of anticipation through her.

"Tell me what you want, sweetheart, and I'll do my damnedest to give it to you," he whispered at her ear.

"I want you to touch me. I want you to love me."

"Where, Annie?—where?" As he asked, his hands moved over her, exploring the smooth, moist skin of her back, the rounded curve of her bottom. Her legs tangled around his, drawing his body closer, pressing her belly against his. Slipping his hand between them, he touched the soft, wet thatch. The tension in her leg slackened as she opened beneath his hand, letting him inside. "Here, Annie?" he whispered.

"Yes." It was more of a moan than an answer.

He rolled her onto her back, but didn't follow her down. Instead, he took his time, kissing her, whispering love words to her, as his fingers stroked and explored. Her head was back, her hair spilling over the embroidered pillowcase, but there was no mistaking the intensity of the pleasure he was giving her. Her legs moved restlessly,

300

opening and closing around his hand, and her hips arched, urging more.

"Please," she moaned. "Kiss me—give me all of it, Hap."

She was going to give him the best time of his life, and he knew it. As her arms reached up to pull his head to hers, he eased his body over her, and her legs closed around him, pulling him down, drawing him into her. This time there was no last-minute fright, no attempt to stop, only the frenzied passion of union, the sound of her panting cries in his ears driving him to ultimate release.

Spent, he collapsed over her. Looking down at her closed eyes, seeing the tendrils of pale hair clinging to her damp temples, he was truly amazed by her. "Reckon that's about as close to heaven as I'll ever get, Annie," he told her softly.

Her blue eyes opened, daring to meet his gaze. "It was easier in the light," she managed.

For a moment he was perplexed. "I always heard most women liked it better in the dark."

Turning her head, she looked at the bright embroidery on the pillowcase. Swallowing visibly, she told him, her voice so low he could barely hear it, "I could see you. I knew it was you. In the dark there are so many nightmares."

His passion gone, he wanted to cry for her. "Don't think about it, sweetheart," he said, stroking her hair where it fell forward over her shoulder. "It's over."

"No. It'll never be over, not until I have Susannah. Maybe not even then."

Easing his body from hers, he lay behind her and drew her back against him. "Would it help to talk about it?"

"No. You wouldn't want to know—you just wouldn't."

"I buried some of those women, Annie. There's not much you could say that I don't already have a fair notion about," he said gently. "I've seen 'em cut inside even. So if it would help to have me listen, I will."

"You'd think I was dirty."

"No."

"Everyone else does. I can see it in their eyes."

"I'm not everybody, Annie." Wrapping his arms around her, he rested a hand on her breast. "I'm your husband. I reckon I love you enough to want to take the pain. If keeping quiet is easier, do that. If not, I'm right here." When she said nothing, he added, "By rights you ought to be dead from what they did to you, but I figure God had a reason for sparing you." Nuzzling her hair with his chin, he said softly, "I'm kind of hoping I'm that reason, Annie."

"So am I," she whispered.

"You don't have to go back up there." As he said it, he felt her stiffen in his arms. "No, hear me out. I don't want you having to look at those bastards, having to remember what they did to you."

"I have to go—I have to."

"I can ride up to Sill. There's supposed to be a few friendly Comanches up there, you know. Maybe I can pay one of 'em to take me up to Llano to look for your little girl. I'm willing to give it all summer, Annie. I'll look in every damned village I can find."

"You don't know her," came the muffled reply. "I'm her mother."

"I'll take the doll. I never knew a kid yet that didn't remember a toy."

There was a moment's silence, then she sighed. "I've got to go, Hap."

"All right." Turning away, he sat up. "We'll be getting a late start, 'cause I've still got to stop over at the stage station and bargain for a couple of mules. Ouch!" Looking down, he saw that the black kitten had a good hold on his big toe. "Damned cat," he muttered under his breath.

"We can't go today," she said suddenly, sitting up behind him. "I can't just leave Spider here to fend for himself. I'll have to take him to Mary's."

Reaching down, he lifted the fur ball by the scruff of its neck. "Cats take care of themselves, Annie. Most of 'em never get inside a house."

"I wouldn't feel right."

Hap looked around, surveying the damage one ball of yarn could do. That cat had managed to string it from one end of the room to the other, catching it on everything in between. He studied the cat.

"You're a little hell-raiser, aren't you?"

It blinked those round orange eyes at him.

"They're like family to me, Hap. When I got back here, they made everything bearable."

"Yeah. Well, if we don't leave out until tomorrow, I reckon I can take him by the Willetts on my way to the station to pick up the mules. That way we can have everything ready for first light in the morning."

"I think it'd be better."

He sure wasn't going to argue with her, not when it gave him another night on that feather mattress. Suddenly he remembered, "I got your coffee boiling—ought to be real strong by now."

"I'll get it. Is oatmeal all right for breakfast? Or I could fry up a little cold mush."

"I'd like mush a whole lot better," he admitted.

"All right."

Covering her front with the sheet, she leaned off the bed to find her wrapper, then quickly slipped it on. He watched her pad barefoot across the floor, thinking it was a wonder how a woman could be everything to a man. There was no explaining how or why he'd come to feel about her as he did, and he guessed it didn't matter much, anyway. But right now he knew he could lay down his life for her. And it wasn't lost on him that he might.

She turned back at the door. "Aren't you getting up?"

"Yeah. While you fix breakfast, I reckon I'll wash up and shave. Then I'll try to figure out what I can put the animal in."

"It's not just an animal, Hap, it's my cat. I wish you had time to get to know him."

He eyed the kitten as it attacked the crocheted edge of a pillowcase. "Yeah, well, I'd probably get along with the other one better. I'm not much for hell-raising animals."

"I've hopes he'll grow out of some of it."

"Yeah, maybe by the time we get back."

Once she left for the kitchen, he went into the other bedroom and poured a little cool water into the washbasin. As he splashed his face, he looked up, seeing himself in the oval mirror. "Nothing like an old fool, is there?" he asked his reflection. But today he didn't feel old at all. He felt like a kid again.

When he came out, dressed and ready to go for the mules, she had two slabs of fried cornmeal slathered with fresh butter waiting for him. Going to the cupboard, she took out a jar of honey and carried it to the table. He noticed she had a cup of water next to her plate.

"Where's the coffee?"

"It had Clay McAlester written all over it," she told him smiling. "I was afraid it would eat the spoon."

"You've never tasted his. Hell, the spoon can't hit bottom in it."

"He must've learned to make it from you."

"Want me to try again?"

"No." She sat down across from him and reached for the honey. Drizzling some of it over a single piece of fried mush, she asked, "Did you find anything to put Spider in?"

"Yeah, there was a carpetbag in the wardrobe. It's already got a couple of moth holes in it, anyway, so I expect he'll be able to breathe in it."

"Good. Just remember to drop him off first. Otherwise, it'll be too hot for him."

"I wasn't planning on listening to him howl any longer than I have to."

"You'd better tell Mary—no, I'd better write it down for her," she decided.

"I don't think she can read much," he pointed out, recalling the woman's letter.

"If I don't put any big words in it." She got up and went into the other room, and he could hear her rummaging in some drawers. She came back empty-handed. "I've misplaced my paper," she said, sitting down again. "I wanted to tell her what he likes and what he won't eat."

"I doubt she's going to cook for it."

"It's not very hard to add an egg to milk, is it?" she countered.

"Well, I can tell her that."

"Pork makes him sick, and so do bones."

"I'll remember it."

"And if she gives him fish, he won't eat it unless it's cooked."

"She'll probably put him in the barn," he reminded her.

"No. He'd starve, Hap. I've never seen him catch a mouse at all."

"Hate to say it, Annie, but he sounds pretty useless," he teased her.

"No. He has great entertainment value, even if he *is* a pest."

"What's she doing with the other one?"

"Twain? Twain's different. He's real easygoing—sort of like you, in fact. He'll eat anything he doesn't have to catch. I've even caught him chewing on raw beans." She cut a piece of mush and carried it to her mouth. "I don't think I packed my stationery. I can't imagine that I did, anyway. I just wrote to Cora the other day, and—"

"I've got paper, Annie. I'll tear a sheet out for you." Having already polished off his food, he got up and headed for the other room. When he came back, he had the tablet and pencil in hand. "Just put down what you want, and I'll see the Willett woman gets it."

"That's some letter you've got in front," she murmured, reaching for the cup of water.

He looked up, surprised. "You saw it?"

"In the buckboard." Seeing that he flushed, she apologized quickly. "I'm sorry. I shouldn't have read it, but there wasn't much else to do sitting under that tree."

"It's not exactly a letter," he admitted. "I, uh, I got this fellow that wants me to write my life story. Got me to

306

thinking maybe I'd kinda like to do it for Clay's kid—they got a kid on the way, you know. Him and Amanda, I mean."

"He means a lot to you."

"Clay? Yeah. Like a son. We've been through a lot together—him being a wild kid, the war, the rangers. But we never talked a lot. Didn't really need to, I guess. I wish you could get to know him, Annie."

"I'd like that."

"Yeah. Anyway, I kinda thought I'd like to put it all down in case I never see the kid—or in case I'm not around by the time he's grown up. I've got a lot to tell him about his pa—and about me. Pretty soon there won't be men like me running around carrying six-shooters and chasing Indians, you know. I'd kinda like to have him know how it was."

"And if it's a girl? What if they have a daughter, Hap?"

"It doesn't matter. I reckon a little girl would like to know about her pa, too. And if it was left to Clay, he wouldn't think it was important. He never knew his own folks, you understand." Hap opened the tablet to rip out a sheet and looked at what he'd written. "Hard to know what to say, though. Hard to know what'll interest a kid."

"Just about everything you've ever done." She reached up for his hand, then drew it against her cheek. "Everybody admires you—you're quite a man."

"Now I know you're teasing me," he retorted. "I never did anything I didn't have to."

She looked up through wet lashes, and her smile twisted. "You're taking me back up there, and you don't have to."

"I made you a bargain," he answered simply. Embarrassed, he drew back his hand and turned to the back of the tablet. "Here," he said, tearing a piece of the paper out. "If I were you, I'd make it real simple."

"Where are you going?"

"To stuff Spider in the bag."

"Be careful!" she called after him.

"He's not a wildcat, Annie."

Picking up the pencil, she considered a moment how to begin her note, then wrote, "Mr. Walker is bringing Spider over this morning. He and I were married yesterday at Baker's Gap, and he will be going with me to look for Susannah. Please love Spider and Twain for me. They have been grand company. Also, please don't let Jim put them in the barn. And whenever you can, please beat an egg into Spider's milk. And don't let him eat any raw fish."

She stopped. She sounded more like the cats' mother than an owner. And Hap was right—if it was too complicated, Mary wouldn't be able to read it. She looked it over, thinking somewhat ruefully that the way she worded it, it sounded like she'd married Spider. But Mary'd know what she meant, anyway. And she and Jim would be so pleased about her marriage to Hap Walker.

After what had happened to Ethan and Jody, she didn't deserve such happiness, but she was getting that chance to start over with a man who loved her. And she felt a pang of conscience for what she was asking of him. Yet she couldn't give up her daughter. All she could do was pray to God that all three of them came back together.

The trail was hot and dusty and dangerous in places, but they'd made remarkable time in the last several days, coming up from San Angelo, following the North Concho toward the Big Spring, then skirting the east side of the mountains, crossing a number of rivers and streams on their way north to the Prairie Dog Fork of the Red River. Their ultimate goal was to reach the eastern side of the Llano Estacado, the heart of the Comancheria. Those high grasslands where the buffalo grew fat, and those deep, winding canyons with Comanche villages stretching along streams for miles. A no-man's land for an Anglo.

He'd been seeing signs of Indians ever since the Big Spring, and for all he knew they were being shadowed by them now. That was the thing about the damned Comanches—they could follow a man for days before they struck, playing a game with him, sometimes even creeping almost to his campfire without his knowing it. He'd once had a horse stolen while he'd had it tethered to his foot, and still he'd woke up with his hair. On foot, but alive. Knowing they were just waiting like vultures over a dying animal, he'd turned the tables, creeping to the edge of the Comanche camp to steal back his own horse. By some miracle he'd gotten away with it.

He was so hot that his shirt clung wetly to his skin while his buckskin pants stuck to the sides of Old Red. He cast a sidewise glance at Annie, but she was riding as stoically as an Indian. He'd give her that—her three years with them had been hell, but she'd sure learned how to travel like them, without complaint. It was almost like tracking across the desert with Clay. Almost, but not quite.

After more than two weeks of marriage, Annie held him more in thrall now than ever. When the going was roughest, he found himself thinking ahead to when they'd be stopping, how much water he could afford to use to make himself acceptable, how good it would feel to roll up in his bedroll with her in his arms. Even at night, when the lovemaking was over, he'd lay there, looking up at the stars, listening to the not so distant howls of the coyotes, thinking how lucky he'd been when he'd stumbled onto Bull Calf's camp in that blizzard. If he never came back from the Llano, he knew he'd die feeling that way.

Seeing the cat panting pathetically, he reached for his canteen, unscrewed the lid, and poured a little water on its head. Then he cupped his hand, making a place for it to drink. It had to be hell being a long-haired black cat in the desert. As hot as it was, it crept back to drape itself behind his saddle horn, positioning itself against his inner thigh.

The damned thing had adopted him, and there hadn't been much he could do about it. When he'd left it at the Willetts', it had tried to follow him. Finally, he'd turned back, handed it to Mary, then ridden on over to the stage-coach way station to buy the two mules. Hot and thirsty, he'd come back by Buell's Crossing, where a downright civil Lake had sold him a beer and apologized about Annie. By the time Hap got home that night, a tired Spider was waiting to get into the house. It had walked more than five miles just to come back. The other one, the cat Annie'd missed so much, hadn't been nearly as adventurous. It was still at the Willetts'.

Finally, rather than make another trip, and faced with an adamant Annie, Hap had spent hours cutting and braiding a rawhide lead and a collar for the little critter. Now he'd been out in the sun himself so long that he was beginning to like it. When they stopped, while Annie fixed food, Hap found himself watching Spider attack anything that dared to move.

"Do you want me to take him?" Annie asked.

"No, he's all right. It's just too damned hot out here, that's all."

"I couldn't leave him to starve, Hap."

"You've got a soft heart, Annie."

"I'm not the one holding him."

"Hell, I haven't even had a dog since I was a kid," he protested. He looked down at the hairy ball cuddled against him. "Cat's not much of a man's animal, you know," he muttered.

"Whether I know it or not doesn't seem to matter," she countered. "He apparently doesn't."

"Yeah, well, when we get back, I don't want you telling everybody I rode one of the old war trails with a damned cat in my lap the whole way."

"I won't. It was good of you to let me bring him."

He squinted, scanning the horizon intently for a moment. "Yeah, I just hope he doesn't wind up in a cooking pot somewhere."

"They never ate any cats I knew of, Hap—and no dogs, either. Just about everything else but not that. You must be thinking of the Arapahos or the Cheyenne."

"Uh-huh."

"See anything?" she asked suddenly.

"No, and that worries me," he admitted. "I know they're out there, and sometime tomorrow we'll be cutting west, hitting the damned canyons."

What he wasn't saying was that Clay'd told him there were narrows scarcely fifteen feet wide in places, and with high walls squeezing in on the arroyos, and caves and overhangs above them, there were plenty of places for an ambush. Places worse than along the main war trail coming across Horsehead Crossing on the Pecos. But she probably knew. She'd been up there, and she'd seen the place, while he'd only heard about it.

Thinking Hap regretted coming, she sought to reassure him. "I can speak to them—I can tell them why we're here."

"Yeah, if you get the chance. Pretty hard to say much if you've already got a bullet in you."

"With just the two of us, they'll come for a closer look."

"Yeah, they don't want to miss out on the fun."

"No."

"You've got a lot of guts, Annie—you know that, don't you?"

"And you don't?" she countered.

"I'm a man. And I've never been through anything like

312

what happened to you. I don't know how you can stand to go back."

"They have Susannah," she said simply.

"They're not going to give us any help, you know. It'll be hit-or-miss finding her."

"I know." She was silent for several seconds, then sighed. "You don't think we can do it, do you?"

"Annie, if I didn't think there was a chance, I wouldn't be here," he lied. "I just hope you can take it if we don't. I don't want this to destroy you."

"I don't know. I just have to believe it's going to happen, Hap."

"Annie . . ." He hesitated, then changed his mind. He wasn't going to say anything to disappoint her. It'd happen soon enough, anyway, and then he'd be trying to comfort her. "You look hot enough to faint," he muttered instead. "Maybe if we stopped a few minutes in the shade of those mesquites, you'd feel better."

"I'm all right."

She was driving herself too hard in her eagerness to reach the hunting grounds. Finally, he looked down at Spider. "The cat's not going to make it if we don't cool him off," he said, hoping to persuade her. "He's panting pretty hard with all this hair on him."

"All right."

"We'll rest the animals and give 'em a drink, then we'll go on," he promised. "I don't want to be trying to cross the river at night, anyway. I'd rather have full light."

"I brought my mending kit. Maybe if I cut some of the fur off, he'd be cooler," she murmured, considering the nearly prostrate cat.

"Yeah."

He reined in and swung out of his saddle to walk wide-legged toward the low-branched trees. His buckskin pants were stuck to his skin, glued there by Old Red's sweat. Quickly tying the big black pack mule's lead to a limb, he took down the packs to cool it off. Then he turned his attention to the cat. Unscrewing the lid off his last full canteen, he wet its head again, rubbing the water into its skin.

"Better, fella?" But even as he asked it, he could see it wasn't. "I don't know, Annie. I think he'd have been better off fending for himself."

She brought her sewing box over, then knelt beside the panting animal. Taking out her scissors, she looked up at Hap. "Can you hold him down? He might not like this."

"Yeah."

The result was almost comical. Bereft of great wads of black hair, Spider turned out to be a lot smaller than Hap had expected. By the time Annie finally gave up and put away the scissors, the irregularly chopped fur made the cat look like a miniature black owl with badly ruffled feathers. Still trying to cool him, Hap washed him down from head to tail, so that the uneven edges stood in little wet spikes. When finally turned loose, the indignant Spider climbed the tree, tangling his braided lead in the branches, nearly hanging himself. Balefully eyeing his human tormentors, he clung upside down to a branch, howling.

"You're more trouble than you're worth, you know that, don't you?" Hap said, trying to free him. "She should've named you Trouble." Behind him, Annie giggled. Then he froze, the hairs on his neck standing on end. "Uh-oh."

"What?"

"Company. Don't move. Just keep looking at the cat,"

he ordered, easing his hand toward his holster. "And keep talking like everything's all right."

Out of the corner of her eye, she could see two mounted warriors coming toward them; and for a moment she froze also. Both had their faces painted black, marking them as part of a war party, possibly the advance scouts for it. And the old terror washed over her, making her heart pound, taking her breath away. Then she saw the glint of the sun on the Peacemaker.

"No!" she screamed, lunging for his arm. "Don't shoot!"

As the bullet went wide, both Indians bore down on them, one with his feathered lance lowered. Before Hap knew what she was doing, Annie was racing toward them, waving her hands, shouting in Comanche. Hap broke into a dead run after her, trying to catch her before they killed her.

"Get down, Annie!" he yelled, his heart in his throat. "For God's sake, get out of the way!"

He raised his gun again, then held his fire as the lead rider lifted the war lance. The other warrior circled her, then came to a halt. She stood there, holding her ground, gesturing as she spoke. Finally, after what seemed like forever, the Comanche with the lance rode toward him, both hands up in a gesture of peace. Pointing at Hap, he asked, "Tondehwahkah?"

Hap looked at Annie. "What did you tell him?"

"That Many Bullets has brought Woman Who Walks Far to visit her adopted people."

He looked up at the Indian, forcing a smile. "Yeah." Carefully sheathing the Colt, he kept his eye on the other one. He'd trust the biggest rattlesnake on earth over a Comanche. "What did he say to that?"

"That there are more warriors coming, and they're on their way to Mexico to steal horses."

"They're lying. They're going down to raid the ranches."

"They outnumber us, Hap."

The Indian nearest her spoke up then, telling her something. She nodded before turning back to Hap. "He says there's no good water right now," she translated for him. "Even the Red's bad in places, with too much sand and gypsum in it. And the ponds and pools in the gaps are so bad the horses won't drink from them."

"Full of good news, isn't he?" he muttered.

"They'd give us water, but they're not sure about what they'll find at the Brazos, so they don't want to spare any. I told him it was drinkable, but I'm not sure he believes me."

As they stood there, talking to the two Comanches, the rest of the war party caught up. Seeing the mules tied up, they took the place for a camp, and to Hap's chagrin, all ten of them dismounted to make themselves at home. One noticed Spider and advanced curiously on the little cat. Having never seen an Indian in full war paint with his face zigzagged in red and black, his hair part marked with a yellow line, Spider took exception to the inspection. Arching his back, he hissed and spat, then snarled, giving a full view of his fangs. Startled, the Comanche drew back, and his companions roared with laughter.

Within minutes, the Indians had a small mesquite fire going and were spitting hackberry balls on sticks. One of the Indians approached Hap, gesturing to his packs.

"They want to know if you'll make some coffee for them," Annie explained. "I told them I'd do it. They want to share their food with us."

"Mighty nice of 'em," he observed sarcastically.

"They said it was an honor to eat with Tondehwahkah. But they're traveling light—it'll just be pemmican and hackberry balls. If you've never tried them—well, they're not too bad."

"Yeah, Clay used to make 'em. Tallow and berry paste. I guess it's all in what a body gets used to. Me, I could've gone a lifetime without eating any, but he'd get a real hankering for 'em.'

"At least they're better than a lot of things they could be offering us," she pointed out. "They could be killing a horse and handing it out in raw pieces, you know."

"I've seen Clay eat that, too, but that doesn't mean I'd want any."

"I expect they'll be moving on as soon as they eat."

"Learn anything else? Like where they're from, or where they're going?"

"They're Noconis—from Ketanah's band. They don't know where the Quahadis are, only that Quanah's somewhere up on the Llano. There are a number of bands camped along the Great Canyon, but they can only say that most are Comanche with a few Kiowa mixed in."

"Reckon maybe that'd be the Palo Duro," he decided.

"I don't know. There are a lot of deep holes up there. Anyway, we'll have to find out for ourselves. They're going on."

"Where?"

She turned to speak to the war chief, then shook her head. "They'll be going down by Fort Davis, as near as I can tell. Usually that means they're after Mexican slaves and horses."

It didn't take long for the smell of burning mesquite and tallow to fill the air. Retrieving one of the sticks from the fire, an Indian buck blew the ashes off the burnt mess on the end, then held it out to Hap. As they all sat in a circle around the smoking campfire, sharing food and coffee, the conversation was animated, with the war chief directing a continuous stream of questions at Annie for Hap. Had Tondehwahkah come to smoke peace after years of making war? Where was Nahahkoah? Why did they no longer see Nahahkoah riding in the desert? In turn, she asked them if they knew anything about any white children held by the Quahadis. But after much shrugging and conferring, they assured her they didn't.

"They're lying about that, too," Hap told her. "They don't want the soldiers coming into their villages."

By the time the campfire was buried, and the Indians moved on, the sun was a white-hot disk in the cloudless sky, and the heat rose in undulating waves from the ground. It had to be near ninety, and it was only April. If they hadn't been facing another river, Hap would have liked to wait until it was cooler to travel.

Then he wondered why the war party had gone on, because most of the Indians he'd tracked traveled at night like Clay. Despite their seeming friendliness, he had to wonder if they'd double back and attack come nightfall. But if they'd wanted to kill him and Annie, they could have done it easily, he reminded himself.

He wanted to wash up, to cool off before he got back into the saddle, but if things were as bad as the Indian had said, he couldn't afford to waste any water. Reluctantly, he threw the packs back onto the mules, tied them down, and gathered up the outraged cat. Tonight, if they pressed on, they might make it to a cedar-fringed shelter where they crossed through the mountains, but that'd be

318

pushing it. Still, the notion of lying with the smell of cedar surrounding him was an inviting one.

It was nearly three o'clock by the time they reached the sinuous, low-banked North Pease River. He could smell it even before he saw it, and he knew the Comanches had told the truth about the water at least. Winding alongside it was a thick line of reeds, willows, and stinking sedge grass. The ground, where he could see it, was crusted with more gypsum than he'd ever known it to have.

To make matters worse, if possible, a herd of buffalo had passed through, leaving an equally strong stench of urine and excrement. He knew he wasn't going to camp there. Hell, he wasn't even sure he wanted to swim across it. And looking over at Annie, he could see she was revolted by the smell.

"Want to go upriver awhile and look for a better place?"

"No. When it's like this, there isn't."

She looked too tired, but he knew she wasn't going to give in. By the time they got across, they were both going to smell like an outhouse. No, they'd just have to go on and pray that the Indians had been wrong, that there was a spring somewhere in the gap. Before, when he'd traveled with men, it hadn't mattered so much, but now he had a wife. He guessed if worse came to worst, he could strip and roll in the dew-soaked grass tonight to take part of the stink off.

"All right." Knotting his rein over his fist, he got a good grip on the cat, wondering how the hell he'd get Spider across without looking like a nearsighted berry picker by the time he came up the bank on the other side. Knowing it was going to hurt like hell, he thrust the frightened creature inside his shirt. "Reckon I'd better go first," he muttered. "If I get into any trouble, don't come after me. I'll yell if there's quicksand."

With a whoop he eased the reins and kneed Old Red. The horse plunged into the water, then tried to drink. He kicked it with his spurs, urging it on across, dragging a fighting mule behind him. At the moment he'd hit the water, the cat popped out of his shirt, took a look at the predicament it was in, and promptly dug every claw it had into Hap's neck and shoulder. Hanging on, it howled all the way over, then let loose and bounded up the opposite bank, its leash trailing behind it. Cursing, Hap tried to grab it, but it was gone.

When he looked back, Annie was having a devil of a time getting her mule out of the water. Nearly mad with thirst, it wanted to drink the foul stuff, founder, and die. Holding his nose, Hap slid from his saddle, hit Old Red on the rump, letting it drag his pack animal on up, then eased down the slimy sand back into the water. It wasn't deep, just nasty. Grabbing the mule's lead, he pulled it, thrashing and kicking across the shallow, sandy riverbed. When it nipped him, he drew his Colt and hit it hard with the butt right between its eyes. As he slogged up the marshy bank, Annie was waiting with Old Red.

"I hate this damned river," he muttered, struggling to stand as his wet clothes sagged. "Never got across it easy yet." Sinking down for a moment in the crusted mud, he caught his breath, then remembered the damned cat. "Spider's gone, Annie," he managed. "Couldn't hold him."

"He's right here."

He looked down, seeing the blood on his shirt where the animal's claws had ripped his skin, and he didn't know whether to be glad or not. She followed his gaze, then decided, "I'd better get the balm."

"Yeah."

He laid his wet gun down and stood up, smoothing his soaked clothes downward, squeezing the excess water against his skin. He knew he smelled so bad that a polecat wouldn't want to be around him. Stripping his clothes, he flung them on the ground, then looked around for anything to clean himself with. Annie'd been a whole lot luckier, and when her horse had hit the water, she'd brought her knees up, keeping everything but the hem of her dress dry.

As he stood there, buck naked, she let the cat down, and it dragged its leash between his legs, rubbing against his wet legs affectionately. "No need to come around now," he growled. "Reckon I've got a good notion of what you think of me, you little varmint." But even as he said it, he bent down to pick the sorry black mess up. "Here now," he said gruffly as it began washing his face with the sandpaper tongue. "You'll make yourself sick."

"He's probably trying to make up," Annie observed, carrying the jar of balm over. Taking off the lid, she dipped her fingers into it. "This may smart a little, but cat scratches get infected."

"Yeah, well, the river water doesn't help much." Turning his head away, he spat on the ground, trying to get the taste out of his mouth. "Must be ten tons of gypsum in there."

"At least. Here . . ." Instead of doctoring the scratches, she handed him the jar, then went to the packs where she found a dry cloth. Pouring a small amount of the precious drinking water on it, she rubbed a bar of lye soap into it.

When she came back, she held it out. "It's strong soap, so maybe it'll help."

Scrubbing himself, he got most of the crusty stuff off, then found a clean shirt and pants. Pulling the shirt on, he left it open so she could treat all the holes and gouges. As she worked, he squinted up at the sun, measuring its position in the sky. "I was kinda hoping to make it into the gap before we bedded down." Turning back to her, his smile was lopsided, reminding her of a little boy's. "I can make a real soft bed out of cedar."

Feeling the heat rise in her cheeks, she had to look away. "By tonight I probably won't need it. I'll probably be able to sleep anywhere."

Disappointment washed over him; then he reminded himself that he was further ahead already than he'd expected to be with her. For a man who'd never had a woman with any regularity before, he was getting damned greedy. It seemed that all he had to do was look at her to get the notion.

He took a deep breath, then nodded. "They kinda brought it back to you, didn't they? Those Indians, I mean."

"Yes." She closed her eyes briefly, then dared to meet his gaze. "I think it was the war paint."

"You were real brave, Annie—you didn't show it."

"But I thought it, Hap. When the first one came riding down on me with that lance, I thought it." Taking one last dab at his neck with the balm, she closed the jar. "I thought he'd kill you, and—" She couldn't bring herself to say it.

"Then why the hell'd you go running out there like that?" he demanded. "I had a good bead on him."

"I had to. I wanted to know where the Quadahis are.

And I had to prove to myself I could look them in the face," she added soberly. "In my mind I was sure they wouldn't hurt me, but in my heart I was afraid. And I knew if you killed him, they wouldn't listen to anything I said."

"You'll never know how much I wanted to pull that trigger, Annie."

"Believe me, if you ever have Two Trees in your sights, I won't stop you. It'd almost be worth dying just to see him pay for what he did to Gretchen."

"And to you."

"And to me. But I've always hoped he died somewhere, that somebody made him pay before now. I know it's not right, but I've prayed for that since the day he took me away."

The pain in her eyes was so real that he wanted to take her into his arms and hold her, but he knew if he did, they'd never get on down the trail. And they had to. Right now they were sitting ducks on the riverbank, and there was no guarantee the next Comanches would be friendly.

"If you don't mind, I'd like to get away from this smell," she murmured.

"The balm?" he teased.

"The river."

Bending down, he retrieved the Peacemaker and spun the cylinder, removing the bullets from the chambers. "Soon as I get this dried out and a little oil on it, I reckon I'm ready. I can't afford to let it get fouled up." He scanned the open area around them, then made up his mind. "I'd better check the Henry, too, 'cause I reckon you'd better carry it from here on. You know how to use it, don't you?"

She closed her eyes again, remembering the urgency

she'd felt firing Ethan's, and she nodded. "Yes," she answered low.

"I'll get it. Then we'd better get around. I never did like this place."

Later, riding beside a silent and decidedly sober Annie, he thought a lot about how hard it was for her to forget, about how no matter how passionate she was in his arms, there were still times when he saw fear in her eyes. There were still times when all he could do was hold her through her nightmares.

"What if he's still alive, Annie? What if you come face to face with him again?" As soon as the words had escaped, he wanted them back. He hadn't meant to remind her again, not after what she'd said.

"I don't know." She sucked in her breath, then let it out slowly. "No matter what I said back there, I wouldn't want you to die for killing him. So I guess if I had to face him again, I'd ask him again to tell me who he sold Susannah to. I know he knows, Hap—I know he knows."

"Then I'll wring it out of the son of a bitch," he promised her. "Right before I kill him."

And he meant it. He didn't know how, or where, or when, but someday he was going to find and kill Two Trees. As slowly as possible. And even then that wouldn't be enough compensation for the hell the Comanche had put her through.

"He said it was a Quahadi," she said suddenly. "But he may have lied. At the time I didn't know one Indian from another, but later I learned there had been Noconis—and even some Kiowas—with the war party. But Two Trees said he sold her to a Quahadi," she remembered painfully. "Yet when I asked him who it was, he wouldn't give me any name. Dark Water taunted me that it was a Kiowa, and that he'd killed her, but I never believed it. She hated me, so she would say anything."

"Dark Water?"

"His oldest wife. He had two—they were sisters. The younger one was called Burns His Supper, but she was named that before he married her. She wasn't any better than Dark Water."

It was the most she'd ever said about her captivity. Hoping she'd tell him more, maybe get some of it out in the open, he didn't interrupt her. She'd kept it bottled up inside her too long, and maybe if she talked about it, she'd heal.

"If he'd let them cut me, maybe it would have been different, but he wouldn't," she said slowly. "He told them he was going to sell me for many horses because of my hair. He liked my hair—and Gretchen's—because it was pale. He used to terrorize Gretchen, telling her how it would look on his scalp pole. He liked to see her afraid. And she was."

"God."

"He kept me for a different reason, because I wouldn't show him I was scared. It became a game, I think, because he had to win, he had to make me give in. And then there was the obvious reason," she added tonelessly. "But no matter what he did, I made up my mind, I wouldn't scream or cry. I wouldn't let him win."

"Annie—"

It was as though she didn't hear him. "I think that's why Dark Water hated me so much. She was afraid he'd marry me, and I'd have the same status she and Burns His Supper enjoyed. To them it was inconceivable that I didn't want it. They made me lose a baby because they were afraid he'd want to marry me, but he wouldn't have. He hated me. But when it happened, as painful as it was, I was glad. I would have rather died than have his child."

Her voice was low, monotonous, devoid of emotion. And suddenly he was afraid to hear any more. The emptiness was worse than tears. It haunted him.

"Annie," he promised quietly, "I won't let you go through that again. If anything goes wrong, and it looks like I'm done for, I'm taking you with me. You'll get the next to the last bullet."

It was as though she came out of a trance. Recovering, she shook her head. "It'll be different this time, Hap. I'm coming to them, and I can speak enough of the language that I can make them understand. I even have a name to give them now—Saleaweah, Woman Who Walks Far. Without Two Trees or Dark Water and Burns His Supper to dispute it, I'll be considered *Nermernuh*. Just like Clay McAlester."

"It's different—you're a woman, Annie."

"No." She looked over at him, forcing a bitter smile. "If you survive long enough, most of them eventually come to think of you as one of them. Even the white women. Big Thunder's wife had been a captive, but after he married her, she was treated as though she'd been born Comanche. When she died in childbed, he wailed and carried on, and the women in his family cut their breasts and hair in mourning. Dark Water was the only Comanche I knew who complained she didn't deserve the honor." She considered for a moment, then allowed, "Not all of them were like Two Trees, you know."

"Big Thunder took a white woman captive," he reminded her harshly. "He took her away from her family."

326

"No. He was like Bull Calf—he didn't take captives because he thought they were a lot of trouble. He just bought her out of pity, because a Kiowa was mistreating her. And he was kind enough that when he brought her two horses, she took them, accepting his proposal. That was another reason why Dark Water hated me—Big Thunder tried to buy me from Two Trees."

"Remind me to write up a commendation for him," Hap muttered.

She hesitated, then looked at Hap. "There was a time when I wished he *had* bought me, as shameful as that sounds. I would have done anything to escape the hell I was living. I suppose that shocks you, doesn't it?"

"No. I always kinda figured nothing a body did to survive was wrong. You did what you had to, and I still admire you for it."

Hot tears stung her eyes again, and her heart was full. She swallowed painfully. "Thank you," she managed gratefully. "I don't know anybody else that would have said that. You make me feel so very lucky, Hap."

He ought to have felt good about that at least, but there was something missing that struck at his very core. He didn't want gratitude; he wanted her to love him. He wanted to hear the words, and he never had. Not yet, anyway.

But all he could bring himself to say aloud was: "Come on, we've probably got another ten to twelve more miles of daylight. And I'd sure like to get to that cedar, whether you're interested or not. I'd kinda like a soft bed."

The Llano was a rugged, isolated area stretching across the border between New Mexico and Texas, then almost up to the Indian Territory in Oklahoma. And it was known almost exclusively to the Comanches and the Comancheros who traded with them. In a few months Colonel Ranald S. Mackenzie and his Fourth Cavalry would be coming up here, but as Hap looked across the high, grassy plains, he didn't see how the hell Mac was going to manage it. The supply problems alone would be formidable.

The land itself was deceptive, with grasslands going along for miles, then suddenly they'd end in sheer drop-offs, yawning chasms that looked like the earth had been split to its core. And down at the bottom would be some little stream that had been carving that ravine for a hundred thousand years. There were nine rivers crossing the Llano from east to west, and at all of the headwaters, arroyos, deep canyons, high escarpments, and sheer buttes dotted the landscape with a barren, almost frightening beauty. It was the heart and soul of the Comancheria.

Looking for a particular group of Indians here was like looking for a pebble at the bottom of a muddy creek, but Annie wouldn't give up. For well over a month, they'd been going up dead-end ravines, isolated canyons, climbing steep, almost impossible walls of rock. But while they'd encountered a number of small Comanche and Kiowa encampments stretching along the streams and the Prairie Dog Fork of the Red River, they'd found no white captives of an age to be Susannah Bryce. The most promising lead, provided by a Kiowa named Two Owls, had turned out to be a ten-year-old Mexican girl from south of Sonora.

For all her fear of individual Comanches, particularly the men, Annie had proven herself a diplomat far beyond anything Hap would have expected. Armed only with the language and her conviction, she'd managed to convey the notion that she was more or less a relative come home to visit, bringing her warrior husband with her. To his chagrin, he'd been recognized, admired, and feted in every little camp between the Pease River and Palo Duro Canyon. He'd watched her play Indian with amazing success, and his pride in the way she handled herself was nearly boundless. She had more guts and will than any man or woman he'd ever known, except maybe Clay.

But they were no closer to finding her little girl than if they'd stayed home. It was as though the child, and the nameless, faceless Quahadi who'd bought her, had fallen off the face of the earth. They could be anywhere, but it looked like they were nowhere. As determined as she still was, it was getting harder for Annie to hide her discouragement. And all Hap could do was watch her disappointment build, and wait for her to finally give up the search.

But the journey had provided a catharsis of sorts. Having faced the Comanches in their villages and being welcomed by them seemed to have brought respite from Annie's bad dreams. She no longer woke up beside him screaming and shaking in the dead of night. Now only lightning and thunder still terrified her.

Daybreak found them in the bowels of the Palo Duro, camped along a stream, shaded by hackberry and cedar. Already awake, Hap lay behind her, his arm over her shoulder, drinking in the seeming peace of the place, watching Spider cavort with a bug at the end of his tether. That had to be the gamest cat he'd ever seen. Easing closer to his wife, he turned his attention to her. He could tell something was bothering her.

She'd been up once to start the cooking fire and tend to nature, but instead of fixing breakfast, she'd crept back to the fragrant cedar bed, and now she lay still and silent, lost in thought. Thinking to distract her from obvious melancholy, he caressed her nipple with his thumb, feeling it harden. Usually that was enough to get her to turn over, but not this morning.

"Don't."

"I'll make it good for you," he whispered close to her ear.

"I don't want to—not now, anyway."

Sighing, he rolled away and sat up. "All right, do you want to talk about it?"

"No."

"Annie—"

Bursting into tears, she hugged her knees to her chest and rocked. "She's out here somewhere, I know it!" she sobbed. "I know it! Can't you understand, Hap? I know it!"

"Hey, have I said I want to turn back?"

"No, but you don't have to!" she cried. "You don't believe anymore! You think she's dead!"

"Annie . . . Annie . . ."

"Go ahead, say it! You're thinking it, aren't you?"

He'd thought it for a long time, but he knew he couldn't admit it. "I'm still looking, you know," he said quietly. "I haven't said anything about quitting, have I?"

"Hap, it's nearly June! Pretty soon the soldiers will come, and when that happens, I'll never find her!"

Lying back down, he stroked her hair where it touched her shoulder. "I'm willing to give it the rest of the summer, Annie. I'm willing to look that long."

"I haven't even found anybody I know, Hap. I just keep asking strangers. Every time we stop somewhere, I keep thinking it'll be the place where I find out something, but there's nothing—nothing at all."

"Shhhhh." At a loss for a means to comfort her, he drew her closer and nuzzled her hair. "Don't, sweetheart," he whispered. Reaching around her, he found the neck of her dress. "We'll keep on," he promised, working the button.

Pulling away, she struggled to sit. "Is that all you think of?" she demanded angrily. "It's not the answer to everything! Don't you think I know what you're doing? You just want to make a baby so I'll forget her—but I won't!"

Stumbling away from the blankets, she caught a hackberry branch, leaned her head against it, then was sick. By the time he got to her, it was over. But she was still pale, ashen, and her skin was clammy to the touch. The heat he'd felt moments ago was gone, replaced by guilt.

"Why didn't you say you were sick?" he demanded. "All you had to do was say it, Annie. I'm not some kind of animal, you know."

"I wasn't, until just now—until I sat up," she choked out. "It's the heat—I can't stand the heat."

"Here, let me get you some water," he offered, going to the packs for a cloth. "Just hold on, and I'll be back." Walking to the stream, he bent down and wet the rag, then wrung it out. When he turned around, he felt sick himself. Dropping the rag, he lunged for her and the Henry at the same time.

"Cheyennes!" he gasped.

For a moment she was paralyzed with fear. Then he pushed her toward a mound of rocks and boulders. "Take cover—and keep your head down. They haven't seen us yet," he told her urgently.

"Spider, they'll get Spider! They'll eat him!"

"You can't get him, Annie."

But she'd stopped and was turning back. Cursing himself for a fool, he pushed her down into a crevice between the rocks, threw the rifle in after her, then he went sliding down the craggy hill. He didn't even have time to save Old Red, but he was going back for that damned cat.

Crossing beneath the cover of cedar, he passed the horses and mules, cut the tethers, then stood up, shouting, "Yeehaw!" The big roan, having caught the scent of the oncoming Indians, took off down the canyon, with the other animals following him. Dropping down again, Hap crawled on his belly to the hackberry where he'd tied Spider, grabbed the cat and his gun belt, then scrambled back up the rocks, diving under a boulder just as the Cheyennes thundered past in pursuit of the horses and mules. He could feel four sets of claws tearing into his chest.

Pulling the cat loose, he thrust it down to Annie. "Here's your damned cat," he muttered. "Keep it quiet—they'll be back. And for God's sake, lie low." Crouching, he drew the Peacemaker and spun the cylinders, adding a bullet to the sixth chamber. "Don't fire the Henry unless you have to," he told her. "The sound'll echo, and there's no telling who'll hear it. If it looks like they're going to find us, I'm taking off up there. No matter what happens, you stay put, you hear? I'll come back for you."

"Your leg—"

"I can make it. If I don't, then you wait until it's over before you hightail it back the way they came. Whatever you do, don't try to come after me."

"Hap—"

"Shhhh. Just keep the cat quiet." Reaching down, he clasped her hand, massaging her fingers, feeling his father's ring. "Look, it'll be all right," he tried to reassure her. "But if it looks like they're going to pin us down, I want 'em to follow me up that cliff."

"I don't want you to leave me, Hap, not now."

"I aim to stay, if I can." But he could hear the Cheyenne war party coming back. He took a deep breath. "Look, whatever happens, I have no regrets, Annie. I want you to know that. I've loved you since I woke up during that bath you were giving me. I saw that hair and thought you were an angel."

"Hap, I—"

"Shhhhh."

He felt her fingers tighten around his, drawing his hand

to her cheek. It was wet. Then she pressed her lips into his palm and whispered, "I love you more than anything."

He'd never wanted to die, but he'd always thought if it happened, it wouldn't matter much. But now he wanted to live more than anything, and it didn't make any difference if he spent the rest of his life on that farm. As long as he had her, he didn't need anything else. Moving his head ever so slightly, he peered around the edge of the boulder that shielded him.

They were down there, going through his things, emptying the packs, dragging out Annie's two extra dresses, taking what they wanted. He held his breath, knowing they knew he and Annie were either up here or down in one of those narrow fissures in the canyon wall. Several painted bucks began the search on foot, turning over the cedar boughs he'd cut, kicking through the brush.

One of them gave out a sharp, startled cry and backed away. An Indian with him fired an ancient gun, and a rattlesnake writhed in a loop, then was still. As the report reverberated off the rocks, Hap knew the place was going to be crawling with Indians in a matter of minutes. There were too many little camps strewn along the canyon floor, and fearing attack, the warriors would be pouring out of every one of them.

There were about ten or twelve Cheyennes down there, and they were dividing up. One pointed directly toward the boulders where Hap and Annie hid; then he and several companions began climbing, carefully picking at the rocks, ascending the steep hill. If they got too close, he'd have to kill them. Then all hell really would break loose.

One Indian was probably within twenty feet of him now. Easing his fingers from Annie's, Hap cocked the

Peacemaker and waited to make his break. He had to time it right, to surprise them into following him. He twisted his neck, looking upward, trying to decide the best way to go. When they got above her, he didn't want them to be able to see her.

He couldn't wait any longer. Praying that the damned cat stayed quiet and that Annie stayed put, he stood up and fired, catching the closest Cheyenne between the eyes. The bullet slammed him backward and sent him rolling down, knocking a companion over. Then his body slid into a crevice and lodged there. Taking advantage of the momentary confusion, he cut sideways across a ledge, then fired again, wounding another Indian. He had to get them as far away from Annie as possible, and he had to keep them looking at him.

But he'd given himself a damned poor place to make a stand. The ledge ended in a sheer drop, and there wasn't any way up either. Cursing fate and his leg, he grasped an overhang and tried to pull himself up. A bullet nicked the limestone within inches of his hand. He was probably the best target they'd had in a long time. Summoning every last ounce of strength in his shoulders, he heaved his body upward, threw his foot over the edge, hung there for a moment, then half rolled onto a rock shelf, dragging his bad leg behind him. While he caught his breath, he replaced the two cartridges.

When he looked down, his heart nearly stopped. A handhold away from Annie, a buck was coming up. He took aim, fired, and missed. But at least he'd warned her. As the Cheyenne looked up at him, he got off another shot, this time hitting his mark. The Indian rolled, screaming all the way down the hill.

Thinking they'd seen her, Annie rose and fired the Henry, picking off a man just starting up the steep, rocky wall. To Hap's horror, she was going to try to come up after him. Clasping the cat against her breast, she fired several shots as she ran, gaining the rock where he'd started.

"Behind you, coming up the other side!" he yelled.

Her foot slid as she tried to turn around, and for an awful moment he thought she was going to fall into the Indian's arms. And he didn't have a clear target. He squeezed off a shot at a rock nearby, splintering a piece off it. As the Cheyenne ducked, she scrambled higher, clawing her way up on the ledge Hap had nearly stranded himself on.

This was it. Armageddon. Mounted Comanches were pouring around the bed in the canyon, and before long the whole wall would be swarming with them. And they wouldn't be wanting to listen to anybody now. But he wasn't going easy—he was going to take as many as he could with him. He reloaded, looked down again, and saw that Annie realized her predicament.

"Cover me. I'm coming down!" he shouted.

"No! They'll get you!" she screamed back. "Go on up!"

"Not without you!" As he said it, he lowered his body over the edge, then dropped down in a hail of bullets. "Whooeee!" he managed, ducking back on the ledge. Hearing the buzz behind him, he swung around. A western diamondback lay coiled, ready to defend its territory. It was the biggest he'd ever seen. "Damn."

As she raised the rifle to shoot it, he had another idea. Taking the gun away from her, he jabbed at it. As it struck for him, he caught it with the barrel and flung it over the side. An Indian below bellowed in pain as it struck him.

There were shouts coming from the canyon floor, then the shooting stopped. Taking advantage of the lull, Hap checked the Henry's magazine and reloaded. He didn't know what they were planning, but he knew he wasn't going to like it. Putting his arm around Annie's shoulder, he sat there, waiting.

"I shouldn't have asked this of you," she said, her voice low. "I'm sorry, Hap."

"For what? For giving me the best six or seven weeks of my life?" he countered.

"For getting you killed." She bit her lip to still its trembling, then leaned her head back against his shoulder. "I shouldn't have come. I should've known it wouldn't happen, but I had to hope, Hap. I couldn't let go of her."

"Hey, it's not over yet, Annie."

"There must be a hundred Indians down there." Twisting her head, she tried to see his face. "I didn't want to believe it, but I'm never going to find her. She's just gone."

"You don't know that."

She swallowed hard, trying to force down the lump in her throat. "I had no right to ask this of you."

"It's all right, Annie. I never had much until I had you, you know. I never had an Ethan or a Jody or a Susannah, but I've got a notion I'd do my damnedest to get any kid of mine back. I always wanted one, you know."

"You'd have had one. Sometime after the first of the year. I'm sorry, Hap. I didn't meant to cheat you out of that, too."

He sat very still, holding her, trying to take in what she was telling him. "How long have you known?" he said finally.

"About two weeks." She swallowed again and closed her
337

eyes. "I was afraid you'd make me go back if I told you. I was afraid once you knew, you wouldn't care anything about finding Susannah. I think I was wrong, wasn't I?"

"Yeah."

"You'd have gone on, anyway, because you gave your word."

"Yeah."

It was too quiet out there, as though nothing was moving, nothing was happening. Easing a little closer to the edge, he looked down.

"Well, I'll be damned," he said softly. Turning back to her, he was grinning.

"I don't understand. What . . . ?"

"Look for yourself."

"You're not making any sense."

"You've got yourself a friend down there."

She peered cautiously, then drew back. "Bull Calf!"

"Sure looks like him, anyway."

Not knowing whether to laugh or cry, she shouted down, *"Wyitepah!"* waving at him. As he shaded his eyes to see her, she added, "Saleahweah! Nermernuh!" pointing to herself.

The ugly Comanche raised his hand in the sign of peace, then gesturing toward Hap. "Tondehwahkah!" Turning to those gathered around him, he pointed up again. "Tondehwahkah!" Several of them began holding their hands up, showing peace also. The ugliness evaporated.

Annie clutched Hap's arm. "It's all right, we're going to make it. We're going to get to go home, after all, Hap. We're going to get our chance." Seeing that he frowned, she sobered also. "What's the matter?"

"I'm wondering how the hell I'm getting you down from here."

"The same way I came up," Then she understood. "I knew if I told you, you wouldn't want me to do anything. And it's not like that at all. I never had any trouble carrying Susannah or Jody."

"Yeah, but you're older."

"And I'm healthy. That's all that counts, you know."

"I'll go first," he decided. "At least that way I can catch you. And give me that damned cat." Retrieving the hissing animal, he stuffed it inside his shirt. "Scratch me again," he warned it, "and it won't be Cheyennes eating you."

By the time they'd slipped and slid down the rocks, the Penetaka chief had dismounted and was waiting for them. His piercing, black-eyed gaze took in Hap, then her before he spoke. Leaving the white man out of it, he engaged in a lengthy conversation in Comanche with Annie, punctuating his words with his hands. After a number of exchanges and much head shaking, he finally turned to Hap.

"You come." It sounded more like an order than an invitation. Before Hap could respond, he barked out something to a Mexican slave. "You come," he repeated. "Bull Calf give gift."

It was Old Red. The wily Penetaka was giving him his own horse. That and his life, Hap reminded himself. If old Bull Calf hadn't shown up, he'd have been parting with his hair. As it was, the Cheyennes who'd just gathered up their dead didn't seem too happy about that turn of events, but they weren't arguing either. Walking to the mules, he knew he had to make a real gesture. Behind him, Annie said low, "He'll take us to Quanah—he's seen Quanah."

Quanah Parker, the scourge of Texas. As many times as Hap had crisscrossed the state tracking Indians, he'd never gotten a look at the half-white Quahadi war chief who had such a bitter hatred for everything Anglo. And it was something he could have stood missing, but he realized the significance of Bull Calf's offer. This was what they'd been hoping for, and one way or another, maybe it would answer the question of whether Susannah Bryce had survived.

"Well, I guess you've finally struck paydirt" was about all the could think to say.

Aware of the longstanding enmity between the Texas Rangers and the Quahadi war chief, she said quietly, "You don't have to go, Hap—you can wait for me. Bull Calf said he'd bring me back."

"Like hell." His forced smile twisted. "I'm in this for the full haul, Annie. Ever hear of 'whither thou goest'?"

"That was Ruth and her mother-in-law," she reminded him. "But Quanah's on the warpath. Bull Calf says he's smoked the war pipe with the Kiowas and the Cheyenne. And I guess even some of the reservation Comanches are coming down to join him."

"And Mackenzie's going to cram it down his throat," he muttered tersely. Rummaging through the few things that had been left in the packs, he found Annie's sack of coffee, his tablet, and his dirty clothes. Hiding his anger at being robbed by the Cheyennes, he turned back to Bull Calf. "Tell him he can have the mules, if he can get 'em back for me," he directed Annie.

She repeated the offer, drawing a wide grin from the

Comanche. After a quick conference with their earlier attackers, he managed to persuade them to return most of what they'd taken, even the animals. As painted Cheyenne warriors mounted up to continue along the war trail, and Comanches melted into the canyon, the Mexican promptly took possession of Bull Calf's new mules.

"You'd better take what you want, Annie. I'm going to have to give 'em the rest. Reckon it'll be pretty light traveling from here on out."

"Bull Calf says we'll have to hurry, Hap. He says Quanah's going to be moving down to the Big Spring before long."

"Maybe we should've waited for him down there."

"It'll be a big war party. There are hundreds of them, I guess."

And he had no way of stopping them. After all his years of fighting the damned Comanches, he was going in to Quanah Parker's camp, acting like some sort of relative. And knowing they were going to be raiding the farms and ranches he'd fought so hard to protect would stick like a bone in his craw. But for her he was going to do it. Then just as soon as he could get up to Sill or over to Richardson, he was going to tell the army where to find Quanah.

"What did you tell him about me?" he asked finally.

"That you're my husband. He knows why we're here, Hap—I just told him. But he can't promise anything except that he can get us to Quanah. He says we'll be even then."

"Yeah. Well, I won't be telling any of 'em. Hell, I can barely sign enough to keep my hair on." Walking back to the packs, he began stuffing his clothes and shaving gear into one of the pouches. "When does he want to leave?"

"Now. The others are going on without him, and I think he hopes he can catch up."

"How far is it?"

"He didn't say—only that he's been there, and he knows where it is. There are a lot of places in this canyon to hide, Hap." She hesitated for a moment, then said somberly, "He says there are a lot of Noconis in Quanah's camp. I, uh, didn't ask him anything about Two Trees."

"You don't have to worry about the son of a bitch. All you've got to do is point him out to me."

"You can't kill him, Hap. You wouldn't get out alive."

"I'll find a way." Clasping her shoulder, he turned her to face him. "When I get riled, I've got a real mean streak in me, Annie. And every time I think of what he did to you, I get real riled."

"I'd rather have you alive than anything, Hap—than anything else in this world."

Even there, in front of Bull Calf and his Comanches, he wasn't proof against those blue eyes of hers. A slow, confident smile spread across his face. "You didn't marry a fool, Annie. We've both got a lot to live for now."

After more than two days of searching through the huge Quahadi camp, Annie finally conceded she'd done all she could. As she and Hap were walking back along the river, she gave up. She was tired, sick, and there was no longer any reason to believe that Susannah was alive. That, coupled with the fact that the camp was swelling with more Cheyennes every day, made it difficult to stay where sentiment ran high against Hap. It was only Bull Calf's influence and Comanche reluctance to murder a guest that kept them from killing an old enemy.

She'd been silent, lost in thought so long that she startled him when she spoke up. "I think we ought to go home, Hap."

As much as he'd wanted to hear those words, he ached for her. "We don't have to, Annie. The summer's not over," he said gently.

"No, it's over. You were right in the first place, you know. She probably didn't live through that first awful winter."

"Annie—"

"I'm all right, Hap. I looked as hard as I could, and I can live with that."

"Yeah."

There were no words of comfort to say. Later, when she lay in his arms, he'd try to ease the pain, but right now there was nothing. Instead, he took her hand and walked slowly back to the tipi Sun in the Morning had set up for them. Now there wasn't any sense prolonging her agony.

"We'll leave in the morning at first light," he decided finally.

"Yes."

His hand tightened around hers, pressing his father's ring into his fingers. "We've got the baby to think of now. When I get home, I'm going to try my hand at making a cradle. I know I haven't said much about it, but I didn't want you to think I didn't care about Susannah," he went on. "I would've really liked having a daughter, Annie, I want you to know that."

"Yes."

"I always wanted a kid, you know, but I never really thought it'd happen. I know you're hurting, but I kinda feel like I've got everything a man could want. Maybe I'm an old fool, but I'm looking forward to seeing what it's going to look like, how it's going to grow, who it's going to be."

"You want a son, don't you?"

"It doesn't matter. To tell the truth, if it gets my hair, I hope to hell it's a girl."

"I don't know why you hate it so much. I've always liked it—it makes you look like a kid yourself, you know. And there's nothing wrong—" She stopped dead in her tracks to stare at a group of half-naked Indian children splashing

344

in the water, and for a moment there was no mistaking the yearning in her face. Then she recovered. "I almost thought . . ."

He followed her gaze, looking them over with what had become a practiced eye. While he couldn't see all of the faces, none of them looked white.

"What?"

"I don't know. The way that girl turned her head—" She sighed, then settled her shoulders. "I can see now I was mistaken."

"Yeah."

"I've wanted to believe so many times that my mind plays tricks with my heart, I guess."

"There's nobody over there that looks like you, Annie."

"I know."

"You probably ought to lie down for a while."

"I will. But first I'm going to tell Bull Calf we're going."

"Yeah, I thought he wanted to catch up to that war party," he recalled.

"I think he was afraid if he left, Tondehwahkah might not get out of here alive." Sighing again, she admitted, "I don't want him to die, Hap. I know what happened at Sill gave him a bad taste of the reservation, but he's got to go back, and I'm going to tell him that." Spying Sun in the Morning outside Bull Calf's tipi, she stopped. "I'll be along directly, but first I'm going to try to convince her, too."

It was over. It was as though a heavy weight had been lifted from his shoulders, and he could go home with a clear conscience. He hadn't found Susannah Bryce, and he hadn't killed Two Trees, but he was taking his wife home, and that counted for more than anything. Right now, as he ducked through the borrowed tipi's flap door, he didn't care if he ever saw another Indian for the rest of his life.

It was too dark, too close, and too hot inside. He stood there, leaning against a lodge pole, looking around. Then he went to his saddle bag for his tablet. He hadn't written much in his book lately, and now he had two reasons to write it. By now Clay's kid had come into the world, and sometime after the next New Year, his would, too.

As he put the bag back, he noticed some yellow silk hair hanging out of Annie's pack. She'd brought the doll he'd found that September day, and apparently Spider'd discovered it. The damned cat had been chewing on it. Taking it out of the pack, he smoothed the hair, straightened the new calico dress Annie'd put on it, then replaced it in the pack. It was a real nice doll—maybe someday his daughter would be playing with it.

"Suppose you want to go outside, huh?" he asked the cat.

In answer it stretched its body and hooked its claws in his pants leg. Sticking the pencil in his pocket and tucking the tablet under his arm, he scooped up Spider and headed for the open air. He had a lot of catching up to do. Where he'd once thought he couldn't fill twenty pages, now he kept thinking up things to add.

Settling down beside the river, he tied the cat's lead to his belt, then opened the tablet. Wetting the pencil, he started in where he'd left off. While the animal climbed all over him and played beneath his knees, he lost himself in his memories.

It wasn't until his hand cramped that he looked up. A half dozen little brown faces watched Spider with obvious fascination. Picking up the cat, he held it out, then demonstrated how to pet it. Spider started purring.

"Go on, try it," he offered the closest kid.

The little boy reached out, touched the soft fur, then drew back. A little girl peered around him, and Hap felt the world stop. As brown as a berry, with dirty hair that fell in greased, feather-trimmed braids, she had eyes as blue as Annie's.

"Susannah?" he asked cautiously.

She blinked, then pointed at herself. "T'sana," she said.

His heart raced. T'sana. Susannah. They sounded enough alike to be the same thing. Maybe the little girl remembered. "Wait here," he insisted, picking up the cat. To be sure they stayed, he reached into his pockets and took out a handful of copper pennies. "Here." As they divided up the prize, he fairly ran back to the tipi, tied the cat to one of the lodge poles, retrieved the little china doll with the gold silk hair, and hurried back to the river.

His heart sank almost immediately. There was an Indian woman with them now, and she had her hand on the little girl's shoulder. Taking a deep breath, he approached them, anyway, and held out the doll. The child's eyes widened, either with pleasure or recognition, he wasn't sure which. Then she reached out, snatched it from his hands, and ran away. The woman spoke sharply, but the child kept going. Finally, the boy caught her and wrestled the doll from her arms. Her face grim, the woman ordered him to give it to Hap.

"T'sana?" he asked, pointing to the child.

She nodded. "T'sana."

Trying to keep them there, he touched his shoulder.

"Hap—Tondehwahkah." Forcing a smile, he pointed at her. "Who? Who you?" he tried to ask. Then he repeated the name the Indians had given him. "Tondehwahkah."

"Tondehwahkah," the woman echoed, nodding as though she knew it.

"Yes. You?"

She hesitated, then touched her breast lightly. "Asabeti."

"Asabeti," he tried, rolling it off his tongue, hoping he'd be able to remember it. "Asabeti." He wanted to ask if she lived around there, but it wasn't even proper for her to be speaking to him. Instead he held out the doll, then pointed to the child. "For T'sana." She shook her head. "For T'sana—from Tondehwahkah. You give."

Finally, she allowed the little girl to take the doll, then apparently ordered both children to leave. The child ran around a tipi and disappeared, but not before he'd seen the way she'd held the doll. Not like an Indian, but close to her breast like a white woman.

Annie was still talking to Sun in the Morning when he found her. Not wanting to say too much in front of Bull Calf's wife, he asked quickly, "Is T'sana a Comanche word?"

"It means rose—like the flower."

"Oh."

"Actually, it's a wild yellow rose." Seeing his disappointment, she asked, "Why?"

"Those children you saw, the ones by the river . . ."

She didn't move a muscle, not even to blink. "Yes?" It was more of a whisper than a question.

"The little girl's white, Annie."

"White?" she echoed, her eyes widening.

"She's got blue eyes." Afraid he could somehow be wrong, he looked away. "Yeah, I gave the doll to her."

"What?"

"I wanted to see what she'd do—if she'd recognize it."

"I see." She couldn't think. He was telling her that he'd found a white child called T'sana. For a moment she couldn't even breathe, then she had to know. "Where? Where did you find her?"

"By the river. But you'd better look at her first."

"But you think it's Susannah, don't you?"

"I don't know, Annie. Maybe I just want her to be. But yeah, I kinda think so. There was something about the way she held that doll. Like maybe she'd held it before."

"I want to see her, Hap. I've got to see her."

Turning back to Sun in the Morning, she made her excuses. Then barely hiding her excitement, she all but ran for the river where she'd seen the children. They were gone, and now only a couple of women waded in the cold, shallow water.

"Did you see where they went? Do you know where they went?" she asked anxiously.

Approaching the women, she asked if any had seen a little girl named T'sana, if they knew anything about her. Both of them regarded Annie suspiciously, then shook their heads.

"The mother's name is Asabeti—at least that's what it sound like to me," Hap offered.

"Asabeti?" she asked quickly, getting a glimmer of recognition from them. Splashing into the water, she confronted one of the Indian women, asking this time for Asabeti's direction. Coming back, she pointed toward where Hap had seen the child run between the tipis.

"They're from another band of Quahadis just come in," she said, unable to hide her excitement. "There's a boy, a little girl, and a baby—and his name—Asabeti's husband, that is—is Waseca," she said breathlessly. Hurrying past him, she whispered under her breath, "Please, dear God, let it be Susannah."

"Don't say anything to them. Just look," he cautioned her. "Don't let 'em know why you're wanting to see her."

They were in luck. The little girl was sitting cross-legged in front of a tipi decorated with a large vermillion sun, and she was holding the doll, stroking its hair, crooning Indian words to it. As they approached, she looked up, and Annie felt a shiver of excitement all the way to her soul. Forcing herself to speak calmly, she moved closer to the child.

"T'sana?" she asked softly. Telling her it was a pretty name, she dropped to her knees and touched the doll's china face, asking its name. When the child shook her head, she suggested, "Molly."

"Mowi?"

"Molly."

"Molly," the little girl repeated solemnly. "Molly."

It was hard to tell if she remembered or not, but Annie was sure she was looking into her daughter's face. For a moment she studied every inch of it, taking in those blue eyes, the curve of the child's cheek, the chin that reminded her of Ethan. Then she reached out with shaking hand to touch the small shoulder.

"Susannah, do you remember me? It's Mama. Oh, dear God, Susannah—it's Mama!"

"Annie, don't."

Her hands slid down the slender arms as she fought back tears. "We've found her, Hap—we've found her!"

"T'sana!"

Asabeti came out of the tipi, then stopped cold when she saw the white woman. Recovering, she grasped the child's arm, pulling her away, then gave her a quick push toward the lodge. Facing Annie, she angrily demanded to know why she'd been touching T'sana. Recovering, Annie assured her she'd been admiring the doll. But the explanation came too late. The Comanche woman turned on her heel and went back inside.

Annie stared for a moment, then turned and ran toward the main body of the camp before Hap could stop her. Racing after her, he caught her from behind.

"What the hell do you think you're doing?"

"I'm going to Quanah. I'm going to tell him she's mine. I'm going to ask him to help me," she gasped. "They can't keep my daughter from me!"

As she struggled to get loose, he wrapped his arms around her, holding her. "That woman's not going to give her up without a fight, Annie."

"But she's mine! I'm not leaving without her. Now that I've found her, I'm not leaving without her!"

"We're going to steal her. Hold still, will you?" he said, tightening his embrace. "Now, listen to me—and get a hold on yourself."

She took a gulp of air before nodding. "All right."

"They've had her a long time, Annie, and it's pretty obvious that Asabeti's real proud of her. You go around asking about her, telling these people she's yours, and all hell's going to break loose. You know that, don't you?"

"Yes."

"So we've got to make plans, kinda figure out how we're getting her out of here without having a couple hundred Comanches chasing after us. So I reckon we'll kinda have to keep our distance, wait for a chance, then just take her. But I'd kinda like to do it when there's something to distract 'em, so we can get a good start on 'em before they miss her."

She nodded.

"So don't go saying anything to anybody—not even to Sun in the Morning or Bull Calf. Or to the other wife, either."

"All right."

"And now that you've seen her, you've got to stay away from her. You don't want 'em to hide her out somewhere."

"No. But I told Sun in the Morning we were leaving tomorrow."

"Tell her the baby's making you sick, and you don't feel like going," he suggested, releasing her.

"All right. But I don't see how—"

"I'll keep an eye on the kid. I reckon I can do it while I'm writing. None of 'em act like they've seen a cat on a rope before, believe me."

"What do you want me to do?"

"Nothing. Visit around, act like nothing's different. And wait. I don't aim to take long at this, I can tell you that much. I aim to have her out of here within the week. Then we're going home—you, me, and the kid. By the time we get there, I expect I'll have a real hankering to farm the rest of my life. Hell, I *know* I will."

But when he got his tablet and Spider and returned to the place by the river, there was no sign of any kids, only women getting water for cooking pots. Still, he found himself a spot, sat down, and wrote several pages of his life story. By the time he got finished, nobody was going to believe it, he decided. He'd done a lot more in thirty-seven years than he'd realized. In another month or so he'd be thirty-eight, but that didn't bother him anymore. He had too much to look forward to now. Annie. The little girl. The baby.

When they got home, he had a whole list of things he wanted to do. Whitewash the house. Make that cradle. Get to know Susannah. Buy a real wedding ring for Annie.

Civilizing the kid wouldn't be easy, but at least he'd done it before. At least he had a notion what to expect. Comanches didn't raise children like white folks, and there was something about that freedom they never got over. Of course, it might be a little different with a girl, because they learned to do most of the real work.

But the first thing on the list was the wedding ring. And he wanted to get a nice one, one that told her what his sometimes awkward words never quite said what he wanted them to. Every time he thought of Baker's Gap and that grim, dirty, one-room house, he could kick himself all over again. She'd deserved a whole lot better than that.

She'd given him everything, but she probably wouldn't look at it like that. She might even think it was the other way around, but it wasn't. Without her, he'd be drifting along, dissatisfied with damned near everything. With her, he had a pretty wife, a family, and a place he could call home. A whole lot more than a man like him had a right to ask for.

The damned cat kept climbing onto his lap, settling

right on top of his tablet. Pushing it off for the fourth or fifth time, he happened to notice somebody was taking a tipi down, loading in onto a travois. And he had a pretty fair notion it was Asabeti and her husband fixing to leave.

Shifting his body against the tree for a better look, he could see the little girl helping carry things, the woman deftly lashing everything down, while a fair-sized Comanche warrior watched from a place in the shade. A round-faced baby with black hair slept in a cradleboard propped against the man's leg, while the half-naked boy darted around, firing sticks from his bow at anything that moved. A rangy dog got up, checked out an empty pot, then dropped to the ground again.

Two white folks and a doll had set them to running. On the one hand, it was going to upset Annie, but on the other, it wasn't a bad thing. As long as they didn't lose sight of Asabeti and her family, they'd probably be a whole lot better off trying to steal Susannah someplace that wasn't swarming with Indians. This way if anything went wrong, all he'd have to contend with was Waseca and the woman. But once he got the kid, he'd still have to ride like hell.

Throwing Spider onto his shoulder, he rubbed his cheek against the soft fur for a moment, murmuring, "Reckon you'll be damned glad to get to where you aren't tied down, won't you, fella? And the time's coming. 'Course, then you're going to have a mighty rough little girl wooling you around," he warned the cat. "Kinda serve you right, won't it?"

As he walked back with the cat perched there, trying to wash the hair over his ear, he decided he must be getting soft. He was actually going to feel bad about running off and leaving old Bull Calf in the middle of the night. But he couldn't afford to say anything about it. Not when he was this close to getting Annie's kid for her.

It seemed that they were going farther north, up toward Tule Canyon. Following at a safe distance, Hap was determined not to let them disappear again. Every hour or so, he'd climb up a hill with a spyglass to make sure they weren't getting too far ahead.

"Well, if they don't hook up with anybody before nightfall, I reckon this is about it," he told Annie, coming back. "As soon as they make camp, we'll try to get ahead of 'em, then I'll double back for the kid while you wait, ready to ride as soon as I get back in the morning."

"I want to go with you, Hap."

"No. We're going to need at least one rested horse for you and the kid. And you need to get some sleep, because I expect we'll be riding hell for leather if Waseca figures out which way we're heading."

"We're heading for the San Saba, aren't we?"

"No, not yet, anyway. Coming north like they have, we'd be going back down through the Comancheria. 'Way I've got it figured, I'll try to make 'em think like that, then we'll head up to Fort Sill. Maybe visit a few days with

356

Doc Sprenger while you and Susannah get reacquainted."
Trying not to think how tired he was, he squinted up at
the late afternoon sun. "You know, it may not be easy, Annie. She may not thank us for this. We may be hauling
her kicking and squalling the whole way there."

While part of her realized that, she didn't want to believe it. "She's my daughter, Hap."

"She's been with 'em awhile. It may take some time to
civilize her even after we get her home."

"I know."

"Do you? I haven't forgotten bringing Clay back, you
know. At the time he hated me for it. Hell, I couldn't even
turn my back on him for fear he'd try to kill me."

"I'm going to make her remember me, Hap. I'm going
to make her remember Ethan and Jody."

"Yeah. For your sake, I hope you can."

"Why are you saying this now?"

"I don't want you to get hurt too bad if it's not like
you've dreamed it, Annie. You've got to give it time, and
you've got to accept she's not the kid she was almost four
years ago."

"Don't you think I know that? But no matter how much
they've tried to change her, she's still my little girl. They've
got no right to her."

"I didn't say they did. I'm just saying we're the outsiders
now, and it'll take some time to change that." Straightening his shoulders, he stepped into the stirrup and swung
his aching leg over the saddle. "But I'm here to help you
do it, you know. In some ways I reckon I've got more riding on this than you."

"You'll be careful, won't you?"

"I wasn't meaning that." He mouth twisted into a wry

smile. "Eventually she's going to accept that she was born to you, that you're her mother. But I've got to make her want to be my little girl."

"I don't doubt for a minute that you can do that, Hap," she said softly. "If you're even half as good to her as you've been to me, she can't help but love you."

The night was dark, moonless, providing him with cover as he crept toward the small campsite. Certain they'd not been followed, Waseca and Asabeti hadn't bothered to picket the horses or take any precaution against attack. And given the heat, they'd chosen to sleep in the open rather than set up the tipi. It was about as good a chance as Hap was ever going to have.

They'd brought a number of horses with them, and a small paint picked up his scent just before he reached it. As it whinnied nervously, he cut it loose, then quickly went to the others. Waseca turned over and grunted in his sleep. Hap counted as he severed the ropes. Thirteen animals. Yeah, he had all of them.

Moving through them, he dropped down, then crept on his knees toward the sleeping family, stopping at each pallet, trying to make out each occupant. Waseca. Asabeti and her papoose. The boy. The girl was behind them, closest to the cold firepit. His hand closed over her mouth. Then as the terrified child tried to struggle, he pulled her blanket over her head and came up running.

"Uh!"

Waseca rolled from his pallet to grope for his gun, while Asabeti screamed. The boy tried to scramble for cover and managed to run into his mother, knocking her down. As Waseca got off a shot, Hap began firing over the horses, stampeding the frightened animals. Finding Old Red where he'd left him, he threw Susannah in front of his saddle and swung up behind her. Frantic, the child tried to dive over the other side, but he pulled her back over the pommel and horn, slid an arm across her chest, and held her tightly.

Jamming the Colt back in his holster, he dug his spurs into the horse's flank and rode like hell for the place where he'd left Annie, with Waseca's calls for his horses echoing in his ears. The kid writhed and kicked and screamed herself hoarse, but he couldn't relax his hold for fear she'd bite him.

He splashed across the stream and came up a narrow ravine, then headed south long enough to leave enough sign for Waseca to follow. Then he doubled back up a worn rock trail, came up behind the rimrock, and cut across hard-baked ground. Reining in, he tried to listen, but if there was anything out there he ought to be hearing, Susannah was drowning it out.

"Here now, that's enough," he said gruffly. "Reckon you're going to have to get over this, else I'm going to be stuffing my kerchief in that mouth."

It didn't help. If she understood English, she wasn't letting on. And he was pretty sure he didn't want to know what she was saying in Comanche.

"Look, you and me have got to come to an understanding," he told her. "You either straighten up, or I'm going to stop and paddle your backside, you hear?"

She fell silent for a moment, letting him think maybe she knew what he'd said. "Yeah, Susannah."

"T'sana!"

"They're both pretty names—sound a lot alike, in fact."

Shifting uncomfortably on the pony's back, he tried to ease her more toward the middle. "Owww! Damn! Now, what did you have to do that for?"

She'd sunk her teeth deep into his forearm and clenched her jaws to keep them there. He could feel blood running down his elbow, but there wasn't a damned thing he could do about it. And he knew it was going to get a whole lot worse. Reaching around her with his other hand, he pinched her nose shut.

"All right, now let's see how long you can hold that breath," he muttered. "Old Tondehwahkah isn't going to put up with much more of this," he warned her. Finally, she let go and so did he. "You know, your ma's gone through hell to get you back, don't you? Yeah, she's been looking at every kid between here and the Concho hoping she was going to find you. You've got to give her credit for that—it ought to mean something to you. She's been real worried about you, Susannah."

"T'sana!"

"Yeah, well, you weren't always a heathen. Time was when you were a little white girl living on a farm down along the San Saba River with your ma, your pa, and a baby brother. I reckon everything was pretty nice for you back then, huh?"

He could tell by the stiff set of her shoulders that she was just waiting for him to make another mistake. And he wasn't about to do it. Instead he just kept talking.

"Your little brother's name was Jody—yeah, Jody Bryce—and you were Susannah Bryce. Your ma's name is Anne, but we call her Annie. And that little doll I gave you—it used to be yours, you know. You named it Molly."

He didn't know how long he talked, only that he never

stopped, all the way back to where Annie was. The summer sun was coming up by the time he got there, and every muscle and every bone in his body ached, but there was no time to stop for anything more than a bite to eat and enough of a walk to stretch his legs.

She was up and waiting for them, running across the flat, grassy land the moment she saw him. And the look on her face made everything worthwhile. She caught his bridle and stood there, her eyes wet with unshed tears.

"I got her for you, Annie. She's a mite tired from hollering, but she's in good shape."

"Susannah?" she said softly, touching the child's leg.

The little girl came awake kicking as Annie reached up to her. "Watch out, she'll get you real good if you don't," he warned her. "Here now, stop that."

"You look tired enough to die, Hap," Annie said.

"I'm all right." Sliding from the saddle to the ground, he reached back up for Susannah. And as the blanket fell away, he could see she still held the doll. Her blue eyes regarded him warily for a moment, then she leaned into his arms. "That's better. You know, you're almost as pretty as your ma." As he set her down, he looked to Annie. "If you've got any, I could sure take some coffee."

She nodded. "And I've got mush made. I thought maybe she'd eat it, that it would be close enough to the boiled meal Asabeti would have fixed."

"Yeah. And you'll probably want to delouse her before we go on. Wash her up some, get a good look at her." Yawning, he sank to the ground and leaned his head back against the trunk of a tree.

"Are you all right?"

361

"Just going to rest my eyes," he mumbled. "I'll be ready to go in a few minutes."

When he woke up, the sun was midway up in the sky, and steam was rising from the grass. Rubbing his eyes, he looked around, then stumbled to stand. Then he saw Annie. She was sitting beside a blanket, her knees drawn up under her skirt, singing softly. And Susannah was asleep on her stomach, one arm around the doll, the other around Spider. Swinging his arms to ease aching shoulders, he walked over.

She had the kid cleaned up and wearing his shirt, and he could see now that her hair was a darker blond than Annie's. Asleep, the little girl looked about as sweet and innocent as any kid he'd seen. He could feel a lump in his throat.

"She looks a whole lot better, doesn't she?"

Annie looked up at him. "She doesn't remember anything, Hap, but I think she will. When I started speaking Comanche to her, she calmed right down, so I've been sort of mixing it up a little, telling her about me and Jody and Ethan in the language, then singing songs I used to sing to her and Jody in English." She swallowed visibly. "If I live to be a hundred, I'll never be able to repay you for this, Hap."

"You already have, Annie. In a hundred ways."

"**C**ome on, Comanche Rose," he murmured, lifting the little girl from her mother's arms. "I know some folks that are going to want a good look at you."

Cora Sprenger had been on the porch waiting for them, but before Hap set Annie down, she was hurrying across the yard. "My goodness—if you all aren't a sight for sore eyes!" Stopping when she saw Susannah, she wiped back tears. "Oh, Annie . . . you found her!"

"Hap did."

"Looks like you've done all right for yourself, Hap. Leg working like you'd want it to?" Will Sprenger asked, coming up behind him.

"Yeah."

"Limp's better?"

"Yeah."

"Will, this is Susannah," Cora spoke up. "They found her."

"Well, if you aren't a pretty little thing," Sprenger said, turning his attention to the sober child. "You look just like your mama, don't you? What's that you've got there?"

"A damned cat," Hap answered for her.

"A cat?"

"Yeah—all the way from San Saba, Doc."

"My God."

"Oh, I don't know," Hap conceded, "it's been pretty game about the whole thing. The kid hasn't turned loose of it in three days, and so far it's not scratched her."

"You don't say?"

"Yeah. It's made that part easier, anyway."

"She's getting along all right?"

"It's been up and down, but it's getting a whole lot better." Turning to where Annie stood, her hand in Susannah's, he nodded. "It's going to be all right. She's not nearly the hell-raiser Clay was. In fact, she's a little on the bashful side, but I figure to change that. Probably when she starts speaking English, I'll be wishing for peace."

"You look happy, Hap," Will decided.

"Luckiest man on earth, Doc—luckiest man on earth. And about to get a whole lot luckier. I reckon the next time I see you there'll be four of us."

"Well, if that's not something! I'm real glad for you—for both of you—and I mean that."

"Thanks."

"Guess the old Rangers are really settling down," Will observed. "I read in one of the Texas newspapers where Clay has a baby daughter."

He didn't know why, but Hap had always sort of expected Clay to have a boy as wild as himself. But it didn't matter—a man took what God gave him. Yet as the notion took hold, he couldn't help smiling. "Nothing like a little girl to make a man proud, Doc. 'Course I've been writing a book for his boy, but I guess maybe his girl can read it just as well. Same way with mine."

"A book?"

"Yeah. Some fellow wanted to know what it was like being a Texas Ranger back in the old days, so I thought I might tell him. Kinda straighten him out, maybe."

"I'd like to see it."

"Why not? But right now I've got a little business to take care of first; then I'll be back over to wash up. I kinda wanted to check on something over at the store." Motioning to Susannah, he said, "Want to come with me? Let's go get something real pretty, eh?"

The child regarded him solemnly, saying nothing. Yet, when he held out his hand, she took it. As they walked toward the post store, they were an odd sight, the limping ex-Ranger and the little girl with the black cat looking over her shoulder.

Will watched, shaking his head, thinking of all the things in his life that had surprised him: Annie Bryce's marriage to Hap Walker was right up there near the top of the list. But now that he'd seen them, he could tell that it was right, that it had given them both a fresh start in life, something they'd both desperately needed. Out of the corner of his eye, he caught the expression on Annie's face as she looked after her husband and daughter. If she wasn't a woman in love with her man, he'd never seen one.

"Cora, you'd better get her out of that sun," he said suddenly. "Make her a little tea, then see that she lies down."

"Where are you going?"

"Looks like Hap's lost—he was going to the store, but

he's headed for the chapel. Maybe I'll go straighten him out," Will said. "Besides, I've got ten cents that says that little girl needs some horehound candy."

Wherever he'd been, Hap came back all cleaned up, his face shaved, his hair slicked back, reeking of lilacs. And somewhere along the line, he'd managed to buy or borrow a blue dress, white pinafore, black stockings, and button shoes for Susannah. As proud as she seemed of her finery, she was having trouble with the shoes, walking like a greenhorn cowboy in a new pair of boots.

"My, Susannah, but don't you look pretty!" Annie exclaimed. Turning to Hap, she wondered, "Where on earth did you find her all those things?"

"Preacher's wife took a shine to her, and they've got a girl about a year older. I don't think the shoes are much of a fit, though," he condeded. "But once she got 'em on, I couldn't get 'em off her. Then we walked over to the store, and I let her pick out whatever she wanted."

"You shouldn't have spent so much—that cameo locket must have cost a small fortune."

"Isn't every day a man gets a daughter," he responded, shrugging. "And she seemed to like it. Besides, I got money, Annie—I just never had much I wanted to spend it on before."

Annie's gaze returned to Susannah, who was still fingering the small locket lovingly. If she hadn't been browned by the sun, she'd have looked every bit as delicate as Annie had remembered her. But right now, her brilliant blue eyes seemed almost startling in that sun-bronzed face.

"Thank you, Hap," she said softly.

"For what?"

"For everything—for Susannah—for being you."

At that moment, Spider had apparently finally had enough wooling, for he decided to make his escape, and leaped for the open door to the Sprengers' bedroom, where he disappeared under the bed. "Maaa-maaa!" Susannah called out, pointing.

"Better go get him—no telling what he can get into in there," Hap told Annie.

As soon as mother and child were gone from the room, he called Cora outside, where he conferred conspiratorially with her. When they came in, Cora picked up the broom, shooed Annie out of the bedroom, and joined Susannah on the floor to rout the cat. Alone in the parlor, Hap just stood there for a moment, smiling. Finally, he cleared his throat and sobered visibly.

"Reckon I've kinda got something I've been wanting to say to you, Annie," he began.

Her eyes widened at the serious tone in his voice, but she let him go on. He shifted his weight off his bad leg, then reached to take her hand.

"It wasn't right the way we got married, Annie."

She could almost feel her heart stop.

"I owed you better, but I didn't want to wait. I guess I was afraid if you got a chance to think about it, you might change your mind."

She had to bite her lip to still its trembling. "I'd have been a fool if I had," she managed to say.

"I guess now I'd like to think we've got something real to build on, that if you had the choice now, you'd do it all over again."

"Yes."

"I thought I was too old to love anybody like I love you,

Annie—I thought life had kinda passed me by in that. But you taught me different, you know."

She could scarce swallow for the lump in her throat. "You don't have to say this, Hap."

"Yeah, I do. I love you more than life, Annie—and I'd like to do it right." His blue eyes intent on hers, he asked softly, "Would you marry me all over again, Annie Walker? Would you say the words in church?"

But the words echoing in her mind weren't the vows they'd exchanged in a dingy room in Baker's Gap. She'd heard them in her kitchen. *I'm what you need, Annie—I can be as mean and ornery as they are. And I've never been a coward. Anything I've ever said I'd do, I've done.*

"Hap Walker, I love you more than my life," she whispered back. "You make me proud to be your wife."

"Is that a yes?"

For an answer, she stepped into his embrace and raised her face to his. As her lips touched his, she murmured, "Yes."

His arms tightened around her shoulders, drawing her closer. "Cora's finding you a dress," he whispered against her lips. "And the preacher's waiting for the word."

"Do you, Horace, take this woman to be your lawfully wedded wife, to have and to hold from this day forward, for better or for worse, for richer or for poorer, in sickness and in health?" the chaplain asked.

"I do." Hap's voice was strong, ringing out through the small chapel.

"Will you love and cherish, honor and keep her, forsaking all others, so long as you both shall live?"

"I will."

"And do you, Anne, take this man to be your lawfully wedded husband, to have and to hold from this day forward, for better or for worse, for richer or for poorer, in sickness and in health?"

"I do," Annie whispered. Then, clearing the ache from her throat, she managed to repeat more loudly, "I do."

"Will you love and cherish, honor and obey him, forsaking all others, so long as you both shall live?"

"I will."

"Do you have the ring?" the chaplain asked Hap. Seeing that he did, he directed him, "Place it on the third finger of her left hand and repeat the words I say."

Sliding his father's ring from her hand, Hap palmed it, then replaced it with a beaded circle of gold. "With this ring I thee wed. . . ."

His fingers were warm, strong, just like the man. As Annie looked up at the softly curling brown hair, the bright blue eyes, the straight nose, the solid chin, she felt the wonder of her love for him. Out of loss and despair, he'd single-handedly made a new life for her. And within her. Now she had everything to live for.

The Honourable Thomas Mannering awoke to a full cavalry brigade rampaging through his skull. His stomach churned in protest at the least movement and his mouth had apparently been used as a nesting site by a flock of untidy birds. Altogether, a normal morning.

What was not normal was the lumpy mattress. Squeezing his eyelids tight, he burrowed into the pillow, avoiding the light he knew from vast experience would only worsen his condition. Where was he? What activities had he indulged in this time? He groaned as memory returned. Of course—the unwanted journey; the mental battle between images of Alicia and Josephine; and that moment when he could go no further. . . .

Desperately needing a drink, he had left the mail, reserving the last seat on the next coach. But the drink or two needed to restore his courage had stretched to several bottles. His last memory was a buxom barmaid brushing suggestively against his arm.

He shifted, suddenly aware that he was not alone. One arm was draped over a deliciously soft body, his fingers cupping a generous breast. This triggered another memory—nuzzling his face against that same breast as he drifted to sleep.

Had he taken the barmaid to bed? It would hardly surprise him, nor was she an antidote like some he had lately encountered. In recent months he had cut a wide and indiscriminate swath through the muslin company, even accepting the questionable services of street prostitutes in his quest for nirvana. It was a wonder he remained healthy. But another of his increasingly common blackouts left no memories of this particular liaison.

Shielding his eyes, he cautiously cracked one lid open, then heaved a sigh of relief. The light was too dim to hurt. He carefully turned his head to inspect the girl. Was she clean enough to risk another romp?

Pain knifed his neck.

Pain was something new, but he had no time to assess its cause. Astonishment exploded through his stomach, sending him reeling to the chamber pot without a moment to spare. Following an unpleasant interval, he grasped his swirling head and hesitantly approached the bed.

His eyes had not lied. The woman was both a stranger and seriously injured. Her head was swathed in bandages, as was the arm that lay atop the coverlet.

"Damnation!" he muttered angrily, looking for some clue as to where he was. The sloped roof and peeling walls hinted at the top floor of an unfashionable inn. Nothing unusual about that . . . The tiny apartment was furnished as if for servants, containing the narrow bed, a single rickety chair, and an equally decrepit table. At least a fire burned in the mean grate, though doing little to suppress the January chill. Two valises rested atop a small trunk. Thankfully opening his own, he extracted a traveling flask and took a long pull to settle his stomach and clear the cobwebs from this aching head.

His eyes returned to the woman in the bed. Who was she? How had she gotten into his room? And why he was in a room? he asked in shock. He was supposed to be on the mail, heading for Devon to pay his addresses to Miss Huntsley. A presentiment of doom was building. He could almost see the sword of Damocles poised above his head.

"Who the devil are you?" he demanded, prodding her shoulder.

No response.

His gaze sharpened. The visible hand was smooth with artistically long fingers, certainly not that of a servant. Her complexion was clear, but even in sleep he could not reconcile her features with a barmaid. Nor did she fit the mold of a prostitute. Her bag and trunk were worn, but of good quality. Paradoxically, the cloak hanging on a peg beside the door was muddy, torn, and smelled strongly of brandy.

He prodded her again. What was she doing in his room? In his bed? How had she been injured and who had bandaged her? Why had he no recollection of any of this? Usually by now he at least managed a hazy outline of his evening.

"Bloody hell! What is going on here?"

His head pounded. He prodded harder, frantic when he could raise no response.

Her left hand rested atop the coverlet. She wore no rings. That precluded a widow or a wife. Terror welled in his throat as he shook her. Still no response. Acute pain knifed through his neck and for the first time, he examined himself.

"My God!"

A bandage wrapped one leg, which was surprisingly sore. Scrapes covered both hands. He peered into a cracked looking-glass and gasped in shock. One eye was swollen and a long graze extended from forehead to cheek. Pain again stabbed from his neck to his right shoulder. Twisting before the glass, he discovered an ugly bruise. The agony was too great to remain in this contorted position for long, but he could not reconcile his injuries with a fight.

"An accident?" he wondered. "Bloody hell!"

But why was he sharing a bed with an unknown and apparently unmarried female? How long had they been here? That elusive snippet returned to tantalize him even as shudders racked his body. What had occurred in the dark reaches of the night? He loosed an exhaustive and highly imaginative stream of invective, until a groan cut him off in mid-curse.

"Anne?" whispered a voice. "My head aches so. Could you bring me some water?"

He collapsed in despair as the Damoclesian sword fell, stabbing his soul. Though weak and barely conscious, she was obviously well-bred. What had he done?

"Anne? Are you here?" whispered the voice again.

Thomas rose and poured water into a cracked cup, holding it to her lips. Remembering that he was nearly naked, he slipped beneath the coverlet, taking care not to touch her. Then he waited for her to open her eyes, waited for her to tell him why they were together, and prayed that somehow his deductions were wrong.

* * *

Caroline swallowed a sip of water from the cup Anne held to her lips. No, not Anne, she acknowledged as memory returned. Her head ached abominably. She reached a shaking hand to the bandage that had slipped down over her eyes.

There had been an accident. She remembered now. The coach had gone faster and faster until it had finally overturned. She had been on the bottom and must have been knocked senseless. Where was she?

In bed.

Someone was with her, someone who had just settled onto the edge. Was she so badly injured that a nurse had been left to attend her? But how could she hope to pay for such an extravagance? She had only a few shillings, assuming her reticule had not disappeared.

Shakily she pushed the bandage up so that she could see. The room was dimly lit, but not with wavering candlelight. A window covered with sparse ivy admitted minimal light from an overcast day. With difficulty she turned to see who rested on the bed.

"You!" she gasped before clamping one hand over her mouth in horror. She lunged away in a reckless attempt to escape, discovered she wore only her shift, grabbed the coverlet, and retreated to the chair under the window.

Thomas jumped as though shot, remembered his own state of undress, and donned the sheet. He backed into the far corner and stared warily at the lady huddled in the coverlet. Wide, terrified eyes stared back. Her reaction was not encouraging. *What had he done?*

"What are you doing in my room?" she demanded icily. "Haven't you caused me enough trouble?"

375

"I have no idea," he admitted with a grimace. "I could ask the same of you. What are you doing in my room?"

"Are you still foxed?" Her nose led her eyes to the uncovered chamberpot and she sighed in resignation.

Thomas rubbed his sore shoulder. "Let us start at the beginning," he began slowly. "The last thing I remember is sitting in the taproom at the Laughing Dog. To the best of my knowledge, I have never seen you before. Who are you?"

"You must have been even more foxed than I thought," Caroline murmured in disgust.

She raked him with an objective stare. Not much older than herself, he looked as though he would clean up rather nicely. Well-cut black hair curled riotously around his face. Despite the bruises, the two-days' stubble of dark beard, and his generally dissipated appearance, he had an aristocratic face of the more handsome variety, highlighted by a wide, sensual mouth and brilliant green eyes under indecently long lashes. But his expression declared him a spoiled society buck accustomed to getting his own way and ready to ride roughshod over anyone who crossed him. Did he really have no memory of recent events? How odd. Her face snapped back into a frown.

"I am Miss Caroline Cummings, third daughter of the Sheldridge Corners vicar. I am on my way to Cornwall to take up a post as governess. We met—if you can call it that—as I was boarding the mail coach. You knocked me down, draped yourself all over me, were odiously and lengthily sick, then passed out in my lap. Being unable to shift you and obtaining no assistance from our fellow passengers, I was forced to endure your presence for some considerable time until the driver lost control of the team and sent us tumbling down an embankment. Now I find you still insinuating your presence on me by invading my room. Please leave this instant!" She finished this recital on a note of barely suppressed indignation that raised her voice until each word pounded into his head with the force of a blacksmith's hammer.

"This situation is worse than you know, Miss Cummings," Thomas ground out, staring despairingly at the dowdy miss in front of the window. Her only redeeming virtue was height. He usually towered over women. But the few wisps of hair sticking out from under her bandage seemed dull brown, as were her eyes. The rest of her features were plain, with freckles dotting her nose. Nevertheless, he would have to make the best of things. A vicar's daughter. Devil take it, she was gentry. If this imbroglio became known, it could ruin his sister's Season. He took a deep breath.

"I am the Honourable Thomas Edward Alfred Mannering. I admit to being on the go last evening—at least I assume it was last evening—and have no recollection of boarding the mail. I can only apologize and hope that my illness did not disturb you too greatly."

"Well," she conceded, "you did make it to the window—over my poor body."

He groaned at the picture her words painted.

"Again," she returned to her original complaint, "what are you doing in my room?"

"I could ask you the same question. I fear that someone has carefully placed us here together," he explained. "I awakened to find myself sharing a bed with you."

She reddened, then her face paled. "What—"

He shrugged helplessly. "I have no idea," he admitted,

"but I was three sheets to the wind rather than senseless so anything could have happened."

She was visibly shaking.

"We will have to marry, you know," he added resignedly. "Neither your reputation nor my honor as a gentleman would survive otherwise." Which was the worse sin? Ignoring honor's demand? Or disgracing his family by wedding beneath him? Unfortunately, honor delivered the more impassioned plea. But how could he survive being shackled to vicarage prudity? *Oh, God, Alicia! How could fate have turned so badly against us?*

Caroline stared as if he had gone mad. *Surely this is a dream. Soon I will awaken, safe in the room I share with Anne. We will laugh at such a fanciful nightmare and finish packing my trunk for Cornwall.* But Mr. Mannering was still there, partially wrapped in a dingy and slipping sheet, and try as she might, she could not wake up. Must she really spend her life with the perpetually foxed stranger who blithely admitted that when in his cups he would of course expect to ravish any female foolish enough to cross his path? He was touched in the upper works.

"But who would ever know?" she protested desperately.

"These things have a way of getting out," he said. "There is no telling how many people are aware we spent the night together. Think it over. I will try to discover where we are and what has happened. Mayhap I can learn how we find ourselves in this fix. Not that it will improve our situation any."

She merely nodded and turned to stare at the ivy-covered window.

Once he departed, she numbly proceeded with her own *toilette*. There must be some way to escape this coil! But she could remember nothing beyond the accident. Not the faintest glimmering. Someone had carried her to an inn, removed her clothing (her cheeks reddened), dressed her wounds, put her to bed. That same someone must have done the same things to Mr. Mannering. Her blush spread clear to her toes. But who would have assumed that they were wed? She slumped dizzily onto the bed. At least nothing had been stolen. Her few coins still lay in the reticule she found tucked among her clothes. Except her virtue, mocked that inner voice she hated.

Mr. Mannering returned with a breakfast tray, keeping his expression carefully neutral. Dowdy didn't begin to describe her dress. Never fashionable, it was at least ten years old, having originally belonged to someone both shorter and stouter than Miss Cummings. Innumerable washings had softened the fabric until it hung like a muddy, brown tent. The bandage bleached her face even paler. And her right hand was nearly as scraped as his own.

"The innkeeper's wife fixed this for us. It is dusk, by the way. We are at the Blue Boar, some forty miles west of Sheldridge Corners." He placed the tray on the table, drew it nearer the bed, then seated himself on the chair.

"What did you learn?" She poured coffee. He was already quaffing ale. This parody of normal dining set her teeth on edge.

"I spoke to a thin young man who was another passenger."

She nodded in confirmation to the question in his eyes.

"He claims that the driver was well into his cups, at least according to the guard. The fellow's betrothed had just jilted him for a soldier and he has repeatedly been criticized for failing to average the nine miles per hour mandated for mail coaches. Slowness is one thing the company will never tolerate. But all tales are hearsay. The guard departed, along with the king's mail, some hours ago. No one really knows why the coachman forced that sudden burst of speed. The accident broke his neck."

Caroline shuddered.

"I owe you a vast number of apologies, it seems," he continued ruefully. "According to report, my attentions were far worse than you implied. So familiar did I act that Miss Spencer was convinced that we are married. She so informed our rescuers and as neither of us was able to contradict her, they placed us in a room together."

"Is she the spinsterish lady?"

"Right."

"That would explain why she glowered at me while delivering her diatribe against the low company allowed onto the mail these days."

He cringed. "Again, my heartfelt apologies. But we must settle our future. Your father is a vicar. Have you other relatives?"

"Papa was the fourth son of the late Lord Cummings, so there are numerous aunts and uncles on that side. But no money. He had to make his own way and preferred the church to the army or the government. He met my mother while assigned as a curate in Lincolnshire. She was the old Earl of Waite's second daughter but was disinherited for marrying so far beneath her, so I know little of that family. You might learn from her example. I have no dowry at all."

So her breeding was actually quite good, he reflected in surprise. Which made his own behavior even worse. But such a connection would not reflect badly on his family.

"That matters not. I see no possibility of explaining away the past eighteen hours, Miss Cummings. I have hopelessly compromised you. There can be no solution but marriage."

"Who will ever find out? No one knows my name. I spoke to none on the coach. I can simply continue my journey."

"Word will get out," he insisted. Honor aside, the more he considered Miss Cummings, the better he liked the idea. While no beauty, she was an improvement on the horse-faced Miss Huntsley. A governess surely had more sense than that brainless widgeon. And she would probably not complain over conditions at Crawley, never having known luxuries. Clearly she had few sensibilities. Most ladies of his acquaintance would produce week-long hysterics after what she had been through. It seemed that fate was offering at least a partial reprieve. All he had to do was convince her of the inevitability of their union.

He flashed the most understanding of his stock of charming smiles.

"The accident has delayed your arrival and your injuries will be impossible to hide. Once it is known you were on the coach whose driver died, someone is bound to connect you with Mr. Mannering's mysterious wife. They know me, you see, having checked my card case. Who would overlook such a scandal involving their governess, Miss Cummings?"

She cringed. "But you cannot wish to marry me, Mr. Mannering. You know nothing about me. Nor I of your, for that matter."

"True, though that can be easily remedied. I will not deceive you, Miss Cummings. I am no bargain," he began.

"To give you the words with no bark on them, I have spent the bulk of the past year in continuous dissipation, surfacing only recently to find myself deep in the River Tick. That is the worst of it, however. I am the second son of the Earl of Marchgate and have a small estate of my own, though it is in considerable disrepair. My father had decreed that in exchange for bailing me out, I must stay on said estate and see to its restoration. The only capital I can obtain is an inheritance from my grandfather that comes to me upon my marriage. But my recent misbehavior has not helped my reputation any. Father claims that Lord Huntsley would welcome my addresses to his youngest daughter. I had not yet given him my answer, deciding in my cups two evenings ago to first travel to Devon and see whether she is really as disgustingly inept as I remember. Frankly, your advent is a blessing. Already I know and like you better than Miss Huntsley."

Hardly a complimentary declaration, but acceptable under the circumstances, she reflected. He obviously had no desire for a wife but must accept one for financial reasons. So their compromising situation would not become a bone of contention in the future. He seemed to consider her an improvement in his fortunes.

"I will be equally frank, sir," she countered, pacing the room restlessly. "I am the third of twelve children. Times are bad and Father can no longer afford to feed such a brood. I accepted a position as governess, planning to send a portion of my salary to my family. That remains important, so in addition to bringing no dowry, I would constitute a modest drain on your admittedly straitened circumstances. To my credit, I am excellent with children and well-versed at running a household. I even know a bit

382

about estate management. However, my education will seem shockingly broad to the polite world for I am the worst sort of bluestocking. And while I have acquired all the manners expected of one in my position, I have no idea of how to go on in higher circles and cannot produce the inane chatter acceptable to drawing rooms. I still cannot accept that marriage is the only solution to our predicament. And I have no desire for a husband who is both an admitted gamester and a drunkard."

He reddened. "Plain speaking indeed, though I had not previously shown a penchant for gaming and believe that I have now come to my senses regarding my recent behavior. As for drinking, after last night I have a profound antipathy to over-indulging ever again. But speaking of last night, I do not know exactly what happened. Nor do you, seemingly. However, we must proceed on the assumption that the worst occurred, with the worst likely consequences."

She blanched.

"Precisely, my dear Miss Cummings," he confirmed. "And if there are to be no long-term repercussions, then we must marry immediately."

"All right. But how am I ever going to explain this to Papa?"

She burst into tears.

From *The Rake's Rainbow* by Alison Lane

BREATHTAKING ROMANCES YOU WON'T WANT TO MISS